As soon as he set her on her feet, she threw herself at him. She tugged at his shirt with hungry hands until she yanked it off. Her small fingers ran up and down his chest, her mouth following the trail.

He bunched his hands into her soft, silky hair as her hot, velvet tongue lapped hungrily at him. "You're killing me, Princess." His voice was hoarse with need. Deciding he needed to turn the tables, he started to nuzzle her throat. She sighed happily as she leaned her head to the side in order to give him better access. He cupped her round bottom with one hand while he unzipped her dress with the other. He smiled when he saw she wore a little, white teddy underneath it. It was barely there, just covering the small swell of her breasts while hugging her flat stomach and her curvy waist. She wore matching white thong panties.

"You like?" she asked shyly.

"I love," he told her as his fingers trailed over the top of her breasts.

She closed her eyes, her body swaying into his. He cupped her breasts through the fabric. She hissed in pleasure as she leaned even closer to him. Slowly, her fingers trailed down under his waistband until she touched his cock. She hesitantly ran her fingers on it, pulling back when he groaned. "Did I hurt you?" Her face was alarmed.

He answered by taking her hand and putting it back. She giggled and grew bolder, her long fingers working magic on him. Finally, he had to stop her or else it would be over before it even begun. Taking back control, he picked her up and threw her on the bed. Her green eyes widened in shock before she reached up and pulled off his pants. When she struggled with the garment, he clumsily helped her, throwing them to the side once they were off.

This book is a work of fiction. Names, characters, places, and incidents either are products of the author's imagination or are used fictitiously. Any resemblance to actual events or locales or persons, living or dead, is entirely coincidental.

Angel Warriors
Copyright © 2008 Stephani Hecht
ISBN: 978-1-55487-119-3
Cover art by Angela Waters

All rights reserved. Except for use in any review, the reproduction or utilization of this work in whole or in part in any form by any electronic, mechanical or other means, now known or hereafter invented, is forbidden without the written permission of the publisher.

Published by eXtasy Books
Look for us online at:
www.extasybooks.com

Library and Archives Canada Cataloguing in Publication

Hecht, Stephani, 1972-
    Archangels / Stephani Hecht.

ISBN 978-1-55487-119-3

    I. Title.

PS3608.E286A74 2008   813'.6   C2008-905602-7

Archangels

Book 1 - Angel Warriors

Book 2 - Captive Angels

By

Stephani Hecht

To Ken, Cody, Joie, Jackie, Dad and Mom. Thank you for believing in me.

Angel Warriors

Book 1

To old friends!
Stephani Hecht

PROLOG

"Just stay down," Forcas yelled, then delivered a hard kick to his ribs. He stood back and brushed black hair out of his cold, dark eyes. "Don't make me have to destroy you."

Abdiel ignored the request and slowly staggered to his feet. Forcas growled in anger before he delivered a spinning, roundhouse kick. Abdiel's head snapped sideways and blood spurted out of his mouth, but at least he remained standing. Straightening his head, he turned to the group of angels who watched the whole beating. Mixed among the proud warriors was everyone who ever meant anything to him—his parents, aunts, uncles and childhood friends—not caring that he was getting his ass royally handed to him. He decided to ignore all of them, leveling his gaze on the leader of their group.

Lucifer wore a half smile on his face that did not reach his hazel eyes. Surprisingly, he was the smallest one present. His head of thick brown hair barely reached Forcas's shoulders—but he carried himself with so much authority that, despite his size, he demanded respect and fear from his followers.

Abdiel wiped blood away from his bottom lip and appealed to his leader. "It's not too late to stop this, Lucifer. If you call your angels back now, He will forgive you. If you go forward with this rebellion, you and I both know, it'll be the end of you and your followers."

The evil angel turned to the crowd and held his arms up, mockingly. "Does anyone here agree with Abdiel? Are there any that wish to join him in his crusade?" When no one stepped forward, Lucifer laughed.

"You haven't seen what I have, Abdiel. He has grown soft and weak. Ever since the creation of the humans, He panders to them. He should remember that we were created first! We are the perfect creation. Those humans are nothing but pathetic sheep compared to us. Now is our time to show Him that we will not sit back and accept second place! If we act now, we can show Him that we are stronger than He ever thought. He will see we are now even more powerful than Him."

"How can we be more powerful than Him?" Abdiel spat at Lucifer's feet The group of angels unleashed a collective gasp at his blatant show of disrespect. "Do you forget He made us? Lucifer, you are an even bigger fool than I first thought."

"How dare you speak to your master that way?" his oldest brother, Douma, interrupted. He looked almost identical to Forcas, right down to the dead, empty eyes. He stepped forward and went to strike again.

Abdiel lashed out and wrapped his hand around his brother's throat. Not since he was a mere child could any of his brothers defeat or overpower him one on one. They always teamed up on him, just like moments earlier.

"Don't you see, Abdiel? He could never value a great archangel like you as I could." Lucifer's voice soothed. "You will always be second to Michael or Raphael, always their lap boy. Join me, and you will be head archangel, as is your right."

"Flattery from you, Lucifer?" Abdiel looked at him, his hand still wrapped around his brother's throat. "I didn't know you looked away from the mirror long enough to notice anyone else."

Lucifer roared. Lifting his hand, he hurled a bolt of energy at Douma and sent him crashing to the ground.

Abdiel looked as his empty hand, then cocked his head at his brother. "You have so much love for your angels." His words dripped with sarcasm. "It's no wonder the other two thirds haven't followed you as well."

Lucifer responded with an energy bolt. The power painfully coursed through him an instant before his body slammed into the ground. *Yeah, that's going to leave a mark. Well, it looks like the time for words is over. Now, it's time to play.* With a low growl, he rolled up into a crouch, then launched himself at Lucifer. *Rules be damned. I'm going to rip his throat out.* As soon as he was close enough to throttle the lead angel, his two older brothers seized him by the arms. Although he fought against them, they effectively held him immobile.

"Now that..." Lucifer strode forth and backhanded Abdiel. "...was unwise. I will make you suffer as you have never thought possible." He turned and crooked his finger.

In answer to his summons, a female angel immediately came forward. Her dark brown hair, long with an abundance of curls, framed her small, pixie-like face. Large brown eyes, surrounded by dark, heavy lashes, blinked. Perfect pink lips formed a sinister smile as she slowly wrapped her arms around his neck.

Lucifer laughed evilly, then roughly pulled her into a deep kiss.

With an angry roar, Abdiel lunged. His brothers tightened their grips.

"I can see why you are so infatuated with Persephone," the evil angel mocked as his hands ran over the female.

Abdiel had hoped to wed her one day.

"In fact, she was so delicious, after I took her, I shared her with several of my archangels. Do you know that after all that she still begged for more? You sure picked a feisty one."

Anger surged through him and granted Abdiel the strength needed to break free of his brothers. Reaching behind him, he drew his sword from its scabbard. Before he could reach Lucifer, however, both of his brothers and his best friend, Beelzebub, pulled their own weapons and moved to protect their leader. Any one of them alone, Abdiel could have beaten—but together, that was a different story. It didn't stop him though. He never backed down from a fight before, and he was not ready to start now.

"Beelzebub, you forget who helped you master that sword," Abdiel goaded, trying to provoke them into a mistake. "As for you, my brothers, I am so going to enjoy tearing you two apart, bit by little bit."

The three rushed him simultaneously. They wouldn't attack him one at a time and give him half a chance. That would actually be honorable.

With a grunt of aggravation, Abdiel brought his sword up to parry their thrusts. They were fast, but he was faster. Moving with a speed no other angel matched, he met all three opponents, sword to sword.

Lucifer watched, his mouth twisted in a smile. After several minutes, he grew bored as the fight continued too long for his liking. "Mammon," he said to his second in command.

A tall male with blond hair stepped forward.

"Finish this now before Abdiel hurts one of these fools."

Mammon nodded, withdrew a dagger from his belt and flung at Abdiel. It buried itself deep in his chest.

The archangel yelped in pain and looked down. The lodged position of the dagger severed the muscle and clamped the nerve control of his blade arm. Dropping his sword, he crumbled to the ground. His brothers and Beelzebub fell upon him, slashing him again and again with their swords. When their arms tired of swinging, they switched to kicking his battered body without mercy.

Unlike humans, angels are immortal—but they can feel pain and bleed, both of which he currently suffered. The only way to kill an angel is to destroy totally, to injure so savagely and leave one in so many pieces no healer can make him whole again. Abdiel grimly realized his former friend and brothers tried to do that to him right now. Through all the pain and damage to his body, his heart felt ripped from his chest when he realized he'd been given a death sentence.

"Enough," Lucifer bellowed. "We have work to do and this piece of nothing has wasted more time than he is worth already. Now everybody come and say goodbye to Abdiel."

His brothers and Beelzebub each gave him another vicious kick before they walked away. His foggy mind brought up fantasies of some day ripping off their legs and beating them with them. When

Persephone walked by, he turned his head for he didn't want to look at the female angel. It wasn't until his parents approached that reaction rose. They had the twins with them. With his last bit of strength, he pushed his broken body up to his knees.

"Please, Father, they are just children, leave them with me." He looked at his little brother and sister. They looked so much like him, with their dark hair, although their eyes were a deep blue to his brown. Those blue eyes now wide with fear and filled with tears.

His father's only response was to spit in his face before sister, Rachael, cried pitifully while his baby brother, Appolion, tried in vain to fight. Their father roughly grabbed the twins by the backs of their necks and dragged them away. The last thing Abdiel heard before unconsciousness stole him was his father smacking the twins.

Abdiel lay wounded and unconscious all through the epic battle. It was not until days later, after Michael and his archangels finally defeated Lucifer and banished the evil angel and all his followers to Hell that they found him. He woke up only long enough to see Michael standing above him, his brown eyes filled with grief and concern.

Michael knelt and gently pushed the black hair back. "It is known that you were a hero, that you alone would not betray Him. Rest well, Abdiel. He is proud of you."

Before he closed his eyes, the sound of a female weeping brushed his ears. Certain he must be losing his mind, he knew his lover, mother and entire family were all gone. There was no one left to weep for him, no one who cared for him. He truly was all alone.

Chapter One

Present Day

"Gabi, there's someone here to see us." Camael's usual teasing banter was gone.

Only one thing could make him that somber—Michael came to give them both the news they dreaded. Michael was the most supreme archangel as he was one the first angels ever born and the most powerful. Because of that, he was the Chief of all the other angel warriors. That is, the angels who lived as humans on Earth in order to protect mankind from Lucifer and his demons. He handpicked his warriors from infancy, sorting through each newborn angel, looking for the specific skills he needed. Once he found the ones meeting his criteria, he made sure they were properly trained.

At adulthood, they each made a sacred vow to protect their mortal brothers from demonic intrusion. Giving up all the luxuries and comforts of their former lives, they lived as humans in regular homes on Earth, ate human food and dressed in current fashions. Aside from a few short visits here and there, they no longer called Heaven home.

At the moment, only two angels were in their household—Gabi, the healer, and Camael, the empath. They needed a new archangel, and Michael was there to tell them who it was.

"Well, should we go see what big bad Mike has to say?" She hoped to lighten the mood.

"Come on, Gabi, we both know he's sending us a new archangel."

"Well, it has been a month, Cam. I'm surprised he waited this long."

"Who do you think it will be?" Camael tried for a casual tone, but the nervous fingering of the buttons on his shirt betrayed him.

"Just so long as it's not one of your brothers, I don't care."

"Hey," he protested with a laugh. "You know the council doesn't let family members serve in the same household."

"Don't worry." She reached out and ruffled the younger angel's hair in a motherly fashion. "He won't send another one like Charoum."

Their previous archangel, Charoum, made Cam's life miserable. The stuffy, older angel could not abide the way the younger angel embraced the human world and how he lived life like a human just out of high school. The fact Cam tended to shoot his mouth off before he took the time to think first, did not help matters either.

Instead of training Cam like he was supposed to, Charoum let him go out unprepared. Cam really tried, bless his heart, but all his instruction was as an empath. He possessed very little combat knowledge and tended to wing it whenever in battle. The empath suffered injuries more times than Gabi could count. It was totally humiliating to the young angel.

The few times Gabi managed to get Charoum to take Cam to the gym to train were terrible. The archangel used the opportunity to slap the empath down on the mat time and time again. She healed just as many injuries from his so-called training sessions as from demon attacks.

What Cam did not know was Gabrielle went to Michael and asked him to transfer Charoum. She loved Cam as if he were a younger brother and would do anything for him. It tore her up inside to see Cam wince whenever the archangel yelled at him.

Gabi was more worried than she let on. She mentally sorted through all the available archangels in her head and could not think of one that would be able to tolerate Cam. It was like the empath was trying to make a career out of being an oddball.

Cam's wardrobe consisted of ratty old jeans and rock tee -shirts. He wore his blond hair in a messy, spiked fashion and his left ear boasted a small gold hoop earring. The empath did not crave manna, the food of angels, but pizza and burgers. His idea of an evening off was loafing in front of the television watching reality shows, sports or some bad movie on the sci-fi channel. He actually asked to be assigned to Detroit because it was the home of his favorite hockey team, the Red Wings.

He was defiantly unique.

They walked into the living room where Michael sat on the couch, watching the TV, a look of horror on his face. "What is this?" He pointed to the set.

"*Night of the Living Dead*," Cam muttered, ducking his head. He started to pull at his hair.

It was a nervous habit of his that really annoyed Gabi. She groaned at his behavior. How could Cam have forgotten to turn off the TV? At least he didn't have a CD blaring. The last thing they needed was for Michael to hear the empath loved alternative rock.

"It's about zombies who attack humans and eat their brains." Cam hoped to get himself out of his mess, but only dug himself in deeper. "It's a classic horror movie."

"Why would they eat brains?" Michael frowned.

Gabi caught the teasing glint in his eye.

"I dunno." Cam's gaze was still on his shuffling feet.

"Correct me if I'm wrong, Michael." Gabi decided to bail out her poor empath. "Didn't you and I see this at the theater when it first came out?"

"Now Gabrielle," Michael chided. "If you give away all my secrets, how will I keep Camael afraid of me?"

Gabi laughed.

Cam looked up, a shocked expression on his face. He cracked a half smile, but refrained from shooting off his mouth.

It was good to see there was one thing that would shut him up. Maybe she should invite the archangel over more often.

"Gabrielle." Michael stood, then handed her the remote. "I am sure you two know why I am here?"

"A pretty good guess," she answered. "We're getting a new roomie."

"It hasn't been easy," Michael drawled, looking over at the young male angel. "Most of the available archangels would as soon beat you, Cam, as work with you."

"Michael..." Gabi began to protest.

Michael held up a hand. "I didn't say I agreed with them. Me, I happen to favor the boy. He makes life interesting, but his mouth does tend to get him in trouble."

Too intimidated by their leader to argue his case, Cam looked down, bit his bottom lip in frustration and played with his button.

Gabi admitted that, at first, his blond, spiked hair and earring were a bit offsetting. But they did not know Cam like she did. He was the sweetest, most compassionate angel she knew. Like a mama bear, she rose to protect, "I would take Cam over any of them." She met Cam's gaze and saw his gratitude. "There is nobody I trust more."

"Peace." Michael held his hands up in surrender, "I wouldn't want you to take your crossbow out on me. Do you two want to know who your new roommate is or not?" When they nodded, he simply replied, "Abdiel."

Gabi felt as though someone punched her in the stomach. *Anyone, please, anyone but him.* For the first time in her immortal life, a real, honest to goodness panic attack built inside her. She kept her face calm to avoid upsetting Cam.

"I thought he worked in the armory making weapons," she said, her tone deceptively composed.

It was common knowledge that, ever since he lost his family to Satan, Abdiel never fought. He shut himself off from any contact with other angels. The only one he ever let get close was Michael.

Many angels still didn't trust him and thought him no better than his family. After all, he had been one of Lucifer's angels along with them. To make matters worse, his demon brothers were very aggressive in their war against the angels. There wasn't an angel family that did not suffer a casualty because of Douma or Forcas. The mere sight of Abdiel reminded too many of his heritage. As far as they were concerned, the apple didn't fall far from the tree.

Abdiel didn't make matters any better with his sullen ways. He never smiled or talked with anyone. His dark hair and eyes matched his disposition and seemed to make him more sinister. Angelic mothers warned their children away from him while male angels never looked him in the eye. They called him the Dark Angel behind his back. In short, he was disliked by most and feared by all. Abdiel was the bogeyman of the angel realm.

"Yes, it is true, he's been working in the armory since the battle in Heaven," Michael assured. "But I've always made sure he kept up with his training. It's time he became an archangel again. You should be honored. There aren't many who can match his skills."

"Are you sure he is ready for the human world?" Gabi asked carefully.

"I'm sure Camael will be more than happy to tell him all the joys of the human world. Get ready for him. He'll come tomorrow." With those words, he disappeared from the room.

Gabi and Cam stood there for a moment, both of them shocked.

The younger angel finally turned and looked at her. "Why are you so upset?" His blue eyes searched her face.

"I'm not," she fibbed. Aware such rarities were overlooked with a frown from above, but understood when used to protect, she sighed. There were times when she hated living with someone who picked up on her every mood.

"I can feel your anxiety, your fear."

"Nobody likes a nosey empath," she snapped, not wanting to share her worries. She immediately felt guilty for taking her anger out on him. It wasn't his fault that her life was about to go into the crapper.

"Have you ever met Abdiel?" Cam still tried to read her feelings.

Damn his hide. "We knew each other as children," she hedged. "Ever since he lost his family, he kept to himself. No one really knows him anymore."

"I know he makes good weapons. All my brothers use him."

"You and your brothers also think *Deep Blue Sea* was the best movie ever made. Excuse me if I happen to doubt your opinions."

"I can't wait to call them about our new archangel. Wait until they hear," Cam chattered as they walked into the kitchen.

Gabi was relieved he no longer probed her feelings. "Are you going to tell Ana?" She referred to Cam's older, overprotective sister.

"Tell her what?" Cam made horror music noises and wiggled his fingers at her. "That we have the Dark Angel coming."

"Stop it." She laughed. "Don't you have one of those human college courses to go to?" For some insane reason, Cam insisted on enrolling at the local college. He always said it was because he wanted to learn as much as he could about humans. Gabi knew better. Cam loved the human race and truly enjoyed mingling with them, being one of them.

"Yeah, I have religious studies."

"Cam, you're an angel. You *are* religious studies."

"I agree." He shrugged on his backpack. "But Ana insisted, and I must always obey my big sister." With that, he grabbed a Coke out of the fridge and turned his iPod on. He flashed her a peace sign, then ran out the door.

After a few moments, she heard his motorcycle gun up. Leave it to Cam to rely on human transportation. Any other angel would simply flash to his destination. Gabi smiled. He rebelled against everything an angel was supposed to be and she would not change him for the world because she did, too. That was why they got along so well. Although she would never admit it to him, she loved those horrible sci-fi movies just as much as he did.

As soon as she thought about Abdiel her smiled faded. Of all the archangels in the world, why did it have to be him? Old feelings of hurt she thought long gone, suddenly washed over her.

She loved him ever since she first set eyes upon him, even though they were both just small children at the time. He was such a cute little male, too. He had the sweetest dimples. To make sure he knew her intentions, she did as any other small girl, and kicked him in the shins. He retaliated by yanking one of her dark braids.

As they grew older, her feelings strengthened. The year before they graduated from school, she sat across the room from him and spent the entire time sneaking glances at him like a lovesick puppy. She still had the folder she wrote *Gabi loves Abdiel* on in her room.

Gabi was such a klutz around him. She would be walking across the classroom and trip over a desk because she was looking at him instead of looking where she was going. Whenever he did talk to her, she would always stutter back. Yeah, she Miss Smooth around him all right.

She remembered Abdiel's dark, soothing eyes that sparkled whenever he teased someone. His black hair was always cut collar length, but one lock always managed to fall over his eyes. Even though he was young at the time, he had a muscular build that put most archangels to shame.

However, he never even knew she existed. He stayed close to his inner circle of friends and was head over heels in love with Persephone. Abdiel never so much as looked at her.

Her throat closed up at a particular painful memory. They were all teenagers at the time. Angel teens could be just as cruel as human ones. The real kicker was, angels went through *that awkward* stage for several years. *Those lucky mortals only have a few years of agony. Nothing like living through several of being the dork to kill one's self-esteem.*

After school one day, she made her way across the courtyard toward home. She walked with her head down, her hair shielding her from taunting looks. The females who had hung out with Abdiel loved to tease her because she was royalty. Even though she was a princess, she did not look like it, and they made sure she knew it. To make matters worse, Gabi did not have her mother to turn to for advice and support as she was raised her entire life by different nannies.

"Hey Gabi," Persephone called. "Come here. I have something to show you."

She should have known better, but wanted them to like her so badly. Nervous, she joined the females. When she peeked at Abdiel, she saw him engrossed in a conversation with the males. He paid no attention to the females.

Persephone handed her a folded piece of parchment.

Gabi giggled and opened it. Her smile quickly turned to horror at the drawn picture. It was a crude likeness of a naked male.

As the females laughed, the males turned around to see what was going on. Abdiel wore a small frown on his face. Beelzebub looked at the parchment and snickered. Beelzebub was one of her biggest tormentors. Half the time when she tripped, it was because he either bumped into her or stuck his foot out as she walked by.

"Come on, your Highness," he snipped. "You have an older brother. Surely not even you are that naïve."

"Leave her alone guys," Abdiel interjected.

Gabi dropped the parchment, then turned to run. Of course, being the klutz she fell flat on her royal face. Her dress flipped up and flashed her royal hot pink panties. Frantic, she scrambled to her knees and gathered the scattered rolls of parchment. Abdiel knelt and helped. She still remembered his words.

"I'm sorry, little mouse."

Tears welled at the fact he called her a rodent. That hurt worse than the scathing laughter from the others. He thought of her as some dirty, ugly mouse. She remembered the day they found Abdiel, bloody and unconscious. He fought bravely, but was cut down like a dog. She never saw an angel that badly injured. It was a miracle he wasn't destroyed. It was only because he was the angel he was that he survived. His own family and friends betrayed him, butchered him and left him for dead.

All the healers were summoned to help. They included her even though she was just barely out of her specialized training. She was in the room while he talked to Michael

"Abdiel, the healers are never going to be able to totally heal you unless you want them to. You must find the will to go on." Michael sat on the edge of the bed.

"How can I, Michael? I lost everything I ever loved."

Gabi strained to hear.

"I am sorry about your family." Michael started to touch his shoulder, but stopped.

"It's more than that, Michael. Persephone betrayed me. I loved her and she threw that away. I'll never be able to trust anyone again."

Those words promised no chance with him. She mistakenly thought if she rushed to his side in his time of need, he would finally realize she was the one for him. Gabi couldn't be more wrong. Even though Persephone was gone forever, he still loved her. Hot tears fell unchecked as her world crumbled and her heart was torn from her chest.

After that, Abdiel completely isolated himself from everyone. She didn't really blame him when she imagined the devastating pain she would endure if her own mother and father did such to her. Nonetheless, it destroyed her when he did not turn to her.

Gabi forced herself to forget him. Instead, she focused on her skills as a healer. She worked hard, and none could match her skills now. Over and again, she told herself she was over him, that it was time to move on. Now he was coming here and everything would change.

With a firm shake of her head, she headed off to the gym to work off some of her aggression. She was no child and refused to allow herself to be controlled by her emotions any longer. If that arrogant angel thought he could come back in her life and turn it upside down, he had another thing coming! Gabi would show him who the master of *this* house was.

Chapter Two

ABDIEL WALKED TO THE FRONT OF THE ARMORY. LEATHER GEAR protected him while he worked. Not bothering with the apron, he stripped the gloves from his hands and impatiently wiped the sweat from his brow. He wondered what Michael wanted him for. Although he already had a pretty good idea what it was, his gut tightened in anticipation.

He found the Chief Archangel seated on a bench. As usual, even in Heaven, Michael was dressed in human garb. He wore a pair of blue jeans with a red plaid shirt and was tossing a baseball up in the air and catching it. His dark blond hair was cut short and a pair of sunglasses hid his brown eyes.

"You wanted to see me?" Abdiel crossed his arms and gave a droll smile.

"It's time, big guy." Michael tossed him the ball.

As Abdiel caught it, the smile faded from his face. He knew this day would come soon. Although satisfied with his occasional solo job in the past, the Chief hinted lately that it was time for a permanent position. That did not mean he was happy about it though. "I hope it's another solo job." He tossed the ball back.

"Nope, you'll have an empath and a healer, just like all the other archangels. It's time you learned to live with others."

Abdiel bit back a curse. Accustomed to being alone, he did not look forward to associating with others. He was happy being lonely and miserable. That was the way things had been for centuries, so why change them now? "I don't think that's a good idea, Michael." He made sure his expression showed his uneasiness.

"You'll like these two, I promise. They won't bite. They might even give you a room where you can go and be all alone and brood." Michael smiled.

"Who are they?"

"I'll let you be surprised by that one."

He hated when Michael became bossy. If it weren't for the fact that his Chief could easily destroy him, Abdiel would pummel him for it. It was almost worth it. "Will you at least tell me where I'm going to be stationed?" His resigned sigh filled the air.

"Detroit, Michigan. You'll like it. The city sees a lot of action." Michael gave a wry smile. "Of course, they have a terrible winter season. You might want to pack extra gloves."

Abdiel cursed at the mere mention because he hated snow and cold, and the Chief knew it. If he didn't know better, he would have thought Michael had it out for him. "When do I leave?" He threw his arms up in surrender, as even he must obey.

"Tomorrow. I did not want to give you time to make up any excuses."

"Fine, just note, for the record, that I think this is a bad idea."

"Noted." Michael grinned. "At least you get to pound some demons into the ground. That should cheer you up."

Abdiel gave a sarcastic salute, then slipped his leather gloves back on.

The Chief laughed at his impetuousness. Few angels dared to give him such guff. "Trust me, Abdiel." Michael became serious. "There is going to be some bad stuff going down in that city. You're the only one I can count on to stop it."

Abdiel was slightly taken aback by the Chief's sudden somberness. "You're the only one I trust."

"I know I was really hard on you, harder than any other archangel. I have my reasons. You're about ready to find out why."

"Ah, man, I hate it when you talk in riddles." Abdiel realized he spoke to empty air because Michael already flashed out of there, leaving the archangel grumbling to himself.

THE NEXT DAY, ABDIEL hesitated before the door of the enormous house. He still could not believe he let Michael talk him into this. It would have been better for everybody if he just kept working in the armory. He did not play well with others, plain and simple. Knowing his luck, the healer and the empath he had to live with would hate him. Or worse, they would fear him. He always preferred hatred to fear. Hate was an emotion he could relate to.

Abdiel dreaded walking down the streets of Heaven. He would hear the whispers of *The Dark Angel* and feel the sidelong glances of fear. Females actually crossed the street to avoid passing him. Worse, young angel children cried at his approach. *What was Michael thinking?*

Before he could change his mind, he knocked on the large, wooden door. When it opened and he looked at the young male angel. Hard pressed to hide his shock, he looked behind him, half expecting Michael to jump out and say, *Surprise, joke is on you.*

The youth was dressed in baggy, jeans at least three sizes too big, tightly cinched at the waist with a belt. He wore a bright yellow tee shirt with a cartoon character on it, his blond hair was spiked up high with enough hair gel to supply an entire angel warrior battalion. *Good, God, he has an earring, too.* The little punk was even chewing gum. If not for the fact that this kid could see him, Abdiel would have sworn he looked at a human.

"Hey, you must be Abdiel." The young angel grinned and put his hand out. "I'm Camael."

Abdiel shook the proffered hand, smiling as he recognized the name. So the angel in front of him wasn't deranged after all. He was just a member of the Lehor family.

The group of eight brothers and one sister were always referred to as the *Lehor Family*. Not because that was their last name, angels do not use them. Lehor was their mother's name, and it was always easier to reference the large bunch by one name.

Anachele was the oldest and the only female. She took care of her eight younger brothers since their parents were mentally destroyed by a demon who captured and took them to Hell. Although they were eventually returned to Heaven, the damage was already done. Their bodies remained intact, but they were catatonic and lived in the angelic equivalent of a human mental ward. It was a danger that all empaths faced if they got too close to Hell as all the agony and pain that was contained there overloaded their systems.

Anachele was very overprotective of her little brothers. She clung to the task of raising them seriously and never took any time out for her own enjoyment. It was not an easy job either. The Lehor brothers were known throughout Heaven for their antics. The six oldest brothers were famous for getting into fights, and all eight of them were known for blurting out the most inappropriate things.

Camael was the second to youngest and, as such, one of family's babies. To make matters worse, he and his younger brother, Barakiel, were empaths like their parents. So Ana watched them like a hawk, while their six older brothers protected them fiercely. The elders greatest fear was losing them like they lost their parents. The only reason they let Cam leave home was because Michael insisted it was time to let their young brother grow up.

"Your sister speaks highly of you, Camael." Abdiel smirked when the younger angel's jaw dropped and a flicker of surprise passed over his face.

"Really? She usually calls me a pain in her..." he drawled the last bit deliberately.

"Yes, she's said that as well." As they both laughed, Abdiel was shocked that he found himself at ease with this young angel. Camael hadn't acted like he was disgusted by his presence. Even better, the empath seemed not to fear him.

"Come on. I'll give you a tour, and call me Cam," he said good-naturedly.

"Okay, just don't call me Ab."

Cam laughed again before he led Abdiel around the house.

As the kid showed him all the rooms, including his bedroom and the big gym for training, Abdiel was relieved to see how large the house was. He was used to having his own space and he valued his privacy. When they walked back into the kitchen, Cam opened the door to something he called a fridge and tossed him a cold metal object.

"It's a can of cola," he supplied when Abdiel looked at it strangely. "When we live on Earth, we eat as humans. Try it."

Cautious, Abdiel took a sip. "Not bad." "Human food is awesome." Cam grinned. "There are so many different flavors and textures. I can never get enough of it."

"That good, huh?" Abdiel chuckled at his enthusiasm.

"Just don't drink any alcohol. For some reason it makes us puke our guts up. One time I took just one drink of beer and I was kissing the can all night."

"Kissing the can?" Abdiel arched a brow in puzzlement.

"Yeah, and Gabi was yelling at me the whole time, which made things even more fun. She can yell louder than Ana."

"Gabi?" He hadn't heard that name in years.

"Oh yeah, that's right, you haven't met Gabi yet. She's our healer. She's the most skilled one ever," Cam declared proudly.

Abdiel shook his head, trying to take in all of Cam's rambling when she walked in. Actually, she glided more than walked. His jaw almost dropped when he saw her for the first time in centuries.

Gabrielle's long, black hair was tied in a thick braid that ran down her back, the raven locks so dark they appeared almost blue. Her bright green eyes were wide and surrounded by long lashes that nearly brushed her rosy cheeks. She was dressed in all black—a leather jacket ended at her tiny waist and pants of the same fabric hugged her curves, accenting her softly rounded bottom. A crossbow slung across her back, along with several arrows, told of her prized weapon.

Abdiel tried not to stare, but it was hard. Her parents were seraphim, the highest order of angels, so that made her royalty, and she sure carried herself like it. She was easily the most beautiful angel. He wanted to pull her into his arms for a kiss and a taste those full lips. More than that, he wanted to see if she still wore hot pink panties. Several deep breaths steadied him. It had been nearly forever since a female affected him this way.

Abdiel remembered her from when they went to school together. She was a shy little mousy thing, cute as a kitten, but skittish as one, too. This female angel certainly outgrew that for she was full-grown. Her tall, curvy body screamed that fact.

"Hey Gabi," Cam said. "This is Abdiel."

"I pretty much figured that," she replied. Her soft and hypnotic voice brought forth images of sex and silk sheets.

"He said not to call him Ab. Since he's pretty big, and he is the Dark Angel, I guess we better listen."

Abdiel didn't know if he should laugh or box the kid's ears. He couldn't help it as he was actually beginning to like the little brat. Nobody ever dared say such things in front of him before. They always whispered it behind his back. Cam's blunt honesty was refreshing. "You're all grown up, Gabrielle." Abdiel redirected his attention to her and became instantly lost in her green eyes.

"You remember me?"

"Sure I do. You kicked me in the shins the first day of school. How could I forget you after that?"

Cam laughed.

Gabi reached up and smacked him on the back of the head.

Abdiel could tell this was not the first time she cold-cocked the empath by the casual, practiced way the movement was executed.

"Sorry to interrupt the introductions," she said casually. "But we have work to do."

Dear God, her voice was so mesmerizing Abdiel hung on her every word.

"Something wicked this way comes?" Cam reached for his backpack.

"You tell me. You're the empath." A small smile curved her lips.

Cam closed his eyes and sent himself outside his body, searching. When he touched the evil minds, he shuddered. It was always hard for an empath to touch an unclean mind. Coming back, he slowly opened his eyes. "There are four of them, and they mean to kill. They don't care who. They just want to have someone suffer so they can enjoy the pain." His face scrunched as if he smelled something bad. "You know, *Survivor* is on tonight. Can't they take one night off?"

"So you feel demon's nearby, too?" Abdiel didn't feel a thing. He didn't know what the empath meant when he talked about *Survivor* either, but decided not to display ignorance by asking.

"Not nearly as well as an empath. We can all feel little twinges. Don't worry. When you get adjusted to being on Earth, you will feel them, too."

"Is that normal?"

"It takes some weaker archangels days to adjust to being around so many demons." She raised her head haughtily. "Do you think you can handle a fight tonight? I know it's been a long time since you had a real battle."

Cam's mouth dropped open in shock as he waited for Abdiel's reaction.

Gabi didn't show any weakness. She met Abdiel eye to eye, waiting for an answer, her chin tilted up in an arrogant way, reminding him again of her royal status. What was the nickname that they dubbed her again? Oh yes, Ice Queen, and it sure as hell fit. He shouldn't have been surprised by her actions around him. Most angels treated him with disdain and distrust. They assumed since all the other angels in his league turned, so would he. Suddenly, he was reminded why he stayed away from everybody all these long years.

He was an idiot to assume she would think any differently. Gone was the shy little teenager he remembered. A hellcat replaced her. It felt like she kicked him in the shins all over again. "Well, I guess there is only one way to find out." His expression determined, he grabbed his sword and scabbard and headed for the door. When he got there, he opened it and stopped. "You two coming or what?" His voice took on its hard edge again as his anger built.

"You just dissed the Dark Angel, Gabi. Great way to make friends," Cam hissed under his breath, then headed for the door.

With a growl of frustration, she followed.

GABI WAS STILL MAD at the little traitor, better known as Cam, an hour later while they walked deep into the city streets, unseen to human eyes, as night fell. Angels always cloaked themselves and the battles from human sight so, the human race was never to know the many conflicts that happened every day between good and evil. All angels felt it their sacred duty to protect humans from this horror.

Cam took the lead, mentally seeking out the demons.

"Does he know where he's going?" Abdiel glanced around.

"Yes, he's better than a navigation system," Gabi spoke quietly, not wanting to distract Cam.

"A navigation system?"

Gabi rolled her eyes. "You really need to watch some TV, read some books—you know, catch up with the rest of us."

"What's TV?" Abdiel looked at her like she spoke a foreign language.

"Michael sent us a dinosaur. When was the last time you were on Earth?"

"Around the Civil War to round up a rogue angel."

"So you've never fought a true demon?" Suddenly aware her mouth was open in shock, she clamped it shut.

"No, the council was too afraid of me running into my family."

Gabi felt like an idiot. *Of course they had been.* "Right, sorry. Didn't think of that."

At that moment, something swooped from the sky, hit Cam and

knocked him to the ground. A yelp of surprise accompanied the slam of his body onto the wet pavement.

The female demon pinned him and beat him about the face and body. For a split second, she paused to look up at Abdiel and Gabi with glowing red eyes. While her body possessed curves in all the right places, that was the only normal thing about her. Her skin and long ratty hair were both dark as midnight and her black dress was ripped up both sides. The tattered split showed off her long legs, which tightly squeezed Cam's hips and kept him in place.

The young angel tried to fight back, but his skills were undisciplined and weak at best. The female quickly detected this and unleashed a whoop of delight. Her long claws gouged deep scratches in his chest. Cam tried to buck her off him, but he was a scrawny thing, and the demon had at least fifty pounds on him.

Abdiel drew his sword and ran forward to help, but two more demons materialized and blocked his way.

The smell of decaying flesh filled the air and Gabi heard him gag. It was common knowledge demons smelled like death, but this was probably the first time he experienced the stench. If that threw him for a loop, then Gabi could only imagine how shocked Abdiel must be at the demon's hideous appearance. Once they had been beautiful angels, but sin twisted their appearances and turned them into monsters.

One was red with bright yellow eyes. Two jagged slits marked his nostrils, a distorted mouth boasted several rows of razor sharp teeth, demonic legs looked goat-like, but much larger and muscular. Red demon bore a kris, the uneven edge of the sword's blade glinted in the moonlight.

Gabi saw dried blood on it. *Now that's no way to take care of a weapon.* It never ceased to amaze her how slovenly demons were.

The second demon was no beauty queen, either. Dark blue with blood red eyes, his body was long, angular and poised for battle. A forked, blood red tongue repetitively darted out of his mouth like that of a lizard. Blue wielded a chain whip, which he slowly swung around.

Although it was no sword, the whip was a deadly weapon. The metal links easily snatch limbs.

Gabi knew this demon did not take any better care of its weapon than the other. Hunks of flesh were embedded in the chain, along with old blood.

Unwilling to wait for introductions, Abdiel pulled out his long sword and charged. He ducked so Blue's chain whip missed him and matched swords with Red. The blades flashed as the two warriors battled.

Blue used the distraction and hit Abdiel fully on the back with his chain whip. Abdiel hissed with pain as it cut deep into his body. Gabi sucked in a breath as she saw the fabric of his black shirt grow darker as blood soaked through it. Blue quickly hit him in the back again, laughing with glee at the archangel's blood.

Pushing Red forward when they next crossed swords, Abdiel spun to Blue, kicking him full in the throat. As the demon fell to the ground gagging, the archangel pivoted and deflected another thrust from Red's kris. Blue recovered and lashed Abdiel's back again. The demon swung its whip again and again.

The healer in Gabi felt Abdiel's strength drain with each blow—in fact, she felt both males in her angelic team weakening. With her bow raised, she watched for a clear shot at the attacking demons. Fear of missing and hitting one of the angels stayed her hand.

Still on the ground, Cam struggled with the she-demon. Finally, managing to push her off, he scrambled on all fours toward his backpack. Before he got to it, the demon grabbed his ankle and dragged him back, pinning him once more.

"You are a cute little empath." She stroked his cheek with a claw.

"Sorry, I don't do demon," Cam rasped, trying to pull back.

"Too bad for you, I am going to have me some angel tonight." The she-demon licked his face.

Gabi's stomach rolled at the sickening sight of demon drool on her empath friend.

"Agh, that is so wrong." Cam fought to get away from the female's wandering fingers. He tried to hit her, but the demon pinned his hands and hissed in his face.

Gabi almost unleashed a triumphant yell when a clear shot at the female demon opened. The fourth demon swooped down. The she-demon slammed right on top of Gabi and her head smacked painfully on the ground. *Damn it, I forgot Cam said there were four demons. How could I have so stupid and let my guard down? Yeah, the two of us must be making a wonderful first impression on Abdiel. He's probably going to go running for the hills because he is saddled with Sir I Dunno How to Fight and Lady Can't Count.*

Since her head hurt already, she head-butted the new she-demon as hard as possible. When the demon staggered back, stunned, Gabi grabbed her crossbow, sat up and shot three arrows into the demonic heart. The she-demon crawled a little way, then disappeared in a flash, back to Hell.

Gabi twisted and sunk two more arrows in the throat of the Blue attacking Abdiel's back. It didn't disable the evil one, but it gave Abdiel enough time to put his sword through Red's heart before spun to Blue and stabbed him as well. Both demons vanished.

Gabi sprang to her feet to help Cam who was being molested by the she-demon. Ready to run, she froze as Abdiel yanked the beastette off Cam. He stabbed it, too, dispatching the demon back to Hell.

Abdiel knelt down and examined Cam's face. A swollen right eye hindered the young angel's vision, and his face bled in several places. Deep cuts where the demon's claw dug in decorated his chest.

The empath inhaled several shuddering breaths and shifted his gaze to the side, too ashamed to look at the archangel.

"Cam, who was your last archangel?" Abdiel demanded softly.

Gabi saw the anger on his face and shared it. The poor kid was defenseless.

"Charoum." Cam rolled over and vomited blood.

"Why didn't he train him?" Abdiel watched Gabi kneel and rub the empath's back.

"He didn't appreciate Cam's unorthodox way of living," she spat. There was no love lost between her and their old archangel, and she saw no reason hide it.

"That doesn't surprise me," Abdiel grunted. He gave a sympathetic look as the empath vomited even more. "Charoum has always been an ass. It still doesn't excuse him sending Cam out totally unprepared. I'll make sure I knock some sense into your ex-archangel next time I see him."

"Sorry I keep puking." Cam wiped his mouth. "Us empaths upchuck more than super models."

"That's okay, kid. You don't ever need to apologize to me for something like that. You can't help it."

Shocked at the compassion in his voice, Gabi was even more impressed when the archangel reached down and pulled Cam to his feet. He shouldered the young male's weight, even though the blood soaking through his shirt, his obvious injuries serious.

"Are you okay, Gabi?" His dark gaze searched her for evident injuries.

"Just a little knock on the noggin, nothing like you two." She tried to ignore the little skip of her heart.

"Come on, Cam, let's get home. We have a lot of training ahead of us." Abdiel flashed away with Cam.

Standing there alone, Gabi tried to make sense of everything. She thought all these years that Abdiel was some cold, unfeeling angel. Yet, he instantly saw that Cam was a good kid and was going to take him under his wing. He was going to train him to fight when every other archangel refused.

She thought back to the way Abdiel fought. She never saw anyone fight so well. He was quick and powerful and it amazed her how cool and efficient he was. Even though he was wounded, she never doubted his ability to defeat the demons.

Afterward, he was gentle and caring, his first thought for his angels.

He didn't yell at Cam for messing up, instead, he comforted the young empath. She recalled the way he looked her over for injuries, concerned for her, too.

She blushed when she remembered the way she treated him earlier. Even though she acted like he was garbage, he still worried about her and wanted to protect her. She was a jerk and she knew it.

As she thought of those dark, liquid eyes, and how that lock of hair still fell over them after all these years, she licked her lips. He became even better looking over time. When she first saw him in the kitchen, an insane urge to run her hands over his arms—just to feel if those muscles were as hard as they looked.

No, she couldn't afford to feel for him again. He was just a good-looking angel—okay, a good-looking angel with an amazing body—but that was it. Gabi wasn't going to set herself up to be hurt again. She'd been down that road and had the tee shirt to prove it.

She flashed herself back to the house. She needed to heal both Cam and Abdiel. But, knowing her luck, Mr. Super Hero Dark Angel could do that, too.

Chapter Three

SHE FLASHED INTO CAM'S ROOM, FULLY EXPECTING HIM TO BE IN there waiting for her to heal him, only to find it empty. Surprised, she went to Abdiel's room and discovered it empty as well. *Those two stubborn males probably did not think they needed healing.*

Gabi followed the sound of their voices to the kitchen. Cam sat at the table, a wet cloth to his face, while Abdiel leaned against the counter laughing at something the empath apparently said. She gave a very unladylike snort of frustration. "You two should be upstairs lying down. Instead, I find you both bleeding all over my kitchen. Now I am going to have to heal you just so you can clean up your own mess."

"Sorry, Gabi, I'll try to bleed less." Cam grinned.

"Do I dare even ask what was so funny?" She raised an eyebrow. Her question made both males laugh again.

"I just told Abdiel not to feel bad for me. When that she-demon attacked me, it was the closest I ever got to scoring." Cam winced in pain.

"That thing nearly ripped you into a million pieces and you think it's funny?" She couldn't believe that the two of them joked like a pair of teenagers.

"I thought she was really beginning to like me. She wanted me to be her baby's daddy."

"Yeah, I could tell she was warming up to you by the way she was beating your face. For your next date, maybe she'll use a whip." Abdiel winked, and both of them erupted into laughter again.

"I'm going to have to disinfect him after that she-demon

manhandled him."

"It wasn't really that bad, honestly, Gabi," Cam said with false sincerity. Both males hooted in laughter again.

Gabi just stood there and shook her head in confusion. "When you two *children* are ready to be healed, let me know." She stalked out of the kitchen and went to Cam's room and paced while waiting for them. Although, she really should be as angry as her act, she was impressed with the way Abdiel put Cam at ease after the fight. Hearing them come up the stairs, she turned.

Abdiel helped Cam into the room before he playfully pushed the empath onto his bed. "Let Gabi heal you. Tomorrow we start your training. Next time it might be a male demon who gets frisky." He pulled off Cam's grubby tennis shoes and tossed them in the corner.

Gabi reached over and touched Cam, compelling him to sleep. It was always much easier to heal him when he was resting. Otherwise, he never stopped talking.

"Thank you, Abdiel." Cam drifted off.

"No problem, kid," he responded quietly. "Michael was right, I do like you."

"How are you doing?" Gabi noticed his back still bled.

"Take care of Cam first," he replied. "I've had worse." He walked out of the room.

Gabi watched him, a small frown on her face. Yes, he suffered a lot worse. She witnessed such.

LATER THAT NIGHT, ABDIEL lay on his bed and reviewed the evening's battle in his head. It felt good to finally get back into action. Although, the demons' appearance was unsettling. It was the first time he battled a true demon—and damn, the things were ugly.

Before the fall of Lucifer, all the archangels battled were lone outlaw angels that broke laws and needed brought to justice. He was more cop than warrior. The wrongdoers weren't much more than mere petty criminals. Even the rogue angels he rounded up later, after the fall, were nothing like the things he met tonight. The rogues either had not gone through the transformation yet or were so early in the transition they showed few physical changes.

These things he fought tonight were different. Not only had their evil deeds transformed them into hideous beings, the evil poured off them like a fetid stench. He was no empath, but he still felt the hate that rolled off them. *I wonder what my family looks like now. What if Rachael and Appolion have turned into monsters, too? If that is the case, then I don't know if I can handle seeing them again. Especially since I should have been able to keep them safe. I'm their big brother after all. I'll never be able to forgive my father for taking the twins from Heaven and me. Even after all these years I still feel like I failed them and I'll never be able to get that blight off my soul.*

A soft knock interrupted his troubled thoughts.

Gabi opened the door and came in. She changed out of her fighting clothes and now wore a pair of jeans and white tee shirt. Her hair was free from the braid and hung loose. The ends of the slightly curly, dark locks just reached the top of her delicious-looking backside. Not that he was checking out her ass or anything. *Who are you kidding? You are checking out her ass. Every single chance you get.*

"If you're ready, I can heal you now." She walked to the side of the bed.

As soon as she got close enough, the scent of roses invaded enveloped him. "How's Cam?" He winced as he sat up. The ridiculous urge to bury his nose in her neck so he could drink in that rose scent taunted. *Down boy, remember she's a princess and you're nothing but an archangel.*

"He'll be fine. He's been hurt a lot worse than that before."

"How many times?" He fought to keep the anger out of his voice, lest she think it directed at her.

"More times than I can count." Her green eyes filled with tears. "I've always been able to heal his external wounds, but I know it hurt him inside even more."

"It's totally unacceptable that no one has trained him yet. Every archangel knows how exposed and vulnerable empaths are. It's a miracle he hasn't been damaged like his parents."

"You know about Cam's parents?" She looked surprised.

"Yes, Ana is a good friend of mine."

"Oh." Full lips pressed tightly together as she looked at the carpet.

If he didn't know better, he could have sworn she was jealous. A part of him wanted to tell her there was nothing between him and Ana, but he stopped. Running his hands over his face, he cleared his thoughts and chastised himself for being an idiot. There was no way that someone as wonderful as her would be jealous over some moron that came from a family of demons.

"Thank you for being so kind to Cam." She smiled.

When she gave him her first real smile, he felt like a giddy schoolboy. It was like she gave him a precious gift. He must be losing his mind, maybe one of the demons knocked something loose. "Cam's a good kid. He just needs some training." He kept his face neutral.

"You're the first archangel who has thought that. The rest couldn't tolerate poor Cam."

"Cam's just honest to a fault. I happen to like that."

"It's been so hard, Abdiel. Every time he goes out there, he gets hurt."

"Not anymore. I'll make sure he never goes out there unprepared again."

"I tried to train him myself." She looked at her hands in shame. "I'm a healer, though, and he needed training from an archangel."

"I know you tried, Gabi. It was the first thing Cam told me when we got back." He cupped her chin in his hand and forced her to look him in the eye. "I don't blame you." Although, he knew he should not be touching her like this, he couldn't help himself. Somehow, he was drawn to her like a bee to honey. Abdiel was never this enamored with a female before, not even Persephone.

"Cam's like a baby brother to me. It has been so hard to see him get hurt all the time." She was whispering, almost in fear of ruining the intimate moment.

Using the pad of his thumb, he gently stroked her bottom lip with light, feathery touches. At first, she stiffened, but eventually relaxed and closed her eyes. Her beautiful full pink lips parted slightly in a small gasp of surprise. Reveling both in the petal softness of her lips and the heat of her breath against his hand, he almost lost it and groaned with desire.

"I'm sorry about the way I treated you earlier." She still didn't open her eyes.

"That's okay, I'm used to it." He licked his lips and thought about what her luscious mouth would taste like.

"No, it's not okay. You're my archangel and we are a team. I should show you respect."

"Somehow I don't see Miss Beautiful Princess bowing down to any archangel." He brushed her hair from her face.

"You think I'm beautiful?" Her eyelids snapped open and shock filled her expression.

"I've always thought you were beautiful, even when you kicked me in the shins."

Her jaw dropped at that comment.

Unable to hold himself back any longer, he pulled her into his arms. He expected her to push him away, but instead she threw her arms around him. As soon as her hands touched his back, he hissed in pain.

She released him and jumped back.

An emptiness accompanied her absence. Part of him wanted to draw her back, pain or no pain. Hell, part of him wanted to throw her down on the bed, rip off her clothes and bury himself deep inside her. It would only take one time, and she would be his forever. Angels mate for life.

GABI STOOD ON THE opposite side of the room gasping for breath as she gaped at Abdiel. *Stupid, stupid, stupid,* she chastised herself. She promised wasn't going to fall for him again, and in less than twelve hours, she was literally throwing herself at him. "Take your shirt off so I can see the damage." She tried to keep her voice emotionless.

When he peeled his shirt off, she gasped in displeasure. His back was a crisscross of deep cuts, some going all the way to the bone. If he were mortal, he would be dead. He must be in horrible pain, yet, he made sure Cam was healed first. Then he talked to her to make her feel better. She sure as heck didn't help matters either when she practically tackled him.

"Lay down on your stomach." She knelt by the bed. When he complied, she placed her hands on his back. Closing her eyes, she recited the healing chants that were as old as time. Using her powers, she knitted the flesh back together and left no wound unattended. She pushed out the infection the filthy demon weapons left behind.

When she finally sensed it done, she urged him to sleep, then came out of her trance. He needed his rest after such grave injuries. His naked, muscular back was irresistible and she had the insane urge to run her tongue along his spine to see if he tasted like he smelled—earthy and spicy. Heat flushed her face. She could just imagine what Michael would say if he caught one of his healers licking an archangel they were supposed to be treating.

"Why are you here on Earth, Gabi?" Abdiel mumbled sleepily.

"Like you, I have a job to do."

"You're seraphim, like your parents. You could be living in the highest order of Heaven with them. Instead, you stay here and take care of everybody else." Without opening his eyes, he grabbed her hand and rubbed his thumb softly against it.

"You're not the only one who feels that they have to make up for past mistakes, Abdiel."

"What horrible mistakes could you have possibly made, Princess?"

"That is my business, not yours." She jerked back her hand and walked out of the room. She probably should tell him of her past sins, but she was afraid and she couldn't bear for him to know the horrible things she'd done. Not even Cam knew. They were her sins, and she would bear it alone.

It wasn't until the next evening that Abdiel woke up. He went downstairs and found Cam in front of the TV. The empath lay sprawled on the couch, his body slumped like he possessed no bones. Abdiel sat down next to him. "What's this?"

"Hockey. The best thing about being assigned to Detroit is the Red Wings." Cam never took his gaze from the game.

"What are Red Wings?" Even more confused, Abdiel studied the screen in hopes of some clearer explanation.

"The red guys are the Red Wings. They're the good guys. The other guys are the Avalanche. They're the bad guys."

"You watch these humans all the time?"

"My whole family's hockey junkies." Cam shook his head. "Besides, Chris Chelios is not just any human. He is a super hero. He's the good guy with the big, red twenty-four on his jersey."

After a few minutes of watching, and with the young angel explaining the rules, Abdiel found that he actually enjoyed the game.

Pretty soon, Gabi came in and flopped onto the other end of the couch. Like the empath, she lay limp, relaxed.

He found himself smiling at the way she cheered and yelled at the TV. When two of the players got into a fight and the Red Wings won, she actually stood and clapped her hands together. He loved the way her hips moved when she did the victory dance. Then the two of them introduced him to something called pizza. It tasted so good that, before he knew it, he had eaten more than Cam. In Heaven, all angels ate was manna. Cam was right. It was nice to try new flavors.

Cam ran to the kitchen for another soda.

"Do you two do this every night, Gabi?"

"Every night we're not out saving the world from evil nasties."

"It must be nice." He couldn't remember the last time he just sat and relaxed around others as he did tonight. It was, well...nice.

"See, it's not so bad living with others." She propped up her feet and opened the top button of her jeans.

He glimpsed her flat belly and smiled at the sight of a princess sitting there with her gut hanging out. It was absolutely adorable. "Not everyone is as nice as you and Cam."

"I know some archangels look down on you, Abdiel but not all of us think like that. I was one of those who found you that day. I saw what your family did to you."

"I did not know you were there."

"I was just beginning in my healing duties. I tagged along with my brother, Raphael, whenever he was sent on a mission." She shrugged.

"It was you, wasn't it?" Realization slowly dawned. "You were the one crying. Why?"

"I don't know what you're talking about." She shifted to get up.

He grabbed her and pulled her back onto the couch. "Tell me the truth, Gabi." He reached down and brushed her hair away from her face.

"What do you want me to say?" Tears welled in her eyes. "That I was a stupid, naïve child who was infatuated with someone who didn't even know I existed?"

"You were infatuated with me?" He couldn't keep the amused smile off his face.

"Like you didn't already know that."

"Honestly, I had no idea."

"Liar."

"Come on, Gabi." He chuckled. "It's not every day that a princess falls for some common archangel."

"You did *not* see me as a princess." Her green eyes snapped fire. "You called me a mouse, remember?"

"That was a compliment. I thought you were so cute and little."

"You *thought* I was a rodent."

"You, a rodent? Never. You're anything but, Princess." Abdiel lowered his head to kiss her. She started to reach up to meet his advance, then stopped. Her body stiffened. When he looked into her eyes again, he almost cursed in frustration. They were cold and distant.

"Don't worry, bud, I am so over you," she snapped.

Figuring he had nothing to lose, he leaned down and kissed her softly on the cheek.

She gasped in shock, then jumped to her feet and fled the room. Her face was flushed and her eyes wide.

He enjoyed getting a rise out of her. This game was fun. He laughed when her growl of frustration drifted back to the living room.

Hours later, Gabi remained hidden in her room. Fully aware she was being a coward, she couldn't bring herself to face Abdiel and couldn't believe she admitted her childhood crush on him. She spent hundreds of years telling herself she was over him, and in less than one night, she acted like the same lovesick puppy all over again.

"Get a grip, Gabi." She picked up a juicy romance novel and figured she just needed to take a time out and get lost in a good book. Her concentration on reading was hindered when her mind drifted back to Abdiel and how nice his lips felt against her cheek. *How would feel on other parts of my body?*

"We're going down to the gym to train," Cam called from the other side of the door. She jumped out of her carnal thoughts.

"Ya coming?"

Knowing that Cam would be disappointed if she didn't, she left her room and followed him down to the gym. Abdiel was already waiting.

Cam hesitated at the doorway, nervously tugging his hair.

"Don't worry. Remember, you like Mr. Dark Angel," she whispered and nudged him forward.

"Come on in, Cam. I promise not to bite," Abdiel teased.

"That's not what has me worried. I just don't want you to see how much of a dork I am when I try to spar."

"I promise not to laugh at your dorkiness. Why don't you show me your weapon? I never saw it last night."

All empaths possessed one weapon they specialized in that was custom made for them in the armory. Cam opened up his backpack and pulled out a pair of tonfa. The wooden weapons resembled a police baton, but were twenty inches long and designed to be held one in each hand.

"I remember when your sister ordered those," Abdiel said.

"She totally wigged out when Michael gave me an assignment and said she was going to have the best weapon maker she knew make these. I guess that was you, Abdiel, huh?"

"Yes, it was me. First rule, whenever you are on the street tracking demons I want you to have those in your hands ready to go. When your new girlfriend attacked you last night, she caught you totally unprepared. Until you learn to use your fists, these tonfa are your best friends."

"Charoum told me that I shouldn't carry a weapon, that it was my duty to be a good little empath and focus on my job," Cam said defensively.

"Second rule, forget everything Charoum ever told you. He's a complete idiot." As Cam laughed, Gabi marveled at the way Abdiel put the empath at ease. For the first time ever in the training room, the young angel relaxed and actually got something good out of a lesson. Not wanting to interfere, she sat in the corner and watched the two. Abdiel was patient with Cam, never once ridiculing or getting angry. He was so kind and caring she didn't know how anyone could ever think him anything but good.

Then it hit her. She had never stopped loving him. In fact, since she spent the last day with him, she grew to love him even more. It felt as if someone punched her in the stomach. Oh heaven help her, she couldn't let herself be hurt again. What was she going to do?

GABI BOLTED UPRIGHT IN her bed as she tore herself out of her nightmare. Her breath came in raspy, fast huffs, making her lungs burn from effort. The smell of her fear and sweat clung in the air. Brushing a lock of damp hair out of her face, she got out of bed. She wore a pair of boxer shorts and a white tank top, so the night air was cold on her skin. As soon as her bare feet touched the cool, smooth wood floor, goose bumps danced on her arms.

She went into her private bathroom and got a drink of water from the sink, then looked at herself in the mirror. Her face was pale and dark circles lurked under her eyes. The nightmares always took a big toll on her body. And the bad dreams surfaced whenever she allowed herself to feel too much.

They were always about the same thing—her mission in Sodom and Gomorrah. She had been called to the cities right before their destruction. The demons released a horrible plague that turned humans into demons. The mortals went insane, then morphed and killed other innocent people. Her job was to heal as many as possible. However, when she arrived, not only was there no cure for the plague, but it was ready to spread to other cities. Scores of humans would perish if that happened.

The council's order was swift and quick. She led a battalion of archangels and decimated both Sodom and Gomorrah. They made sure nothing was left behind, that every last bit of the disease was eradicated. She remembered the screams of the dying. As a healer, it was in her nature to save lives, not take them. Deep down she knew it was the only way to save humanity, but it still felt so wrong.

For centuries, she carried the pain deep inside her. She never had anyone to turn to for comfort. Since both of her parents were seraphim, they resided in the highest realm of Heaven, protecting human souls. Once her parents took their thrones, they left forever. Gabi and

Raphael were raised by a slew of nannies that seemed to change on a daily bases. They were never loved and coddled like other children.

As a result, they grew up to be cool and aloof. Gabi knew that for years, her name was the Ice Queen, and she carried it proudly. After being hurt by Abdiel, she didn't want to even think about letting anyone else into her heart. Her life was healing and that was it.

Then she met the Lehor family and everything changed. They embraced her into their fold and taught her how a real family was. If not for Ana and the boys, Gabi would still have an empty shell of a life. After she met the Lehors and started her work as an angel warrior, her nightmares all but faded. Until tonight.

She blamed Abdiel. If he hadn't come and brought up old memories, she wouldn't have had the dream. Well, if Michael wanted the two of them to work together, then Abdiel would have to learn to keep his hands to himself. She'd just go and tell Mr. Dark Angel that right now.

She marched down to his room and flung open the door without even bothering to knock. He bolted up the instant she entered, but she still kicked at the bed. They looked into each other's eyes as she tried to think of something clever to say.

He finally tired of waiting. "You wanted something, Princess?"

"I would appreciate it if you would keep your hands to yourself in the future." Palms on hips, she tried to strike her best royal pose. "It's very distracting, and I don't like it." She pivoted and flounced out of his room. No sooner did she make it into her own room, then her door slammed wide open and banged against the wall. She spun around, her hands balled up, ready for a yelling match. Abdiel was about to find out she was no weak, simpering female that backed down. "Get out," she snarled.

He ignored her and walked a slow circle around her, looking at her P.J.s. His tone was a soft warning, "If you want me to keep my hands to myself, Little Mouse, then I would suggest you don't come to my bed wearing next to nothing."

With a loud gasp, she realized he was right. She barely wore any clothes and the white tank top left little to the imagination. Embarrassed, she crossed her arms over her chest. Even worse, he was half-naked, too. His dark blue flannel sleep pants hung low on his lean hips and he wore no top, which provided a great view of his muscular, tan chest.

He opened his mouth, but stopped and looked around her room.

She winced, realizing what was coming next because she was an avid collector of angel memorabilia made by humans. If it had wings and a halo, she had to have it. There were bears, dolls, posters, blankets and countless figurines littering her room.

Abdiel picked up a big, pink, stuffed bear with a golden halo and wings. "I see that humans still think we have wings." He shook his head and put the bear back. "Interesting collection you've got there."

"Thank you…" She growled. "Don't change the subject. I meant what I said. I don't want you touching me anymore."

Moving like a lion, he stalked forward, causing her to back pedal until her back was flush against the wall. He put his hands on either side of her head, slowly leaned forward and breathed on her neck.

Despite her best efforts to stay angry, she shivered with desire when his hot breath cascaded over her shoulder.

"I'll make a deal with you," he whispered in her ear. "I'll stop touching you, if you stop touching me."

"I'm not touching you now," she argued breathlessly.

"Could have fooled me, Princess."

Gabi was shocked to find her hands buried in his hair. The only thing separating their bodies was the thin material of her top. When her hardened nipples felt the heat and strength of his chest, her knees threatened to buckle. She never before felt pure, raw desire like she did now. It terrified her. "I can't do this again, Abdiel." She was appalled to realize that she was crying. "I won't allow myself to fall for you again."

He immediately dropped his hands and went to the other side of the room. "Look, I didn't mean to upset you. I'll promise to keep everything professional from now on. I'm sorry. I forgot my duty is to be your archangel, and not to romance my healer. I'll keep my hands to myself. Just don't cry anymore." He walked out of the room, his hand crossed over his chest.

Gabi knew she hurt him. She didn't need Cam's empathic skills to tell her that, the look that passed over Abdiel's face clued her in. It was a mixture of self-loathing and sad acceptance. *Way to go, Gabi. You just dissed the Dark Angel, again.* A little sarcastic voice taunted in her head. She released a small scream of frustration, then threw herself face down on her bed.

Chapter Four

Over the next weeks, the team settled into a regular schedule. They ate, slept and trained. Abdiel spent every spare moment working with Cam. Before long, he formed a genuine friendship with the empath. He liked the kid so much, he even found himself willing to trust someone at his back besides Michael.

He really enjoyed Gabi's company as well. Her quick wit and gentle ways made it easy for him to let his guard down. Although, he still had to fight the urge to take her into his arms and claim her as his. He gave her his word he would keep his hands to himself and he would stand by it, even if it killed him. In order to take his mind off his feelings for her, he concentrated on his job. Every night he took his crew out to hunt demons. There was definitely no shortage of evil in Detroit so it was easy to keep busy.

At first, when they would have to fight, Abdiel would keep Cam close to protect him. However, Cam quickly improved under Abdiel's tutelage and the archangel let him loose. What the empath lacked in strength, he made up in quickness and agility. Abdiel was surprised at how fast the young angel caught on. Soon, he was standing shoulder to shoulder with Abdiel, more than holding his own.

When Cam would go to school, Abdiel watched TV and read any book he got his hands on. Now that he was living among humans, he wanted to learn everything about them that he could.

It was easy for Abdiel to see Cam's fascination with the human race. They were diverse and very interesting. He even became a hockey geek like his empath. Abdiel loved to watch TV. Nick at Night was his favorite, followed by reality shows. Finally, when he asked Gabi for pork chops and applesauce for dinner ala Brady, she threatened to cut him off.

Abdiel got used to not living alone and being around them. In fact, one day Cam was at the movies and Gabi was nowhere to be found, he actually began searching the house for her, wanting her company. He located her in the gym, working out with a punching bag. He watched her for several minutes, admiring her skill. Her lithe body moved in a way that would make even most archangels envious. His gaze traveled down and settled on her legs. Sweet damn, they seemed to go on for miles. "You want to spar?

She jumped, obviously surprised at being watched. "Ya think you can handle it?" She recovered quickly and flashed him a saucy smile.

"It's a risk I'm willing to take."

They went to the center of the gym and faced off. They opted to use no weapons and fight with their fists instead. At first, they only hit each other lightly, playfully. Soon the competitive side got the better of them and they were full-out fighting. He had to admit she was good.

He grabbed her wrist. Spinning her around, Abdiel pinned her against him. They both froze the instant their bodies touched. His arm pressed against her chest and her full breasts heaved against him as she breathed hard from exertion. He hardened as he fantasized about cupping them in his hands and teasing the nipples to full points.

After a moment, she got a hold of herself and tried to take him down. Their legs tangled and they both fell to the mat. He landed on top of her, both of them still panting from the workout.

Her soft curves felt so good under him. Their bodies molded together as if custom made for one another. His erection pressed against her thigh and he made no move to hide it. He wanted her to know how much she turned him on. *Damn, even though I have no right, I want her so badly it hurts.*

"Abdiel, let me up," she whispered.

"Just give me one kiss, Gabi. That's all I ask for." Even as he said the words, he knew he was lying. He wanted a lot more from her.

They both knew it.

When she didn't argue, he leaned down and captured her full mouth with his. As soon as they met, he was lost. It was the most passionate and beautiful kiss he ever experienced. He used his thumb to nudge her chin down so that her lips fully parted. In that instant, he invaded her mouth with his tongue. Ever gentle, he explored the inside, reveling in the sweet taste she offered. He almost came on the spot when her small tongue started to dart around, too. The velvet heat from it threatened to drive him crazy.

Abdiel left her mouth and tasted her neck. When she moaned, he laughed. He needed to remember that Little Princess liked that. Moving lower, he alternated bites and sucks on her collarbone. Although, he knew giving her a hickey was childish, but he wanted to mark her as his.

Suddenly, she stiffened.

He almost cursed. She was pulling away from him again. He rolled off of her and got to his feet. "I'm sorry, I should have remembered my place." He helped her up.

Gabi gaped, her mouth open to speak. She must have changed her mind because she clamped it shut and ran out of the room.

He stopped himself from following her.

A FEW NIGHTS LATER, Gabi sat in the kitchen reading while Abdiel and Cam practiced, yet again, in the gym. All was right in the world—she had her coffee, cookies and a steamy romance. Her moment of peace vanished when an angel flashed into the house.

Usually, manners dictated you didn't just flash into someone's house, unannounced. Just because you could pop into any room at will, didn't mean that you shouldn't respect other's privacy. You knocked on the door. Obviously, this angel was too angry to follow protocol.

The tall, willowy female's blonde hair was pulled tight into its usual bun. She was dressed as all female angels dressed when in Heaven, in a long white dress that gracefully flowed around her body. Her usually cold blue eyes now flashed fire. "Where is my little brother?" Ana spat.

"What did he do now?" Gabi glanced up from her book. This wasn't the first time Cam's sister came for his hide, and it would probably not be the last time either.

"He flunked religious studies." Ana held up a letter from the school.

Gabi quickly ducked her head behind her book, then smiled. She snorted in an effort to suppress her laughter. *How could he flunk religious studies?*

"It's not funny, Gabi. He never takes anything seriously. None of my brothers do." Ana sat at the table.

"Come on, Ana, it can't be that bad. I would love to have a little brother."

"You wouldn't if you dealt with what I do. Imagine having to live with eight Cams."

"Wow, I never thought of it that way. I am so sorry." Gabi almost felt bad for her.

"So where's my brother?" She reached over for a cookie.

"He's in the gym with Abdiel."

"So, how is it, living with the Dark Angel?"

Ana was a justice angel. They were the ones who looked into another angel's soul to see if it was pure or not. Justice angels were just a little more sensitive than empaths. They were also the ones that condemned the guilty to Hell. Once a justice angel announced their verdict, the chosen archangels swiftly and mercilessly followed their orders. There were no appeals in Heaven.

While a lot of angels gave Ana a wide berth out of fear, a chosen few found her good to talk to. Cam dubbed her the Heaven's Top Shrink, and he was right. Gabi spent many nights on the phone with Ana, talking about her problems. She was one of the few close friends Gabi had.

Ana was the only one Gabi confided her secrets to. Ana knew Gabi carried a torch for Abdiel all these years. She darn well knew what Gabi thought of him, but she wasn't going to give her the satisfaction of admitting it. "Your brother worships him," Gabi replied, deliberately avoiding the true meaning of her question.

"Why would my brother admire him so much? Cam usually enjoys tormenting archangels."

"Abdiel's different. He's so patient and kind. He always puts others needs before his own. You should see him fight. I have never seen anyone that could come close to matching his skills. Just the other day..." She stopped, angry she was tricked her into admitting too much.

"Everybody deserves a second chance, Gabi." Ana reached over and grabbed her hand.

"I can't stand to have my heart broken again."

"What do you think will hurt worse—taking a chance and failing, or not trying at all and never knowing if it could have been?" Ana bit into another cookie, rolling her eyes in pleasure.

"It's not that simple, Ana."

"Sure it is. He's a gorgeous male specimen and you love him. Any normal female would already have him wedded and bedded. Now, go get him already."

"What if he doesn't want a real relationship with me?"

"Have you looked in a mirror lately? You're beautiful. Besides, I happen to know for a fact he won't turn you down."

"How can you be so sure?" Doubt still plagued Gabi.

"Let's just say you're not the only one who calls me with your problems."

"Abdiel called you?" Gabi shook her head. "Should I be jealous?"

"Please." Ana snorted. "With eight brothers I have enough males in my life."

"Let's go find Cam so you can beat him." Gabi set down the book and stood.

"Don't think we are done with this conversation. When I said everybody deserves a second chance, Gabi, I meant you, too."

Gabi felt her heart skip a beat. What if Ana was right? Did she dare hope for a future with Abdiel? Totally confused, she left the kitchen.

After grabbing a big handful of cookies, Ana followed.

Abdiel and Cam sparred with six-foot Bo staffs. The two females watched as Abdiel attacked. Even though the archangel held nothing back, Cam matched his skills for several minutes before Abdiel disarmed him and knocked him to the ground. It was obvious Cam was no longer some weakling who could be pushed around.

"How? When?" Ana stared, her eyes wide with shock.

"He's got a great teacher," Gabi replied proudly.

"But it's only been three weeks and Cam actually seems to know what he is doing?"

"Hey Ana." Cam gave her his cutest grin and tugged nervously at his shirt.

"Don't *hey Ana* me and you can get that puppy dog smile off your face, too. I just got your grades."

Another angel flashed into the room. The male looked a lot like Cam, but older and taller. This new male possessed the muscular build of a warrior. An archangel's sword was strapped to his back and a couple of daggers were tucked into his belt. His blond hair was cut in a short, military style.

Abdiel's irritation escaped in an annoyed sigh. "What is going to happen next? A big clown car rolling up with the rest of Cam's family tumbling out?"

"Hey, Ramiel." Cam lifted one hand in a nervous half wave.

"Don't beat him yet, Ana. I get first dibs," Ramiel growled. His lip was bleeding, and his left eye sported a nice shiner.

"What did I do to you?" Cam rolled his eyes in exasperation.

"I just had a little chat with Charoum." Ramiel ignored Ana's snort of disgust. It was no secret she hated when her brothers got into brawls. "That wretch was boasting to his buddies about how he handled you. You should have told me he treated you like dirt."

"Why, so my big brother could come in and save the day for me once again? I need to learn how to stand on my own two feet."

"Come on, Cam, we all know you can't fight your way out of a paper bag. It's time you went home with Ana. Everybody knows you tried. There's no reason to be ashamed. You just aren't up to fighting demons."

"Cam," Abdiel yelled, interrupting the stream of curses the empath was directing at the intrusive brother. "Why don't you show your brother what you've learned?"

Cam caught the Bo staff Abdiel threw. Ramiel shook his head in disgust before he caught his. The two brothers went to the center of the gym and faced off. They moved in a slow circle. Ramiel jabbed at his brother a few times with his staff. Cam easily deflected each thrust, but made no move to attack. The older brother started to lash out harder with his weapon. It was obvious, by the choice words he muttered under his breath, that Ramiel was annoyed with his brother. Cam, for his part, just kept calm. Finally, when Ramiel ran at him, he caught his older brother in the stomach and threw him over his head. Cam was not even winded.

Ramiel jumped to his feet and attacked Cam again, only this time he didn't hold back. "Okay you little snot, if you want a real fight I'll give it to you." He growled at his little brother. Unfortunately for Ramiel, no matter how fast he came at Cam, the empath deflected his blows before knocking him on his butt again and again and again.

"Ouch, he's down. That's what, five times?" Gabi smiled.

"Seven. This is more entertaining than a Red Wings game." Ana took another bite of cookie. "These are so much better than manna. Those humans sure know their food."

ABDIEL LOOKED AT ANA in shock. He couldn't decide which one in their family was more crazy—the two brothers who started laughing, even while they were trying to destroy each other, or their older sister who sat there acting like they were all at an ice cream social.

"Okay, I cry uncle," Ramiel said after Cam knocked him on his humiliated tush one last time. Cam helped his brother to his feet. Ramiel crushed his younger brother in a hug. They thumped each other's backs roughly. The two laughing like idiots despite the fact Ramiel was bleeding even more now.

"I don't get it." Abdiel shook his head. "Your brothers are a bunch of morons."

"Don't try to understand them." Ana smiled. "After a couple hundred years, I just gave up. Now if you two will excuse me, I need to have a little talk with my brother." She marched over to Cam and jerked him by the ear. He instantly turned compliant, letting her drag him out of the room, his grades in her hand.

"Can I have a word with you in private, Abdiel?" Ramiel whispered.

"Sure," he responded.

They walked to the other side of the gym. "Thank you for helping, Camael. All of us have been so worried about him."

Abdiel looked at Ramiel and saw the love he held for his brother. Abdiel wondered for a moment how it must feel to have a family that cared for you. Even before they left Heaven, neither one of his older brothers would have gotten in a fight for him. In fact, his brothers used him as a punching bag until he learned to fight back. The twins adored him, but he didn't have them anymore. "It was nothing. He's a good kid," he responded gruffly.

"I just don't understand how you did it all in just three weeks. Not to diss my brother, but he was pathetic." Ramiel looked a little nervous as he shifted back and forth on his feet. "You know that five of us brothers are archangels and we all tried to train Cam without any luck. The kid never seemed to get it before now."

"It wasn't too hard. He's a natural. I've never seen anyone catch on that fast. If I didn't know better, I would have pegged him as archangel materiel. He must just be a late bloomer, that's all."

At his words, Ramiel actually turned green.

"What are you hiding from me?" Abdiel grew irritated that the other angel beat around the bush.

"Look, Cam doesn't even know this. He's different than other empaths."

"I know he's got a mouth and the uncanny knack for using it at the wrong times. But I have a feeling you don't mean that, so just spit it out."

"He doesn't just feel emotions like other empaths. He goes inside other's heads and reads their thoughts, their past and sometimes their future. Not only that, but he can touch objects and know things about the people that held them before him. Lately, he's been talking to us in our minds, although I don't think he realizes he's doing it."

"The only angels that can do that are shifters." Abdiel knew shifters were angels that took the form of animals. Almost every day there was a story about how dogs led some lost child from the wilderness or a dolphin saved a swimmer from drowning. That was all the work of shifter angels. Since talking animals tended to scare people, they all communicated with each other telepathically.

Suddenly, it all made sense. Abdiel remembered on his first night how Cam knew what the demons were going to do. *They mean to kill. They don't care who. They just want to have someone suffer so they can enjoy their pain.* No normal empath could have known that. Cam must have read the demon's minds in order to find out their intentions.

"We've always told Cam that all empaths could do what he does," Ramiel continued guiltily. "We thought that after what happened with Mom and Dad, the last thing he needed to find out was that he is different. Not a lot people know it, but our mother was a very powerful telepath. That was probably why she was attacked in the first place. For some reason, physic angels attract demons. We're afraid that if all of this comes out about Cam, there will be a huge target on his back."

"You have to tell him. It's not fair to keep him in the dark." Abdiel tried not to be angry with the Lehors. They thought they were protecting their little brother, but this was a huge thing to hide from him.

Ramiel nodded. "I'm really concerned about him, Abdiel. All of a sudden, Cam is some super fighter, and now his physic abilities have exploded. I don't believe it's a coincidence. There has to be a reason and it can't be good.

"Michael did say that there was going to be some serious crap going down. Maybe a part of Cam senses it too and is getting ready."

"There's more you need to know. Cam can..."

An angel flashed into the room. It was, yet, another Lehor brother. This angel was thin like Cam. His blond hair was longer than Ramiel's, but was still in a neat, clean-cut fashion.

Abdiel actually looked around for the clown car before he realized the angel was injured. The brother's face was covered in blood and his ripped clothes were streaked with mud. Several weeping wounds were visible on his body.

"Derel, what happened?" Ana screamed from the door before she ran to her brother.

"They attacked us, and we didn't even know they were coming. There were so many of them." Derel was hurt so badly he could only whisper.

Ana held him in her arms, tears in her eyes.

"Where is your archangel and empath, Brother?" Ramiel asked in a strained voice as he and Cam knelt on the ground next to him.

"Gone. My archangel, Haniel, tried to fight them, but they outnumbered us. I tried to stop them, but I'm just a healer. When the demons took the others, I came for help."

"Why didn't your empath warn you?" Cam inquired. "He should have felt them coming."

"Beliel didn't feel anything until it was too late."

Cam looked up and met Abdiel's eyes. The empath's face was a mask of fury, the hand that held his brother shook.

Abdiel nodded at Cam to let him know he had the same thought. There was something fishy about this whole ambush.

"Cam, I came to you because Abdiel's your archangel. I have heard all the rumors about him. I know he can help." Derel grabbed Cam's shirt, pulled him down and looked him the eyes.

"Of course we'll help." Cam grabbed his brother's hand and held it tightly.

Derel looked at Abdiel. "We were guarding an orphanage that is run by missionaries. For some reason, the demons want one of the kids in there. You have to stop them."

"We'll stop them, healer, I promise," Abdiel vowed.

"You did good, Derel. You managed to get away and go for help. Mom and Dad would be so proud of you," Ana reassured, tears falling down her face. She flashed both herself and Derel out of the house and to the healing rooms up in Heaven, where some of the strongest healers could help him.

"I'll round up my crew and meet you there," Ramiel said grimly. "From the sounds of it, you guys are going to need some help." He, too, flashed away.

"Come on, Cam, let's get ready." Gabi laid a reassuring hand on Cam.

"The empath turned rogue. There is no way that he did not feel that many demons nearby," Cam growled between clenched teeth.

"I agree." Abdiel looked at Gabi. "The empath betrayed them."

Cam looked down at his shirt, covered with his brother's blood. Unleashing a roar of rage, he turned and punched a hole in the wall.

THOUSANDS OF MILES AWAY in Columbia, a small group of rebel guerrillas lay sleeping. Slowly several demons slithered to them, looking like a disgusting mixture of snakes and wisps of smoke. As they reached the humans, they started whispering in their ears.

"Kill the children. The children are bad. They must die. Kill them. Rip them apart. Kill the children. Leave no one alive."

Chapter Five

THE THREE OF THEM FLASHED TO THE SIGHT OF DEREL'S AMBUSH, deep in the jungle of Columbia. The hot, heavy air reeked of blood and the lingering stench of death that always clung to demons. Abdiel braced, waiting for attack, but no demons appeared in the immediate area. All he saw was the violent evidence left from the earlier battle.

Blood was everywhere, great pools of it soaked into the ground and it was splattered on the nearby plants. In the dirt, he saw deep gouges where someone clawed the earth as they were dragged away. Weapons were scattered around, left by the angels taken prisoner. Haniel's sword was among them. That alone showed how desperate the situation was. You just don't separate an archangel from his sword without one hell of a fight.

The angels stood in a circle, weapons at the ready. Cam mentally scanned the jungle. He signaled that it was clear, then knelt on the ground and picked up the sword. As soon as he touched it, he released a loud breath, like someone punched him in the stomach.

Abdiel knew the empath connected with Haniel simply by holding the archangel's sword. *Damn, Ramiel was right about the young angel's unique skills.* He stole a glace over at Gabi and saw a confused frown on her face.

Cam looked at them, his blue eyes, normally full of life, flashed with anger. "We were right. Beliel has turned rogue. He led his own crew here to be cut down like sheep. Taken completely by surprise, Haniel and Derel hadn't stood a chance. The demons have Haniel in Hell. They're torturing him, even as we speak. Derel just barely escaped. They almost got him, too."

"I'm sorry, Cam," Gabi said. "But you need to remember that Derel was able to get help and he's going to be all right."

"They trusted Beliel and he used that against them." Cam gritted his teeth. "How could he do that to his own crew?'

"I want everybody on alert," Abdiel ordered. "If they were able to take down an archangel as strong as Haniel, then we are dealing with some pretty dangerous demons." He looked at Cam. The empath breathed hard and shook from head to foot. The anger he felt, in addition to the emotions the two ambushed angels left behind, overwhelmed the kid. Abdiel knew that he needed to bring his empath back into focus and quick, before Cam got so sick he was no good to anyone. "Cam, you don't even have your weapons out yet," he spoke loud enough to get the angel's attention.

Cam looked down at the pair of tonfa in his hand with a *duh* expression on his face. "Have you been doing 'shrooms? They're right here." He spun them in his hands to prove his point.

"Just look in your backpack." Abdiel rolled his eyes in exasperation. Why couldn't he have an empath that followed orders?

With a confused shrug, Cam complied. When he looked inside his bag he stopped, his mouth in an *O* of surprise. After glancing up at Abdiel with a smile, he slowly pulled out a new pair of tonfa. His blue eyes were wide as he drank in the sight of them.

The new weapons were almost like his old set, the big difference being the ones Abdiel gave him were outfitted with a blade on the outside of each shaft. The blades were razor sharp and deadly and would easily cut through an enemy, but could accidentally injure the one wielding them. Only someone who was highly skilled with the tonfa would dare use them. Abdiel custom-made them for Cam. The weight and length were set with his measurements in mind. No other angel would be able to wield them as efficiently.

"Wicked," Cam breathed. His face looked like a child's on Christmas morning. "Thanks Abdiel, they're awesome."

"I figured it was time to let you run with scissors."

Abdiel was glad to cheer Cam up. It was more than just needing him battle ready. For the first time since Appolion, another male angel looked up to him. In fact, Abdiel was only slightly surprised to find he cared for the empath as a brother. It was easy to see why Gabi stuck by Cam for so long. He wondered if Ana really knew what a good job she did in raising her brother.

Six more angels flashed in and joined them in the clearing. Ramiel brought along his angel warrior crew. His empath was a female with long, red hair so curly it looked like a wild mass of flames. Bright turquoise eyes contrasted milky white skin. A black leather top just barely covered her breasts, leaving her toned stomach exposed while skintight pants hung low on her hipbones. Abdiel wondered how the empath managed to bend over, let alone fight. She held a long whip coiled at her waist. The healer of the crew was a young male with light brown hair. He stood behind Ramiel, casting fearful glances at Abdiel.

"Don't be afraid, Daniel." Cam snickered. "Mr. Dark Angel only eats one stupid angel a day and he had one for breakfast already."

"Is he... he's not serious is he?" The healer swallowed uneasily.

"Yes, I'm sure Michael would let an archangel snack on other angels. Don't be such an idiot." Ramiel rolled his eyes.

"You're still the same punk you were in school, Cam," Daniel snarled. "Everything is just one big joke to you. Well, you can just bite me."

"Ya know that's what your sister said to me last night."

Ramiel seized the collar of his lunging healer. Cam stood his ground, a smirk on his face. He laughed as the healer cursed at him in several different languages.

"Now, now, children. Let's save the fighting for the demons," the archangel from the other group of warriors said.

As soon as Abdiel looked at the other archangel, he groaned. Blue eyes and blond hair were unmistakable. It looked like the clown car just delivered another one of Cam's brothers. Like Ramiel, he brought his healer and empath. They stood close to their archangel showing that they were a tight crew.

"Heads up everybody." Cam spun his tonfa. "We have company coming."

"How many, Cam?" Gabi aimed her crossbow at the sky, her gaze scanning the area.

"I can't tell. There are too many. All I know is that they are mad and bad."

"Are you sure?" Ramiel's uneasy female empath shifted. "I don't feel anything."

"If Cam says they're coming, then they're coming." Ramiel drew his sword. "My little brother is never wrong."

"But..." The female gawked. "Okay, he's right. I feel them now. Wow, he's good."

All of the sudden, the trees and plant life around them shook violently. It was like a thousand hands grabbed the earth and jerked it beneath their feet. They widened their stance to keep their balance.

Around them, disembodied voices whispered and the language of demons swirled. Mixed in were human voices that screamed and begged for help. The three empaths shook as the suffering mortal's cries overwhelmed their senses.

A strong wind whipped through the clearing, bringing with it the death scent. It kicked up dirt and leaves. The debris blew into their eyes and made it difficult to see. The wind strengthened until it was almost impossible to breathe.

"Where are they, Cam?" Ramiel yelled to be heard.

"I don't know," Cam called back. "It's like their playing ring around the rosy. They keep moving. I can't get a steady fix on them."

The nine angels formed a circle, their backs to each other. As the wind finally started to die down, Abdiel gripped his sword tightly as he waited for the inevitable attack. They all stared into the forest, tense and ready. The only sound now was their ragged breathing.

Suddenly, a swarm of black snakes slithered toward them from all directions at a supernatural speed. The things had glowing red eyes and hissed in a demonic dialect. Their undulating forms looked like tendrils of smoke and their smell so strong and vile Abdiel tasted the bile rising to the back of his throat.

The red-haired empath shrieked in fear and hid behind Ramiel. Gabi hissed in disgust and moved forward, equal with Abdiel. Pride welled up within him. She wasn't going to shame him by showing how much the snakes disgusted her.

"I really, really hate snakes," she muttered low enough so only he heard. "I had a bad experience with one once."

He gave her a small, reassuring smile before he turned back to the demons.

The snakes formed several withering piles. As the serpents slithered around in circles, faster and faster, they grew larger. The demons pulsated and glowed dark green color as the smell of burnt reptile drifted up. Angelic eyes watered. In mere seconds, the groups of snakes formed into the shapes of hideous eight-foot tall demons.

The demons still had the heads of snakes, but their tall, muscular bodies were that of males. Scales covered their black skin, along with some disgusting greasy matter. Their hands ended with a set of razor sharp, six-inch talons. Abdiel was reminded of the sinister characters portrayed in Cam's comic books.

Their hideous bodies were dressed in the style of an ancient Egyptians. They even wore gold arm cuffs and breastplates. On each of their waists was a small, black dagger. However, none of the demons moved to draw them.

"Presto Change-o," Cam snapped. Not even the sight of dozens of demons morphing shut him up. "Hey, Mom, look what I can do."

"Neat little parlor trick they got going there." Ramiel gave a low whistle.

"You think they do birthday parties?" Cam drawled.

Abdiel laughed. Leave it to the Lehor brothers to keep shooting off their mouths even when they're getting ready to do battle. At that moment, the demonic horde attacked en mass. Abdiel brought his sword up to strike the fiend charging him and caught sight of Cam and Gabi out of the corner of his eye, engaged in battle.

Abdiel swung his sword sideways and sliced at the demon's belly leaving a deep gash. The beast swung with razor sharp claws. He ducked just in time. Coming up, he stabbed it in the heart. With an ear-shattering yell, it vanished.

As soon as he finished that one, another took its place. None of the beasts used their weapons. Their claws and teeth were lethal enough by themselves. The fact Daniel already bled from three vertical slashes on his cheek proved that.

Ramiel's female empath was knocked to the ground by one of the demons. She went to strike at it with her whip, but the monster slapped her arm and the weapon was knocked from her hand. As the beast loomed over her, she squeaked in fear, totally helpless. It raised its claw, ready to strike.

Before Abdiel or Ramiel could go to her aid, Cam was there. He placed his body between the female and the demon, his tonfa flashing as he struck the monster. The female rolled out of the way so she wouldn't get trampled.

The battle between the empath and the demon happened so fast it was almost impossible to follow. Every time the demon lunged at Cam, the angel dodged and struck back with his tonfa, leaving behind a bloody wound. Cam moved with a skill and grace that put most archangels to shame.

When it looked like the demon had him pinned to a tree, Abdiel got worried.

However, Cam used the tree to launch into a backward flip. He flew over the demon and landed behind it. The fiend shrieked in frustration as it turned and attacked the young angel again. Cam dodged the beastly claws and blows as he continued to hit the demon time and time again with his tonfa. Finally, he wounded the demon enough, it disappeared back to Hell.

Abdiel grunted his approval even as he continued to fight his own opponent. His arms ached from the many blows parried from the beast. He was right. There was no way Haniel and Derel stood a chance fighting these powerful minions from Hell with just the two of them. Not only were these strong demons, but there were so many of them.

Luckily for the angels, they had more warriors on their side this time and they were stronger. It was difficult, but the nine angels finally defeated all the creatures, dispatching them back to Hell. After the last little beastie vanished, they all stood there, trying to catch their breath.

"That was fun." Cam shot an evil grin toward his brothers.

"So what do you think of our little Cammie, Nathaniel?" Ramiel looked at the other blond archangel.

"Ooh lookie wookie at Cammie Wammie," Nathaniel teased, pulling Cam into the classic big-brother-tortures-little-brother noogie. "He can fightie wightie now."

"Oh come on, knock it off." Cam pushed him off.

"You know," Ramiel said with mock seriousness, "it's going to be impossible to live with him now. He actually beat me in sparring."

Nathaniel laughed and patted Cam on the back.

Cam smiled, obviously proud he impressed his brothers. He wasn't considered a baby anymore.

"Let's see you take on Mael, then I'll really be impressed," Nathaniel challenged. Mael was by far the toughest Lehor brother. He fought the dirtiest, too.

"Ooh, I'm shaking in my boots." Cam held his hands out to his side and shook them. When the female empath giggled at his actions he turned and gave her his most charming smile.

"You're a cocky, little bastard all of the sudden." Nathaniel put Cam in a headlock and tried to pull him to the ground.

Ramiel joined in and helped take their little punk brother down.

After several moments of tussling, the brothers got up and Nathaniel pulled Cam into a hug. Nathaniel was a few inches shorter than Ramiel, but was just as muscular. His blond hair was cut collar length in the back and the front was long. Unlike Cam, he didn't spike his hair up, but let it fall in soft waves.

"I'm Nathaniel." The older brother offered his hand to Abdiel. "This is my empath, Donel, and my healer, Liam. I don't know how you managed, but my hats off to you for showing this smart-aleck some moves."

"I'm Abdiel." He laughed and shook hands. "Actually, it has been a pleasure working with Cam. I've never had a pupil catch on so fast."

At his words Nathaniel and Ramiel exchanged guilty looks and he wondered what else there was that they weren't telling him. His head started to pound. This family was going to drive him crazy.

GABI UNLEASHED ANOTHER BORED sigh and shifted her aching butt. She had been stuck sitting on this rock for the better part of an hour while the archangels continued to scour the jungle for a clue that would tell them why the demons planned to attack the orphanage in the first place.

Ramiel's female empath was obviously sick of waiting, too, because she got up and sauntered over to Abdiel. "So you're the Dark Angel," she cooed. "My name is Anfial."

Gabi bristled as Anfial looked at Abdiel like she wanted to devour him. That little strumpet actually licked her lips. All of the sudden, Gabi had the childish urge to grab Abdiel by the arm and say, *Mine* like a kid claiming the last cookie. Gabi was thrilled when Abdiel barely looked at the female.

"I prefer to be called Abdiel, thank you."

Anifial's smile faded and turned to Cam. "Thank you for saving me during the battle."

"No problem," Cam muttered, turning red.

"I've never seen an empath fight that well before. If I didn't know better, I would have sworn it was an archangel who defeated that demon."

"Nope, I'm just a plain old empath like you."

Gabi frowned at his words After what she saw him do today, she had a nagging suspicion that there was something different with Cam. No empath she knew could touch an object and tell the past like he did earlier with Haniel's sword.

Anfial walked over and placed a hand on his arm. "There is nothing plain about you, Cam." She swayed her body so her breasts brushed against him.

Oh no. She likes him, Gabi thought. The day that Ana dreaded finally came. All the older Lehor brothers attracted females like bees to honey. Like humans, female angels were drawn to the bad boy type, and that definitely was what the brothers were. Up until now, Cam remained in the shadows of his brothers, ignored by females. Now that he was showing some serious battle skills of his own that was obviously going to change. Ramiel seemed to notice the same thing Gabi did. He frowned with a low growl and jerked Cam to his side.

As the males continued to talk, Anfial sidled up to her. "Now I know why you're serving with those two." She pointed at Cam and Abdiel.

"Whatever do you mean?" Gabi scowled.

"Everybody knows you're the Ice Queen. Why else would Michael put you in the same house as two hot males?"

"Please," Gabi made sure the angel saw the disgust on her face. "Cam's young enough to be my son."

"What about Abdiel? Only someone as cold as you would let a male like that walk around unclaimed. Maybe I'll show him how a real female appreciates a warrior. He is more than an archangel—he is *the* archangel. I wonder what it would be like to kiss those fine lips of his."

"Don't you dare touch him," Gabi hissed.

"Ooh, looks like the Ice Queen does have feelings after all. All right, I'll be nice. Cam it is. Abdiel is much too old for me anyhow. I like my males young and eager."

"You're nothing but a pit viper." Anfial was one of those females that wanted to see how many male warriors she could get to fall for her. Gabi witnessed countless females like her before. Anfial walked away and Gabi continued to fume. She was no ice queen. She just kept her emotions in check. Just because she didn't throw herself at every good-looking male didn't mean she was some cold fish.

Or did it? No! I am not like my parents and Raphael. I have a heart and they never will. An urge to scratch out Anfial's eyes overcame her. *How dare she make me doubt myself?*

"Gabi, you okay?" Abdiel walked over to her, his dark eyes filled with concern.

"Fine," she replied with a smile. Just the sight of him warmed her heart. The anger and frustration she felt before melted away. How was it that he made her so happy? "That was sweet what you did for Cam. He loves his new toys," she told him. "Is that where you've been disappearing off to lately, getting them ready at the armory?"

"Yes, but it's no big deal. He's earned them and then some."

"Still." She resisted the urge to brush that lock of dark hair back from his eyes. "It was so nice, I could just kiss you."

"Well, why don't you?" he challenged. He immediately seemed to catch himself. "Sorry, Gabi, I shouldn't have said that."

She thought about what Ana told her. She did deserve a second chance, and she was no ice queen regardless of what anyone thought. Before she changed her mind, she stood on tiptoe and pressed her lips to his.

Shocked at first, Abdiel wrapped his arms around her and pulled her close. With a possessive growl, he deepened the kiss.

She gasped and he used the opportunity to slip his tongue past her lips. He stroked the inside of her mouth, and she whimpered. When he ran his hands down her back, dangerously close to her rump, she was hard pressed to remember their audience.

Finally, the two of them pulled away, their breathing labored. Looking deep into her eyes, he gently brushed a loose lock of hair away from her face.

"Do you and the laser need a room, Mini Me?" Cam asked in his best Dr. Evil voice.

"Shut up, Cam!" Abdiel and Gabi said in unison.

Cam laughed as he bent down to touch one of the daggers left behind by the demons. He sucked in his breath and dropped the weapon like it burned him. "We have to get to the orphanage, now!"

"Are you sure, Cam?" Ramiel asked.

Cam nodded as his light blue eyes widened with panic.

Gabi felt a wave of confusion wash over her all over again. Cam always was a good empath, but he never showed skills this advanced before. She darted a glance over to Ramiel and Nathaniel, but they refused to meet her gaze. Those dirty dogs knew something.

"The demons were just to distract us. They've sent humans in to kill the children," Cam announced.

"How does he know that?" Anfial asked with awe.

"Good question. I wouldn't mind knowing the answer to that one myself," Gabi said.

"The humans are evil to begin with. With demons urging them on, they'll stop at nothing." Cam looked at Abdiel. "They're on their way now. When the humans are done, not one child will be left alive."

Chapter Six

WHEN ALL NINE ANGELS FLASHED THEMSELVES TO THE ORPHANAGE, nothing looked out of the ordinary. There was no sign of danger. All looked safe. The yellow lights softly shone through the window of the building, illuminating the night. Children's laughter echoed from inside. A radio played soft classical music. The notes floated through the air, giving the entire area a homey feel. There was no telltale demon scent, just the warm aroma of the jungle.

But, Abdiel didn't doubt Cam for a minute. If Cam said trouble was coming, well then, trouble *was* coming.

"They'll be here." Cam returned the glare some of angels shot him. "Trust me."

"Where are they then?" Daniel shot back, obviously still smarting from their earlier argument.

"The humans are coming this way," Anfial snapped at the male healer. "I can feel them now. I couldn't feel them before though. You have awesome skills there, Cam."

"It's no big deal." Cam peeked at her from under his lashes. The *come-hither* look worked well. Anfial actually took several steps forward before Ramiel grabbed her by the arm and pulled her back.

"You wanna give me some lessons on how to improve my skills?" she asked Cam coyly, completely ignoring her archangel.

"Anfial!" Ramiel ordered. "Stay away from my brother. He's a bad influence."

Suddenly the calm of the night was interrupted by the sound of jeeps and trucks closing the distance. Abdiel cursed softly under his breath when he saw what they were carrying. In addition to several hardened soldiers, the vehicles were loaded down with guns and machetes. In short, the humans were armed to the teeth.

"What do you want to do, Abdiel?" Gabi asked, her eyes wide with panic. Angels fought demons not humans.

"Empaths," he commanded. "Use your powers and urge the humans to leave."

The three empaths closed their eyes and went into a trance. However, the soldiers continued to move forward. Cam cursed as they opened their eyes.

"The demon power has closed their minds off to us. We can't get through!" Anfial shuddered.

Abdiel weighed his options. If only they could squash the humans, but Michael would have his hide. The council forbade any archangel from physically hurting any human let alone engaging them in battle. The warriors were there to protect their mortals, not interfere with their lives. Humans were not even supposed to know angels existed. If Abdiel and his crew so much as touched a hair on any of the soldier's heads, the justice angels would be on them like white on rice.

Why does everything have to be so difficult? An idea struck Abdiel. *Maybe we can scare off the humans without even having to lift a hand.* "Show yourselves and your weapons."

"Are you sure?" Ramiel asked, doubt lacing his voice.

"Do you have any better ideas?" Abdiel retorted.

"No." He gave a mischievous grin. "I just want to be able to tell Michael I tried to change your mind in case this bright idea of yours goes into the pisser."

"Just do as he says," Gabi snapped. "I trust Abdiel. He would never lead us astray."

"I trust him, too," Cam chimed.

Abdiel looked at his crew, a smile of gratitude on his face. It looked like the two of them decided to keep him. It kind of made him feel like a stray puppy though. He reached out and grabbed Gabi's hand. His heart sped up at her tender smile.

"I don't know, Nathaniel," Ramiel drawled. "Should we trust Cam? He's been wrong in the past."

"You're probably right." Nathaniel chuckled when Cam returned a murderous look. "Remember when he was a kid and thought that chocolate milk came from brown cows?"

"Don't forget he was the one who was afraid that if he sat on the toilet an alligator would come up and bite him on the butt, too."

"Don't listen to either one of them, Anfial." Cam smiled. "Just remember that at the end of the night, they are nothing more than two psychos with bad haircuts."

Anfial gave a girlish giggle even as the two brothers bombarded Cam with rude hand gestures.

"I think I just vomited a little in the back of my throat," Gabi whispered to Abdiel. She slugged him in the arm when he laughed. "If you boys are ready," she called, gaining their attention. "We have some humans to scare."

As soon as Gabi and the others made themselves visible, the humans stopped dead in their tracks.

Even though the angels didn't make a threatening move or say a word, the soldiers dropped their weapons and ran in the opposite direction. Gabi could only imagine how frightening angel warriors, with their swords and battle gear, must appear to the humans. Even she and Anfial were taller than the humans, and they were females. Ramiel, Nathaniel and Abdiel probably looked like fierce giants to the men.

She sighed in relief when the humans scrambled back into their vehicles and tore out of there. Abdiel's plan worked.

THE NEXT AFTERNOON, ABDIEL went to Gabi's room. Knocking on the door, he entered to find her sitting on the bed reading another one of her romance novels. She had that stupid pink angel bear clutched to her chest. She wore a pair of faded sweatpants and a large, red tee shirt with a picture of a carton dog on it. On her feet, a pair of thick gray socks bunched at her ankles. Her dark hair, pulled up in a messy ponytail, was a totally sloppy look. On her, it looked perfect.

"Can I ask you for help with something?" It was an innocent question—one he had not dared ask anyone for hundreds of years.

"Of course." She put her book down.

"I need to speak with Cam and it's not going to be an easy conversation. I could really use a hand with this one."

"I know. Ana called me today and told me that she asked you to talk with him." Even angels used cell phones. In fact, Michael insisted that each of his angel warriors carry one and keep it on at all times. "She said Cam is a telepath and a really strong one, too."

"Did you have any idea?" He already knew the answer. She never would have kept Cam in the dark.

"I should have." A guilty expression claimed her face. "I just always assumed he was a darned good empath. I was so stupid not to have figured it out. It wasn't until the other day in the jungle when he started reading objects that I suspected something was different about him."

"You have nothing to feel bad about," Abdiel assured as he reached down and grabbed her hand. He lightly kissed her knuckles. "I don't think there has ever been an empath with Cam's gifts. How could you know?"

"I've lived with him for years. I shouldn't have taken him for granted."

"Up until recently you were too busy trying to keep him in one piece, Gabi. You didn't have time to think about anything else."

"Why do you always do that?"

Her green eyes darkened with what he hoped were desire. Her little, pink tongue darted out and moistened her lip. "Do what?" he choked out the words, fighting to get himself under control. He didn't want to scare her away again, not when she just opened herself up to him.

"Know exactly the right thing to say." A shy smile tugged at the corner of her mouth.

Abdiel reached down and ran his thumb along her bottom lip. *What in the hell is wrong with me?* Never accused of being the touchy feely type, yet here he was unable to keep his hands to himself. This was the type of female he should keep his hands off. She was royalty and he was from a family of demons. He didn't deserve her, and he knew it. Yet, that wasn't going to stop him from having her. She was his. She just didn't know it yet.

"Let's go talk with Cam," he said, gruffly getting control of himself before he did something stupid. *Something stupid like going on my hands and knees before her and begging her to love me like I love her.*

Abdiel wanted her so badly that his hands shook. The fact that she was right there, already on her bed made it worse. In his mind, he envisioned easing her back on that bed. He could almost feel her soft, naked body pressed against his as he imagined what it would be like to bury his nose against her throat, inhaling her scent as he plunged himself into her soft, velvet heat and she gasped in his ear.

When a male angel found his mate and made love to her for the first time, he marked her, claiming her as his forever. The male did this by placing the palm of his hand on some discreet area of his partner and branding her with his unique mark. Although Abdiel never saw one up close, he heard they were beautiful intricate artwork forming the male's family symbol. Right now, the urge to mark Gabi as his was so strong that the palm of his hand started to burn.

He was surprised to find that he had indeed fallen to his knees in front of her. He placed one hand on either side of her hips and leaned forward. Fully expecting her to stiffen like she had in the past, he was delighted when she wrapped her arms around his neck and drew him to her.

"I can't fight this anymore," she confessed.

His angel trembled just as much as he did. "Then don't." He slowly inched his way toward her, waiting for her to protest. When she didn't, he gave her a tender kiss. Using his tongue, he outlined her lips before he dipped into her mouth. Running his hands through her hair, he freed the dark, silky masses so they hung free. "I love your hair, especially when it's down," he murmured. A tear slip from her eye. "Why are you crying, Princess?" his voice cracked with concern.

"I'm so happy." She gently pushed back his hair. "I've waited for this moment my entire life."

Abdiel kissed the tear away, savoring its salty goodness. Slowly, he lowered her onto the bed, settling his body on top of hers. Her small hands caressed his back, showing him that she wanted this just as badly as he did. She ran the bottom of her foot up and down the back of his leg.

His lips left Gabi's mouth and went to that sensitive spot on her neck. She arched into him as he gently nipped at her. When her breasts pushed against his chest, he could tell she wasn't wearing a bra. He tentatively brushed a hand over her breasts, waiting for her to protest. When she didn't, he cupped her through her shirt and gently teased the nipples. She whimpered and he pulled back.

"Please." She pulled on his hair gently. "Don't stop, if you do, it will destroy me."

Abdiel pushed up her top, so that the cartoon no longer looked at him, and exposed her perfectly formed chest. Not believing the beautiful gift she was giving, he bent down and suckled one of her nipples into his mouth. He nipped and laved as she thrust her back up so he could take her more easily.

Growing bolder, he slipped his fingers under her sweatpants and past her panties until he was touching the very center of her. Gabi was so hot and ready for him that he almost lost it right then and there. When he slipped a finger into her velvet heat, she shuddered with pent up passion. Using his thumb, he gently feathered over her clit. She gave a keening cry as her juices coated his hand.

Urged on by her panting and mewls, he continued to make love to her with his fingers. She almost threw him off her a couple of times because she was bucking so hard. Just when she was ready to come, he left her breast and covered her mouth with his, absorbing her scream.

There was no sense in Cam knowing what they were doing.

Abruptly Abdiel tore himself away from her and sat on the edge of the bed as he tried to get himself under control. If he didn't stop now, he was going to take her and mark her. Then she would forever be linked to him and his family and that was something he couldn't do, no matter how strongly he wanted to.

"Why did you stop?" Gabi came up behind him, wrapping her arms around his broad chest.

"If I don't stop now, I'm going to go all the way and claim you as mine, Gabi," he admitted hoarsely.

She got up, walked over and stood in front of him. She took off her shirt, and with a sexy little shimmy, lost her pants and underwear, too.

He whimpered as he took in her beauty. *Holy moly, she is actually offering herself to me.*

"So help me, Abdiel," she said in a deep, husky voice. "If you don't finish what you stared, I'll shoot you with my crossbow."

Then she knelt before him. She tugged at his black tee shirt, and he lifted his arms so she could take it off. Her hands fumbled clumsily with his fly, so he helped her undo it. He got up just long enough to tear off his black jeans and toss them aside.

Completely naked, Abdiel grabbed her in his arms and tumbled onto the bed, landing with her underneath him. The sensation of her silky smooth skin touching his made him groan. He separated her thighs and eased between them, just as he was about to enter her, he stopped short. "Are you sure, Gabi?" Sweat beaded on his forehead as the pressure within him built.

She answered him by wrapping her legs around his waist and drawing him to her.

That move shattered all his resolve and he plunged into her heat. When he felt how small and tight she was, he closed his eyes and forced himself to be still.

She hissed in protest and dug her nails into his back, urging him to continue.

"I don't want to hurt you, Princess. You're so damn tight."

"Please Abdiel," she whimpered. "I am hurting, but not from that. I want you so bad it's almost killing me. Please, finish it."

Well, who could argue with that logic? He started to slowly move inside of her, almost drunk with pleasure. It was everything he thought it would be and more. After being lost for so many years, he finally found his place and it was in her arms. He braced one hand against the headboard and grabbed her right hip with the other.

As his thrusts grew faster, he felt the hand that held her grow warm. Now that he started to mark her, nothing could stop him. He would destroy anything that came between them. She was his mate, his beloved, his heart. Right before he climaxed, he heard her yelling his name as she came. He threw back his head and found his own release, his hand burning as he claimed her as his forever.

Afterward, Abdiel rolled off her so that he would not crush her.

As soon as she was free, she twisted around so that she could look at the mark.

He reached out and gently traced it. It looked like an intricate tattoo. His family symbol was a black long sword standing on its hilt. Two black snakes, their eyes bright red, spiraled up the length of the sword, heads facing each other at the point. "I'm sorry," he said softly. "I know you hate snakes."

"Abdiel, shut up." She kissed him. "It is the most beautiful thing I have ever seen."

"Gabi, I..." he started.

She put her hand over his mouth and stopped him. "Shhh, it's all right. I have no regrets. We can talk about this later. Let's go take care of Cam first."

He nodded his agreement, letting her think she had a say in the matter. He already knew that no matter what, he would never let her leave his side now. He already lost everyone that he ever loved and he was damned sure not going to lose her, too. He was just going to have to convince her that he was worthy of her.

THEY FOUND THE YOUNG angel in front of the TV watching *The Amazing Race*. He wore ratty jeans and a Green Day tee shirt on. As usual, Cam was stuffing his face with junk food. As soon as they walked in, the empath's eyes grew wide and his head snapped in Gabi's direction.

All male angels instinctively knew when another male marked a female, even without seeing the mark. Abdiel was glad Cam kept this tidbit of information private.

"Cam, we need to talk," Gabi said as she sat down next to him on the couch.

"I don't like this." Cam glared at both of them suspiciously. "You guys look just like Mike and Carol Brady right before they sit Greg down and have a heart to heart with him"

"I promise Cindy didn't tattle on you." Abdiel sat in a chair facing the couch.

"Okay, let's get this over then." Cam turned off the TV with the remote. "What did I do now?"

"Nothing." Gabi assured. "You're not in any trouble, I promise."

"Why is it that I know I'm still not going to like this chat?" Wary, Cam looked at them.

"Because you're not going to like it," Abdiel replied bluntly. Cam was always truthful with him, so he owed the same to the empath.

Cam puffed out his cheeks. "Okay, shoot."

"Have you ever noticed you know things other empaths don't?" Abdiel asked.

"So?" Cam looked confused. "I just listen better."

"That's just it, Cam," Gabi said gently. "Normal empaths feel emotions. They don't listen to others' thoughts."

"Of course they do." Cam gave a nervous chuckle. "Did my brothers put you guys up to this?"

"Cam." Abdiel gave him a steely stare. "You have telepathic

abilities."

Cam laughed. "In case you didn't know, only shifters have that ability. Since I don't howl at the moon, it's pretty safe to assume I am not an animal."

"We didn't say it made any sense," Gabi snapped. "Ana and your brothers have known all along."

"See, I knew they put you guys up to this." Cam said triumphantly.

"Your mother was a very strong telepath according to Ramiel." As soon as Abdiel mentioned Lehor, Cam shot him a dirty look.

"Don't bring my mother into this idiotic conversation," he growled.

"Cam, tell me why the demons wanted to kill the children the other night?" Since the young angel would not listen to reason, Abdiel was going to have to slap him in the face with cold, hard facts.

"They wanted one of the boys dead," Cam replied. "The others were just in the way."

"Why did they want this boy dead?" Abdiel pressed gently.

"Because the boy is going to grow up to be a great leader. He will lead Columbia out of poverty and war."

"How did you know all this?"

"I just scanned the demon's minds and read why they were sent there and… aww crap." Cam's face turned pale. "I'm not supposed to be able to do that, huh?"

"No other empath can do that," Gabi admitted.

"Why did Ana hide this from me?" Cam snapped angrily.

"She was worried that if the demons knew you were special they would go after you like they did your parents," Gabi answered.

"She had no right. I'm not some child that needs coddled." Cam was up now, pacing the floor.

"You're right." Abdiel got up and put his hand on the younger angel's shoulders. "They should have told you. But they only thought they were doing what was best for you. They love you, buddy."

"Do you think Michael's gonna make me leave now? I'm not an empath—I'm some freak." Cam looked between the two of them, worry on his face.

"I think Michael will let you stay here, in the *Land of Misfit Toys*," Abdiel assured him. "And you always were a freak. Nothing has changed."

"Thanks." Cam gave him a crooked smile. "If you two will excuse me now, I have to give my dear, big sister a call." He ran up the stairs to his bedroom.

"Thanks a lot." Gabi gave his arm a light slap. "Since when am I a misfit toy?"

"You are the only princess I know who lives on Earth and mingles with other angels," he drawled.

"You haven't asked me about that since the first night that you came here. Why?" she asked softly.

"I figured you would tell me when and if you wanted to."

"I'm afraid to tell you."

"What could possibly be that bad, Gabi?"

"I let them down, Abdiel." Gabi's beautiful green eyes filled with tears.

"Let who down?"

"The humans. I was supposed to be guarding Eden and I let Lucifer sneak in." She admitted her sin as she looked at the ground. "Uriel and I were stationed at Eden's gate," she continued, the words tumbling out. She was afraid if she took her time, she wouldn't be able to go on. "We were supposed to be protecting the humans. I was so young and cocky. I thought the assignment was beneath me. I couldn't believe that someone of royal blood was reduced to guarding mortals. In short, I was a snobby idiot."

"Don't be so hard on yourself." He tried to comfort her, but she shook her head and continued.

"Some young child came up and told me he had a message for Adam. I should have known better. I barely gave the male child a second glance. I just let him pass. It was Lucifer in disguise and I didn't even see through it. I let him get in and corrupt Adam and Eve." The tears now flowed freely down her face.

"You can't think like that, sweetheart," Abdiel whispered, his heart breaking for her. "Satan is the best deceiver out there."

"No, I thought humans were beneath me, so I didn't guard them like I should have. I made the biggest sin an angel could make. I let down our mortal brothers. That was the day Satan introduced sin to man. All this suffering today is my fault." She breathed in gulps as her sobs grew stronger.

"Gabi, stop thinking like that. Even angels make mistakes." He grabbed her shoulders and made her look at him. "Satan has fooled many. One third of Heaven's angels fell for his honeyed words. He would have eventually found a way in, even if you had stopped him that day."

"He didn't fool you though. You saw right through him."

"Yeah, and then he handed my butt over to me on a silver platter," he drawled as he wiped the tears off her face. "I'm glad you decided to stay on Earth, however."

"Why?" she whispered.

"Because I might have never realized how much I love you."

"Don't say things that you don't mean."

"It's true," he said gruffly. "You're all I think about. The other day, I asked Cam if all angels smelled as good as you. I thought he was going to slug me."

"If this is some kind of joke, it's not funny Abdiel." Her voice trembled. "You don't have to say this because of what just happened in my bedroom earlier."

"Trust me, Gabi, this is no joke."

She gave a slight shake of her head. "You still feel that way, even after what I just told you."

"I love you because of stuff like that, Gabi. You're a caring and wonderful female. All these years you have put your own needs aside in order to help mortals."

"Thank you."

"Thank you?" he echoed, his smile soft. "I tell you I love you and you say *thank you*."

"I'm sorry. I should say that it's about damn time. I've loved you since we were children."

"What?" His jaw dropped in shock. "I thought you said you were just infatuated with me and that you were over it."

"I under-exaggerated to you for pride's sake. I've loved you ever since I could remember. But you didn't even know I existed."

"I'm sorry." He pulled her into his arms. "I was an idiot."

"Yes, you were," she agreed as she snuggled into his chest.

"If it's any consolation, I've always noticed you."

"Please." She blew a raspberry at him. "I was such a dork in school."

"But you had the sweetest tush." He smiled at the memory. "With the cutest, hot pink panties."

"That was so humiliating." Her cheeks were as pink as those panties.

"No, it was downright sexy."

"You're a big, fat liar." She stood on tiptoe to brush back the lock of hair that always fell over his eyes.

Abdiel turned serious. "Why would you want me, Gabi? You know what my family is."

"You are not your family, Abdiel. You were the only one who dared to stand up to Satan. If there's anybody who doubts you after all you've gone though, well then they aren't fit to even look at you."

As Abdiel bent down to capture her sweet lips in a kiss, he could feel his heart galloping with excitement. She loved him. The sweetest, most beautiful angel ever loved him. "Let's have a formal mating ceremony." He hoped he wasn't rushing things. He was just afraid of losing her. "I want all of Heaven to know that you're mine." His little princess responded like any other female in history. She jumped into his arms with a squeal of delight.

"Yes, yes, yes." She punctuated each yes with a kiss.

"Can we do it right away?" Abdiel asked.

"You have to give me some time. I have so much planning to do," she cried out, running up the stairs. "Cam, quit yelling at your sister. Give me the phone. I need to talk with her."

Abdiel laughed as Cam walked down the stairs with a scared look on his face.

"Never get between a female and her best friend when there's news be told." Cam shook his head.

"It might be a little while before you get your phone back." Abdiel couldn't get the goofy smile off his face.

"So, unless I was mistaken, you've finally marked her, huh?"

Abdiel nodded. "Is that going to be okay with you? Serving with a mated couple?"

"Please, it will be so much better than you two mooning over each other. It's about time you guys came to your senses."

As the two males laughed, Abdiel realized that he had something he hadn't in hundreds of years. He had a family.

Chapter Seven

AFTER SHE STEPPED OUT OF THE SHOWER, GABI WIPED THE STEAM off the mirror in Abdiel's bathroom. She twisted around to get a better look at his mark now forever on the back of her hip. She smiled as she traced it with her finger.

When she stripped and dropped to her knees in front of him, she was terrified he would refuse her, but he hadn't. In fact, he acted like she gave him the best gift ever. She was so glad she followed Ana's advice and gave Abdiel another chance.

She dressed and went back into his bedroom. He was lying on his stomach sound asleep. The white sheet covered only the lower half of him, leaving his tanned, sculpted back exposed. Her faced grew a little heated when she saw the small scratch marks she left behind. She offered to heal them for him, but he refused saying that he earned them and wanted to keep them.

His face, when he took her the first time, was filled with such tenderness that she scarcely believed it was for her. His dark eyes burned with passion, yet were soft with love. No matter how long her immortal life lasted, she would never forget that moment.

Last night there was no question of her going back to her own room. He simply held out his hand and she took it, then he led her to his bed. They spent the entire night making slow, delicious love as they got to know each other's bodies, inch by inch. She sat down on the bed and gently stroked his face. He slowly opened his dark eyes and gave her a lazy smile.

"Come back to bed," he coaxed, pulling her by the arm.

She playfully smacked him on the shoulder. "Your mate needs food. Do you realize that it's already afternoon? We've slept the morning away."

"It's not like anyone is going to miss us. Cam went to a training class this morning, so we have the house all to ourselves."

"I'm starved. If you come downstairs, I might even cook for you or, at least, call Cam and tell him to pick something up on his way home."

"Fine, let me take a shower first." He got out of bed, not bothering to hide his naked body from her.

Gabi felt her insides turn to jelly at the sight of the angel warrior's fine butt.

He caught her staring and fixed her with a hot, smoldering look. "Be a good, little angel, or else we're never going to leave this room," he growled as his dark eyes burned with passion.

She leaned back on the bed and crooked one finger at him.

He didn't need any further invitation. Reaching the bed in two strides, he pinned her to the mattress and started ripping off her clothes.

Food is so over-rated, she thought.

"I'M NOT GOING BACK Ana and that's final," Cam told his sister as he walked into the kitchen and set down a couple of fast food bags in front of his housemates.

"You have no choice, Cam," Ana shot back, her cheeks pink with anger. "You need to develop your new skills and Hayyel can teach you."

Ana and Cam stood in the middle of the kitchen facing each other, ready for battle. Even though the empath was scrawny, he was tall. Ana barely reached his chest. That didn't faze her in the least, however. She just stood on tiptoe so she could stare him down.

"He's a wolf, Ana."

"He's a shifter," she corrected.

"I swear he smells like wet dog. I'm always afraid that he's going to smell my...you know what." Cam motioned over his groin area in case anyone had any doubts about what he referred to.

Abdiel laughed at Cam's last remark.

"Don't encourage him." Ana rolled her eyes.

"I did just fine on my own before. Why is it that now that I know I'm a telepath you think I need tutoring?" Cam grabbed a Coke from the fridge and held the can to his head.

"Because I'm sick of you popping into my head uninvited." Ana grabbed the can from him and opened it, before handing it back. "The other day I was in a council meeting and all of the sudden your voice is in my mind telling me the score of the hockey game."

"Sorry, I meant to tell Nathaniel."

"See, that's what I'm trying to tell you. Geez, Cam I recorded that game and you ruined it for me."

"Sorry, Ana," He gave her one of his famous smiles. "I've got tickets to next week's game. I'll take you to make up for it."

"You can't buy me off with tickets," Ana said sternly, although there was no mistaking the glint of excitement in her eyes.

"Come on Ana." He reached into a drawer, pulled out a bag of candy and held it out as a peace offering.

"Fine." She snatched the candy from his hand. "But you still have to go to your lessons with Hayyel."

"Woof, woof," Cam held his hands up in surrender.

Abdiel turned to Gabi with a flabbergasted look.

She just shrugged her shoulders in response. She was used to the Lehors.

"My head hurts," Cam complained, rubbing the heel of his hand into his eye.

"I'm sure it will go away the more you use your telepathy." Gabi smiled.

"It's not from that. It's from Hayyel hitting me on the back of the head."

Ana laughed. "That's something I'd like to see. I have another council meeting, so try to stay out of my mind, little brother." She disappeared.

Cam was about ready to say something smart, but stopped short.

As he closed his eyes and went into a trance, Gabi groaned, she was really didn't feel like hunting today.

"Your brothers are out, Abdiel, and they're looking for you," Cam said, his eyes still closed. "Boy, are they pissed. They... Oops."

"Oops? What do you mean oops?" Gabi stood up and walked over to him, her stomach doing little flip-flops.

"Your oldest brother is Douma?" Cam asked Abdiel with a weak smile.

"Yes, why?" Abdiel had a leery look on his face.

Cam started tugging at his hair. "Because he just told me to get out of his head and tell his little brother it was time to come out and play."

As ABDIEL PATROLLED THE streets, he thought back to the last time he saw his brothers. It ended with him on the ground crying like a girl and them trying to hack him into a million bitty angel pieces. Call him crazy, but it was something he didn't want to repeat. *Been there, done that* "Are you sure it was just my two older brothers?" he asked Cam again. He was worried that the twins would be with them. He didn't know if he could bring himself to fight Rachael and Appolion, no matter what they became.

"For the millionth time, yes." Cam rolled his eyes. "Why don't you just ask me if it's your little brother and sister? I can hear the question bumping around your thick skull."

"You know what? I think Ana was right. Get out of my head."

"No one has seen the twins," Gabi tried to reassure him. "Not since they were taken from Heaven."

That should have made him feel better, but it didn't. The fact that they remained unseen for all these centuries led him to wildly speculate what might be happening to them. *What if they were being held prisoner and tortured?* Rachael was a full-grown female now and Hell was full of rapists. A cold, hard fury built up inside of him as he thought about her being violated.

"Are you going to be okay?" Gabi always read him like a book.

"Sure, just peachy, I can't wait for the family reunion," he said sarcastically.

"That's just it, Abdiel, you haven't fought any of your family members yet. I've seen your brothers. They're different, changed."

"It's not like we were close even before they turned. Their favorite game when we were children was Kick the Tail of the Abdiel."

"So," Cam drawled. "I guess we can cross them off our Christmas card list."

"Oh, too bad," a voice hissed at them. "I was hoping we could get close and lovey dovey just like the Waltons."

They looked up above them toward the sound of the voice. On a fire escape, they could see the shadowy outline of two demons.

I didn't sense a thing, I'm sorry, Cam communicated telepathically with both Abdiel and Gabi.

Abdiel hissed in displeasure. If his brothers managed to shield their presence from Cam, then they were in big trouble. Only the strongest demons could hide from empaths.

Douma and Forcas leapt off the fire escape. They did a neat flip in the air before they landed on their feet, right in front of the three angels.

"Neat trick," Cam shot out as he twirled his tonfa. "You guys work for Cirque Du Soleil? What do you think, Abdiel? They could name their act, *The Grimm Brothers.*"

Abdiel couldn't say anything smart back. He was seeing his brothers the first time since their banishment from Heaven and Gabi was right. They had changed.

Douma's body looked like Godzilla bred with the Terminator. His dark green skin was covered in scales and muscles popped out all over him. His eyes turned blood red in color and they glowed brightly in the night. He was completely bald, the shiny skull bare except for a pair of black horns. Very large, pointed ears seemed to sprout from the side of his head. They had several chunks missing as if something had bit them.

Forcas was smaller, but just as ugly, with skin that was pale gray. Matted and snarly long, white hair trailed down his bony back. Large, droopy eyes that were pure black, reminded Abdiel of a shark's. His fingers tapered off into huge claws. While Douma wore nothing more than a loincloth, Forcas had on a pair a tattered jeans and a tight, white wife-beater shirt.

"You guys are in serious need of an Ambush Makeover," Abdiel breathed out, disgusted.

Cam gave a whoop of laughter.

Forcas hissed right before he blasted the young angel with a bolt of energy. Cam went flying into the unyielding wall a building, his body slamming hard before sliding to the ground.

"You should teach your empath some manners." Forcas glared at Cam like he was something foul that the demon just stepped in.

Abdiel forced himself to remain calm. He could not afford to let his emotions get the better of him, even though the sight of Cam on the ground was enough to make his blood boil.

The empath moaned as he started to move around a little.

Slowly Gabi walked backwards toward Cam, her crossbow aimed at the two demons the entire time. When she reached the empath, she knelt down and touched him. "You okay, Cam?" she whispered.

Cam surprised everyone by getting to his feet. "I'm fine, Gabi." He snatched up his tonfa, then went and stood shoulder to shoulder with Abdiel.

"What a brave, little empath you have there," Douma said to Abdiel. "He's going to regret not staying down."

Forcas and Douma each held a long sickle in their hands, a heavy chain attached to their weapons. They started to swing the chains.

Forcas looked at Gabi and smirked. "Oh isn't that just precious?" He curled his upper lip in disgust. "Abdiel marked the female."

"Wonderful." Douma licked his deformed lips. "Right before we destroy our precious brother, we'll take the female in front of him."

Abdiel knew they were trying to goad him into making a mistake. He felt Cam stiffen beside him before the young angel relaxed as well. The archangel was pleased to see his training was paying off. Douma attacked Abdiel while Forcas took on Cam. The two demons moved so fast that they were just a blur. However, the two angels were ready for them.

Abdiel brought up his elbow to meet Douma's face. The demon shrieked with anger as he arched his sickle around to strike the archangel. Abdiel swung his sword up to deflect it. Sparks shot out as the two weapons matched with an ear-grinding shriek.

Forcas charged. Cam jumped up and grabbed the fire escape, pulling himself up as the demon stumbled forward in a missed lunge. When Forcas turned around to see where he was, the empath swung his feet around and kicked the demon in the face.

"Come on, you idiot, he's just an empath," Douma chided. He turned and fired a ball of energy at Abdiel.

Abdiel threw up his hand, conjured up a shield and easily deflected the ball.

The demon's face instantly filled with a mixture of shock and fear. He didn't expect his most powerful weapon to be useless.

"A little trick Michael taught me." Abdiel grinned at his shaken brother.

"A worthy opponent," Douma admitted begrudgingly. "Unfortunately we didn't come to play, we're here on a mission."

Both demon brothers pulled out several small throwing stars. Douma chucked his at Cam. A successful hit sent the angel whimpering in pain to his knees. Small keeling cries grew into full-blown screams as he ripped at his skin, his hands tearing chunks of flesh from his body as he tried to pull the stars free.

Forcas threw his stars at Gabi. Abdiel dove in front of her, most of the stars hitting him. The archangel was unconscious before he even hit the ground. His massive body landed on top of hers, blocking her from the demon's view.

Gabi shrieked in pain as three of the weapons buried themselves in her flesh. It felt like acid burning its way into her body. Poisons were not supposed to affect angels, but this was something new. She found the stars that were in her, ripped them out and tossed them aside.

Gabi looked at Cam and gasped. He still dug at the stars embedded in his flesh. His hands were coated with his own blood and he foamed at the mouth. The empath's eyes glazed over and he shook his head back and forth.

"Shut up, shut up, shut up," Cam chanted. He clasped his hands over his ears and yelled, "Shut the fuck up!"

Finally, Cam slammed his head on the ground. The sickening sound of it echoed off the deserted street. He gave another cry of agony the tortured sound broke Gabi's heart. The demons watched him with curious smiles on their faces. They obviously enjoyed the show.

Gabi was shocked at how quickly Cam was incapacitated. The poison affected Abdiel in a different way as it knocked the archangel out. He still hadn't moved. Gabi felt dizzy and her vision dimmed. She knew she was about to become unconscious, too, and shook her head, desperately fighting it. She didn't dare nod off because then Cam would be alone.

The two demons walked over to Cam. Forcas grabbed the young angel by the hair and forced him to look up at them. The empath's blue eyes moved back and forth, wildly.

"Please," Cam begged. His nose trickled blood. "Please, make the voices stop."

"Tell us what you feel, empath," Douma demanded, his voice laced with compassion Gabi knew he didn't really feel.

"I feel despair." Tears ran down the angel's face. "The voices are in pain. They're crying for help."

"You can hear the voices?" Douma asked, his voice oddly intrigued. "Only telepaths can do that."

Forcas roughly released the angel.

Cam rolled into a ball. Holding his head in his hands, the angel rocked back and forth.

The demons just stared at the empath in a cold, detached manner. "What do you think?" Forcas asked his demon brother.

"None of the test subjects reacted this way. This is defiantly unique." Douma continued to look at Cam like he was a lab rat.

"Do you think he could be part of the Order of Four?"

Gabi shook her head. *What the hell was the Order of Four?* She needed to get Cam away from those two sons of bitches.

"I think that is a very good possibility." Douma said thoughtfully.

"So that would make Abdiel the Control then." Forcas nodded with satisfaction.

"Let's take all three to Mammon. Let him decide."

Forcas knelt in front of Cam. "Come with us, little one. We will ease your suffering."

Cam gave the demon a grateful smile. "Yes, that will be good. I'll go anywhere with you. Just make the screaming inside my head stop."

Like hell, Gabi thought. There was no way she was going to let those monsters touch Abdiel or Cam. She slipped her cell phone out of her pocket and pressed the one speed dial button that she thought she would never use, her brother Raphael. When she heard his voice answer, she could only manage a little croak of response before she slumped over on the ground next to Abdiel.

ABDIEL WOKE UP WITH a groan, every muscle in his body aching. It felt like a bus hit him. A bus driven by his brothers. He slowly opened his eyes and only saw blurry images. He furiously scrubbed at his face trying to wash away the fog. Slowly his vision cleared and he realized he was in an opulent room that was all white and gold. The voices of healing angel chants drifted all around him, soothing him all the way down to his soul. He was lying on a large, soft bed, and he was wearing white linen pants with a white shirt.

He was up in Heaven in the healing chambers. "Gabi? Cam?" he called out, panicking as the memories of the fight came back to him. Both of them had been hurt, and now he didn't know where they were.

"They are being healed," a strong voice said behind him.

Abdiel turned and saw a tall, male angel with short, straight, black hair and the same green eyes Gabi had, except his eyes were cold and unfeeling where hers were always dancing and full of life. Although he didn't appear to be that much older than Abdiel, the stranger carried himself in a way that demanded respect. It was obvious he was a very powerful and ancient angel.

"I am Gabrielle's brother, Raphael." He inclined his head formally.

"What happened to us?" Abdiel rubbed his head.

"Your brothers dipped their weapons in demon's blood. It is something we have never seen before, and it obviously acts like a poison to us."

Abdiel forced himself to his feet and walked out of the room. He needed to see Gabi and Cam for himself. Raphael appeared to understand and took no offense as he followed him. He found Cam's room first.

Ana and Derel were with him. Derel sang the healing chants while Ana held a bucket for Cam as he projectile vomited. All of a sudden, the empath turned on his brother and shoved him away with a roar that could only be described as demonic.

"Back the fuck off," he snarled. "That damn singing of yours is driving me crazy."

Raphael instantly shifted into head healer mode. He went over and helped Derel to his feet. "Do you need me to take over?"

"No, that won't be necessary, sir." Derel rotated his arm, working out a kink. "He'll come out of it in a minute."

"How many spells like this has he had, and how long do they last?" Raphael asked as he knelt down to look at the empath more closely.

Abdiel was stunned when Cam growled and snapped at the head

healer. What shocked him even more was the way his empath looked. Cam had two black eyes and bled from his nose and ears. He was deathly pale and shaking, his blond hair slicked back with sweat. The feral look left his face as quick as it appeared. His eyes grew wide as he looked at his brother.

"Oh crap, I'm sorry, Derel," he moaned. "I did it again, didn't I?"

"It's all right, little brother. I know you didn't mean it." Derel reassured. He turned to look at Raphael. "The spells are happening further apart and are less frequent. The healing seems to be working."

"What's happening to him?" Abdiel bit out part of the lump in his throat.

"The demon's blood affected him the worst," Raphael said. "We don't know whether it is because he is an empath or a telepath. I suspect that it is because of both."

Abdiel walked across the room and knelt by Cam. "How you feeling, bud?"

"Just do me a favor and shoot me in the head." He moaned before he vomited again.

"His body is trying to purge the demon's blood. It is extremely toxic to him," Raphael explained. "He almost entered a catatonic state. Luckily, he has a very strong will."

"Did you hear that, Cam?" The archangel tried to encourage. "You did really good."

"Can't talk now, must puke." Cam sat up and did just that.

"I'm so sorry," Abdiel whispered to Ana.

"Not as sorry as your brothers are going to be once I get my hands on them," Ana snapped out as she rubbed her brother's back.

"Is he going to be okay?" Abdiel asked.

"Of course he is. Derel's taking care of him. Now you go rest, I promise to get your empath back to you, and he will be as annoying as ever." Ana leaned over and gave him a peck on the cheek.

As Abdiel started to leave, he stopped and looked back at Cam. He should have kept him safe. He failed his empath. Now the young angel was suffering for it and Gabi was hurt, too. *What kind of archangel are you anyway? You can't even protect the ones that you love.*

"He's not Appolion," Raphael said, the expression on his cold face never changing.

"What's that supposed to mean?" Abdiel snapped back, aggravated his thoughts were so obvious.

"You think you failed him like you failed the twins. What befell Cam was no more your fault than what happened to Appolion or Rachel. What happens, happens. We have no control over fate."

Abdiel wasn't sure if he liked his future brother-in-law or not. He couldn't help but wonder how this robot angel and Gabi could be related. It was obvious when personality was being handed out she got it all. Raphael led the way to Gabi's room. As soon as Abdiel saw her, his heart stopped.

She looked so helpless lying there. Her dark hair was fanned out over her pillow and her cheeks were flushed. She wore a white gown. The fabric hugged her skin, showing off her luscious curves. Her hand was tucked under her cheek.

"How did we get away?" Abdiel sat on the bed and brushed his fingers through her hair.

"She called me," Raphael replied. "She did not want your brothers to hurt you again."

Abdiel smiled at that. It must have been hard for his proud, little princess to go running to her big brother for help, but, she did it for him. She opened her eyes and looked up at him.

"Abdiel," she breathed. "You're okay."

"Thanks to you, Princess, yes."

"What's the Order of Four?" she asked.

He exchanged confused looks with Raphael. "I have no idea," Abdiel finally said. "Where did you hear that?"

"Your brothers. They said Cam was part of the Order of Four and that you were, too. They said you were the Control."

"Do you have any idea what they could have meant?" Abdiel

directed his question to Raphael.

"No, I will have to do some research on the subject." The ancient angel's face filled with concern.

"Michael told me some big things were going down in Detroit," Abdiel admitted.

"Unfortunately, your Chief only shares information when he deems it fit." Raphael ran his hand through his hair in frustration, the first real show of emotion Abdiel witnessed.

"You'll get no argument from me there." Abdiel was all the sudden feeling drained. The poison had taken a toll on his body and he still was not one hundred percent.

"Give me a couple days to consult with some of the other elders. Let me see what I can come up with." Raphael placed his hands on Gabi and scanned her making sure that she was healing properly.

"Is there any way to fight this poison?" Abdiel was almost afraid to hear the answer.

"Not at this time." Raphael moved away from Gabi, obviously satisfied with her progress.

"So we are helpless against it."

"Yes, and now your brothers know it."

"That's one hell of a weakness, healer," Abdiel shot out angrily.

"We are working on an antidote."

"Until then, we're sitting ducks." Abdiel bit back a foul curse. He was in Heaven after all.

"Yes it is. I must go now. I have a lot of work to do if we are ever going to find a way to fight this new weapon." Raphael and left. He didn't kiss his sister, let alone say goodbye. After being around the Lehors so long and seeing the way they were so affectionate it bothered Abdiel a little. He started to get up to grab Raphael and demand that he show his baby sister some attention, until she tugged on his hand.

"Stay with me. I need you to hold me."

Abdiel didn't argue. He stretched out on the bed and spooned her in his arms. Soon the two of them were sleeping peacefully.

Angel Warriors

Chapter Eight

SOMEONE SHAKING HIS SHOULDER AWAKENED ABDIEL. DECIDING to ignore whoever was bugging him, he snuggled deeper into bed. Pulling Gabi closer, he savored both her soft curves and the way her silky hair tickled his cheek. Maybe if he just kept pretending to sleep they would go away.

"Wakey, wakey, time for eggs and bakey," Cam's voice sang out.

What in the hell is Cam doing here bugging me? He should still be in his own room, puking his guts up.

"Awh, isn't that just so sweet? They look so cute there snuggling," another voice chimed.

Abdiel thought it might be Derel's, although he could be wrong. It was so damn hard to immediately place each brother. There were so many of them.

"So, I guess everyone knows that he's marked her, huh?" Cam asked.

"Are you kidding me? It's all anyone is talking about in Heaven, that Mr. Dark Angel and Ms. Ice Queen are together. No one thought that they would ever find a mate period, let alone each other."

"Gabi is not an ice queen," Cam spat, instantly protective of his healer and friend.

"Look, you don't have to tell anyone from our family that. We all love Gabi just as much as you do. I was just telling you what everybody was saying is all."

"Everybody is wrong about them. They're perfect for each other. If I ever find a female that loves me half as much as they love each other, I'll consider myself one lucky bastard."

"They got it that bad for each other, huh?"

"Oh my God, Derel," Cam groused. "Their voices are consistently in my head going on and on about each other. It's a good thing that I'm learning how to block voices or else I'd be privy to their every sexual encounter. That would be a real T.M.I. moment."

Both of the brothers laughed when Abdiel flipped Cam off with his eyes still closed. Finally realizing that they were not going to go away, the archangel opened one eye and saw Cam standing over the bed. Although the black eyes were gone, Cam's face was still pale and drawn. Derel was holding him up, the empath leaning heavily on his brother's shoulders. Abdiel was relieved when Cam gave him a lopsided grin. The side effect that made him angry earlier obviously wore off.

"We have to go," he told Abdiel. "The council has sent for us."

"You need to be in bed. I'll tell the council they need to wait," Abdiel said gruffly as he got out of bed careful so as not to wake Gabi.

"I tried to tell them to wait," Derel replied. "But this demon blood thing has their panties all in a bunch. They won't even listen to Ana, and she's one of them."

"It won't do them any good if Cam passes out at their feet either," Abdiel argued.

"I promise not to give those bastards the satisfaction," Cam replied with a weak smile. "Besides, you know that we can't exactly refuse a summons from the council. I don't know about you, but I've no desire to be banished to Hell for disobedience."

Abdiel gave a sigh of resignation as he reached over and softly shook Gabi awake. Although he hated to admit it, Cam was right. It was never a good idea to tell the council to go take a flying leap. It tended to make them cranky.

"Cam." Gabi yawed and stretched her arms as she woke up. She had just a smidgen of bed head, and it made her look cute. "How are you doing?"

"I feel like somebody tied me up and forced me to watch the Avalanche beat the Red Wings." The empath swayed a little causing his brother to tighten his grip.

"Ouch," she giggled, wrinkling her nose. "That bad, huh?"

"Just let me put it this way," Cam said dryly. "I am so going to kick Forcas's and Douma's teeth in next time I see them. That demon's blood really did a number on me."

"What are you doing out of bed?" she asked. "No offense, but you look like hell."

"He doesn't have a choice. The council requests our presence," Abdiel informed.

She surprised them all by swearing. "I suppose those nosey, busybodies think we're tainted now." She rolled her eyes.

"I take it you're not a fan of the council," Cam said with a grin.

"They have sticks up their b—"

Abdiel clamped his hand over her mouth. "Here I thought I was going to have to worry about your smart mouth getting us in hot water. Her highness is going to get us all in trouble," he told Cam.

Gabi pushed his hand away. "I'm sorry. You guys have never had to deal with the council before. I have. For the most part, they're just using the proceedings to fit their own agenda."

"Hey, my sister is on the council," Cam protested.

"I said for the most part. Of course, I'm not including Ana. She's my best friend," she defended.

"Michael and Raphael will be there as well," Abdiel reminded her gently.

"You forget Jehel is the head of council," she snapped. "He hates all three of us."

They could not argue that point. Jehel never made it a secret that he didn't trust Abdiel. He also always made it clear that he thought Gabi should behave like all good princesses and not be mixing with humans. As for Cam, well Cam was Cam and that was enough to set Jehel off.

"We are so screwed," Cam moaned.

"Ana won't let anything happen to you," Derel promised. "Now come on, let's get this over with.

AFTER GABI FIXED HER hair, they made their way to the council chambers. The floors that they walked on were made of gold as were the set of closed double doors that stood at the entrance of the chambers. Abdiel moved to take Cam from his brother, but the angel shook his head and refused the assistance.

"Thanks, but I will face them on my own two feet," he said.

"I'll be waiting for you out here," Derel told him. "For God's sake little brother, just keep your mouth shut. You know the rules. It is forbidden to speak unless you are asked a question."

"I know, I know." Cam rolled his eyes. "Ana already drilled that fact into my head."

The three of them pushed open the doors and walked in together. The sound of their feet marching forward echoed through the chamber. Besides that, it was eerily quiet as several gazes followed their every move. When they reached the front, they knelt down on one knee and formally bowed. They stayed in that position, with their heads down, waiting for permission to rise.

The council chambers managed to seem large and oppressive at the same time. The walls were made of solid white marble and there were pillars in every corner. Several rows of long podiums stretched across the front of the room, staggered theater like. Several justice archangels stood at attention at various places, much like bailiffs in a human courtroom, there to both guard the council and to take any angel judged guilty away.

The council was comprised of archangels, elders and justice angels, like Ana. They were feared and respected by all. Their word was law. Whenever someone received a summons, they were instantly filled with terror. If the council wanted to see you, it was never good news.

The council made up the laws and guidelines that all angels were expected to follow. They were ruthless with those that broke the law. The council was not known for its mercy. Cam compared them to the

Gestapo and Abdiel completely agreed.

They were still kneeling on the ground, not able to get up until they were acknowledged by the council. Abdiel was seriously starting to get pissed off at them. The fact that they were making his Gabi grovel on the floor made him seriously think about doing something stupid and rash like standing up and demanding to know why they were even summoned in the first place.

You need to calm down, Cam's voice admonished in his head.

Crap, if Cam could feel me projecting anger, then the other empaths that are on the council will be able to feel it, too.

Don't worry, Cam sent, picking up on his thoughts. *I'm blocking your emotions from them. In fact, I'm shielding all of our minds. They won't be able to feel anything from us.*

How in the hell are you managing to do that? Abdiel shot back, careful to keep his head down.

I dunno, I just thought about it and was able to do it, go figure.

"You may rise now," Jehel stated. The leader of the council sat in the middle of the front row. He had long, white blond hair and very cold, pale gray eyes.

Is it just me, or does he remind you guys of one of the elves from Lord of the Rings? Cam asked silently as they got to their feet.

Abdiel snuck a glance at the empath and saw that Cam directed his gaze to the front of the room. His face was completely innocent looking. As he scanned the group of angels, Abdiel quickly spotted Ana in the crowd, her brow creased with worry. He also picked Michael and Raphael out of the crowd. He hoped that they would be allies.

The three angels stood silently, facing the council, as they waited to be addressed. They were not offered chairs.

"We have a serious matter to discuss today," Jehel finally announced breaking the silence. "We have three angels that are tainted with evil. As such, we must consider banishing them."

The announcement immediately caused an uproar. Half the council was appalled at the suggestion while the other half vigorously agreed and nodded their heads.

Abdiel gritted his teeth as he fought the urge to tell Jehel to go screw himself. Somehow he knew that comment wouldn't help their cause any.

"I think that's a bit harsh." Michael narrowed his eyes in anger.

"They've taken demon's blood into their bodies, never before has this happened," Jehel replied, his voice clipped and detached. "They're no longer pure. Who knows what they may be carrying inside of them?"

"I've scanned them all," Ana snapped. "I detected no evil in them."

"I'm sure you scanned your brother thoroughly," Jehel replied sarcastically.

"What are you suggesting?" Ana hissed out slowly. "That I don't know how to do my job?"

"My apologies." Jehel put his hands up, although his face still held a condescending smile. "We still must not forget that they have been compromised. Do we want to risk having them around us? We do not know what may happen."

"Why don't you get down to the real reason why you gathered us all here, Jehel, instead of beating around the bush?" Raphael didn't hide the annoyance from his voice.

"I decree, as head of the council, that these three angels be declared rogues and banished to Hell. For all we know, they could have already turned and be spying for Lucifer," Jehel announced.

The council buzzed, even louder this time, with conversation at this. Abdiel stole a quick glance at his team. Gabi's cheeks were flushed with anger and her green eyes shot daggers. Cam was biting his bottom lip, probably so he wouldn't curse out loud.

"My brother would never turn!" Ana yelled out. "He has proven himself loyal time and time again."

"The same goes for my sister," Raphael called out. "She is from an ancient and royal line. It is obscene to even suggest that she would betray us."

"What of Abdiel?" Jehel asked. "He has no family to stand up for him and why? Because they have all turned. Is there anyone willing to guarantee that he will not do the same? Who will stand up for him?"

"I will," Ana said, getting to her feet. "In front of this council I proclaim Abdiel my family. My brothers and I accept him of our blood. He is one of us."

Abdiel was shocked. What Ana just did was huge and not to be taken lightly. By speaking them in front of the council, they were binding, and she knew it.

Cam placed his hand on Abdiel's shoulder, showing the council he agreed with his sister.

"Abdiel is my sister's mate," Raphael added. "Therefore, he is of my family as well. Unless of course, Jehel, you would suggest that I would willingly give my only sister to a traitor. If you go ahead with this madness and banish them to Hell, I will do everything in my power to bring you down. I strongly suggest that you rescind your verdict."

Jehel turned pale. He didn't dare oppose Raphael. Gabi's brother was one of the most respected and feared angels. "Well, I suppose we can postpone final judgment until we are sure of the long term effects of the poison," he said stiffly.

"I agree that this new weapon the demons have is worrisome," Michael told Jehel. His look was as venomous as Raphael's. "But you can't blame my angels just because they had the misfortune to be Lucifer's first test dummies. There is much we can learn from them."

"I agree," Raphael added. "As the head healer, I do have some questions I would like to ask."

"We would be honored to answer your questions," Abdiel told him as he bowed his head formally.

"Camael," Raphael asked, ignoring the way the young angel winced when addressed by his proper name. "Tell the council what happened when you were poisoned."

"At first it just burned. But as it traveled through my bloodstream, my whole body felt like it was on fire," Cam replied.

Abdiel noticed that his voice was weak and thready, probably from the effort it took to stand on his own combined with the energy he was using to shield their emotions.

"But, that wasn't the worse part of it, was it?" Raphael prodded.

"No," Cam gulped, looking pale. "There were voices in my head, voices of the damned souls from Hell. They cried and begged for mercy. I couldn't turn them off. It wasn't until I was brought to the healing chambers that they ceased."

Having spent so much time around the young angel, Abdiel was able to read him like a book. He could tell that there was something that the empath was not telling. By the concerned look on Ana's face, he knew she sensed it, too.

"Yet with my sister and Abdiel the blood just weakened them and rendered them unconscious. Did the poison affect Camael differently because he is an empath or because he is a telepath? We must find this out," Raphael never took his gaze off Cam even as he talked to the council.

"Are my brothers free to go now?" Ana asked. "They are both still very ill and in need of their rest."

It took Abdiel a full minute to realize she was talking about him, too.

"For now," Jehel replied. He didn't look pleased at all that his wishes weren't carried out.

Once they walked back out into the hallway, Cam allowed himself to collapse.

Derel ran forward and caught him before he hit the ground. The male healer staggered a little under his brother's weight, but managed to keep a firm grip on him. "How did it go?" he asked them, even as his hands scanned Cam looking for fresh injuries.

"We have a new brother. Ana adopted Mr. Dark Angel." Cam smirked.

"Only Ana would adopt someone hundreds of years older than her." Derel chuckled. "I hope you know that now she is going to boss you around, too, Abdiel."

"Cammie!" a voice shrieked behind them.

They all turned and saw Anfial running towards them. She threw her arms around Cam, almost knocking both him and Derel to the ground. Today she was wearing a tight, baby doll tee shirt and short, black miniskirt. "I heard what those mean demons did to you. I was so worried I cried," she gushed.

Cam awkwardly put his arms around her and gave her a hug, all the while shooting a *Help Me!* look over her shoulder.

Derel and Abdiel snickered as Gabi rolled her eyes.

"I'm all right. It was no big deal really," Cam mumbled, embarrassed.

"You just say that because you're so brave. I can feel all the pain coming from you."

"I wonder if she can feel my stomach rolling over," Gabi whispered.

"Be nice," Abdiel whispered back. "She loves her Cammie."

"I brought you something," Anfial declared as she held her backpack up for Cam to see.

"Is that what I think it is?" Cam asked, his face lightening up as he caught a whiff of the bag.

"One Big Mac and a large order of fries," Anfial confirmed. "Ramiel told me it was your favorite."

"You are awesome," Cam told her.

She bounced on the balls of her feet, showing how happy she was that she pleased him. "It gets better." She pulled out an iPod. "I downloaded the new episode of Lost. I figured you probably missed it."

"Thank you. That was so thoughtful of you."

When Cam gave the young female one of his smiles, Anfial blushed. She grabbed his arm and took him from Derel.

Abdiel was beginning to feel his own stomach roll over.

"You need to be resting. Come on back to your room, and let me feed you." She led him away.

"She's going to ruin all of my healing." Derel shook his head and watched them leave.

"She's good," Gabi admitted. "She knew the way to Cam's heart—

junk food and prime time TV."

"Well, now that she's taken him off my hands, I better go get ready." Derel walked away. "Michael says he has a new assignment for me."

Abdiel felt for the healer. He couldn't even imagine how hard it would be to lose his team. He reached out and grabbed Gabi's hand for reassurance.

"Don't worry. You're never getting rid of me," Gabi told him.

"I thought Cam was the telepath," Abdiel told her with a crooked smile. "How is it you always seem to read my mind?"

"I love you, Abdiel. I don't have to be a telepath to know what you're thinking."

He pulled her into him and kissed her. She wrapped her arms around him, bringing him even closer. He felt, more than heard, the little whimper that slipped from her.

"Abdiel, let's do the mating ceremony tomorrow," she whispered into his ear. "I don't want to wait any longer to formally be your mate."

"Are you sure, Gabi?" he croaked out, all ability to speak normal robbed as she rubbed him through his pants. When she bit him softly on the earlobe, he nearly jumped out of his skin. Although they were alone in the hallway right now, anyone could discover them at any moment. He was trying to keep his cool, but she was not making it easy.

"I'm very sure," she purred. "Now, I don't think I can wait much longer to be with you. Meet me back at my room." She slowly trailed her fingers down his chest before she turned and walked away, her hips swaying seductively.

Now it was his turn to whimper.

"Remember," she called. "Angels mate for eternity. We're going to be together forever."

"I'm going hold you to that promise." He ran to catch up with her.

MAMMON WAS PISSED, AND he made sure everybody in Hell knew it. Contrary to popular belief, Hell was not full of fire and brimstone. In fact, it was the exact opposite. Since Hell was located in a series of underground catacombs, it was cold and damp. However, the demons went to great lengths to make their home as opulent and beautiful as Heaven. They almost succeeded.

"You mean to tell me that you part of the Order of Four within your grasp and you let them go?" he snarled at Douma and Forcas. Mammon was second only to Lucifer and was feared by all the demons. He was a master of torture and pain and did not hesitate to use it on anyone who displeased him.

"All is not lost," Douma said, hurriedly trying to placate his leader. "Now that we know where this empath is, we can set up a trap for him. We also know that his weakness is the demon's blood."

"Somehow I don't think you brother Abdiel is going to just let you walk in and take this empath," Mammon spat.

"Abdiel's weakness is his heart," Forcas interjected. "He has a soft spot for both his healer and his empath. Our little brother has always been too kind for his own good."

"Lucifer always wanted to take Abdiel prisoner and punish him for his disobedience," Mammon said thoughtfully. "Perhaps we can use the empath as bait and capture them both."

A third demon walked out from behind Mammon's chair. He laughed snidely at the three others. Unlike the other two demons, he showed no fear of their leader.

"What's so funny, Beelzebub?" Forcas snarled.

"You all underestimate Abdiel. I was his best friend and I know him better than all of you. He could crush both of you and not even be winded."

"Get out of here, Beelzebub!" Mammon yelled. "When I want your opinion, I'll ask for it."

Bub held up his hands in surrender. He walked out of the chamber and shut the door behind him. Walking down the hallway he entered another room. This room was much smaller. It was mostly taken up by a large bed. A small female angel lay in the center of it sleeping.

The girl's eyelids were closed, but then they were always closed. She had not opened them in centuries. She hadn't moved either. The girl was frozen in time.

"You need to stay out of my head, little one," Bub hissed.

The girl looked so innocent. Long, dark hair fanned out on the pillow. Her face was pale and dark circles were around her eyes. Her small, white hands were clasped on her chest.

"Do you hear me?" The demon persisted. "Leave me alone."

Let me go then, demon, the girl sent the command, although she never moved a muscle.

"No, you belong here."

Let me go! The angel screamed in his head.

The screams grew louder and louder. Bub grabbed his head and started to scream along with her. He knew that his yells sounded tortured and manic, but he no longer cared. His sanity slipped away from him long ago. Only a shell was left.

Chapter Nine

"OUCH, THAT WAS MY EYE YOU KNOW." GABI GIGGLED AND blinked furiously, trying to ease the hurt.

Ana pulled back the eyeliner pencil and gave her a mock glare. "Well, stop wiggling around then. If you don't sit still, you're going to go out there looking like a raccoon and we can't have that happening at your own mating ceremony."

Gabi complied and let Ana finish putting on her makeup. They were the only two angels in the large room set to the side of the ceremony hall. Gabi heard the murmur of voices outside, indicating other angels were assembling to witness the mating ceremony. "Ana." Gabi gave her best friend a grateful smile. "Thank you for convincing me to give love a second chance. Without you, none of this would have ever happened."

"No problem, you guys belong together." Ana gave her a sly look. "Cam told me that Abdiel has already marked you. Naughty, naughty, not waiting until the official mating ceremony."

"I know, Ana, but it just happened. It was so beautiful, too. He was so gentle and patient with me. He's just so perfect."

"Wow," Ana breathed. "I wish he had a brother he could introduce me to. I mean, besides the ones in Hell. Are you going to show me the mark or not?"

Gabi giggled, lifted her dress and bared her hip.

Ana's face filled with awe as she looked at the mark. She reached out and briefly touched it. "Snakes. I guess that shouldn't be too surprising considering who his parents are." Ana talked almost as fast as Cam did when he was excited. "That's so pretty. Now I'm really wishing Abdiel had an available brother."

Gabi let her dress drop and covered the mark. "Why is it that you haven't found yourself a male yet?"

"Please, who would want to have to deal with my brothers? Besides, I haven't met anyone that makes me feel anything remotely close to what you feel for Abdiel." There was a soft knock on the door and Ana went over and opened it.

Gabi was floored when she saw Raphael. Her brother was never one for public displays of affection of any kind, check that, make it *any* displays of affection, even the private kind. She was shocked that he was even bothering to show up for the ceremony at all, let alone taking the time to see her before.

"Ana, it's good to see you," Raphael said formally, with a nod.

"Raphael." Ana gave him a small curtsy. "I'll give you two some privacy." After Ana left, the room became enveloped in an awkward silence.

He held a rectangular, red, velvet box in his hands and shifted it back and forth, obviously nervous. It shouldn't have given her any satisfaction to notice his discomfort, but it did. It was nice to know that her brother was capable of having any kind of emotion. She was seriously beginning to suspect that he was some kind of robot.

"You look real beautiful." He finally broke the silence. "But then you always do."

Ooh, an actual compliment along with some emotion! she thought nastily. She was half tempted to ring up Douma and Forcas and ask them to take a look around to see if Hell froze over. "Thank you for standing up for us the other day in front of the council," the words sounded clipped and plastic, even to her own ears.

He gave her an angry scowl before he caught himself and made his face neutral again. "I'm your brother. Of course I'm going to protect you."

"Did you find anything out about the Order of Four?"

He shrugged. "Michael knows something, but he refuses to tell me.

He said that we would know when the time was right."

"Thank you for trying."

That finally succeeded in getting a rise out of him. His green eyes snapped with fury. "Damn, it Gabi, quit thanking me. You're my sister. I would do anything for you. Look, I know I'm not good at showing it, but I do care.

"You could have fooled me," she scoffed. "Until the other night, how many years had it been since I saw you? You probably don't know the answer, but I do because I hoped each and every day that you would finally realize that you had a sister and that you actually gave a damn about her."

He looked completely crestfallen. "Is that what you really think of me? No, don't answer that, of course that's what you think. Gabi, I have always loved you. In fact, you are the only one that I do care about. I certainly don't give a rip about our parents. I resent Mom and Dad for leaving us just as much as you do. The reason I don't visit more is because I honestly don't know how to have a normal relationship thanks to them. It scares me to realize that I am becoming just as cold as they are."

Gabi could not respond because it was as if all the air were sucked out of her lungs. Raphael always seemed to be in total control of everything around him, almost as if fate never dared to challenge him because he would kick it in its butt if it did. The revelation he felt as lost and lonely as she did sometimes was shocking to say the least.

Raphael sat in the chair that Ana vacated and gave her an earnest look. "When you called me and all I could hear was Cam screaming in the background, it nearly destroyed me. Then when I got there and saw you lying on the ground, I was so afraid I lost you forever. Now I understand Abdiel's pain from losing his little brother and sister because I felt it that night."

Gabi saw that he wanted to hug her, but didn't know how to approach her. She took matters into her own hands and threw herself into his arms. She felt him give a shuddering sigh as he held her tight in his arms. Her heart broke when she realized he was starving for affection.

"We're both such a mess, aren't we?" She wiped away a tear from her cheek.

He held her by her shoulders and looked her in the eye. "Please, be careful. I'm very worried about you. I have a bad feeling that Michael is right. There is something big getting ready to happen. I also think that your empath, Cam, is going to be right in the middle of it."

"Cam? No, you must be wrong, Raphael. Up until a few weeks ago, he could barely fight off a puppy. Now you're saying he's going to be in some big demon battle."

"When we first got Cam here, he was so bad off that I personally had to heal him. When I scanned him, I found a huge source of energy that's being barely contained within him. That kid has a lot of powers about ready to pop. I've never seen anything like it before in any other angel, and I've healed Michael. It's more than just telepathy, too, if I'm right, Cam is going to be one of the most powerful angels in Heaven. I think that a part of him somehow senses that there are going to be hard times ahead, and his body is getting ready."

"Look, I love Cam, but you don't know him as well as you think." Gabi shook her head, still refusing to believe him. "Do you want to know what he did Thursday? He burped the alphabet all day long. He wouldn't stop. Don't forget that angels can speak every language ever known to man. He burped those alphabets, too. Do you know how annoying it is to hear the French language butchered like that? Besides, I've scanned him myself a hundred times and I've never detected anything."

"I'm telling you the truth, Gabi," he said adamantly. "Maybe the powers chose to show themselves now because he was exposed to the demon's blood, or maybe it was because of the rigorous training that Abdiel put him through. For all we know, the little brat might just be a late bloomer. All I do know for sure is that, burps and all, Cam is more powerful than anyone could imagine."

"So the demons were right." She suddenly felt the urge to take Cam and hide him in his room so nothing could touch him. "He is part of this Order thingy they talked about. They said Abdiel was, too. Do you think they were right about that as well?"

"Michael has always made it a point to train Abdiel harder than any other archangel. I wouldn't be surprised if the Chief knew all along that your mate is destined to be part of the Order of Four. I wouldn't worry about Abdiel though. He's the most skilled archangel I know." Raphael gave a lopsided grin.

"You said Cam was bad when you first saved us. How bad is bad?" She looked down at her hands, almost not wanting to know the answer.

"Gabi, he was begging the demons to take him to Hell when we first got there. He was on his hands and knees pleading with those monsters. When we finally did get him here to Heaven, he turned wild and tried to attack us. I think that if it had been any other empath but Cam, they would have gone insane."

"Oh no, Raphael." She all of the sudden realized how dangerous the poison really was. "They're going to use this on other empaths, ones that won't be able to fight it like Cam did. If we don't find an antidote then the angel warriors are going to suffer terrible losses."

"Don't worry. I have my best healers already hard at work in the lab. We'll find a way to fight this. But don't think about that today. This is your special day, and you should only have happy thoughts on your mind. Here, this is for you." He handed her the velvet box.

"What is it?"

"Mom sent it for you." He smiled ruefully. "By messenger, of course. She didn't even bother to send a note for either of us with it."

Gabi opened the box and pulled out a gold tiara. Several emeralds were set into it. She knew that it was the piece her mother wore when she married her father. Gabi was half tempted to toss it aside. She was four years old the last time she saw her mother, and she certainly didn't need anything from her now that she was an adult.

Raphael sensed her thoughts. "Those emeralds will look really great with your eyes. Wear it for that reason alone."

"Raphael." She grabbed his hand. "Will you walk me to the mating pool?"

He gave her a tender smile. "Nothing would please me more, little sister."

Derel poked his head in the door. When he spotted Raphael, he bowed slightly. "Sorry for the interruption, but it's time to get started."

"How's Cam doing today?" Gabi asked.

"He's doing much better. He's just nervous that he's going to drop Abdiel in the pool."

"Derel." Suspicious, she crossed her arms. "Where would Cam get that idea?"

Derel didn't even have the good graces to look guilty. He shot her a sly look. "Because we put it there. It's so much fun tormenting that little dork. To top it off, Ana is about ready to go ballistic. Barakiel dyed his hair black. He said that he didn't want Abdiel to feel left out of the family because we are all blond."

"Who is Barakiel?" Raphael wore the confused look most angels did when they were around the Lehors.

"That's the youngest brother." Gabi supplied. "He's always changing the color of his hair or piercing some body part. Just be thankful he's an empath and not a healer."

"I still got stuck training that one." Raphael pointed at Derel. "He may be one of the best healers I ever taught, but he still drove me crazy."

The complement seemed to shock Derel for he obviously did not known that Raphael thought so highly of him.

Gabi smiled. *Welcome to the club, kiddo. He's just full of little surprises today. Maybe I should get poisoned more often. It seems to bring out the teddy bear in my brother.*

"So are you guys all set then?" Derel directed his question to Raphael.

As Raphael nodded, Gabi fought back the tears. The brothers wanted to make sure that she had someone to walk her to the mating ceremony. She knew that if Raphael were not there, one of them would have done it. They wouldn't have let her go alone.

Raphael settled the tiara on her head. "Let's go, little sister. Your mate awaits you."

EVEN THOUGH HE BEEN born and raised in Heaven, there were still times that the sheer beauty of the place awed Abdiel. The wedding chamber was a perfect example of this. The enormous hall was luxurious without being gaudy, a perfect balance between elegance and taste.

There was no ceiling in the wedding chambers. Instead, there was the open sky above their heads. It was a clear blue and white billowy clouds were scattered throughout. Once in a while, a bird could be spotted swooping through the air. A slight breeze blew through the room, bringing a fresh, fragrant floral scent. Ivory towers stretched up as far as the eye could see before disappearing into clouds. Gold, chiffon fabric draped the towers offsetting the solid gold floors.

There were many stone statues depicting various famous angels engaged in battles. Abdiel had been dumbstruck when he noticed that one of the statues was of him battling Lucifer on that fateful day. He never thought of himself as some hero, but obviously whoever made it, thought differently.

Several small fountains dotted the chamber. They were fashioned out of white marble. Several different types of flowers floated in the sparkling blue water in each of them. The fountains surrounded a large, shallow pool seated in the center. Marble steps led up to it, followed by more steps on the inside that went into the water. Unlike the fountains, this pool was not adorned with flowers.

This large, white marble pool was the marriage pool. It was angel custom that the couple was baptized as part of the ceremony, their past lives washed away as they became one.

The hall was filled to capacity. Many came because Gabi was royalty and, much like humans, angels liked to see the rich and famous. Others came to get a glance at the infamous Dark Angel. In truth, most of the angels attending were complete strangers to the couple. Besides Raphael, Gabi had no family present. The only *family* Abdiel had was the Lehor family. Well, technically the Lehors belonged to both of them, lucky dogs that they were.

Gabi stood in the pool facing Abdiel. Her dress was all white, light and gauzy with long sleeves that opened just at the elbows. The fabric flowed gracefully around her knees pooling in the water.

Abdiel wore a white, button up shirt. The top two buttons were undone showing off a glimpse of his chest. His white trousers were rolled up in order to keep them dry. He couldn't take his gaze off of her. She was the most beautiful angel ever made. He still could hardly believe she was going to be his. Forever.

Ana stood in the pool as well, she was standing up for Gabi. When Gabi asked her to do the honor Ana cried, a rare show of emotion for the justice angel. Cam stood on the other side of Abdiel. He looked more nervous about being in the spotlight than Abdiel. The empath was shocked when Abdiel asked him to be his best man.

Michael stood in the middle. He was the one who was going to preside over the marriage. Any other high-ranking angel could have done the ceremony, but Gabi and Abdiel would have no one but their leader do the honors. He was the one that finally brought them together after all.

Michael started the ceremony and Abdiel could feel Gabi grip his hand tighter in anticipation. They looked into each other's eyes, sharing the deep love they for one another.

As Michael droned on and on, angel weddings were notoriously long, Abdiel knew he should be paying attention, but he couldn't concentrate. He couldn't believe she was all his. His beautiful Gabi was giving him her heart. He never imagined in his wildest dreams that he would ever be so fortunate.

"Abdiel," Michael's voice snapped him out of daze.

"Huh?" he stammered. He was caught mooning over her like some dope.

Cam stifled a laugh. All the females *Awed* their approval.

"It's time to kiss me." Gabi bit her bottom lip shyly.

Abdiel swooped her into his arms and did just that. It wasn't until Michael cleared his throat that he remembered the audience. He reluctantly pulled away.

Ana and Cam dunked them under the water. Cam was so nervous he inadvertently sent out mental thoughts so strong Abdiel picked them up.

Don't drop Abdiel. Everyone will think you're a super-dork if you drop the Dark Angel on his big day.

He gave him credit though. Cam didn't drop him. Once they were baptized as husband and wife, the ceremony was over. Then they stood in a reception line while everybody gave them their well wishes and blessings. Abdiel thought it would never end. Gabi, however, was a natural. She greeted every single angel warmly and easily made conversation. Finally, Ana came up to him. She smiled when he gave her a grateful look

"Go ahead and take your bride home," she whispered.

"Did you get everything ready?" he whispered back.

"Yes, I fixed your bedroom just like you asked. Cam will be staying with me the next week in case you need him."

"I thought he was staying with Ramiel."

"Please," she rolled her eyes. "Like I would leave him alone with Anfial. That she-demon would just love that."

"Thank you Ana, for everything."

"You're our family, Abdiel, and not just because I said some stupid words in front of the council. My brother's and I care for and respect you."

"Come on, Ana, don't get mushy on me," he chided playfully.

"No, I'm serious, Abdiel. I have always known you were a good soul. That's why I asked Michael to send you to be Cam's archangel."

"You what?" he asked. Ana's meddling seemed to have no bounds.

"I knew Cam needed a new archangel, so I asked Michael to send you. My little brother was lost and needed someone who would be firm, yet kind." She walked away, then she shot over her shoulder. "Besides, you and Gabi were apart far too long. If I hadn't have butted in and forced you two together, who knows how many more centuries would have gone by before you guys came to your senses?"

"Cam is right. She is like a shrink," he muttered under his breath. But, he hadn't missed the sad look in her eyes. Being a justice angel tended to drive away any male suitors. Well, that and eight very overprotective brothers. Ana must have felt feel lonely at times. He turned and grabbed Gabi by the wrist. He led her behind a pillar, away from prying eyes.

She immediately grabbed him by the hair and pulled him into a passionate kiss.

He pinned her to the pillar and took the kiss even further, splaying his hands over her ribcage so he could *accidentally* brush against her breasts. "Let's get out of here," he told her, his breath labored.

She giggled, then threw her arms around him. While kissing him, she flashed both of them back to their house. Ending up in the kitchen, they tumbled backward until he landed in a chair. She sat down in his lap and continued the kiss. "Oops," she said, finally coming up for air. "I meant to flash us to the bedroom. I've never been that far off before."

"That's okay," he told her, taking the tiara out of her hair and setting it down on the table. "I'll get you there." He stood up with her in his arms. Raining small love bites down her slender throat, he started up the stairs. When he felt her hands slip under his shirt to stroke his chest, he stumbled. "Be good or else we'll never get there." He growled.

She responded by taking his ear between her teeth and suckling it. She giggled wickedly when he cursed and stumbled, yet again.

Finally, he made it to the bedroom, pushing open the door, and carried her inside. Several candles were lit. The shadows from the flames flickered on the walls. Rose petals lay scattered over the bed. The fragrance they gave off reminded him of her. A platter of chocolate-covered strawberries stood on the nightstand. Yeah, it was a good thing he asked Ana to set up the room and not Cam. The empath probably would have set them up with corn chips and soda.

As soon as he set her on her feet, she threw herself at him. She tugged at his shirt with hungry hands until she yanked it off. Her small fingers ran up and down his chest, her mouth following the trail.

He bunched his hands into her soft, silky hair as her hot, velvet tongue lapped hungrily at him. "You're killing me, Princess." His voice was hoarse with need. Deciding he needed to turn the tables, he started to nuzzle her throat. She sighed happily as she leaned her head to the side in order to give him better access. He cupped her round bottom with one hand while he unzipped her dress with the other. He smiled when he saw she wore a little, white teddy underneath it. It was barely there, just covering the small swell of her breasts while hugging her flat stomach and her curvy waist. She wore matching white thong panties.

"You like?" she asked shyly.

"I love," he told her as his fingers trailed over the top of her breasts.

She closed her eyes, her body swaying into his. He cupped her breasts through the fabric. She hissed in pleasure as she leaned even closer to him. Slowly, her fingers trailed down under his waistband until she touched his cock. She hesitantly ran her fingers on it, pulling back when he groaned. "Did I hurt you?" Her face was alarmed.

He answered by taking her hand and putting it back. She giggled and grew bolder, her long fingers working magic on him. Finally, he had to stop her or else it would be over before it even begun. Taking back control, he picked her up and threw her on the bed. Her green eyes widened in shock before she reached up and pulled off his pants. When she struggled with the garment, he clumsily helped her, throwing them to the side once they were off.

She wrapped her arms around his neck before she lay down on the bed, bringing him with her.

As he slowly undressed her and revealed her glorious body, he thought he was going to die with pleasure. As soon as he freed her breasts, he took one of her nipples into his mouth and gently ran his tongue over it. He used his fingers to tease the other nipple, bringing out a cry of pleasure from her. She grabbed his head with both of her hands and tugged at his hair, holding him tight to her as she whispered encouraging words to him in several different languages.

He forced himself to tear his mouth away from her breast and started to make his way down her body with his lips, tongue and teeth. He paid particular attention to her navel, circling it slowly with his tongue. He felt pure, alpha-male satisfaction when he saw her flat belly quiver in response. Twisting her body slightly, he switched his attention to his mark on her hip. He could have gone on tasting her skin forever, the mixture of the salt from her sweat combined with the scent of roses was better than any manna Heaven ever produced.

"Please," she panted. "I need you now, Abdiel."

He needed her, too, dear God, how he needed her. If he didn't get inside of her soon, it would destroy him. Giving the mark one last lick, he moved down and used his teeth to pull off her panties. She whimpered and begged some more.

He used his knee to separate her legs and settled himself between her milky white thighs. When he entered her, he almost came right then. Pausing for a moment, he gathered himself and regained some control. Slowly, he began to thrust into her.

He growled with satisfaction at the sight of her beneath him panting. When she wrapped her legs tight around his waist and dug her nails in his back, his growl turned into a whimper. She whispered hotly in his ear, demanding more. He complied as he thrust into her harder and faster. He felt her muscles tighten around him as she found her release. After a few more strokes, he joined her.

"Wow," she breathed out when he collapsed next to her.

"Thank you." He kissed her on the tip of her nose.

"Is it always that good?"

"I hope so," he replied. Like her, he never knew any other lover.

Angels mate for life. Short of taking a human mate or a female demon, they only know one lover. Having sex with humans was strictly forbidden. As for demons, only the bravest male angels dared that. Even female demons were unpredictable and violent. An angel could get seriously maimed.

She gave out a squeak of surprise when she felt him harden again. "Can we again? Already?" she asked.

"That's one of the benefits of being an archangel. We have great stamina." He rolled on top of her.

THE NEXT MORNING, HE lay on his side, playing with her hair. She finally fell asleep an hour ago, exhausted. They made love the entire night. As he thought about what he had missed all those lonely, dark centuries, he silently cursed himself for taking so long to realize that she was his mate.

He shifted his weight and winced. They defiantly made up for lost time. There wasn't one position that they hadn't tried. He was pretty sure that some of the things they did were illegal in certain areas of Earth. If not, then they should be. He paused as the hairs on his neck stood up. Something was not right. He sensed danger. Naked, he got up and walked to the window.

As he stared out, he knew what it was. His brothers were nearby. It felt just like Gabi told him it would, a little twinge. Nothing like Cam felt by any means, but he knew demons were near and he knew it was Forcas and Douma. Cursing, he turned and started to get dressed in his leather pants and a long sleeved, black shirt. He went and gently shook Gabi awake.

She sat up with a start. Her eyes were wide and her breaths came out quick and shallow, showing that she felt the demons, too.

"Your clothes are in the dresser," he told her. "Ana moved them for you." There was a knock on the door. He opened it a crack to find a sheepish Cam on the other side.

"Sorry, I hate to interrupt you the day after your mating ceremony, but we have to go," he said urgently.

"What's up, Cam?" Gabi called from behind Abdiel. She was already up and getting dressed in her battle gear.

"Someone is calling out for help. I think it's Derel's old archangel, Haniel," Cam spoke louder so Gabi could hear, too.

"It's Douma and Forcas. They have him," Abdiel told him.

"You know this telepath thing sucks," Cam complained. "I feel like a 911-call center."

"Go get our weapons. Gabi, and I will meet you downstairs." He shut the door and turned to her.

"Those two have real bad timing," she huffed as she put on her jacket.

"I'll make sure and tell them. Maybe we'll get lucky and they'll realize that they're being rude, apologize and go home."

"Well, you could tell them that they could've at least waited another hour because I wasn't quite finished with their little brother yet."

"Let's go get this over as quick as possible," he said, with a wry smile. "Just the sight of you in that outfit turns me on."

They went downstairs. Cam paced as he waited. He was pale and shaking. "Good, you're here," he snapped before he handed them their weapons.

"Are you feeling okay?" Gabi shared a worried look with Abdiel.

"I'm fine. Haniel just won't shut up," he growled as he grabbed their wrists and flashed all three of them out of the house.

They appeared on a deserted street. Haniel was there. At least Abdiel thought it was Haniel. The angel in front of him was unrecognizable.

He was hogtied, and his body was a bloody mass of wounds. His eyes rolled up into his head, and he let out gurgled moans. Gabi and Cam immediately knelt by his side.

"Guys," Abdiel snapped. "I have a bad feeling about this."

"What the hell?" Cam pulled a greeting card off Haniel's chest.

Abdiel took it from him. As he read it, he cursed.

"What does it say?" Gabi asked.

"It's a wedding card from Forcas and Douma. They said Haniel is our wedding present."

"Those sick bastards!" Cam spat. "Why can't they go to the wedding registry like everybody else?"

"We need to get out." Abdiel felt the panic setting into his stomach. "This is a trap."

As if to confirm his statement, a building behind them exploded.

Chapter Ten

The force of the explosion knocked the three angels backward. They landed painfully on the ground, momentarily stunned. Slowly they got up to their feet. Abdiel shook his head in an effort to ease the ringing in his ears.

"What's going on?" Gabi groaned as she held her head.

"My brothers suck. That's what's going on," Abdiel growled.

"Things are about to get a whole lot worse, guys," Cam shouted. "We're about ready to get a lot of company, all of it stinky, mean and demon."

All around them, demons of every shape and size flashed in. Cam hadn't been lying. The smell of death was so overpowering Abdiel gagged. The monsters scampered around like multi-colored cockroaches. Some of them actually trampled on their brethren as they fought their way free from Hell.

Abdiel looked at Cam, worried at how all the demon activity would affect him. The last thing they needed was for their empath to overload because of all the evil vibes thrown around. Cam looked a little peaked, and he seemed to be swallowing down some vomit, however, he quickly recovered. In fact, the young angel actually smiled like he was looking forward to the fight.

The males braced, ready to do battle, but the demons did not attack the angels. They instead scattered in different directions into the city of Detroit. Even so, Abdiel brought his sword around and decapitated the nearest one. It vanished before its head even hit the street. Cam launched throwing stars at another demon. Abdiel wasn't amused when he recognized they were the same ones his brothers poisoned them with. Angel warriors were *not* supposed to use demon weapons.

"What?" Cam played innocent when he saw the archangel's glare. "I'm just being a responsible borrower and returning what was lent to me is all."

"We need to have a serious talk when all this is over." Abdiel was going to get Cam to tell him what he was hiding even if he had to beat it out of the empath. In fact, he would enjoy smacking the kid around. Cam was acting like he was PMSing ever since they been attacked by Douma and Forcas. Abdiel realized he projected that thought a little too hard when Cam scowled at him.

"How many are there?" Gabi yelled, throwing her body over Haniel's in order to protect the injured angel. She grimaced when a demon kicked her on its way out to the street.

Abdiel moved his body between hers and the enemy.

"There are hundreds of them, and more keep coming," Cam spat out. "It's like a demon convention."

"Gabi," Abdiel called. "Flash Haniel out of here. I need every available hand."

Gabi put her hands on the injured angel and sent him to the healing chambers. She then grabbed her crossbow and loaded it. She crouched down on the ground with her weapon trained up. The two males stood in front of her, their weapons at the ready.

"Cam, call your family, and let them know what's happening." Abdiel rolled his eyes when the empath pulled out his cell phone. "I meant telepathically, you dork."

Cam gave him an aggravated look as he flipped his phone shut. He closed his eyes and contacted his sister and brothers. When he was done, he looked at the others. "They're on their way. Ana said she would tell Michael."

"There's too many for us to fight alone," Abdiel said. "We'll just have to focus on damage control until help gets here."

The sounds of sirens tore through the air. They mingled with the cries and yells of humans. Off in the distance, another explosion shook the city.

"Please don't let it be the Joe," Cam whimpered, referring to the Joe Louis Arena, the home arena for the Red Wings. "Any place but the Joe."

They ran out to the main street and stopped, shocked by what they saw. The humans were confused and scared. Even though they didn't see the demons, they could see the destroyed buildings and the fires that dotted the landscape.

There were several cars smashed into each other as the people in them drove recklessly in an attempt to leave. The vehicles blocked the roads, making it impossible for anyone to navigate the city streets. Some of the humans took to rioting and looting. They smashed windows out of stores and stole items. Others set fires to cars and buildings. Although the number of people committing these acts was small, the effect was nonetheless devastating.

Abdiel felt his cell phone going off in his pocket. Looking at the caller ID, he saw it was Michael. With an aggravated sigh, he answered it. "I'm a little busy here," he shouted.

"So I've heard," Michael snapped back. "Look, I don't want any heroics on you guy's part. Find shelter and bunker down until help arrives."

Abdiel pulled the phone back and looked at it in surprise. "We must have a bad connection, Chief, because there's no way you would ever suggest we leave the humans defenseless."

"You heard right, and it's not a suggestion, it's a direct order. This is all a trap that your brothers set up for you and Cam. We cannot afford for either one of you to be captured."

"What do you mean by *we*? How are Cam and I any more special than any other angel warrior? How are we more important than the humans for that matter? We both took vows to protect the mortals, and we can't very well do that if we're hiding like a couple of wussies."

"Wow!" Michael said with a whistle. "That is the biggest speech I've ever heard you make, and it was so full of questions, too. Hanging out with Cam and Gabi has turned Mr. Dark Angel into a chatter box."

"Michael, this really isn't the time to talk about my social skills. We freaking have a demon Mardi Gras going on here." Abdiel winced when he realized he just used freaking, Cam's favorite word. Michael was sure to razz him about that.

"Freaking?" Michael drawled out, not disappointing. "This just gets more and more interesting. What's next, you going to get your ear pierced, too?"

"Maybe I'll add that to my to-do list. Now, you wanna tell me why there's no help flashing in?"

"The council has blanketed the city. Nothing can flash in or out. Help is coming. It's just going to take a little longer. That's why you have to take Cam and hide his scrawny butt. If the demons get a hold of the power he yields, we're in deep trouble."

Abdiel didn't have to ask what powers Michael was talking about since Gabi already filled him in on what Raphael found when he scanned the empath. He looked at Cam who fought a demon. The young angel threw the rest of his demon stars at the beast before he straddled it and started punching it with his bare fists.

Yeah, Cam was something all right. Still, he loved the kid and would do anything to protect him, even play the role of wussie and hide. "All right, Michael, you win. I'll take them both to a safe house and wait for the others to arrive." He listened for a few moments. Finally, he hung the phone up with a silent curse. He whistled loud, and Cam reluctantly left his demon and came over. Abdiel grabbed them both by the arms and dragged them behind a building. "Things are about to get a lot more interesting boys and girls."

"Oh goodie," Gabi replied.

"The council has blanketed the whole city. Nothing can flash in and nothing can flash out."

"Great," Cam shouted as he threw his arms in the air. "Really, great."

"They didn't want any more demons to be able to flash in," Gabi said as another explosion threw debris all around.

"Except now were stuck," Abdiel spoke grimly. "And our help is going to take a lot longer to get here."

"Okay, no big deal," Cam spat, sarcastically. "It's only what? Five-hundred against three."

"The others will get here. They'll just have to drive," Gabi said, lamely.

"Yeah, our kind are just great with cars," Cam continued the sarcasm before he jerked his head toward Abdiel. "Mr. Dark Angel here hasn't even sat in a car, let alone driven one."

Abdiel gritted his teeth. First Michael and now Cam, he was really getting sick of being called that name today. "The Chief wants us to find a safe house and wait until help arrives."

Cam gave him a look of pure disgust. "I am not going to be some pansy and hide while my city is destroyed by demons. Michael can go get bent."

"That was not a request, empath, it was a direct order," Abdiel snapped trying to remind Cam of his place.

"So sorry, archangel." Cam curled his lip in disdain. He walked back several steps, away from the shelter of the building. "This empath is sick of being Michael's whipping boy. If you want to go hide your heads in the sand, that's just dandy. Me, I'm going to go do the job I vowed to do."

Abdiel was half pissed off and half scared shitless that Cam was talking to him this way. He knew that the young angel was trained from the crib to always obey his archangel and Michael. Disobedience was not even in the angel warrior's dictionary. A couple of days ago, Cam would have sooner cut off his own hand before he defied a direct order.

"Camael," Gabi yelled, her quivering voice betraying her own concerns. "You will listen to your archangel. You took a sacred vow to obey and serve, and you will honor it."

"That's easy for you to say, Gabi." Cam walked back a few more steps, then gave a strangled cry. "I'm the one stuck with Haniel's voice screaming in my head, not you. I know every freaking thing they did to him, every last bit of torture inflicted on him. I haven't been able to sleep because every time I closed my eyes, I was in Hell with him."

Abdiel instantly felt all of his anger disappear. Cam was terrified and desperate and that was something that he never saw the empath display. Even before the kid learned to fight, he still went into battle without one hint of fear. Crap, this whole situation was really beginning to scare Abdiel now.

Gabi's face went pale. Obviously, she was worried, too. "Come with me, Cam, I'll heal you and take all the voices away."

Abdiel knew she was lying in a desperate attempt to get the empath to come back to them. Cam was born a telepath and would always be one, whether he liked it or not. However, Cam seemed to buy it, his face softening.

"Promise?" The empath took a hesitant step forward.

"Sure thing, bud," Abdiel added. Yeah, they were big, fat liars all right, but right now, he would do anything to get Cam to safety before the empath did something really stupid like getting himself captured.

Cam took another step forward before he jumped back with a snarl. "Liar, I can read your minds. You're just saying that to get me to come with you. Abdiel, you're nothing but a—"

Something swooped down and grabbed Cam. Abdiel looked up and saw that a black winged demon had the young angel by the shoulders. Cam fought to get out of the demon's grasp even as it flew away with him.

"Cam!" Gabi shouted.

"Well," Abdiel breathed. "That's one way to shut him up." Abdiel's mind buzzed. Cam was in serious trouble. The same overwhelming feeling of despair he felt when the twins were taken surged forward again.

Gabi brought up her crossbow to shoot, but after a moment, she brought it down. She obviously didn't want to risk hitting Cam. The demon carried him further away.

They started to run after him, but another winged demon swooped down and attacked. This one was black as well. It resembled a gargoyle. Its hideous wings like a bat's.

Abdiel grabbed Gabi and threw them both face down on the ground. The demon's claws just barely missed them. The beast shrieked in protest.

"Stay down," he told her. "I'll take care of this." He stood and swung his sword.

The demon just flew higher, out of reach. It gave him a ghastly laugh.

He swung his sword again, and once more it flew just out of reach. Abdiel grunted in frustration. He was going to beat this thing to a bloody pulp. He just needed to get his hands on it first.

An arrow flew through the air and hit the demon. It was followed by several more. The demon fell to the ground. It thrashed around and screamed in pain.

Gabi lowered her crossbow and stood up. She gave him a haughty look. Her eyes snapped with anger.

He responded with a crooked smile. "Nice job, sweetie," he said.

"Nice job?" she echoed before she dropped her voice to mock his. "Stay here, helpless female. I'll take care of this."

"Sorry, next time I'll try to remember I'm mated to an Amazon."

"I prefer Amazon Princess, thank you very much."

"Noted, now let's go get Cam and try to hold out until help arrives."

"Do you think he'll be all right?"

"Gabi, give Cam some credit. He'll probably talk the demon into submission."

CAM STRUGGLED AGAINST THE demon's grip even as it took him higher into the air. Since he was never a big one for heights, his stomach gave a little lurch. He knew it was pretty ironic an angel possessed a fear of heights, but he couldn't help it. It was just a good thing angels really didn't have wings. He released the blade in the tip of his boot, swung his leg up and tried to hit the monster. Since he was being held in an awkward position, he missed by like a mile.

The demon screeched a warning and tightened its grip.

He yelped in pain as its claws dug deeper into his shoulders. The sharp talons punctured his flesh, almost to the bone. He felt blood running down his back from his wounds, sticky and warm. "Let go of me," he grunted, clenching his teeth to keep from crying like a girl. *Those claws hurt.*

Sorry, Angel, the demon's raspy voice filled his head. *Douma and Forcas have demanded that you be brought to them.*

Great, thanks, but no thanks. Tell them to send out an email just like anyone else if they want to talk, Cam sent back. *Now put me down and go away, your claws are hurting me.*

Quit moving and it will hurt less. I have to hold on tight because you're wiggling like a worm. Besides, the pain you are feeling now will pale in comparison to what awaits you in Hell.

The raspy voice was really beginning to irritate him. Deciding the fall would beat delivery to the demon brothers, he started to fight the beast's hold even more. *The fall will only break every bone in my body and hurt like a mother scratcher. No biggie, it's not like it will kill me or anything. I'm immortal. Yeah, it's official, my life sucks now. Why, oh why hadn't I been a good little empath and gone with Abdiel when he asked?*

He struck the demon's talons repeatedly with his tonfa. The demon tried to enter his mind once again, probably to tell him to knock it off, but this time he was ready. He put up a mental brick wall and added a strong telepathic shove. The demon screamed in pain and loosened its grip. Encouraged, Cam gave an even stronger mental push. The winged monster immediately let go as the force in its mind caused it to spin backward. The angel went flying through the air, his arms and legs cartwheeling as he tried in vain to find something to grab onto to break his fall.

Fortunately for him, the demon was carrying him quickly through the air before it dropped him and the momentum from that caused him to fall at an angle rather than just straight down. Instead of slamming into the hard street below, he went toward a building. He curled up into a tight ball before making contact. Crashing through a window, he rolled across a room and slammed into the wall.

He heard his leg snapping even as glass lacerated his body. *Lucky me, the nice building broke my fall. Well, it was better than going splat on the hard concrete below. Nobody likes an angel pancake.*

He groaned with pain as he rolled to a sitting position. His left leg pained him and was disfigured. If human, he would not have been able to stand on it. He slammed it against the wall until it snapped back into place. Biting back the cry of pain, he stood.

He looked around at the room. It was an old, abandoned office building. Cockroaches skittered by, leaving little trails in the dust. The smell of urine and decay was strong. It was not exactly the Ritz, but it sure beat Hell.

The demon crashed through the window.

Cam focused his mind at it and sent another mental, *Back off!*

The demon screamed in agony as it shook its head.

The angel smiled, happy to see he gave the demon one mother of a migraine. Using his telepathy as a weapon took a lot out of him. He grew lightheaded and the stinky room spun a little. The demon was already coming back and this time, he would have to do hand to hand combat.

Cam faced it, only to find he dropped his tonfa when he fell. He saw them across the room. *Okay, I get it. I should not have been a jerk to Abdiel and disobeyed a direct order. Haven't I been punished enough already? I mean, come on. This has got to be the crappiest day of my life.*

He stared hard at his weapons, giving them a filthy look, like it was their fault he lost them. He had the blade in his boot and a veritable armory of other weapons tucked in different areas of his clothes, but none would do as much damage as his tonfa. *My weapons are so close. If only I could reach them.* He continued to glare at them, wanting nothing more than to feel their reassuring weight in his hands. He was shocked when they shifted ever so slightly, scooting a few inches on the floor, moved by unseen hands.

All of a sudden, memories flashed back to him.

He had only been five at the time. Barakiel was three. They were sitting on the floor in their mansion playing with little wooden horses. Ana, Ramiel and Nathaniel were already teenagers at the time, and they were sitting at a nearby table doing homework. The others sibs were not there. They must have been outside playing.

"Cammie, I want juice," Barakiel demanded.

"Okay, Bear," Cam replied, using the nickname they had all called their youngest brother.

Cam simply used his mind and the cup floated through the air and came to his outstretched hand.

Bear clapped his pudgy hands together while he let out slobbery giggles.

Ana immediately rose from the table and ran over to them. "Mom said you're not supposed to do that anymore, Cammie." Even as a young angel she still sounded bossy.

"Why?" he asked in the way only a child of five could.

"Because it's our special secret, baby," his mother said as she came into the room.

God, his mother was so beautiful. Her hair just wasn't simply blonde—it was every shade of blonde. The different hues mixed together to form a long, soft mane that Cam liked to rub into his face as he drifted to sleep. Her eyes were the same light blue as theirs, but hers were always filled with love and understanding.

She knelt down to him and took both of his grimy hands into her clean, soft ones. "Listen, Cammie, you must never, never move things around with your mind again. Only bad angels do that, and my little baby is not a bad angel. You must also stop talking to mommy in her head. Use words only."

Cam tried not to cry. He was only helping Bear out after all. He sniffled as big, fat tears finally won out and fell down his cheeks. "Yes mommy, I is sorry."

She kissed away his tears before she left with his father on a mission. It was their final mission. That was the night they were captured and mentally tortured. He cried for nights alone in his room. He thought it was all his fault because he was a bad little angel. He never tried to move things with his mind again. In fact, he forced himself to forget he could do it.

Until now. *Well, isn't that just a kick in the pants? I have telekinesis as well as telepathy. Damn my family. They lied to me again! I wonder what else they haven't told me.* He stared hard at his weapons and concentrated. He needed his tonfa so he could pay this demon back for his battered body. The pain put him in a foul mood.

The weapons flew through the air right at him. Cam gave a whoop of victory. He reached out to grab them, but they went right by him and crashed onto the opposite wall. *A whole lot of good that did*. Unless he was planning on making the demon laugh itself to death, he was still up the creek without a paddle. He could almost feel Hayyel smacking him on the back of the head.

The demon was now in the room and making its way toward him.

He was totally defenseless. Yeah, his life most definitely sucked, there was no doubt about that anymore. As the demon lunged for him, he put his hand out to defend himself. To his shock, an arch of fire erupted from his hand, shot forward and struck the demon. As the fire left his body, he felt his energy drained from him. He tried to break off the contact, but was unable to do so. The line of fire continued to branch between him and the demon.

The demon unleashed an inhuman cry of agony. Its head started to spin around as its body pulsated. Flesh and blood sprayed him as the demon exploded. The only thing left was smoke, a charred spot on the floor and itty-bitty demon pieces.

That was unexpected. He looked down at his hand as if it held an explanation. "Sweet," he muttered. As dizziness overwhelmed him, he swayed unsteadily. His eyes rolled back into his head. With a loud thud, he hit the ground.

His last thought was, *Crap, not on the dirty floor.*

"CAM'S STILL NOT ANSWERING his phone," Abdiel told Gabi.

They spent hours, scouring the city, looking for Cam, without any luck. Now it seemed every demon in the area knew where they were and gunned for them. Right now, they were crouching down behind a dumpster. Every time they stuck their heads out, they drew a demon.

He was already bloody from a nice dagger slash to his chest. *Yeah, we're super heroes all right, Captain Dumpster and Girl Garbage.*

"I'm really worried about him, Abdiel." Gabi's eyes filled with tears.

"Don't worry, Princess. Cam's changed. He can handle himself now." He kissed her on the top of her hair and hugged her tight. *I just hope that I'm right. I don't think I could live with myself if something happened to Cam.*

"If only we could reach him."

Abdiel wanted nothing more than to continue searching for Cam, but he knew they were in over their heads. They would have to wait until help arrived. The last thing he wanted was for Gabi to get hurt or captured, too. So he made one of the hardest decisions ever in his immortal life. They would hole up and search for Cam later. "Are there any safe houses nearby?"

All angel homes were protected from invasion. Ancient shielding chants said over the dwellings made it impossible for demons to enter. There was no other way they could hold out until help arrived.

"Yes," she said, her eyes lighting up as she remembered. "There's an apartment three blocks over. Michael uses it when he visits."

"Let's go. We're just demon bait sitting out here."

"How do you suggest we do that? The demons will be on us as soon as we show our faces. You're already hurt."

"We run," he said grimly. "Let's just hope we can make it all the way without being taken. That safe house is our only hope."

Chapter Eleven

They left the shelter of the dumpster before walking cautiously onto the street. A bright yellow demon immediately spotted them and gave a hoarse battle cry. It ran towards them, joined by two demon buddies.

"Run," Abdiel told Gabi as he grabbed her by the arm and pulled her down the street.

She fought desperately to keep up. His legs were longer than hers, and she had to take two steps for every one of his. She heard the pounding footsteps of the demons behind them as the monsters drew closer and closer. A sharp pain exploded from her leg. She tumbled forward, her cheek scraping on the hard cement. "I'm hit," she gasped out as she looked at the small throwing dagger still lodged in her right calf.

"Has it been poisoned?" Abdiel knelt by her, his dark eyes full of concern and fury.

"No, I don't think so. It just hurts." A small cry of pain left her lips as she pulled it out.

He took it from her and threw it aside with a look of disgust.

The demons used her injury to their advantage and covered the distance between them.

Gabi knew they were sitting ducks. Abdiel may be the greatest fighter out there, but there was no way he could defeat so many demons all alone. Maybe if Cam was still with them they would have a half a chance, but the empath was God knows where. They couldn't even flash out of there. Thanks to the council blanketing the city, they were trapped. "Damn the council," she said as she tenderly cupped his cheek.

"It's going to be okay, Princess."

But, they both knew that was a lie. They were going to be destroyed right in front of each other. As an angel warrior, Gabi always prepared herself for this, but not now, she just found true happiness. She only hoped they finished her off first so she didn't have to see him destroyed.

She cupped her hand behind his head and brought him down to her lips. She needed to feel him against her one last time. She put all of her fear, sadness and regrets into the kiss. Her body pressed so tightly to his she didn't know where she ended and he began. All too soon, he pulled away.

With a sad smile, Abdiel sat her up against a building and turned to face the demons.

Two more demons joined the original three. They circled the angels. It was hopeless odds, and they both knew it. Gabi loaded her crossbow and dug a butterfly knife out of her boot. They may be toast, but she was going to inflict some damage before being taken down.

A demon lunged at Abdiel and stabbed him in the shoulder. The archangel hissed with pain before he spun and elbowed the offender in the face. The fiend staggered back with a bloody mouth. As soon as he got rid of that demon, two more jumped on him. They pinned him to the ground while a third jumped on his chest. The demon punched him repeatedly in the face. Blood poured out of his nose.

Gabi screamed in protest at the sight of him being hurt. She fired her crossbow and managed to hit one of the demons in the back. Instead of going down, the injured demon ran at her with a roar of anger. The demon moved so fast she didn't have a chance to reload her weapon.

It jumped on top of her and opened its mouth to issue a victorious cry.

"I take it Satan doesn't have a good dental plan for you guys." She gagged. *Ew, that demon has... well, demon breath.*

"Why don't you give me a kiss and see for yourself?" the demon suggested.

The beast lowered its head and started to nuzzle her neck. Gabi fought, but it was strong and pinned her. Helpless, she bit back a scream. That thing was going to rape her. Dear God, that was the ultimate humiliation, the biggest fear of all female angel warriors. She heard rumors of some females who carried black market grenades with them so if they found themselves in this position, they could destroy themselves before the demons violated them. Gabi never understood this reasoning before. Now she did. She'd rather be blown into bits than endure what was coming.

Gunshots rang out. The demon fell off of her with a growl. Opening her eyes, she saw a male with a gun. She breathed a sigh of relief. The cavalry finally arrived. She looked around for more angels, but saw only the lone male. A little surprised, she didn't look a gift horse in the mouth.

Gabi studied the male, trying to place him. She had never him before. He had dark hair, short in the back and just long enough in the front to brush back. Piercing blue eyes seemed to look right into her soul. That gaze swept over her in search of injuries, almost like a healer would do, but his build and stance screamed archangel. In addition to the gun, he held a kris she could have sworn was of demon make.

The male ran over to the group of demons that pinned Abdiel. He pulled off the one punching the archangel and threw him to the ground. When the demon saw the newcomer, its black eyes widened in fear.

"What are you doing here?" it screeched.

"I was just minding my own business," the stranger spoke casually.

Gabi gasped when she heard how much he sounded like Abdiel.

"And poof, it's a big, old family reunion."

"Our fight is not with you." The demon whined, obviously trying to placate the newcomer.

"Now, now, Belair," the male whispered as he crouched down to look the demon in the eyes. "We both know better than that. I remember, all too well, how well you wield a whip."

Gabi gave a muffled squeak when she saw the male's eyes turn a glowing red.

The demon gasped and clutched his throat. Fighting for breath, it fell onto its back. An evil laugh left the stranger's lips.

Gabi pulled her crossbow closer to her, suddenly unsure of this male. No angel that she knew could do what he just did, not even Michael. *Who in Heaven is he?*

"Say hello to my brothers for me, you sick perverted beast." The male spit on the demon before he turned to help Abdiel.

It wasn't until he looked at her again that she knew. Even though his eyes were blue, and not dark like Abdiel's, they were familiar. He even had a lock of hair that fell across his eyes like Abdiel. Holy moly, their savior was Appolion, Abdiel's long-lost brother.

Abdiel and Appolion fought well together. They stood back to back, wielding their swords with deadly accuracy. Appolion didn't have the discipline that Abdiel did, but he fought with a passion and anger that Gabi never saw before. It only took a few moments to injure the demons badly enough so that they couldn't get up again.

"Thank you, we owe you our lives I'm Abdiel. This is Gabrielle."

"You need to get your female to safety." The other angel didn't offer his name. "Carry her, and I will shield us from the demons."

"You can do that?" Gabi asked as Abdiel lifted her into his arms.

Appolion nodded his head. Gabi saw he wore dark blue cargo pants and a jacket with Paramedic written on it. She resisted the urge to tell Abdiel this stranger was his brother, just in case she was wrong. But deep down, she knew she was right. There was something different about Abdiel's brother, something dangerous. She really needed Cam there. He would be able to scan Appolion and tell her everything she needed to know.

But Cam wasn't there. He'd been taken. Gabi buried her face in Abdiel's shoulder and mourned for the empath. Her sweet, innocent Cam was in the hands of some evil demon and she couldn't save him.

She thought about the despair that Ana would suffer when she found out and felt even sadder.

They sprinted the remaining way to the apartment building. Appolion was right. They walked right by the demons and they were not noticed at all. First, he choked a demon simply by using his mind, and now this. It seemed like Appolion could do anything. She wondered dimly if he did windows, too. When they got to the door, the male turned and started walking away. Gabi's heart went out for him. He seemed sad and resigned, like the weight of the whole world was on his shoulders.

"Appolion?" Abdiel croaked out.

Appolion stopped dead in his tracks and slowly turned around. His mouth opened and closed several times, but no sound came out.

It was easy to see the fear on his face, mixed with what, Gabi prayed was hope.

"You're still an angel," Abdiel whispered. "You didn't turn. I prayed that you didn't become demon, and my prayers have been answered."

"No, you're wrong," Appolion said, his voice filled with pain. "I don't know what I am, but I'm not like you."

"Come with us," Gabi spoke softly, using the same tone of voice someone uses with a scared child. "I can sense you are injured. Let us heal you."

"I can't go in there." Appolion looked at the building apprehensively. "It's protected. I can feel it pushing me away even now."

"Where's Rachael?" As soon as Abdiel asked this, his brother's face filled with grief.

"I don't know. They separated us the first day we all were in Hell. I haven't seen her since. We used to communicate telepathically, but not anymore."

"What happened to you, Appolion?"

"They tried to turn me, but I wouldn't let them." He was unwilling to meet their gazes.

"What did they do to you, little brother?"

Appolion looked at his feet. He shook his head refusing to speak.

It was Gabi who answered. "They tortured him," she whispered. "I've scanned him, and he carries many wounds on him, some quite old."

"They kicked me out of Hell." Appolion finally looked up. "I've been living as a human ever since." He walked over and touched Gabi's wound.

She felt the heat from his hands as he started to heal the injury. But, he pulled back before it was completely healed. A slight flush covered his cheeks.

"I'm sorry. I've only healed humans. I guess I can't heal angels," he murmured.

"It's because you're injured," Gabi told him. "An injured angel cannot heal another angel. I knew as soon as I saw you that you were a healer and a gifted one, too."

"Come home with us," Abdiel pleaded.

Appolion actually took a few steps toward them before he caught himself and stopped. He slowly shook his head back and forth, an apologetic look on his face. "Don't you see? I'm tainted. I'm not an angel, and I'm not a demon. I'm not fit for Heaven."

"Michael will help you."

"No, he will send me back to Hell."

Appolion's voice was filled with panic and his eyes grew so big Gabi half expected them to pop out of his skull.

"I can't go back there. I won't."

His younger brother turned around and ran the hell out of there. Gabi never saw an angel move so fast. Soon, he was swallowed up in the crowd. Knowing what little she did about Appolion, he was probably shielding himself from view. That was one wicked talent he there.

"Appolion!" Abdiel yelled.

After several moments, he turned with a defeated sigh and carried Gabi up the stairs to the apartment door. When he got there, he tried the door only to find it locked. He lifted up his foot in order to kick it in.

"Stop!" Gabi shouted before she touched the lock, it unlocked at her touch "We don't need keys."

He carried her inside, went to the bedroom and placed her on the bed. He started to walk to the adjoining bathroom, but she grabbed him and pulled him into her arms. Her gentle touch was his undoing. He placed his head on her shoulder and let the tears come. She stroked his hair as he cried silently, her heart breaking, too.

"I love you," he whispered against her throat.

"You'll always have me, Abdiel," she promised.

"He was so close, and I scared him away."

"Don't worry," she told him as she stroked his arm. "We'll find your brother again."

"He seemed so sad. I feel so helpless." He played with her hair.

"He's not a demon, Abdiel. At least you know that."

"He's lost though, Gabi, and I don't know how to help him."

She held him in her arms as their city fell apart around them. She never felt so helpless.

"There was one thing about Appolion that confused me though." Abdiel kissed the tip of her ear.

"Only one thing? I could think of a million questions I would like to ask him." Gabi said as she looked at him. "But what confused you?

"The entire time we were fighting those demons I could have sworn he was humming the song, *Kung Fu Fighting*. Is that weird or what?"

APPOLION STOOD ON THE roof of a building and looked over the skyline of Detroit. He silently chided himself. *You just to sing Kung Fu Fighting didn't you, you idiot. Now Abdiel knows that you sing your own soundtrack when you fight, great way to impress your big brother there.* He felt like kicking himself. He finally saw Abdiel after all these years and how did he react? He ran away like some little girl. His father was right, he was just a weak fool.

Another explosion tore through the air, and his gut tightened at the thought of more destruction. He really liked the city despite all of its faults. Now he would have to leave. It used to be that the demons left him alone, but not anymore. Now that Douma and Forcas knew where he was, he would be hunted. He would never allow them to take him back to Hell. He shuddered as he remembered his old home.

Abdiel's female was right, he did carry old injuries. He was terribly abused in Hell ever since the first day taken there by his parents. His back hurt constantly from the scars that the whippings left behind. Yet, he dared not go with the angels. Douma and Forcas told him Michael would destroy him if he ever went to Heaven.

Of course they could be lying. They also said Abdiel would attack him and that was untrue. He released a ragged sigh, but couldn't allow himself such wishful thinking. It would only lead to disappointment, or worse, death. He was all alone in the world. That would never change. He started to hum *One is the Loneliest Number."* *Oh God, Appolion, shut up already*, he snapped at himself.

Suddenly, a presence reached out through the night air and touched his mind. He shook his head, denying what he felt. The touch was so familiar, but he had to be wrong. The presence called to him, and his heart responded. Although he knew that he couldn't respond to it, he couldn't turn away from it either. There was no way it could be here on Earth this close, but, he knew at the same time, that until he knew for sure, there was no way he could leave Detroit. He would just play it cool for now and hide in the shadows.

He was damn good at being invisible.

Chapter Twelve

ABDIEL WALKED DOWN THE LONG HALLWAY, NOT KNOWING WHERE IT led. He finally found himself in a small dining room. The only pieces of furniture were a large oak table and four chairs. Cam was sitting there with Appolion. A third chair was occupied by a small female. She had long, dark, curly hair and the same piercing blue eyes that Appolion did.

"Cam, what are you doing here?" Abdiel asked. "That demon took you."

"I dunno." Cam shrugged. "This is your dream not mine."

"I'm dreaming?"

"Well, this sure isn't my dream." Cam rolled his eyes. "If we were in one of my dreams, there would be a dozen female justice angels catering to my every naughty need."

Appolion's jaw dropped. "No way, you guys have orgies? I didn't know angels did that. I've always thought it was just a demon thing."

Cam gave him a wicked smile. "Normally angels don't do that, but all rules can be broken in dream land."

Abdiel groaned. How was it that even in his own dreams Cam still managed to drive him crazy? He looked at the dark-haired female. She stared straight ahead, completely ignoring the males.

"Who is she?" Abdiel pointed at her.

"You already know who that is," Appolion told him. "Look closer at her."

"Is that you, Rachael?" The female refused to answer.

"She won't talk. She can't yet." Cam sighed.

Abdiel threw his hand up in frustration. "Is anyone going to tell me what is going on here?"

"Now you're just being rude." Cam shook his head.

"Is he always like this?" Appolion asked.

"Usually, that's why they call him the Dark Angel."

A tall female walked into the room, bringing a bright light with her. Abdiel never saw her before, although her eyes were identical to Cam's. Her blond hair was pulled back in an intricate braid, and she wore a gold tiara with rubies in it. Her long white gown swayed gracefully around her ankles as she all but glided across the floor.

"Do not worry, archangel," she said, her voice soft and soothing. "All your questions shall be answered in time. Although you may learn that you will not like what you find."

"Hi, Mom." Cam waved with a huge grin on his face.

"How can you be here, Lehor?" Abdiel demanded. "You have been mentally destroyed for centuries."

"You were right. He is rude," Appolion drawled.

"You know, since this is my dream, why don't you two smartasses scram?" Abdiel snapped.

"We can't leave," Cam replied.

"Of course you can, my dream, my rules. In fact, why don't all four of you leave, but we can keep the table. Now all I need is Gabi and a can of whipped cream."

Lehor stormed over and smacked him hard on the back of the head.

Abdiel scowled at her as he rubbed the hurt away before he stopped short. You weren't supposed to feel pain in dreams.

"They must be here because you four are forever linked," Lehor told him. "You angels are our future, our only hope."

Abdiel scowled at her and looked at Cam to see his reaction. The empath ignored him, his attention centered on a goblet full of red wine that was in front of him. The empath picked it up and drained it.

"What the hey? Cam, you can't drink that. It's alcohol. It's going to make you puke your guts up."

Cam didn't even acknowledge him. He just set the empty glass down and silently studied it.

That alone proved that he was dreaming. Abdiel never knew Cam to keep his mouth shut for more than five seconds.

Lehor started to softly sob as she looked at her son.

Abdiel went over and put his arms around her, trying to comfort her. "Don't worry. Cam's going to be all right. He's just going to be kissing the can for a while."

"No, archangel. My son is not going to be all right. He is going to suffer and face great peril, and there is nothing I can do to stop it. I begged Him to spare Cam, but He said that it must be my son that faces this challenge. I'm afraid it just may destroy my Cammie."

Abdiel grabbed Lehor's shoulders. "Go tell Him I will take Cam's place. He's too young and inexperienced, whatever this task is."

She smiled sadly. "Now I know why my children love you so much. Thank you for your offer. However, this is something that Cam must face on his own. All I ask is that you stand by my son and protect him as much as you can. That is why I called you here tonight."

"Why does it have to be Cam?"

"Because he will always have his brothers and sister to keep him from turning. It would be easier for your twins to give in to the evil. We need all four of you or the Order will not be complete."

"Please, Lehor, go tell Him that I will take Cam's place. I would never turn. I have Gabi now, and I'd never leave her."

She reached up and stroked his face. "I wish that I could spare Cam this, but this is the way it must be. You are a good soul, Abdiel, now I know why your mother grieves because she lost you."

"You're wrong about that." Abdiel argued, ignoring the little surge of hope that went through him. "My mother hasn't even given me a second thought ever since she left Heaven."

"No, Abdiel, it's you who are wrong. Your mother has thought of nothing but you. Every day she cries for you and the twins. I must go now, prophet."

The whole room started to fade along with all the angels in it.

"I'm not a prophet," he yelled out to the fog.

Her voice floated back to him. "You are more powerful than you think, archangel. You are the Control, and with that title comes many gifts. Having prophetic dreams is just one of them."

ABDIEL WOKE UP WITH a start, his breath coming out in great gasps. He looked around for Cam and the twins and saw only the dark outline of the bedroom. He was still in the apartment with Gabi. It was all a dream. One big, freaky dream.

Gabi turned over and opened her eyes. She gave him a sweet smile.

He reached down and kissed her, trying hard to ignore the anxiety that was still clawing at his stomach. *It was just a dream.*

"Feeling better today?" she asked.

"Thanks to you." He brought her hand up to his mouth a nuzzled it. Just then, his cell phone started playing *Sweet Home Alabama*. He reached over and snagged it open.

"Hey Abdiel."

Abdiel almost cheered in relief. "Cam, are you all right, bud? We've been so worried about you."

"I'm fine, just a little banged up."

"Where are you? We'll come and get you." He gave Gabi the thumbs up, and she sighed with relief.

"I know you're both injured," his voice sounded tired. "Michael called, he said Ana's on her way. I'll meet you back at the house."

"Fine, just do me a favor, don't drink any wine." He felt like an idiot making such a stupid request, but the dream seemed so real.

"I won't." Cam sounded completely confused. "My freaking head hurts bad enough without adding an angel hangover to it."

"Are you sure you're fine, Cam?" There was a pause over the phone. For a moment, Abdiel thought he hung up.

"Did my family say that I any other gifts?" Cam finally asked.

"No, why would you think that?"

"Ana never said anything about me being a WMD?" he snapped angrily, not answering the question.

"Why would Ana say you're a weapon of mass destruction, Cam?" Gabi, hearing only his end of the conversation, wore questioning look.

He shrugged his shoulders.

"I blew up that demon, Abdiel." The young angel's voice was raw with anger.

"Slow down, Cam."

"No, I will not slow down. I have voices in my head, things flying at me and fire shooting out of my hand." He was hysterical. "I'm some freak, and nobody seems to care."

Abruptly, the call ended. Abdiel frantically called his number, trying to get him back on the phone. His voice mail picked up.

"Hi, this is Cam, can't come to the phone now. Look, leave a message and I'll get back to ya."

The sound of his carefree voice brought a lump to his throat. It sounded so different from the Cam he just spoke to. He was so scared and angry. He thought back to the dream and started to get really worried. What if it hadn't been just a dream? What if everything Lehor told him were true?

CAM SAT ON THE dirty floor, his head between his hands. His broken cell phone lay on the ground next to him. In a fit of anger, he smashed it against the wall. It was a childish thing to do and he knew it, but so what. It's not like he really needed it anymore. He was Mr. Telepath. Ever since the demon blood incident, he hadn't been the same. He was full of hate, anger and lust. It was all he could do to hide these emotions from the others.

The other day he lost control. Anfial sat next to him on the bed. She whispered things in his ear that would have made the old Cam turn red.

Her hands ran up his leg, not quite touching, but dangerously close. All of a sudden, a haze of anger overcame him. With a growl he grabbed her and pinned her to the bed. He even started to rip at her clothing.

I'll teach that fucking dick tease not to play me, he thought.

Luckily for both of them, his old self stopped the new him. He left the room, sickened by what he almost did. He left Anfial behind. She was scared and confused. As an empath, she felt the mass of emotions that surged through him. What would his family think if they knew what he almost done?

Sorry, Ramiel. I violated your empath. In all fairness she shouldn't not have been playing with fire. Yeah, that would have gone over real well. Jehel been right. He was tainted, and it scared him. But he didn't dare tell anyone, not even Abdiel and Gabi.

Cam growled in frustration. There was a demon downstairs. He felt it lurking around for several minutes. Well, he might as well go down and deal with it. Maybe beating something would make him feel better. He slowly made his way down the rickety, old stairs. His leg was still useless, so he dragged it behind him. Every step he took sent a jolt of sharp pain up the entire length of it. This demon was so going to pay for making him move.

It was obviously an old warehouse downstairs. The entire area was wide and open. It was just as dirty as the office upstairs. He wrinkled his nose. It was just as stinky, too. "Come out and play," he called in a singsong voice. He sniffed the air expecting the usual smell of decay, but was shocked when the smell of incense greeted him instead.

A small, female demon slipped from the shadows. She almost looked like a female angel. Long, blonde hair hung to her waist and porcelain skin was pure and unblemished. Full lips were pursed in a slightly surprised look. She wore a red leather corset top and tight, red leather pants.

The outfit left little to the imagination. Her body was so hot! Cam was horrified to feel raw lust rise up in him. He even licked his lips as he wondered what demon meat would taste like. She smiled at him showing off her fangs. Her eyes were a dark green. The pupils were shaped like a cat's. A pair of black wings protruded from her back.

She tucked them in tight as she approached.

None of that turned him off. In fact, it made her more desirable and exotic. He knew everything he was thinking about doing to her was wrong and forbidden and it gave him the hard-on of his life.

"Aren't you a sweet, little puppy?" Her voice was so husky, it dripped sex.

"Why don't you come over here and I'll show you how sweet I really am," Cam said as he spun his tonfa.

"Fine, but first drop your weapons." She opened her hands to show that they were empty. "I am unarmed."

"Fine." He tossed aside his tonfa. "Bare fists it is." *Unless you happen to have a whip handy. You can use that on me any time.* He was so lost in his raunchy thoughts that he didn't even see her coming. She launched herself at him and backhanded him across the face. His lip split open, and blood poured down his chin. She gave him a wicked, seductive smile and, to his horror, he found himself grinning back at her. He must be losing it. Here she was kicking his butt and he was totally into her. He balled up his fist and raised it, but hesitated. She was small and delicate looking. He didn't want to hurt her.

She used that moment to bitch slap him again.

Oh yeah, she's a demon, almost forgot that little tidbit. He tried to spin around and hit her back, but his bum leg gave out on him. He fell to the ground hitting his head painfully on the floor. But on the plus side, when she leaned over him to look in his face, he did have a nice view down her top. He got to see every inch of those delicious breasts.

She threw her body on top of his. Straddling him, she ripped the front of his shirt open and raked her nails down his chest leaving behind bloody scratches.

He grabbed her hips in order to throw her off, but found himself gripping them tight, pressing her body into his, grinding her into his cock.

Leaning down, she licked the blood off his chin. "Mmm," she purred. "Angel blood tastes so sweet."

"That's not the only thing that tastes sweet." His hands left her hips. He hesitantly started to touch her all over.

Seeing him unsure of what to do, she guided his hands to the right places. "I was right. You are a little puppy," she marveled. "This is your first time, isn't it?'

He could only nod in affirmation. She let her hands roam over his body and all ability to speak left him. He knew it was his job to fight her and he was going to do just that. Honest he was, in just a few minutes.

As she unzipped his pants, she dipped her head down toward his mouth.

Cam reached up to meet her halfway. Their lips met in a vicious, hard kiss. His tongue explored her mouth tentatively touching her fangs. Finally, he forced himself to stop. "I'm not supposed to be doing this," he panted.

"Now, now, little one. Didn't anyone ever tell you that female demons were fair game? You can have sex with us all you want, no strings attached."

Yes, right before he left for Earth, Nathaniel gave him the lecture about the angel birds and bees. Humans were off limits and you couldn't touch a female angel unless she was your mate, but female demons were a whole different matter. You just had to be very careful around the demons. There were many a male angel that lost valuable body parts during sex. So whatever you do, don't let them ever touch… Oh boy, she was touching it and it felt too good to make her stop.

He released a sound that was equal parts gasp of surprise and groan of ecstasy. Growing bolder by the second, he reached up and cupped her breasts through her top. She threw back her head and whimpered in happiness. *No babe, the pleasure is all mine.* "If I any sense left in me, I stop this," he growled out between kisses.

"If you want to stop, then stop," she said as she started to nuzzle his neck.

When she sank her fangs into him, he let out a cry. It should have hurt, but instead it drove him over the edge. He sat up and gripped her tightly in his lap, showing her that he was the one in charge now. He fisted his hands in her hair and held her tight to him as she fed off of him. As he unlaced her top, he knew there was no way he was going to stop.

An hour later, he sat on the ground and watched her getting dressed. He only bothered to put on his jeans. He knew he should feel guilty but strangely, he didn't. In fact, for the first time since he was poisoned, he felt relaxed. It felt so good to finally have his emotions in check. A demon did that for him who would have thought it? "What's your name?" he murmured.

"Like you really care," she scoffed.

"No, I mean it. What's your name?"

She stopped and turned to him, a shocked expression on her face. She was obviously not used to being treated with respect. She gave him a small smile. "We both know what I am, little puppy. I'm just a succubus. I am beneath an angel." She turned her back to him.

When he saw her struggling with the ties on her top, he went up and helped her. Silently he laced up the back of her top for her. When he was done, he placed a small kiss on her bare shoulder. Unable to resist, he ran his tongue briefly over her soft flesh. "You're not beneath anyone," he whispered in her ear.

"Stop being so nice to me, Cam." She was crying.

His heart skipped a beat. "How do you know my name?"

"Every demon knows your name. Douma and Forcas have placed a huge bounty on your head."

"What?" He spun her around so she looked at him. "Was all this some kind of trap?"

"At first," she admitted softly. "But don't worry. There is no way I could ever turn you in."

"Are they going to be mad at you?" He didn't want her to get in trouble.

"I have no plans on telling them of our little encounter, and I know you're not going to be telling any of your friends and family either."

He didn't bother to argue with her about that one. Having sex with demons wasn't exactly dinner table conversation.

"You need to be careful, my little puppy. Every demon is looking for you."

Her weird green eyes narrowed with concern. "Why me?" He was confused. He was just an empath, a nobody.

She shrugged her shoulders. Wrapping her arms around him, she hugged him tight.

He stroked her hair as his mind spun.

"I need to go." She wiped her nose and pulled away.

She waved her hand and a small piece of paper appeared in her fingers. She pushed it into his hand. Before she turned away, she gave him a peck on the cheek. "Call me anytime, puppy. You better hurry and get dressed. Your family is right outside. By the way, my name is Lilith." She walked out leaving him alone.

He looked down at the piece of paper and crumpled it up in his fist. He started to throw it away then changed his mind and put it in his pocket instead. Hearing voices outside, he started to panic. He turned to run towards his clothes and cursed when a fresh wave of pain shot through him. The extracurricular activity he just participated in made his leg even worse. He hopped over to his boots and struggled to put them on. He wished he wore his old tennis shoes, but Abdiel told him the boots would be better for fighting. Of course he fell. He looked up to see Ramiel and Nathaniel looking at him with knowing smiles on their faces. He closed his eyes as he groaned.

"How ya doing, little brother?" Ramiel snickered.

He ignored them and pulled on his boots. He reached over and grabbed a fresh tee shirt out of his bag. Before he could put it on, Nathaniel stopped him.

"You let her bite you?" he asked, horror on his face. "Didn't I teach you better than that?"

Cam looked down at his chest and saw several bite marks. He forgot about those. *Oopsie daisy!* He quickly pulled on his shirt to hide them. All the while ignoring his brother's knowing looks. "I don't know what you're talking about," he lied to his brothers.

"Come on, like you're the first angel to get some demon tail." Ramiel laughed.

"Don't tell Ana," Cam snapped.

"Your secret's safe with us." Nathaniel hauled him to his feet. "I'm not suicidal enough to be the one to tell her that one of her baby brothers lost his virginity to some demoness."

Ana came in at that moment. She was dressed as a human wearing white jeans and a white leather jacket. As soon as she saw him, her eyes widened in concern. "We have been looking for you all night. When I found out that some demon carried you away, I was worried sick." She ran over to him. "Oh Cam, you look like hell. I should have brought Derel with us. You need a healer bad."

"You have no idea," Ramiel muttered under his breath.

Cam shot him a murderous glare.

She pulled a tissue out of her pocket. Wetting it with her spit, she started to wipe the blood off his face.

He gently pushed her hand away, suddenly feeling suffocated by her mothering. "I'm fine. Just get me home."

She nodded and started to turn away. Suddenly she stopped and turned around. Her eyes flashing, she pointed to his chest. "What is that?" she asked angrily.

Panicked, Cam looked down at his chest. To his relief he saw she was pointing at the lettering on his shirt. It read *You're just jealous because the voices in my head only talk to me.* He released a breath of relief. "It's just a goof, Ana."

"Everything is just a goof with you, Cam. I mean honestly, can't you take anything seriously?" She stormed off in a huff.

His brothers helped him outside where the car waited. They still couldn't flash anywhere, so they relied on human transportation.

As his sister gave him another angry look, he felt his own fury rise up in him. She lied to him again. How dare she cop an attitude with him? "By the way, Ana, when were you going to tell me the big family secret? Or were you planning on keeping Cammie in the dark forever?"

As soon as he spat out the words, his family looked at him with shock. Their Cam never talked with such venom before.

He pulled out of his brother's grip and turned to stare them down, too. They were there that day, too when their mother told him not to use his powers. They were just as guilty as she was.

"Tell you what?" Ana's voice trembled uncertainly.

Instead of answering her, he held up his hand. A small pebble flew from the ground. All three of his sibs got stunned looks on their faces as they watched it travel. He caught it and showed it to her.

"Oh, that," she said weakly.

"What else are you guys not telling me?" he yelled at her before he threw the rock.

"Nothing, I swear." For the first time that both of them could remember, she was backing up from him.

"Cam..." Nathaniel started.

Cam held up a hand to stop him. "So you mean to tell me that you knew nothing about this?" He turned to an abandoned car. He lifted his hand and released an arch of flame. The car burst into fire, then exploded. Right before he passed out, he heard his brothers cursing.

HE WOKE UP TO Ramiel smacking him on both sides of his cheeks. He realized he was lying down in the backseat of the car. Nathaniel was driving and Ana was in the front passenger seat.

"Impressive," Ramiel drawled. "You fart flames from your hand, then faint like a girl."

"Go screw yourself," he snarled as he sat up and rubbed his pounding head.

"Real potty mouth you developed there," Nathaniel called back. "Very angelic of you."

Cam curled his lip at his brother. Using both hands, he saluted him with his two middle fingers. Ramiel smacked him on the back of his head, making the pounding increase ten-fold. Cam scowled as he rubbed it. Slowly, he became aware of the sobs coming from the front of the car.

"Ana?" Shock took over the anger. "Are you crying?" He never made her cry before. He and Ana were always he closest sibs in the family. Yet here she sat in the front seat sobbing, and it was all his fault. Instantly, all his anger dissolved. Ana was his world. He didn't love anyone as much as he loved her. He felt like such a dweeb.

"I didn't know that you could do that last thing." She hiccupped. "Please, don't hate me."

He leaned forward and reached around the seat to give her an awkward hug. Kissing her hair, he squeezed her. Both of his brothers shot him dirty looks. Not that he blamed them—nobody hurt their sister. "Don't cry, Ana Bana," he used his childhood nickname for her. "I'm sorry I was such a jerk. I could never hate you."

"Only the three of us knew about the telekinesis," Nathaniel told him. "Mom and Dad hid it."

"Why?" Cam asked as he continued to hug his sister. It felt good to be near her. She was always the one to kiss his boo-boos when he was little, and right now he felt like his life was one big, giant boo-boo.

"Every angel that has ever shown the gift has been hunted by demons," Ramiel supplied.

"No one knows why," Ana sniffed. "Not even the council."

"As for that other thing you just did," Nathaniel's voice was laced with concern. "We don't know what that was."

"I blew up that demon that carried me away," he admitted. "It was trying to take me to Douma and Forcas. They've put a bounty out on me."

The car was silent as the siblings tried to digest what he told them.

In all of history, there never been a time when a group of Lehor brothers were that quiet. Finally, Ramiel gave a low whistle.

"I think we better keep this from the council," Ana shocked them all by saying.

"Ever since I was given the demon blood, I feel different," Cam blurted. Confession was good for the soul after all. "I'm all messed up inside. I'm feeling things and doing things that I never would have even thought about before. It's almost like there is some evil thing in me fighting to get out."

"Is that why Anfial is afraid of you all of a sudden?" Ramiel asked.

"I almost…" Cam paused, looking for the right word. "I almost hurt her." Then he felt like a dweeb all over again.

Ana started to cry once more.

When they finally got back to his house, Cam gasped in shock. There were dozens of cars parked out front. Angels milled around walking in and out of the house. Cam wasn't lying when he said angels couldn't drive. Most of the cars were dented and scratched up. One was even rammed into the tree in their front yard.

"Michael is using your house as a command post," Ana explained. "Since nobody can flash in or out, all the angels have to stay here."

"How many are there?" Cam asked.

"A couple dozen, give or take."

"Abdiel isn't going to be happy about this," Cam stated the obvious.

"I said as much to Michael," Ana replied. "It just seemed to amuse him. The Chief just loves to annoy Abdiel."

Ramiel's healer walked out to meet them. He got one look at Cam and smirked.

The anger that Cam contained in the car surged forward again. He tried to put a lid on it, not wanting to make a spectacle of himself in front of all these witnesses.

"Looking good, Cam," Daniel mocked him.

"I'm not in the mood, dumbass," Cam snarled. He needed to put as much distance between him and that jerk as soon as possible. He knew he was about ready to go over the edge.

"Did you kiss your mother with that mouth?" Daniel shot back.

That comment struck a chord and the healer knew it. The prick even started to laugh until Cam turned and looked at him. With a roar that promised retribution, he jerked himself away from his brothers. He attacked the healer, driving him to the ground. Losing control, he punched the other angel again and again.

Daniel was bleeding horribly. He held his hands up to stop the beating.

Yet Cam still didn't stop even when he heard Ana beg him to. "You shouldn't play with fire unless you want to get burned," he yelled. His brothers came up and tried to pull him back. He easily threw them off of him and ran back to the downed angel. He kicked him hard with his steel tipped boots. He was thrilled to hear the healer's ribs break. He was in such a frenzy he didn't even notice Michael come out.

Finally, the Chief went up and grabbed him by the face. He locked eyes with Cam. "It's time to stop," Michael spoke in a low, soothing voice.

"I'm going to destroy the fucker," Cam roared. He lifted his hand. A loud crackling sound came from it as he aimed it at Daniel.

"No, you need to calm down." Michael grabbed Cam's hand and jerked it down.

"He shouldn't have talked about my mother."

Michael placed his hands on Cam's temples and closed his eyes. The Chief archangel eased the anger out of the young angel's mind.

Cam's head fell back, and his eyelids fluttered shut. When he opened them again, all the anger was gone, replaced by a calming white light that soothed him. Until he remembered what he just did. Cam looked at the healer in horror. The angel lay there, beaten to a pulp and unconscious. He did that. He was an empath. He was supposed to ease others pain, not bring it on. He glanced down and saw his hands covered in blood. "I'm sorry," he whispered to his Chief. "Crap, Michael, I didn't mean to do that."

"It's going to be okay," Michael assured.

"I don't think so." Now that the Chief cleared his mind, he realized he almost was lost forever to the rage. He almost became the thing he hunted. "What's happening to me?"

"Go in, take a shower and get cleaned up," Michael urged. "Derel is here. He can heal your wounds. We can talk more later."

Cam turned and started toward the house. The crowd parted to let him through. As he walked by the other angels, he could hear them whispering. A deep shame filled him from the inside out, making him feel dirty and tainted.

Now he understood what Abdiel endured through all these years.

ABDIEL STOOD AT THE window looking out at the city. The other angels finally made it there a couple of hours ago. Already things were turning for the better. It was going to take a few days, but the angels were going contain the demons. Unfortunately, a lot of damage was already done to their human brothers. No angel would ever consider this a victory.

There was a knock at the door. He opened it and saw Nathaniel. His usual dancing blue eyes were dead and listless. Lines of worry creased the archangel's face and the despair that surrounded him was so thick Abdiel didn't need an empath to tell him it was there.

"I'm here to take you two back home," Nathaniel said dully.

"What's the matter?" Abdiel asked as he reached out to grab Gabi's hand for support. Only one thing could be upsetting Nathaniel, Cam.

"Cam lost it and beat the crap out of Ramiel's healer," Nathaniel sighed.

"Is this some kind of sick joke?" Gabi's face was full of shock. "Cam would never do that."

"Come on, all you Lehor brothers fight," Abdiel defended his empath. "Maybe Cam decided to follow in your footsteps."

"No." Nathaniel shook his head. "This was no simple brawl. He really hurt the other angel. Michael had to pull him off."

Abdiel and Gabi exchanged worried looks. Although they didn't tell Nathaniel, they both worried about Cam. "Do you really think he was trying to hurt that other angel?" she asked.

"Look, he's my brother, and I love him, but he's all messed up. I don't know what he's capable of anymore," Nathaniel admitted.

"It's the demon blood, isn't it?" Abdiel knew deep in his gut that his friend was not the same since poisoning.

Nathaniel nodded. They all knew that there would be no more ignoring the obvious. Cam was in big trouble, and he needed them.

"Take me to him," Abdiel commanded.

CAM LAY ON HIS bed and stared into the darkness. Derel healed him a while ago. Afterward, his brother tried to talk to him, but Cam merely grunted in response to all of Derel's questions. Finally, his brother gave up and compelled him to rest. Cam resisted the order. He knew he should be sleeping, but he just couldn't.

What were Gabi and Abdiel going to say when they learned he attacked another angel? Whenever Abdiel trained him, he stressed the importance of keeping one's anger in control. Cam curled up in a ball and cradled his aching stomach. He did a piss poor job of that. If Michael hadn't grabbed his hand, he would've destroyed the healer just like he did the demon.

Abdiel and Gabi walked into his room. Gabi sat on his bed with him while Abdiel just sat on the floor. They were all silent for several minutes.

"Are you guys mad at me?" Cam finally asked.

"No, of course not," Gabi reassured. "We love you."

"You should have told us though," Abdiel said, gravely.

"I was afraid you guys would hate me if you knew what was going on with me," Cam rasped. "I think I'm turning demon."

Abdiel reached out and grabbed the younger angel by the back of the neck. He gently pulled him forward. They met head to head.

Cam was mortified when he realized that he was about ready to cry. When Gabi laid her head on his back and stroked his hair in a motherly fashion, he started to bawl like a baby.

"I won't let that happen, bud. I've got your back," Abdiel said softly.

"Promise me that if I do turn, you'll destroy me, Abdiel. It would devastate my brothers if they have to fight me."

"Stop talking like that. That's not going to happen."

"Damn it, Abdiel, promise me. I'm so fucking scared I'm going to go demon and hurt someone from my family. You have got to swear to me you won't let that happen."

"You're not going to turn Cam," Abdiel declared so firmly Cam had no choice but to believe him. "I won't let you."

Relief swept over Cam. He didn't have to fight this battle all by himself anymore. Abdiel was going to help him and make it all better.

Chapter Thirteen

Cam's mutterings and thrashing woke Gabi. *Oh please no.* He was having another nightmare. She leaned over and touched his brow and he instantly calmed down. Brushing back his sweaty hair, she whispered some nonsense words to him. Even while asleep, anxiety lined his face.

It wasn't until Cam broke down and cried that she realized just how bad off he was. She held him in her arms and rocked him like a child until he finally fell asleep. Even then, she and Abdiel still wouldn't leave him. She curled up at the foot of the bed, and Abdiel stretched out on the floor, one arm reaching up to touch Cam's leg.

Derel healed her and Abdiel when they first got home, and she asked him if Cam was all right. He reassured her that Cam's injuries were taken care of as well. However, he refused to meet her eyes, and she suspected he hid something from her, couple with all the nightmares Cam suffered. She wanted to make sure for herself that he really was healthy.

She laid hands on him and chanted softly as she entered his body with her healer skills. When she got a good gander at what was going on inside of him, she pulled out so fast she stumbled backward and landed on her butt.

She saw the source of energy that Raphael told her about, but now it was huge. It was a great white ball of power, neither good nor bad, and was barely contained. She knew it was to blame for his new gifts. She remembered what he told about destroying the demon and shuddered. Raphael was right, Cam was one of the most powerful angels, and she wasn't sure he would be able to handle that responsibility.

That wasn't the worst thing she found in him though, not by a long shot. The demon blood was still flowing through him. His angel's blood was fighting it, but she didn't know if he could withstand another poisoning. It would turn him catatonic, or worse.

She started to shake with fury. Derel must have found the same things in Cam when he healed him and he never said a word about it to her. She didn't think for one cotton-picking minute Derel overlooked these abnormalities. He was too good of a healer to miss something this big. She got up and went to her old bedroom, where the Lehor family was crashing. She rapped on the door.

Derel answered it. As soon as he looked at her face, his smile faded. He knew this wasn't a social call, she came to him as his leader, not as his friend.

Officially, she was second in command of all the healers, answering only to Raphael. Since she chose to become an angel warrior, she tended to leave all the leadership jazz to Raphael. However, tonight was different. She was going to rip Derel a new one. "Come out in hallway with me, and close the door," she snapped.

"Yes, Mistress," he replied, addressing her formally.

Normally, one of the Lehors using her official title would have ticked her off, but not now. By using it, Derel was showing he knew he was in big trouble and was a little afraid. Good, she wanted him shaking in his boots. Right now, that was a good thing. "You lied to me, healer." She was all Ice Queen now, her tone completely detached and not showing the love she really did have for him. "I just finished scanning your brother."

"I didn't lie." Derel kept his eyes down, shamed. "I just didn't tell you everything."

"You lied by omission, Derel, how could you not tell me? This is huge. If the council ever found out what you did, they'd proclaim you rogue and banish you."

Derel went down on one knee before her and bowed his head. He completely subjected himself to her, showing he acknowledged her leadership and honored her. By angel custom, he could not get up until she released him. She usually hated it when her healers did that, but not tonight.

"I did it to protect my brother, mistress. I'm sorry if I offended you."

She walked by him, leaving him to kneel for a few more minutes and kicked the door open to the bedroom. Ana, Ramiel and Nathaniel all jumped when they heard it hit the wall. None of them went to bed yet, but then they obviously had a lot to talk about. "This ends now," she commanded. "There will be no more secrets kept from me. Cam is not only my empath, he's my friend, and I won't have you lying to me or him anymore."

"We're just trying to protect him," Ana protested, her eyes rimmed in red from crying.

"We could have lost him, Ana. We almost did. The whole reason that demon got him in the first place was because he was having a major meltdown and not scanning the area like he should have been. This whole thing has him scattered, and we need him focused now."

"Maybe he should just go home with me." Ana twisted her hands together nervously.

"He's a full grown male now and not some infant that needs coddled. It's time to cut the apron strings, Ana."

"I happen to think my sister is right," Nathaniel interjected, placing a comforting hand on Ana's arm. "Cam's not safe on Earth anymore. The demons are hunting him down."

"I don't mean to get all Her Highness on you guys, but too freaking bad. We need him too much in this war. His skills are unmatched now, and I happen to think they're only going to grow more powerful."

"That's not fair." Ana sounded half hysterical. "Hasn't our family sacrificed enough? We already lost our mother and father."

"I'm sorry, Ana, but that's the way things are going to be. I have no say in it, and neither do you. I hate to break it to you, but this is only the beginning. You know what's going to happen when the other empaths find out."

"You think they're going to persecute him?" Ramiel growled out, his jaw ticking in anger.

"No, just the opposite. Like Raphael is the leader of the healers and Michael the leader of archangels, your mother was the leader of the empaths. She was so loved and honored they refused to elect a new leader, even though she's catatonic. As soon as they learn that her son is so gifted they will no doubt demand that Cam be their leader."

"There's no way." Ana shook her head. "He's too young for such responsibility."

"He blew up a demon simply by willing it, Ana. I'd say that makes him a big boy now." She grabbed a dagger off her dresser, went back out into the hallway and stood over Derel. He still hadn't moved. At least he knew how to be a polite angel. Not that such would earn him any bonus points right now. She was too angry at him. She handed him the dagger. "Derel, son of Lehor, I demand that you take a blood oath that you will never deceive me again," she commanded.

All of the sibs released a collective gasp. What she was demanding of him was huge. To swear a blood oath was binding and only used on rare occasions. The last blood oath Derel probably had taken was the one to serve as an angel warrior. He didn't hesitate even one second. He took the dagger by the blade and squeezed it tightly in his fist until blood trickled from between his fingers.

"I swear upon my blood never to lie or keep anything from you again, Mistress Gabrielle." Only after that did he look up into her eyes.

"You may raise now, healer." She turned and looked at the rest of the clan. "You guys were my family when I had none, and you taught me to love. I will never forget that. I love Cam, too. Don't you think I feel like locking him up in his room and keeping him safe? But I won't humiliate him like that. He's a warrior—he's taken the same vows we have, and I won't dishonor him by treating him any differently."

"Gabi, there's something else you do need to know," Derel said quietly, he took a towel from Ana and wrapped it around his cut hand.

"What's that?"

"You know that energy source you saw in Cam?" At her nod, he continued. "I found something like that in Abdiel, too. It's kind of like Cam's, but it's different."

Gabi didn't answer because she was already beating a path back to Cam's bedroom. As soon as she got there, she threw herself down on the ground where Abdiel was sleeping and scanned him. Derel was right. There was a white light building up in her mate, too. She stared it down with her healer's eyes, despising and fearing its very existence. She knew that nothing would ever be the same again. Their lives changed and there was no going back. Her breath came out in short, little gasps as a wave panic swelled through her body. She laid her head on his chest and started to cry.

He woke up. "Gabi, what's wrong?"

She found that she couldn't put her sorrow into words. In the end, he just ended up holding her and rocking her like she rocked Cam earlier.

"THIS IS STILL OUR house, right?" Abdiel asked grumpily.

Gabi gave a small chuckle as she patted his hand. They went down for breakfast and found the kitchen full of angel warriors. Abdiel took one look at the gawking crowd and decided Michael would pay for this one.

Cam walked down the stairs and joined them. As soon as he saw the crowd, his lip curled. "I'm going back to my room," he announced. He turned around and started to leave.

Abdiel grabbed the back of his shirt and hauled him back. "If I have to play nice, so do you," Abdiel told him.

"They're all staring at me like I'm some frigging lab rat," Cam complained.

"Well, you did go ballistic on them," Gabi informed tartly.

Cam responded by walking up to the fridge. Grabbing a carton of milk out of it, he proceeded to drink straight from it. He looked around like he was daring someone to say something.

Abdiel went over to him and jerked the carton from his hands. He smacked the punk on the back of the head.

Cam rubbed his head as he shot the archangel a filthy look.

"Excuse my empath folks," Abdiel told the other angels. "He's always cranky in the morning."

"Did you really give it to your brother's healer?" a young dark-haired male asked.

"Yeah, so?" Cam grunted.

"That is so cool," the male exclaimed. "That guy is such a jerk."

"It's about time us empaths stood up for ourselves," a blond male angel chimed in.

A female joined the group. She tucked a strand of long blonde hair behind her ear. "The Empath Guild would love it if you would be our keynote speaker at next month's meeting."

"I don't do well speaking in front of crowds." Cam tried to edge his way out of the room, but the empaths tightened their circle and blocked him in.

"What would be the title his speech?" Abdiel drawled. "101 ways to beat a healer?"

That comment angered the blonde female. She gave him a huffy look. "Like an archangel would understand. Empaths have been getting the shaft for far too long. We're the ones sticking our necks out night after night. And what do we get for all our efforts? A room in the loony bin when we become catatonic."

"What exactly is the Empath Guild?" Abdiel directed his question to Cam. Talking to the female was like talking to a pit bull.

"It's an advocacy group for empaths." Having lost his carton of milk, he grabbed a soda from the counter. The whole conversation bored him. "I've never been to a meeting, but I guess they push for empath rights."

A vision of empaths carrying picket signs flashed through Abdiel's mind. What was next? Healers demanding medical and dental benefits?

The female went over and placed an imploring hand on Cam. "Please, it would be an honor to all of us. You are the most respected empath out there."

Abdiel groaned. These kids were looking at Cam like they worshiped him. He was going to be impossible to live with now. When he finally told them that he would speak at their stupid meeting, they almost fainted at his feet.

He looked at Gabi. Her mouth hung open as she shook her head. It made him feel a little better to know that he wasn't the only one baffled by the weird turn of events.

"Oh honestly," Ana hissed from behind them. She walked into the kitchen

Cam gave his sister a lopsided boyish grin as he pulled her into a hug. She gave him a quick squeeze.

"Feeling better?" she whispered.

"Much," he reassured.

"Michael wants to see you three in the gym." She pulled away.

Abdiel nodded and led his team out of the kitchen. Their gym was converted into an infirmary. Cots lined both sides. It was already half filled with the injured. Michael was kneeling by one of the cots. On the other side sat a female justice angel. She had a beautiful mane of deep red hair. Her bright green eyes were rimmed red from crying.

"What's Haniel doing here? I sent him to the healing chambers." Gabi stared at the injured angel.

"Yeah, that's one of the reasons I wanted to talk to you guys." Michael cast an uneasy look at Cam. "The morning that all this stuff started going down, another team was poisoned."

"Which team?" Abdiel asked.

"The guys from Flint."

Flint was about two hours north of Detroit. Like their city, Flint was seeing a lot of activity lately. It was a little close for comfort.

"They were taken to the healing chamber," the Chief continued. "The empath went crazy and attacked the healers. They tied him down."

"Crap." Cam paled. "It really sucks to be one of us empaths now."

"The council decreed that any poisoned angel must be confined to Earth until they are deemed not dangerous," Michael finished.

"That's ridiculous," Abdiel said angrily. "Haniel is an archangel. Not only that, but he's Jehel's nephew. Why would he banish his own kin?"

"I told you the council had sticks up their butts," Gabi spoke in a stage whisper.

The Chief gave her an aggravated look. "I think you've been hanging out with this one too much." Michael jerked his thumb at Cam.

Cam kneeled down next to the red-haired female. "What is your name?"

"Amadeaha, I'm Haniel's sister." She never looked up from her brother.

"I'm an empath," Cam said softly, his eyes never leaving the female. "Would you like me to ease some of your pain?"

"No," Amadeaha whispered. "I want to feel this pain, remember it. It is the least I can do for my brother."

"Are you sure? Please, let me help you." When the female shook her head in the negative, Cam shrugged his shoulders and stood up. He cast a sad look at the justice angel. He reached out to touch her, but stopped himself at the last moment.

"So how is Haniel doing?" Abdiel asked Michael.

"It's going to take a few sessions of healing, but he'll make it. However, his days of being an archangel are probably over."

"Is that what you called me for?" Gabi walked closer to the injured angel. "To help heal him?"

"Thanks, Gabi," Michael drawled out. "We could use the help. We seem to be one healer short."

"Sorry, Michael," Cam looked down at his feet.

"I know you are, Cam." Michael patted him on the back. "We also need you to read him. He hasn't said a word since you guys found him. We need to know what happened to him."

Cam nodded and went to the other side of the cot. He and Gabi placed their hands on the hurt archangel, and they both went into a trance.

Michael motioned Abdiel over. "The word is that there's a bounty out on Cam." Abdiel didn't ask how the Chief knew as he had a way of knowing just about everything. It was near impossible to keep a secret from him. "Yeah, Cam told me last night."

"Ana wants me to call him back to Heaven."

"We both know Cam would refuse."

"I already told her no." Michael ran his hand through his mane of blond hair. "But, we both know he's not just an empath."

Abdiel didn't argue. Ever since his talk with Cam last night, he suspected as much. The young angel was too powerful and gifted to be only an empath. He had to be more. "Are you going to tell me what he is?"

"He's a strange mixture that I never saw before. He is empath, archangel, and telepath all rolled up into one."

"How long have you known this?"

"I just figured it out yesterday."

Abdiel stopped and gave him a shocked look. "You scan every newborn in Heaven looking for their talents. How did you miss the boat with Cam?"

Michael set his face in a grim expression. "I'm pretty sure Lehor shielded his gifts from me in an effort to protect him. It was a damn stupid thing for her to do. If I'd known all along, I would have seen to his training, so he would have been better prepared for what was ahead. Now the kid is throwing his skills around willy nillly."

"So is he going to be reassigned then?"

"You're the only one that can control him. Right now, he's too volatile. It's all he can do to control his emotions," Michael answered.

Control—that word jarred his memory. It was something Gabi told him his brothers said. "Does this have something to do with that Order of Four thing my brothers mentioned?"

"It's a very old angel and demon prophecy." Michael sighed. "There's going to be a battle that could end all of human kind. Four angels will save the world. Three are archangels that have gifts that have never been seen before. The fourth is the Control, the leader of the other three. I happen to think that you and Cam are part of the Order of Four."

"Come on, Michael, it's just us you're talking about."

"Why do you think your brothers want Cam so bad? It's because they're thinking the same thing I am."

They both looked at Cam. His blond hair was a mess as usual and he wore his trademark torn jeans and rock tee shirt. He removed the hoop earring from his ear and replaced it with a diamond stud. *Yeah, this punk was going to save the world.*

"Okay then," Abdiel said. "Let's just say for sake of argument that you're right about Cam and me. Who are the other two?"

"I haven't figured that one out yet," Michael admitted.

Cam opened his eyes and walked over to them. He tugged at his hair nervously and gave the Chief a furtive look from the corner of his eye. It was obvious Michael still intimidated him.

"They really fu..." He stopped and shot a guilty glance at the Chief. "They really messed him up."

"No shit, Sherlock," Michael snapped.

Cam's eyes widened in surprise. He must have never heard his boss curse before. Abdiel laughed at his stunned expression.

Cam opened his mouth to talk, but only a grunt came out.

"Why don't you fill Cam in on everything we just talked about," he suggested.

"I want to know when Cam was going to tell me that he could obliterate demons with his mind?" Michael gave him an irritated look.

"I won't do it again, I promise." Cam's eyes were wild with fear. "I'll just stick to my duties and not break anymore rules. Please, don't make me go back to Heaven."

"Don't worry," Abdiel reassured. "Nobody's going to send you away."

"It's no big deal," Cam said to Michael. "Every time I do that flame thing, I faint."

"That's because you were injured at the time and already weak. You need to learn how to use your gifts more," Michael stated. "But I only want you to practice around Abdiel. I taught him how to shield energy bolts so he'll be able to stop you if you lose control."

Abdiel was still trying to digest everything Michael just told him. If what he said was true, then life was about to get more complicated. He and Cam were going to be hunted nonstop. They would use Gabi to get to them. By taking her as his mate, he gave away his biggest weakness to his brothers, his undying love for her. Surely, Michael was wrong. There was no way he and Cam could be part of this old prophesy. He worked in the armory up until a few months ago and Cam just learned how to play with the big boys. The mere idea was ridiculous.

Cam stared at Abdiel with a look of horror on his face. He obviously read the archangel's mind and knew everything Michael just told him. Oops, so much for giving the news to him gently.

"Oh, hell no!" Cam spat out.

"You really need to learn how to close off your mind to him," Michael chastised Abdiel.

"Look, I'm no hero," Cam argued. "I'm just some dork who wants to be left in peace."

"Sorry, we don't always get to pick our destiny," Michael didn't sound sorry at all.

"How I am supposed to be an archangel? I've never been trained to be one?" Cam talked so loud several angels turned to look at them, but he was too far gone to care. "I went to empath training. They didn't teach us squat about tactics, or war. All we empaths ever did in school was sit in a circle, hold hands and get in touch with our feelings."

"Is that what they really do in empath training?" Abdiel asked.

Michael and Cam both stopped and looked at him from the corner of their eyes. Both of their faces read *Don't be such an idiot*.

"Look, Chief." Cam shook his head as they looked away from

Abdiel. "I'm going back to my room. Let me know when you freaking come to your senses."

Michael grabbed him by the front of his shirt and started to drag him out of the gym. "Abdiel, grab two practice swords and meet us outside."

Well it was official—Cam was in for it. Abdiel went to the weapons cabinet and grabbed a pair of practice swords. As he ran outside, he glanced at Gabi and saw she was still in a trance, healing Haniel. *Good, she'd have a heart attack if she knew what was about to happen.* By the time, he made it to the front yard, a large crowd already gathered around Cam and Michael. Abdiel handed the swords to Michael.

The Chief tossed one to Cam.

He caught it and looked down at it in horror. "I'm not fighting you, Michael."

"Why not? Are you afraid of what you might find out?"

"I won't fight you for two reasons. One, you are my Chief and my vows won't allow it, and two, because you're Michael. You're the best warrior in Heaven. You could wipe the floor with my puny butt."

The comment brought a round of laughter from the crowd, but Abdiel was too nervous to join in. He felt a small hand gripping his arm, the fingernails digging into his flesh. He looked down and saw Ana, her blue eyes wide with terror. Abdiel put his arm around her, partly to comfort her and partly to keep her from going out and trying to stop the fight. That would dishonor Cam.

Michael didn't give Cam another chance to argue. He attacked him. The young angel barely had time to bring his sword up to deflect the blow. At first, that's all Cam did, deflect Michael's strikes. Soon his natural born instincts took over, and he started to fight back.

"Does someone want to explain to me what this is all about?" Derel never took his gaze off his brother.

"Michael initiates every new archangel this way," Ramiel explained. "It's a rite of passage."

"Does Cam know that?"

"I'm guessing no," Nathaniel drawled. "How long did you last, Ramiel?"

"Three minutes. You?"

"Four. I think our little brother is going to put us both to shame."

"No way," another archangel argued. "He's too small. There's no way he's going to last even a minute."

"Fifty bucks says my brother goes five minutes," Ramiel growled.

"You're on."

Soon all the archangels were placing bets on how long Cam was going to last. Abdiel ignored them and kept his focus on the fight. Damn, he never realized how quick Cam was. Ramiel was right. He would last five minutes easy.

It lasted six minutes.

Michael finally disarmed Cam and knocked him off his feet. The young angel rolled to his knees and panted for breath.

The crowd cheered loudly, Abdiel doubted that Cam even realized the cheers were for him. He went to Cam who still sat on the ground.

Nathaniel went up to him as well, and hauled him up to his feet, then gave him a big, bear hug. Ramiel started to thump him on the back proudly.

"I don't get it," he gasped out. "Michael kicked my butt."

"Camael, I fought every one of my archangels and there was only one that lasted as long as you. That is your good buddy Abdiel."

Cam gave him a horrified look. "This was all some test?"

"Can't get anything by you, Einstein. Now are you going to tell us what you found out from Haniel or not?"

"Jeffrey Dahmer has nothing on demon jailers." Cam shuddered. "They pumped him full of demon blood just to see how he would react. When that didn't amuse them anymore, they used various toys on him. The reason why Haniel hasn't said anything is because he can't. They freaking cut his tongue out, Michael."

"Haniel deserved better than that." Abdiel scowled. "He was a great warrior."

"Douma and Forcas sent me a message." Cam's eyes turned dark with anger. "They said next time it was going to be one of my brothers that I found hogtied."

"You know what I think, Cam?" Abdiel asked.

"What?"

"I think it's time that we went out and took our city back."

Cam grinned wickedly. "Oh goodie. It's time to go demon hunting."

"Let's grab Gabi and get going. We'll explain everything to her on the way."

"SO LET ME GET this straight." Gabi's mind whirled in shock. "You and Cam are part of this Order of Four, and Cam is really an archangel."

They were in Gabi's car, a small red Beetle Bug. Unlike most other angels, she was an excellent driver. In fact, this car was her baby. Cam was sound asleep in the backseat.

"That's what Michael said." Abdiel nodded.

"That would explain what I found in both of you last night."

"Do I even want to know what you're talking about?"

"There is some force within both of you. It's something new, too. I didn't see it when I healed you guys before."

Abdiel rubbed his chest. "Are you sure it's just not some side effect from the demon blood?"

"No, I'm pretty sure that it's what's making Cam grow in power. Have you noticed anything different with yourself?"

He scratched his head. "I've been having weird dreams."

"Weird how?"

"Cam's mom is there, and they seem so real. It's like they're telling me the future."

"You do know that's how Michael knows so much? He has prophetic dreams."

"Great, just what the world needs, another Michael. I'll stick to being plain old Mr. Dark Angel, thank you very much."

She rolled her eyes. "You know I'm kind of surprised they haven't placed a bounty on you."

"There's always been a bounty out for me."

"What?" she shrieked. "When were you going to tell me? I mean I'm only your mate after all."

He put his finger in his ear.

She really hoped she blew out his eardrum.

Cam continued to sleep in the backseat, so exhausted that not even her yelling woke him.

"I thought you already knew. I really ticked Satan off when I wouldn't play his reindeer games."

She swung the car into a parking spot, shut off the car and turned to give him an angry glare. *How dare he be so flippant about this?* "You aren't alone anymore," she yelled. "Believe it or not, I actually care what happens to you. From now on, you tell me stuff like this."

"I think it would be better if you stayed close to the house." He didn't look at her.

"Why? You know I can fight better than almost any healer?"

"My brother's are out for blood now," his voice hitched a bit. "They may go after you because of me."

"It may come as a shock to you, bud, but your brothers would love to get me just because I'm royalty." Her voice dripped venom.

"Are you telling me that you have a bounty on your head, too?" His gaze turned even darker with anger at the mention of her being in danger.

"Not exactly," she admitted. "But demons have always thought it was a big coup to capture any angel of royal lineage. Not only that, but I've made a name for myself even before I met you, Mr. Macho Pants." What she said was true. She was the most gifted healer known, more powerful than even Raphael. She knew and mastered ancient healing chants that confounded every other healer. If she wasn't so devoted to the human race, she probably would be sitting on the council and ruling all the other healers alongside Raphael.

"You know, you're so cute when you're angry." Abdiel gave her his crooked smile, took her hand and started to kiss her knuckles. He leaned over and started kissing her neck.

Damn, Abdiel knows this is my weakness. "Stop," she commanded even as she tilted her head to the side. "Cam's in the backseat."

"He's asleep," he whispered against her throat.

Cam picked that moment to start babbling in his sleep. "Ana, Derel hit me in the tummy."

They both burst out laughing. Cam was sprawled and drool ran down his cheek. He thrashed around, caught up in his dream.

"I don't know why we didn't realize he was an archangel sooner," Abdiel quipped sarcastically.

Finally, their laughter woke him. Cam sat up with a snort. Scratching his stomach, he gave them a curious look. They laughed even harder.

They left the car and made their way through the streets. Although everything was a lot calmer than before, there was still demon activity. There were no humans out in the city. It was completely deserted unless you counted angels and demons.

"Eloa," a strong voice yelled from the distance. "Watch your back they're closing in."

"I'm trying, Derdekea, but they're fast," another voice answered.

"You have to be faster," the first voice chastised. "Muriel, stay back, but keep your bow ready."

They followed the sound of the yelling. Three female angels were fighting a group of demons and the beasts were winning. The angels were hopelessly outnumbered. The enemy had them pinned.

Abdiel delivered a flying kick to one demon that was bringing its sword up to strike one of the downed angels. The fiend stumbled back a few steps before it turned its weapon on him. He dodged the blade as he kicked the wretch full in its ugly face.

The demon fell on its back and started to gag on its own blood.

Abdiel turned to find another demon only to be attacked by two.

Not that Gabi really expected them to stand back and attack Abdiel one at a time. That was only for ninja movies.

Cam tackled another demon that had one of the females pinned. Crouching above the demon, he pulled a butterfly knife out of his boot. Flipping it open, he stabbed the demon in the throat.

His lips curled up into a cruel smile that she never saw him wear before.

Seeing that they were out manned, the other demons turned and ran. Cam raised his hand and, using his telekinesis, sent a dumpster flying across the alley. It smashed the fleeing demons into the wall with a sickening wet thud. "It's not nice to leave a party early, boys," he called out in a fake singsong voice.

Damn! Gabi reminded herself not to ever tick him off. He just finished off six demons and hadn't even broken a sweat. Somehow, she longed for the old, defenseless Cam. This new Cam was scary and unpredictable.

Cam went over and helped the female archangel to her feet. There was no mistaking the look in his eyes. He was raking the female over like she was a piece of prime rib.

Gabi sprinted over and put herself between the two of them. "Are you guys all right?" She tried to ignore the fact Cam panted over the three females.

"How did he just do that thing with the dumpster?" the female archangel, Derdekea, demanded, suspicious.

"Any time you want private lessons, just let me know, baby. I'd love to help you in every way possible," Cam drawled.

Gabi groaned. It seemed the demon blood made him a horn dog in conjunction with his hair trigger temper.

The female's face colored with anger. "You're awfully mouthy for a little, young thing."

"Why don't you come on over and see how little I really am?" Cam smiled wickedly.

Gabi put her hand over his mouth in order to shut him up.

Abdiel came over, grabbed him by the nape of the neck and hauled him off. "Sorry ladies, he was dropped on his head as a kid."

Cam waved at the females as he was led away.

To the shock of Derdekea and Gabi, the other two females tittered and waved back.

"He is so hot," one whispered to the other.

Gabi frowned. *Were all young angels losing their collective minds? Cam was actually beginning to be some cult hero. It seemed even angels had a serious bad boy infatuation.*

SEVERAL HOURS LATER, THEY were still patrolling the streets. Suddenly, Cam stopped dead in his tracks like someone slapped him in the face. He sniffed the air before he took off running at a neck-breaking pace. Abdiel cursed and followed him. What now?

"Cam, get your ass back here. You haven't even scanned the area for danger."

Cam completely ignored him and continued to tear down the road. Abdiel finally caught up with him and tackled him to the ground, giving both of them a nice case of road rash. Cam struggled to get out from underneath him. Abdiel cuffed him on the side of his head in an effort to snap him out of it, but Cam still fought him.

"Let me go, Abdiel I need to go to her." Cam rasped out.

"Stop, you need to calm the hell down."

"She's calling to both of us, don't you feel it?"

No, the only thing he felt was a growing annoyance with him. An unseen force threw him off the empath and sent him sprawling on the street. All righty then, it was obvious that Cam's telekinesis was getting stronger.

As soon as he was free, Cam scrambled to his feet and started hauling ass again, Abdiel hot at his heels. All of a sudden Cam screeched to a dead stop with an *oh fuck* look plastered on his face. Abdiel skidded to a stop next to him and felt the vibe too. A demon was close. Damn close, and they been caught with their pants down.

"Good going, boys," Gabi growled from behind them. "While you two were playing alpha male you didn't bother to scan for enemies."

Okay, point taken, they been idiots. They made their way over to where the demon was, weapons drawn. The street appeared to be deserted.

Abdiel whistled. "Here, demon, demon," he yelled like he was calling the family dog.

A tall, dusky demon walked out with a small female child in his arms. The little angel was unconscious. Her long, black hair hung down. She wore a white, tattered gown, a pair of dainty bare feet poked from under the lacy trim on the hem. "Abdiel," the demon rasped. "It's me, Bub."

"Beelzebub?" Abdiel was shocked. His former best friend was unrecognizable. His once handsome face was twisted with long fangs and jutting cheekbones. Matted black hair hung to his waist, blue eyes were a burning red and filled with pain.

"Gabi." The demon looked at her sadly. "You have grown up to be so beautiful."

"Thank you." Tears filled her eyes and her lips softened into a sad smile.

"I need you to take her." Bub held the girl out like she was some type of venomous snake ready to bite him.

Abdiel looked down at the child, and his heart lurched. It looked like Rachael but that was impossible. His sister should be a full-grown female, not still a child. The demon thrust the girl into his arms.

"She won't shut up. She screams day and night. Since I can't kill her, I must get rid of her."

"What happened to her?" Abdiel asked harshly as he clutched the female tight in his arms.

"What happened to *her*?" The demon snarled out. "She may look innocent, but she has tortured me day and night for centuries. The only reason I'm returning her is because I cannot stand her scrambling around in my head anymore. It's not because I have any kindness left in my heart. That has long ago been drained out of me."

"Oh gee, why doesn't that shock me?" Cam, the Sarcasm King, asked. "Could it be because you're the top general of Satan's armies?"

"I'm going to enjoy bringing you to your knees and watching you grovel," Beelzebub growled.

"Ditto." Cam's glare equaled the menacing one he received.

"What about Appolion? What did you monsters do to him?" Abdiel asked, deliberately leaving out the fact he just recently saw him.

"Don't ask any more questions from me." Bub snarled like a jungle cat. "Remember what I am. We are no longer friends. In fact, I cannot wait for the day when I finally defeat you in battle. That will never change."

His former friend pivoted and walked away. The three of them watched him in shocked silence. Abdiel and Gabi turned when they heard Cam chuckle.

"She says she's cold and that she would appreciate it if you got her inside." He pointed to the female child.

"Is it really Rachael?" Abdiel was almost afraid of getting his hopes up. He already let Appolion slip from his grip.

"Yes, it is. She somehow put herself in some frozen state when she was taken down to Hell." Cam slipped off his jacket and covered Abdiel's sister with it. "There you go, Rachael, that should warm you up."

Gabi walked over and peered down at the child. She leaned down and kissed the girl's cheek. "Welcome home, little sister. Your brother has missed you something terrible."

The way she talked to his sister made his heart melt. She was the kindest most caring soul he ever knew. He was so damned lucky to have her. "I love you, Gabi," he whispered for only her to hear.

"Of course you do." She smiled. "Now, let's get Rachael home."

THEY SNUCK HER IN the back door. Abdiel and Gabi agreed that until they knew more, it was best to keep the return of his sister secret. Of course, that was not going to be easy with a house full of angel warriors.

"Take her to my room," Cam whispered. "I'll go find Ana. She can scan her."

They made their way quietly up the stairs. Thankfully, the upstairs are was pretty deserted and they didn't run into anyone else. They made their way to Cam's room, and Abdiel placed her on the bed.

Gabi tucked her in and ran her hands over her looking for any injuries.

Abdiel raked his hands through his hair, frustrated. "Do you think she'll ever wake up?"

"I honestly don't know." Troubled, she nibbled on her bottom lip. "Whatever is causing this is not physical." She felt so useless. Here she was a healer, yet she could not give him back something that was so important to him. There was nothing she could do to heal his sister. A tear slipped down her cheek.

Cam entered and dragged, Ana with him. "You can't tell anyone, promise," he whispered to her.

The blonde female stopped dead in her tracks at the sight of the child lying there. "Like anyone would ever believe me." Ana sat down on the bed next to Rachael. "You could have scanned her just as easy as me, Cam. Actually, you would do a better job. You're the telepath."

"I thought of that." Cam tugged on his hair. "But I can't be impartial. I like her, too, much already."

"So is that why you freaked on us back there, bud?" Abdiel queried.

Cam gave him a sheepish look. "I'm sorry. I was just drawn to her. It's like she's a missing piece of me. It's nothing sexual, like with a mate or anything. It's just like we need to be together, linked somehow. It's the same thing I felt when I first met you."

"You felt some freaky physic connection to me? Why didn't you say anything about it before now?"

Cam blushed. "I didn't want you to get the wrong idea and think I was getting all *Broke Back Mountain*."

Gabi and Ana both coughed as they tried to hold back their laughter.

Cam gave them a nasty look, his face flush. He crammed his hands in his pockets and cursed under his breath. "I'm not gay. Not that there's anything wrong with that. It's just not my thing. Oh, screw you guys, I'm just gonna shut my trap before I dig myself in deeper." He snapped his head Rachael's direction. "You can stop laughing at me, too, little one. It's partly your fault I went running off half-cocked. You were calling me after all."

"She's been talking to him," Abdiel supplied for a confused looking Ana.

"She's got a real great sense of humor, too." Cam slid down the wall until seated on the floor. He yawned tiredly. "If you guys don't mind, I'm going to sleep here on the floor tonight just in case she needs me."

Gabi smiled at his consideration. She knew then his fears of turning demon were unfounded. He still had his caring nature. It was just buried a little deeper than before.

Ana closed her eyes and scanned Rachael. After several minutes, she opened her eyes and smiled with relief. "She's been around terrible evil. But she protected herself by shutting her body down. That's why she's still young. It's really quite impressive. I've never known an angel to do it before."

"Is there? I mean did you feel any..." Afraid to vocalize his fears, Abdiel stopped short.

"There is not an ounce of evil in her heart," Ana soothed, her expression pure compassion. "She is still an angel."

He sighed with relief. "Thank you, Ana."

"I would stay, but I have three other brothers here besides Cam." Ana stood and started for the door. "I don't trust them not to start up another fight."

Abdiel curled up on the foot of the bed. The earlier battle must have totally exhausted him because he was quickly out of it. Cam followed suit.

Gabi was the only one awake. "You really need to wake up for your brother," she whispered to her sister-in-law.

I'm not ready to yet.

Gabi looked around for the source of the voice. She wasn't surprised to see no one there. She glanced down at Rachael even as she shook her head in disbelief. Yet, the voice was most defiantly that of a young female child. "I must be losing it." Yeah, that was it, she was working too hard and needed a vacation.

No, you are not losing it, silly, the voice was stronger now. *Although a vacation would be nice.*

"I thought you could only talk with Cam," Gabi felt a little stupid talking to a comatose person, but witnessed stranger things these past few weeks.

I can talk to whomever I want. Cam is just the easiest to connect with. But you seemed nice so I made the extra effort to talk to you.

"You should talk to Abdiel. He's so worried about you," Gabi kept her voice low to avoid waking the others. If she was losing her mind, she didn't want an audience.

No, I'm mad at him, the voice in her head turned into that of a petulant child's.

"Why? He's been so worried about you all these long years."

I waited and waited and he never came for me, the voice cried now.

"No, he was so sad that he lost you. Please, he can never be truly happy until he had you back." Even as the words tumbled out of her mouth, Gabi knew how true it was. They could never be truly happy together until he had his life back.

Reacting on pure instinct, Gabi grabbed the girl and held her tight in her arms. She started reciting ancient chants. Nobody taught her the chants. They came from her heart. With her energy poured into the little girl, she didn't care if it completely drained her and made her a cationic shell. This, she would give to Abdiel.

Shocked by a heat buildup in her chest, she feared her inability to help Rachael and yet she pressed on. Even as she continued, she knew how dangerous her actions were. No healer ever attempted what she was doing. Check that, no healer was even capable of doing what she was, not even Raphael. Only she possessed the gifts needed to complete this task.

A great white ball of energy surged between the two of them. Gabi felt her vision dimming, but didn't pull back. She needed to do this. If she ever wanted to have a life with Abdiel, she must help him overcome his past. *Please, please,* she thought franticly. *This has to work. For him it must work.*

Her head spun. Buzzing filled her ears. In the distance, she heard a scream that was not her own. She felt Rachael grab her back right before the darkness overcame her.

Captive Angels:

Archangel Series Part 2

Chapter One

An ear-splitting, heartrending scream exploded through the room. On his feet in a flash, Abdiel stared at several small arches of light spinning around Gabi and Rachael. Bright blue in color, the arches moved in different directions and at varied speeds. They grew brighter and brighter until he saw neither female. "Gabi! Rachael!" As soon as Abdiel touched the blue light, he was thrown across the room and slammed against the wall. Briefly stunned, he slid to the floor in a slump.

Finally, after what seemed forever, the light slowly faded. When it dissipated, Rachael was a full-grown female. She screamed and held a limp Gabi in her arms. Terrified, she shoved the unresponsive female from her and shook her head back and forth. Fear stole her breath and she hyperventilated.

"Gabi, no!" Abdiel scrambled across the room and scooped his wife into his arms. Her half-opened eyes were completely unfocused. With a slight shake of her shoulders, he stared as her head lolled to the side and she remained motionless, catatonic. He glanced up.

Rachael launched herself from the bed, crawled to the corner and wrapped herself into a tight ball. She whimpered and rocked back and forth, her dark hair shielding her face.

Abdiel refocused his attention. "Come on, baby, wake up." Tears formed in his eyes. "Please, don't leave me, Gabi." He was so upset all he could think about was that his love was gone forever as he held her close and started to weep.

Captive Angels

CAM DASHED OVER, GRABBED Rachael by the shoulders and yanked her to her feet. "What did you do to her?"

"Nothing," Rachel insisted. "I'm a good, little angel."

"No, you're not," he snarled. "You're a bad, bad little angel." He stared as she unleashed a shout of anger that sounded half demon, half angel. Her eyes darkened a shade, just like his whenever he was about to lose his temper. Sure enough, she shot off a bolt of energy hitting him square in the chest. With a grunt, he sailed across the room and slammed into the wall.

Grabbing her head savagely between both her hands, Rachael unleashed another bloodcurdling scream. Every window in the room rattled, then shattered one by one.

"You know." Cam rolled to his feet and started toward her. "I really hate it when someone zaps me."

"You're not being very nice," she spat, her hand raised. Several books fell off their shelves and tumbled to the ground. "I don't think I like you."

A picture flew off the wall and shot toward his head. Cam's sideways dive avoided the hit, but slammed his right shoulder into his dresser. The hurt shaken off, he rolled to his feet and directed a hardcover book at her. It hit her in the back, knocking her to the ground. "You're not the only one that can do magic tricks." Cam knew full well his eyes were turning the dark blue, which matched hers. "I think it's time to teach you a lesson in manners, little chickadee." He shot off an arc of flames.

Moving with cat-like agility, she jumped out of the way. She yelled something at him in demon talk before she released another energy bolt.

He moved, but not quite fast enough. It hit him in the arm, lifted him off his feet and spun him around as he sailed through the air. Slammed into the wall, Cam stood up and lifted his hand. Flames started to build up in it again.

ABDIEL CLUTCHED GABI TO his chest. Combined energy built to a hazardous level. The sky darkened. Lightning streaked through the ever-deepening cerulean. The entire house shook violently. Abdiel felt the dangerous energy, but was dimly aware all hell was breaking loose. Completely lost in his grief, he couldn't bring himself to care.

The door blasted open and Michael strode in, fire in his eyes. With a simple wave of his hand, the two angels' powers dissipated. "That is *enough* you two." He didn't yell, but his voice carried sufficient anger to scare both of them into obeying. "Gabi did this to herself."

That alone shook Abdiel out of his stupor. "Why?"

Rachael twisted her hands together nervously. "She wanted to give me back to you. She said you would never be truly happy until you had us back. I tried to stop her, but she was too strong. It's all my fault." She walked over to the bed and knelt on the ground. Bowing her head, she laced her fingers behind her neck and waited.

As soon as he saw the position, he breathed a ragged curse. He remembered the position well. He did it countless times himself as a youth. It was the way their father made them take their beatings. His own baby sister actually thought he was going to hurt her. How many times had she felt the sting of their father's whip against her back? He reached out to touch her head.

She shivered with fear and kept her eyes tightly shut. Her nostrils flared as she took in deep shuddering breaths.

"I will never hurt you, Rachael," he vowed.

She opened her eyes and looked up at him, her gaze disbelieving. "I told her I was angry at you."

"You were angry with me?" This time when he went to stroke her hair, she didn't flinch.

"Every day when they first took us there…" She laid her head in his lap as tears spilled from her eyes, "I prayed you would come and get us. When you didn't, I hated you. I know it was stupid. There was no way you could have entered Hell, but I still blamed you."

"I would have come for you if I could have. I swear it." He gently wiped the tears from her cheeks.

"I know that now. I'm sorry about Gabi." She snuggled against his hand as if she craved a loving touch. "I really did try to stop her, but she wouldn't let me."

"Abdiel," Michael interrupted softly. "Take Gabi to your bedroom. Raphael is here and he knows about the situation. Cam, you watch over Rachel and, for crying out loud, try not to destroy each other."

"How do you know who I am?" Rachael asked him, a small frown on her face.

"Let's just say you and your brother are not the only ones who have weird dreams." He turned and looked at her. "By the way, there was nothing you could have done to stop Gabi. Her heart was set on making you well." Michael walked over to Abdiel. "Don't give up hope yet."

Abdiel picked Gabi up in his arms, holding her gently, afraid of breaking her even more. When he walked by Rachael, she reached up and gave him a shy kiss on his cheek. Still timid about touching him, she refused to meet his gaze.

WHEN EVERYONE LEFT THE room, Cam looked at her. "Why are you so afraid of Abdiel?"

"He's going to beat me," she whispered, although she'd already scanned her brother's mind and found he wasn't capable of doing such a thing. Still, she doubted as her family wasn't exactly the warm and fuzzy type.

"Michael said it wasn't your fault." Cam started to pick up some of the debris in the room, then dropped the book and shoved his hands in his pockets. "Abdiel's not like the rest of your family. He won't hurt you ever. He promised not to and he always keeps his word."

A quick duck of his head followed his swift glance, but not before she noticed the look on his face. Oh God, he felt sorry for her. If it was one thing she hated above everything else, it was pity. She was used to being hated. She and Appolion had grown up cutting their teeth on the preverbal hate stick. But she could never get used to someone feeling bad for her. It made her feel helpless.

Rachael stared down at the raggedy old gown she wore and realized she looked like a war refugee. She ran her hands over the offending material trying to make it stretch out as far as it could go. *Good molly, my legs are barely covered. This is no way for me to make a first impression.*

Cam went to his dresser and pulled out a pair of sweatpants and a tee shirt. As he handed them to her, they locked eyes for the first time and both of them froze.

She sucked in a breath. *Brother.* The thought came unbidden into her mind and, as soon as it did, she knew it was true. Even though they had come from different parents, he was as much her brother as Appolion and Abdiel. They were linked by some higher power and had been since they were born.

Rachael reached up and touched his cheek, gently rubbing her fingers over the lingering road rash. He got that injury fighting Abdiel in order to get to her so he must feel the connection, too. Relief filled her at the prospect of her never going to be alone again. She had found…home. "Thank you for coming to me. Without you I would have been lost forever."

"After seeing the way you handled yourself earlier, I somehow doubt that," he mumbled.

"I sense your pain, your inner conflict, brother." She smiled at his shocked expression. It was going to take them both a little while to get used to being around another telepath.

"Get changed and I'll get you something to eat. I don't think we can keep you a secret anymore. Not since you and I pretty much went postal," he said gruffly.

"What do you mean postal?" She wrinkled her nose. Actually, she already knew what he meant. Rachael had been scanning his mind since the car ride home, plucking little bits of information from his thoughts and memories. However, she wasn't ready to tell him that yet. The first thing she learned in Hell was not to reveal all your strengths or weaknesses.

"Sorry, I forgot you've been vegging out for the past few centuries. I mean since you and I tore apart the house. I think we broke every single window." He gave her a small smile before he left the room.

Rachael quickly took off the gown and pulled on the clothes he gave her. It felt so good to be in regular clothes. She looked over at the old, white dress and vaporized it with her mind. She didn't want anything around to remind her of her time in Hell.

Even though she was full grown now, she noticed with disgust that she was smaller than most females. Cam was no giant by any means, but his tee shirt hung to her knees. She cinched the drawstring as hard as she could on the sweatpants in order to keep them up. Somehow, she didn't think losing her drawers in the kitchen would be a good introduction into the angel world.

Rachael went into the adjoining bathroom and willed herself to look in the mirror. A giant crack ran down the middle, thanks to her and Cam's little spat, but otherwise, it was unbroken. When she saw her reflection, she gasped in horror. She reached out and touched the glass, trying hard to will away the image looking back at her.

Her raven curls went every which way. Her deep, piercing blue eyes were wide and framed by long dark lashes. High, finely arched cheekbones enhanced full lips. She was the spitting image of her mother.

Rachael hissed a demon curse and shattered the mirror with a wave of her hand. She resisted the insane urge to turn the water on and scrub her face until the offending features were wiped away. She would have rather turned into a demon than look like her witch of a mother. She didn't just hate the female, she despised her.

When Douma and Forcas started to do the bad things to her, she went to her mother for help. Instead of helping her, as any other normal mother would have, the witch smacked her across the face and called her a lying whore. *How can a ten-year old female be a whore?* When Rachael refused to retract her story, her dear, old sweet mother gave her a beating that made their father proud.

Cam's voice floated across her mind. *Are you okay? I can sense you are upset.*

I'm just dandy. Hold your horses, I'll be there in a second. She tried to sound annoyed, but wasn't. Ever since Appolion cut contact with her, she had no one friendly to communicate mentally with, until now.

Rachael walked out into the hall and Cam took her hand, led her down the stairs and into the kitchen. There were a couple of males there and they both looked at her with interest. Much to her dismay, she found herself hiding behind Cam. She just couldn't stand to be ogled.

"Be nice guys. This is Abdiel's little sister and you don't want to piss him off by hurting her feelings." Cam squeezed her hand reassuringly and directed her into a seat.

One of the males stepped forward. "Hi, I'm Daniel." He turned and looked at Cam. "Look, I'm really sorry about earlier. I shouldn't have said anything about your mother. That was a real low blow. It's just that I learned my sister was in town and she's up to her old tricks."

"Who's your sister?" Rachael asked as Cam poured them tall glasses of milk and set them on the table.

"My sister is a succubus."

The big swig of milk Cam just took, slid down the wrong pipe.

Daniel groaned. "Oh no, not you, too. I swear my sister has banged every male I know."

"What's your sister's name?" Cam gasped between coughs.

"Ramiakle."

"Then she's not the one I, ah...." He glanced over at Rachael and turned bright red.

"You're such a perv, Cam." She wrinkled her nose.

"Thank God, at least she hasn't gotten her claws into you." Daniel visibly relaxed. "I can tell you have some small injuries. It would be an honor if you would let me heal them for you. It's the least I can do."

"In case you forgot, Daniel, I beat the ever living tar out of you. You don't owe me anything."

Daniel still went over to him and touched his shoulder. Since the injury wasn't too serious, it only took a moment before his arm was back to normal.

When the healer moved to touch her, Rachael instantly tensed up and unleashed a low growl.

"It's okay, he just wants to heal you," Cam reassured. "I'll be sitting here right next to you the entire time."

"Don't worry, little one." Daniel gave her a crooked smile. "I would never want to face the wrath of your big brother, let alone Cam."

"It's not us you have to worry about, healer. Little Miss Muffet there could probably kick both of our asses."

Daniel went over and very gently touched her back.

Rachael scanned the healer's mind and found he meant her no harm so she allowed it. It still terrified her to have a male other than Cam or Abdiel touch her. Cam held her hand the entire time and, before she knew it, her back was healed.

Daniel pulled back from her with a look of awe on his face. His gaze darted between her and Cam before they shifted to one of the shattered windows. "You guys were the ones who caused all that to happen earlier, weren't you?"

Rachael looked over at Cam, wondering how he was going to explain this one away when the sound of pounding footsteps made her turn her head. Another healer, with several more hot on his heels, raced up the stairs. If Raphael called for extra healers, it could not be good.

It's all my fault. I did this to her. If I just stayed in Hell, none of this would have happened. Hot tears stung her cheeks. Rachael had always been taught tears were a weakness. In fact, the more she and Appolion cried, the more they were beat for it.

Stop thinking that way. You are where you belong now. Cam's voice soothed her instantly. *Don't diminish Gabi's sacrifice by thinking you are unworthy of it. Derel and the other healers are going to help her at this moment.*

As soon as they were the only ones left in the kitchen, Daniel fixed them both with a concerned glance. "There is only one thing that could get this many healers upset. Is our Mistress injured?"

Realizing Daniel was deeply troubled at the thought of Gabi being hurt, Rachael told him everything that happened to her. By the time she was done, the healer paled and she felt despair coursing through him.

"We can't lose our Mistress. There must be something we can do." He paced a few more steps before he stopped and ran up to them. Grabbing both of their hands, a smile slowly spread over his face. "Come on, I have a crazy idea that just might work."

ABDIEL REACHED OVER AND stroked Gabi's hair. Raphael, Michael, Derel and Ana stood around him silently. The other healers left the room, carrying the heavy weight of their grief with them. The news of The Mistress' condition traveled quickly and the echoes of screams and cries went through the house as more healers joined in their mourning. They all admired and loved her just as much as the archangels did Michael.

Abdiel gritted his teeth together as he fought to keep his own cries back. Part of him wanted to join the healers. He wanted to throw back his head and yell out his pain for all to hear. True determination and years of holding his feelings in kept him from doing so.

Some insane part of him felt if he did give in and weep, he would be giving up all hope Gabi would wake up and he wasn't ready for that. Although he knew deep down it was hopeless because they tried everything and they couldn't make his Gabi better, he refused to surrender.

Part of him wanted to grab her and shake her by the shoulders. *Don't you realize I can't live without you? Without you, I am nothing.* She did this for him. To make him happy, she sacrificed herself, but he would never be happy again. He lost what meant the most to him. Abdiel leaned down and buried his face in her hair, breathing in her scent.

Gabi lay still under him, her beautiful green eyes dull and lifeless.

Cam burst in with Rachael and Daniel in tow. "Daniel's got an idea, guys."

"It's hopeless," Abdiel replied dully. "There's nothing we can do."

"Cam," Ana said quietly. "We've already tried everything."

"You don't understand," Rachael implored. "Daniel really thinks Cam and I can help."

"No offense, guys." Abdiel didn't look up. "But unless something needs blowing up, I don't think so."

Daniel went over to Raphael and went down on one knee. "Master, I believe we can use the power that dwells within the two of them to rejuvenate The Mistress."

"You mean jump start her like a car?" Michael asked, his voice laced with disbelief.

"That's exactly what he's suggesting." Raphael looked at the healer thoughtfully.

The room was silent as they all took in what Daniel was suggesting. It had never been tried before. But then there were never two angels with Cam and Rachael's gifts before either. They all looked over at Raphael and waited for his response.

"It would be very dangerous," he finally warned. "We could lose all three of them trying."

"It's a risk I'm willing to take," Cam said. "Gabi would do it for me in a heartbeat."

Rachael nodded her head. "Me, too. It is the least I can do."

Abdiel looked over at them, touched by what they were offering to do. They were willing to risk themselves in order to save Gabi. Yet at the same time, a part of him couldn't believe these two were capable of something so great.

Michael looked doubtful, too. "You two don't even have full control of your powers yet. In case you forgot, you almost vaporized the house not even an hour ago."

Cam pointed at Abdiel. "Remember, he's the Control. He can shield our powers if we lose control."

Raphael took charge. "Rachael and Cam, go on either side of Gabi and lay hands on her. Abdiel, hold their hands and try to keep a reign on their energy. Daniel, I want you to go over with Cam and sing the healing chants. Derel, come stand by me and do the same."

Following his instructions, they formed a circle around her. Rachael and Cam looked at each other, nodded, then closed their eyes. They both placed their hands on Gabi and released their energy.

Abdiel was shocked by how strong it was. The air hummed as energy flowed into Gabi. He threw up a shield in order to keep it centered. It pulsated and strained to escape. He fought hard to keep it contained or else the power would surge out of control.

A glowing light settled over them. It felt warm and calming at the same time. Abdiel heard the healers' strong voices combine in a rich melody. The sky turned a deep blue and streaks of lightning beat white paths throughout it. The horizon grew hazy as waves of heat were sucked from the center of the earth and brought up to the surface. The color came back into Gabi's face. Her eyelids fluttered as her eyes came back into focus. She let out a strangled gasp, like a drowning victim revived.

Abdiel reigned in the healing light and the buildup of energy died down. Cam and Rachael collapsed on the ground. They were tired, but otherwise unhurt. Abdiel, found himself panting, exhausted from fighting their powers. It was harder than he'd thought.

"Abdiel," Gabi breathed.

Her voice was the most beautiful thing he'd ever heard. Abdiel scooped her up in his arms and hugged her tight. "It's going to be okay, honey." He kissed the top of her head.

"Did I get Rachael back for you?" She was still worried about him even though she could barely move.

"Yes, you did." He couldn't let her go. "You did real good."

"Where is she?" Gabi struggled to sit up. She followed Abdiel's gaze to his sister. "Why are you letting her lie there on the floor? And why is she wearing Cam's grungy, old stuff?"

He looked down at his baby sister. She looked so small and fragile, yet she was capable of so much. She had given Cam a taste of his own medicine, matching his skills one by one. It was just as hard to keep her powers under control as it was Cam's. Abdiel pulled his sister onto the bed and gave her a big hug. "Welcome home, sister, and thank you for bringing Gabi back."

"You're not mad at me?" Rachael squeaked.

"I could never be mad at you," Abdiel reassured.

She gave him an impish smile before she scooted over to the other edge of the bed and hung her head over the far side. "We did it," she yelled at Cam. Reaching down, she smacked him on the shoulder. "Wake up, sleepy head."

"Leave me alone or I'll remember I owe you one for blasting me," he groaned. "Why is it, Abdiel, that every time I meet someone from your family, they find it necessary to zap my butt?"

"Maybe it's because of your winning personality," Gabi said tartly.

Abdiel laughed, relieved to hear her dry wit. Even though she still looked too pale and tired for his liking, he knew she was on her way to being better.

"Sorry about your windows, Gabi." Rachael did a bouncy movement on the bed.

"Do I even want to know?" Gabi asked. Her eyelids were beginning to droop.

Raphael came over and took her hand. "You need to rest. You've been through a lot today."

Gabi obeyed her brother, closing her eyes. She grumbled in a sleepy voice, "I really want to stay awake and talk. I'm very interested to find out what they did to my windows." Exhaustion won. Clutching Abdiel close, she soon fell asleep.

GABI WOKE UP TO a pair of bright blue eyes staring at her. Startled, she sat up with a gasp. "Rachael, is there something you needed?"

"Oh goodie," Rachael broke out into a huge grin. "You're awake. I was sick of being around boys."

"Where are the boys?" She nearly choked on the last word.

"They're talking about that Order of Four stuff." She gave a wicked smile. "They didn't even ask me about it, and I could tell them everything they want to know."

"Slow down," Gabi said. "What do you mean you know everything?"

"That creep Beelzebub knew all about the prophecy." Rachael gave out a bored, little shrug. "I just scanned it from his mind. He was so easy to read. It was actually pathetic."

Abdiel came in the room to check up on Gabi. "Hey, you're awake."

Cam trailed behind him.

"Yeah," she said drolly. "Rachael was just filling me in on The Order of Four. Seems she knows everything there is to know about it."

Abdiel looked over at his sister, clearly shocked. She was trilling a piece of gum in her fingers as she hummed to herself. "What exactly do you think you know, Rachael?"

"I happen to know the names of all four angels." She blew him a raspberry. "You only know of two."

Abdiel gritted his teeth in frustration and Gabi couldn't blame him. It was like pulling teeth to get any information from Rachael. "Okay, who are the other two?"

"Appolion and me, dummy." She blew another raspberry.

"See, I know right there that you're wrong." He rubbed his head like it hurt. "Appolion wants nothing to do with us."

"That's because he's being a jerk," Rachael scoffed. "You know, he shut his mind off to me. His own twin, the nerve of him."

Abdiel shook his head in disbelief. Gabi felt the same doubt he did. Sure Rachael had some serious mojo like Cam. But she was still a tiny, little slip of a thing. There was no way she would ever be able to fight demons. They would just flick their fingers at her and send her flying.

The door slammed shut with a loud bang. The mirror on their dresser splintered. *Do you believe me now?* Before her brother could even blink an eye, she cartwheeled through the air. Her legs scissored out and caught his, slamming him onto the ground. Rachael opened her hand and a fighting dagger from the dresser top flew to her palm. She tapped him on the head with it. "You should never doubt me. I never lie. Now, do you want to hear the rest of it or not?"

Okay, she had made a believer out of them. Abdiel shut his mouth and held his hand up to indicate she should continue. Gabi bit back a giggle, nothing like having your own sister kick your can to humble you.

"You and Cam are right. You guys are the first two of The Order of Four." Rachael rolled to her feet. She idly flipped the dagger from hand to hand. "Cam, because he can harness fire, and Abdiel, because he is the Control. You know, the one that makes sure the powers of the other three angels don't go out of control."

"What would happen if it got out of control?" Gabi asked.

"That would be bad," Rachael said blandly.

"How bad?" Abdiel's brow creased with worry.

"The entire human world would cease to exist," she whispered.

"That would qualify as bad," Cam muttered.

"What role do you play in the Order?" Gabi asked.

"I can harness lightning and control the weather. That's why I can send out energy bolts."

"No offense," Cam interjected. "But that's not so unique. Douma and Forcas both can zap somebody."

"They just barely make a fizzle in the energy field," she scoffed. "What they do is a hug compared to what I can do. If I'd wanted to really hurt you earlier, I could have vaporized you. Just like you could have blown me off of Earth. We both were holding back when we fought each other."

"Oh great." Abdiel ran his hand through his hair. "You mean to tell me what you guys did earlier was a warm up?"

"Well, I couldn't exactly blow your sister up," Cam admitted guiltily. "I mean it would just be rude."

"But you see, brother, it's not Cam and I you have to worry about, it's Appolion."

"Why would we have to worry about Appolion?"

"The power Appolion has makes Cam and I look like fluffy bunnies. Appolion is the Destroyer." She gripped the dagger blade tightly in her hand, her nervousness about her revelation clear. A small trickle of blood seeped through her fingers.

"I thought you said Appolion is an angel?" Gabi reached over to touch Abdiel's hand, his expression sick with dread.

"He is," Rachael spoke earnestly, eager to defend her twin. "He just doesn't want to believe it yet."

"What exactly is he supposed to destroy?" Cam tugged on his hair, betraying his own unease.

"It has no name. It's a monster worse than any of our worst nightmares." She squeezed the blade even tighter, causing more blood to spill.

Abdiel reached out and gently eased the knife away from her. "Are you talking about a demon?" His voice was strained and his glare concerned, no doubt because she was as pale as a ghost.

"No worse, it's the most evil thing Hell has ever spawned. Douma and Forcas are growing it. When it's ready, they're going to release it on Earth. It'll completely annihilate both Heaven and Earth unless we can stop it."

"You mean to tell me you guys are the only ones that can defeat this thing?" Gabi asked gently.

Rachael nodded. "That *thing* won't be ready for a while yet, but it *is* coming."

"How did you convince Beelzebub to let you go?" Gabi tried not to let her see how much her words had scared her. "I don't care what you say, he's no weakling."

"Neither am I." She ran a shaky hand through her dark hair.

"How can you be so sure you're right about all this?" Abdiel asked.

"You had the same dream I did. You were there with me, big brother. You know I speak the truth."

Gabi and Cam looked over at him, their eyes accusing.

Abdiel held up his hands in defense. "Look, I just thought it was a freaky dream. How was I supposed to know it was all real? Cam and Appolion were in it, too, and they didn't say anything."

Rachael rolled her eyes. "That's because it was our dream not theirs. They don't have that gift, just you and me do. Oh, and Michael."

Abdiel started to pace the room nervously. "If Douma and Forcas find out about Appolion, he'll be hunted down and captured. There's no one to protect his back. He's all alone out there."

"I know." Rachael shrugged her shoulders. "But he won't let me contact him so I can't warn him. He makes me so angry. You know what? I've decided he's no longer my twin brother anymore. Cam is my new brother."

"We look nothing alike." Cam shook his head in mock sadness. "Nobody will ever buy it. You're stuck with Mini Dark Angel."

Chapter Two

The angel warriors banded together, and soon, the demons retreated. Working together with the humans, they stopped the looting and put out all the fires. Healers blanketed Detroit and, because of them, the human death toll was very low. Finally, the city returned to normal.

To Abdiel's great relief, all the visiting angels left their house, leaving only the four of them. It wasn't just the fact he hated his privacy being invaded, but there had been other issues as well. After Rachael and Cam had called attention to themselves by shattering every window in the house, there was no way to keep anything secret anymore. So now, everyone knew not only about Rachael, but also about the Order. Worse yet, they knew about Cam and Rachael's special gifts and had started to look at Rachael like she was a science experiment gone bad.

Cam was a whole different matter, however. The empaths continued to follow him around like lost, little puppy dogs. The archangels accepted him as one of their own and gave him the respect the title deserved. Instead of being flattered with all the attention, it seemed to bother the young angel. It was almost as if he wanted to disappear into the shadows.

Abdiel could tell, even though she fought hard to hide such, it hurt Rachael that the other angels looked at her with a jaded eye. It didn't help matters that she had no control over her energy blasts and kept zapping anyone who even slightly ticked her off.

"Did I do that?" she would ask, dismayed as yet another angel was thrown off their feet.

"Yeah, you did that, Steve Urkle," Cam would drawl back.

The one piece of good news was that with Ana's diplomacy and Michael's bullying, the council decided to look the other way as far as Rachael was concerned, even though Jehel was far from happy with it. He had demanded a vote on the matter, but he lost. The council even lifted the restriction of flashing in Detroit. They were free to travel from place to place in their own way. Although Cam still preferred his motorcycle and Gabi was not about ready to give up her Beetle.

Abdiel and Cam went out patrolling every night. They rooted out any stragglers still left behind from the attack and took care of any locals that showed their faces. Gabi was still too weak to join them, so she stayed home. Rachael was left behind as well. They had all agreed for now they would keep her improved condition a secret from the demons. Well, everyone but Rachael. She was itching to get out there and hand out some payback.

"I know how to fight," she yelled at Abdiel. "I'm not some child that needs to be coddled."

"You could have fooled me," Cam snickered. "Up until a few days ago you were still in Oshkosh overalls."

"How do you know how to fight?" Abdiel asked her. "You haven't had any training."

"I've always been able to sneak into your thoughts." Rachael shrugged as if it were no big deal. "Every battle you have ever fought, I was there with you."

"You do realize that's too frigging weird?" Cam's voice was filled with awe.

They all decided they were going to live their lives as normal as possible. They refused to let Douma and Forcas rule them. That would mean the demons were winning the war. They were not about to close themselves up and live in fear.

It would turn out to be the biggest mistake of their immortal lives.

CAM STROLLED AROUND THE college campus not shielding himself from the humans. He needed to feel like a normal college kid, not some freaky empath angel that wasn't really an empath, but something else never been seen before. Heck, it would be nice to truly be a mortal for a day. He wondered what it would be like not to have to worry all the time about demons and evil. It would be cool to have a life where your biggest worry was whether you would pass the next exam. Instead, he always had to be on alert, ready to play superhero. Oh, and don't forget the fact every demon was on him like one of the superstar Bounty Hunters.

A small female human saw him and waved. She bounded over to him with a toss of her long, blonde hair. "Hi, Cam. We're getting the old study group back together. Are you game?" She flashed him a winning smile displaying her even, white teeth.

"Sure, Becky." Cam smiled. He really valued the friendship he had with the human. "I'll try to make it when I can. I've been really busy at work."

"What do you do again?"

"Social work," he lied smoothly.

"Pam will be very happy to hear you're coming. She really likes you, Cam."

Cam got uncomfortable. That the human was attracted to him was no surprise even if he hadn't been telepathic as she made her feelings obvious. She flirted outrageously with him and used every advantage to be near him. Her hands always seemed to find their way to his arms when they were talking, and she took every opportunity available to accidentally brush up against him, but humans were strictly hands off.

Seeing Cam's unease, Becky turned to him with a surprised look on her face. "Oh my God, you're gay aren't you?"

"What?" Cam rolled his eyes. "No, I just can't get involved with anyone right now."

"Do you already have a girlfriend?"

"No, I just can't get into a relationship. It's not allowed." He inwardly groaned as that little nugget slipped.

"Are you in some sort of weird cult that doesn't believe in sex?" Becky looked horrified such a thing could exist.

"Something like that," Cam muttered. "Don't worry though, I don't drink the punch." His new cell phone rang interrupting the interrogation. He scowled when the number on the caller ID was one he didn't recognize. Excusing himself from Becky, he walked around the corner for privacy.

If this was, yet another empath calling him with another problem, he was going to lose it. Ever since they had found out about his special gifts, empaths had been calling him with everything from advice to gripes about their archangels. At first, he'd purposefully given them bad advice just for grins and giggles, but the calls still kept coming in. Why didn't they just call his Aunt Amiteil? Although she was a cold, heartless bitch who never could spare a moment or a kind word for any of her nephews or niece, she still was the unofficial leader of the empaths. "This had better be good," he growled into the phone.

"Cam, this is Dina."

The voice on the other end was so weak he could barely hear it. Dina was Jehel's only son. *What in the hell is he calling me for, and how did he get my number?* Cam felt his stomach turn over. This could not be good. He tried to scan the other angel, but he slammed into a mental brick wall. He knew instantly it was Douma and Forcas. Not only were they capable of blocking his telepathy, but this whole set up just reeked of them. What was it with those two? Couldn't they take one day off?

"Dina, give the phone to the demons." He realized he was talking to the other angel like he was a child, but his protector gauge had just gone into overdrive. The angel's bloodcurdling screams filled his ear. The old empath part of him took over letting the other angel's pain soak into him. Shielding himself from human eyes, he sank down on a stone bench. A cold sweat covered him as he started to shake.

"This is Forcas," an evil voice hissed into the phone.

Duh, I already guessed that one, jackass.

"Unless you come and meet us right now, I'll torture this angel. I'll direct all the pain to you so you feel every bit of it."

To prove his point, the demon held the phone near his captive. Cam heard a slap right before Dina cried out again. Cam whimpered as he felt Dina's fear wash over him. There was no way possible he could refuse Forcas's demands. They both knew it. They were using his biggest weakness against him. The worst part was it was Jehel's son. Here he was about to sacrifice himself for someone and that someone had a jerk for a father. That just stuck in his craw. "Leave him alone. I'll come," Cam grit out, trying not to get physically ill from all the emotions.

"We're in the park by your house." Forcas laughed evilly. "And don't even think of telling Abdiel. If you try to contact him by phone or mind, I'll know right away and I'll hurt this pathetic angel even more."

Cam flashed himself to them and spotted Dina crumpled on the ground. He launched himself at the wounded angel and placed his hands on him. Flashing the captive to Heaven, he turned to fight the demons. A bolt of energy hit him in the chest and knocked him backward. Before he could recover, they were on him, kicking the crap out of him and wrapping a set of heavy chains around him.

Struggling to his feet, Cam lifted his hand to shoot off flame. The chains around him came to life. Surging with energy, they burned him before they rebounded his own power against him. He dropped to the ground screaming in pain. As the energy bounced around his body, he jerked around on cool earth. *Fuck, I'm in big trouble.* He fell into their trap and knew they would drag Abdiel into it using his pathetic ass as bait.

GABI HAD TAKEN RACHAEL shopping so Abdiel was home all alone, sitting in front of the TV when his cell phone went off. He saw it was Cam. "Hey, Cam, you get registered for all your classes?"

"Sorry, brother." Forcas's voice crept through the phone. "I think he's had a change of plans."

Abdiel jumped up. "What have you done to Cam?"

"He's all right for now. Do you know he willingly traded himself over for another angel? He's almost as noble as you."

Abdiel gripped the phone tight. They had Cam and he had no doubt in his mind they already hurt him and they would do a lot worse unless he figured out a way to get him free. "What do I need do so you'll let him go?"

"Come on, brother." Forcas chided. "We both know what you need to do. Don't make me go into the stereotypical bad guy speech. Just come to the park by your house and get your friend."

Even though he knew it was a trap, he flashed himself where Forcas had directed. It was completely deserted except for his two demon brothers and Cam. He cursed his stupidity for not calling for backup. At the very least, he should have called Gabi and told her what was happening. She was going to have his hide for this, and he deserved it for being a moron.

Cam's hands were tied behind his back. The bindings bit into his wrists turning his fingers blue. A gag was cutting into his mouth. Already the gag was bright red from the blood coming from his cut lip. His eyes were starting to swell shut. Forcas and Douma had obviously beaten him bad.

Yet they hadn't broken his spirit. Staying upright on his knees, he shot them a defiant look from his half closed eyes. His head moved as he tried to shoot off smart remarks around the rag in his mouth.

Abdiel was a little unnerved he hadn't heard his voice in his head. Why was he not communicating telepathically?

Cam's scrawny frame was dwarfed by a set of heavy chains covered in ancient demon markings. With his hands behind his back, he thought the chains were overkill, even for his brothers.

Abdiel saw red. "Let him go, you sons of bitches."

Cam tried to yell something at him, but it was muffled. Douma walked over and backhanded him. Cam tried to shoot off flame at the demon. The chains around him turned white hot and hummed eerily before he was thrown onto his back by an unseen force.

"How many times do we have to tell you?" Douma sneered. "Every time you try to use your powers, the Chains of Containment will turn them back on you."

So that's why Cam is not communicating with me telepathically. These chains are trapping his gifts. The young angel jerked around on the ground from having his own powers turned on him. Abdiel moved forward to help him, but his brothers stepped in front of Cam and blocked his way.

"You have one choice, brother." Forcas came over and stroked Abdiel's cheek with a claw. "Come with us, or we'll pump him so full of demon's blood he'll be nothing but a blathering idiot."

Cam started to yell against the gag once again. Even though Abdiel couldn't understand him, he knew what he was trying to say. He smelled a set up and he didn't want Abdiel to agree to this. What Cam didn't know was Abdiel wasn't about ready to let Cam go to Hell and suffer alone. He wasn't going let him be deserted down there like Rachael and Appolion had been.

Douma held up a silver bracelet. It was an angel harness. A device used by justice angels, it made the wearer incapable of flashing. It was the angel equivalent to handcuffs. With a sigh of resignation, Abdiel held his hand out.

Cam started to yell harder against the gag, pleading with Abdiel, wanting Abdiel to flash out of there and leave him behind.

Douma snapped it shut.

Abdiel knew they had lied. They were never going to let Cam go. Now they had both of them. And Gabi and Rachael were totally unprotected.

As soon as they got the angels to the dungeon in Hell, they chained them to opposite walls. They left the Chains of Containment on Cam, but removed the gag. Now that they had him in Hell, they wanted to hear his cries of agony.

They started beating them, attacking the two angels without mercy or without letting up. It seemed to go on for hours. The worst part for Abdiel wasn't his own pain, but hearing Cam's grunts. Cam never broke though. He didn't give the demons that satisfaction. Abdiel found a grim sense of victory in that.

Finally, the demons stopped and left. The two angels sagged against their restraints panting and in pain. Their blood trickled down and mixed with the dirt floor. The uneven stones that made up the walls of the cell dug into their backs even as their bodies protested the way the chains twisted them. Abdiel tried to shift around to find a more comfortable position only to find there was none.

Cam started to sing Daniel Powter's song *Bad Day* in a weak, broken voice.

In spite of himself, Abdiel laughed. "I'm sorry I got us into this, kid."

"I was the one who went to them in the first place," Cam admitted. "They had Dina and used his pain to draw me out. At least I was able to send him to Heaven before they got me in these damn chains. I was so stupid. Instead of fighting, I went up to the angel and helped him first. His pain and fear just overwhelmed me. I couldn't think straight. I guess I'm just a plain old empath after all."

"That's crap, and you know it." Abdiel spit blood out of his mouth. "If you were an empath you would've overloaded by now since we're in Hell. Yet here you are still shooting off your smart mouth."

The door to their cell swung open and Douma and Forcas strode in. They went to Cam, completely ignoring Abdiel. Forcas grabbed the young angel by the hair roughly. Cam tried to fight, but the chains kept him immobile. Douma held up a syringe for him to see. It was huge and full of demon blood.

Cam's eyes went wide with fear. "No, crap no," he whimpered. He tried harder to fight, bucking so hard against his restraints his wrists bled from straining against the chains.

"Don't, please," Abdiel hated begging his brothers, but he would do anything to stop them from hurting Cam. "I'll do whatever you want. I'll even go before Lucifer and ask for his forgiveness. Just don't put that stuff in him."

"We've been waiting to experiment on this one." Forcas pulled harder on Cam's hair, tilting his head so his jugular was exposed.

Cam continued to struggle wildly.

This was his worst nightmare come alive, and Abdiel knew it. Abdiel also knew he was powerless to stop it. He cursed the day Cam had met him. Everyone he ever cared about had been hurt because of him. First, the twins when they were taken to Hell. Then Gabi when she brought his sister back. Now it was Cam, and all because his damn brothers wanted a lab rat.

Douma plunged the needle ruthlessly into Cam's neck and injected every last drop of blood into the angel. That finally succeeded in breaking him. Cam threw back his head and released a scream of pure agony. It echoed all through the bowels of Hell causing demons everywhere to stop what they were doing and look up in surprise.

"OH, GABI, LOOK AT this," Rachael squealed in delight.

Gabi looked over at the dangerously short miniskirt her sister-in-law held up. "If I let you buy that, your brother will have my hide."

Rachael tucked it over her arm with all the other revealing clothing.

It seemed every time Gabi said something was too skimpy that was incentive for Rachael to buy it. Ever since she'd discovered she had breasts and curvy legs, she seemed intent on showing them off.

Rachael was currently dressed in a short, ruffled red skirt. It was paired with fishnet stockings and a tight, red top that showed off her belly. A pair of knee-high black boots with six-inch heels completed the outfit. Since they were out shopping, they didn't shield themselves to the humans. Several men stopped dead in their tracks in order to get a better look at her. Rachael seemed totally oblivious to all the attention.

"As soon as Abdiel sees what you're wearing, he's going to strangle both of us," Gabi huffed.

"My brother needs to remember I'm not that much younger than him." Rachael never looked up from the rack of clothes she sorted through. "You know, Cam bosses me around, too. I'm older than him, but he still acts like an old granny around me."

Gabi chuckled as she thought about how quick Rachael had picked up on Earth lingo. It had only been a couple of weeks, but she'd assimilated. Obviously, Cam had been a good tutor. "He's just overprotective of you." Gabi took a black leather skirt from her hands and hung it back up. "I'm afraid all the Lehor brothers have decided you are their new sister." Cam had taken her to meet all of his brothers. They all took an instant liking to Rachael. They admired her spunk and quick wit. Not to mention the fact she could chug a whole can of whipped cream without coming up for air.

"Don't remind me," Rachael groaned. "The other day some poor empath tried to talk to me, and Ramiel all but growled at the poor guy." She wrinkled her brow in confusion. "I don't feel Cam or Abdiel on Earth any longer."

"Scan Heaven," Gabi ordered as her heart sped up with fear. "Maybe they went up there for something."

Rachel closed her eyes and went into a trance. When she opened them, they were full of tears. "They're not there either. We need to get back to the house."

Gabi didn't argue. She made them invisible to humans, then flashed them to their house. They were met with deathly silence. Gabi ran one way while Rachael went the other. They both called out for the males and neither received a response. Gabi found Abdiel's phone on the ground. She snatched it up and scrolled through the history. The last call was from Cam. It had lasted thirty seconds. She clutched the phone in her hand desperately needing to touch something her mate had.

Rachael entered the room. She panted, her eyes wide. "I can't touch either one of their minds. There's something blocking me. It's not Douma or Forcas. It's something stronger."

"Here, try this." Gabi shoved the cell phone into her hand. "Sometimes Cam holds something someone has touched and he's able to read their past thoughts."

Rachael grabbed it and jerked backward as the memories slammed into her. She let out a small cry of distress. "Douma and Forcas have them both." She bolted toward the gym.

Gabi ran to keep up with her.

Rachael jerked open a cabinet and started to paw through the weapons stored there. Since Abdiel collected every weapon imaginable, the choices were extensive. The sky tuned dark and thunder rumbled. Rachael breathed hard with anger. "I'm going to go get them back."

"You can't go to Hell." Gabi started to panic. They had Abdiel. They had her mate and she could do nothing to help him.

"Why not?" Rachael spat. "I know the place like the back of my hand."

Lightning split the sky and Gabi realized it was because Rachael was so distressed she was throwing her powers around without meaning to. Gabi grabbed her by the shoulders, "Look I'm just as upset as you are. That's my mate they have. But we can't do this without help." Gabi flashed them to the one angel that could aid them. The mansion was in the heart of Heaven. She pounded on the door. "Michael, we need you."

THEY UNCHAINED CAM SO Abdiel could have a full view of his thrashings. They even took off the Chains of Confinement. There was no danger of Cam using his powers now.

At first, Cam just flopped on the floor, crying out as waves of pain racked him. Then he got up and started to ram his head into the wall again and again, screaming about voices in his head. The demons stood back and watched him hurt himself while in the throes of his frenzy. Douma and Forcas laughed as the blood poured down the angel's face.

Cam rolled on the balls of his feet, holding his head in between his hands. Abdiel could see blood trickle out of both his ears and he foamed at the mouth. Finally, he flipped onto his back with a sickening, bone-crunching sound. He started to convulse violently. His already injured head pounded into the ground.

Abdiel heard joints pop as his body protested the contortions the seizures twisted him into. The archangel fought against his own restraints, desperate to get to his friend. "I'm going to make you pay for this Forcas and Douma."

They just laughed even harder, then walked out of the cell, slamming the door shut.

All Abdiel could do was sit there hopelessly as his adopted brother was slowly destroyed right before his eyes.

Abdiel sat there in the darkness listening to Cam's ragged breathing. After what had seemed like hours, the young angel had finally quieted down some. Cam's face was unrecognizable. Between the beating the demons had given him and his own self-destructive fit, he was a bloody pulp. He still hadn't woken up and Abdiel doubted he ever would.

"Oh no, not my little puppy," a soft voice cried. A small female demon glided into the room. She was really quite beautiful with long blonde hair. She had dark green eyes like a tiger's and an impressive set of fangs. She immediately went to Cam and ran her hands over him.

At the sight of yet another demon touching him when he was so helpless and totally defenseless, Abdiel got good and pissed. "Don't touch him," he snarled. Not like there was much he could do besides trying to down her with a well-placed loogie.

She looked up at him and her eyes flashed dangerously. Her black wings flapped opened as she displayed how much his comments, well...ruffled her feathers. "I would never hurt my little puppy. He's too sweet." She opened the small pouch she had over her shoulder and pulled out some manna. She tried to slip it in between Cam's lips, but he gagged on it. Undaunted, she forced some more into his mouth.

This time, the angel heaved as his body rejected it.

She nibbled on her bottom lip with her right fang before she turned to Abdiel. "He cannot take in the manna. Your friend is too far gone for it to help him."

"How is manna going to help him anyway?" Abdiel growled, still not trusting the demoness.

"One of two ways me and my sisters keep our beauty is by

consuming manna." She rummaged through her bag again.

"What's the other way?" Abdiel asked wearily.

She pulled out a small dagger and a cup. "We drink angel's blood," she confessed. "Just like demon's blood can change an angel, angel's blood can stop a demon from physically turning all the way."

"You're a succubus, aren't you?" He leaned his head against the wall and rolled his eyes. "I don't want to know how you and Cam know each other, do I?"

"Which question do you want me to answer first?" She smoothed back Cam's hair. "Yes, I am a succubus, and yes, little puppy and I know each other because we did what succubi are best at."

"Do you get this close to every angel you know?"

"No, I have never given them a second thought." She smiled gently down at the young angel. "But Cam was different. He knew what I was and still didn't look at me with disgust. That's why I'm willing to risk myself for him."

"You can help him?" He really hoped this demon chick wasn't messing with his mind for jollies.

"How about you? Are you willing to sacrifice everything you have been told for him?"

"Of course I would. He's like a brother to me."

She walked over to him. "I need some of your blood. We have to feed it to him. Otherwise, he'll completely turn demon."

"Is this some kind of twisted joke?" Abdiel was shocked she even suggested such a thing.

"Answer me one thing, archangel." The female looked him in the eye. "How do you think rogue angels last so long without turning? As soon as an angel turns their back on Heaven and embraces evil, they immediately begin the transition to demon. In order to slow down the process, they buy angel blood from the black market."

"You're lying," Abdiel spat. "The council would never allow something like that to take place."

"Please." The demon curled her lip in disgust. "Your precious council has known about the practice of angel blood for centuries. They just hide it from the civilized angel population. They have their own interests at stake."

From what he had seen of the council, he had to admit there was probably some truth in her words. He could easily see Jehel putting politics before what was moral. But Abdiel still blanched at the thought. Even if she was right about rogues, no pure angel had ever drunk another angel's blood. For all he knew, it could make Cam even worse. When he looked at Cam and saw him slipping more into a catatonic state, he made up his mind. After all, what did they have to lose? "If this hurts him more, I'll hunt you down and make you regret the day you set eyes on me."

She cast a doubtful glance at the chains holding him to the wall. "Given your current situation, I don't think making threats like that is very effective." She cut a deep slash in his wrist. Holding the cup under it, she caught the blood that flowed out.

"How much blood do you need?" he complained.

"It's not like you can die from blood loss." She rolled her eyes. "You are immortal, after all." Finally, when the cup was full, she went over and knelt by Cam. She lifted his head and slowly let some of the blood trickle past his lips.

At first, he choked on the fluid. Soon he grabbed the cup with both hands and gulped it in. When he finally drained the entire glass, he opened his eyes halfway. "Lilith, is it really you?"

"Yes, but I can't stay long."

Abdiel was shocked to see actual tears in her eyes.

"Am I going mental or did you just give me blood?" Cam sounded revolted by the idea.

"If I hadn't done so, you would have turned or worse, gone completely catatonic. While the thought of you becoming one of us appeals to me, I knew that would make you unhappy. Don't worry. It was pure angel blood. I would never poison you."

"It still hurts," he hissed as his eyelids fluttered.

"It will while the transformation takes place." She hung her head down while the tears flowed harder.

"What do you mean transformation?" Abdiel shot her a venomous look, the only weapon he could wield at the moment. "You said this would stop him from turning demon."

"He won't become demon, but he won't be full angel anymore either." She dared to look up at him. "He will have to continue drinking angel blood or else he will succumb to his dark urges. There may also be some physical changes as well."

"What do you mean physical changes?" Abdiel felt his heart speed up as panic surged through his body. "What's going to happen to him?"

"I honestly don't know." Her hands twirled around nervously. "The rogue angels chose to let demon power in them. Cam was forced to take it in when he was injected. This is a first."

"What the hell did you do to me?" Cam whispered before his body arched upward and he yelled in pain.

"I had to." She threw her head on his chest. "It was the only way to save you. Once this is all over and they grow tired of you, I'll take you home with me. I promise to take good care of you, and it will only be the two of us forever."

"He's an archangel, not some stray puppy." Abdiel was beginning to get a sick feeling in his stomach. Maybe the succubus had only been helping herself all along. It was suddenly beginning to look like she was trying to make Cam into her slave. Dear God, by giving her his blood, he had helped her.

Cam rolled onto his side and whimpered.

Abdiel was relieved to see the young angel's breathing seemed less labored than before and he was at least conscious. It looked like the danger of him turning catatonic was over. Abdiel just hoped he had chosen the lesser of two evils.

Footsteps paused outside the cell door.

The succubus looked over at him and placed a finger over her lips to tell him not to say anything. He mimicked using a key to lock his mouth before he flipped her off just to let her know he wasn't fooled by her innocent I-just-want-to-help act.

She returned the rude gesture, then flashed out of the cell.

Two demon jailers came in and unshackled him. They went to haul him up to his feet, but he shrugged off their hands and stood up by himself. Abdiel wouldn't be dragged to his own torture session. He would walk on his own two legs for he had no doubt in his mind that was where they were taking him. He remembered what Haniel had looked like when they found him. His stomach turned over. With one last worried look at Cam, he let them lead him out of the cell.

They took him to another cell and roughly ushered him in. In the center was a table with restraints for both the feet and hands. On the wall was a rack that held various instruments of torture. True to every stereotype, there was a plain light bulb hanging in the center of the room. *Oh, goodie this is so going to be fun.*

"Strap him down, then leave us," a voice said from the darkness.

He would know that voice anywhere. There had once been a time he had craved to hear it and it had spoken sweet loving words to him. "Hi, Persephone. Long time no see."

BACK IN THE CELL, Cam swallowed another scream. The pain he was feeling now was completely different. Earlier his body had felt like it was burning from the inside out as the demon's blood had traveled through his veins. Now it felt like someone was tearing him apart bit by bit. Finally, unable to stand the agony any longer, he let loose a yell.

He was barely aware that all his injuries were healing at a phenomenal rate. As his body transformed, bones broke and reset. Every muscle in his body went into spasms as they grew. He rolled up in a fetal position and heard himself calling out for Ana and his brothers as if he was a child again. When the pain became too much, he let the blessed darkness claim him.

Chapter Three

IF NOT FOR HER VOICE, ABDIEL WOULDN'T HAVE RECOGNIZED HER. Gone was the female he once thought he loved. When he'd last seen her, she'd been beautiful and regal with long, curly brown hair and wide, brown eyes, but like his brothers, the evil in her had changed her. A monster stood before him. Her skin, although unblemished, was a dusky shade of red. She had cold, soulless, black eyes and her hair was as dark as midnight. Her hands were long, curled inward and formed claws. There were long talons at the ends of her fingers. On the top of her head was a set of black horns.

She was dressed like some goth teenage boy's wet dream. Her black gown was long and flowed gracefully around her. The outfit was ripped in many places, the holes strategically placed so glimpses of her most provocative body parts showed through. She wore a black studded choker around her neck with a large ring in the front so it resembled a dog collar. A gold snake bracelet coiled around her upper arm and ended just above her elbow. Her vinyl, knee-high boots had long spiked heels and silver buckles that ran the entire length up her leg.

Following her orders, the guards threw him roughly on his stomach on the stone table and restrained his hands and feet. When the fetid smell hit him, he tried to pull his face away as he gagged. The table was covered in dried blood. Some was a fresh, bright red. The rest was dark, and obviously, old. It seemed housekeeping wasn't top on the list of priorities for demons.

"Do you know what my specialty is, Abdiel?" she asked.

He looked down and didn't answer her, refusing to be baited. Seeing how she had pulled out a whip and he was spread eagle on a rack, it was a stupid question. She'd always been a little dense now that he thought about it. How could he have ever thought she was so great? Gabi was right. He'd been a stupid idiot.

"I torture others. I'm very good at it. In fact, I'm the best there is in Hell." She pulled his head up by his hair, forcing him to look at her.

"Good for you." He decided to use sarcasm a weapon. "I'm the Texas Hold 'Em Champion three years running in Heaven."

She bared her fangs and hissed, her eyes burning with fury. Smacking him on the cheek, her talons left several scratches.

Seeing stars, he shook his head to clear them away. Obviously, she had no sense of humor, but she did have a mean left hook. Her claws sliced away his shirt and bared his back. *Damn, that was my favorite one, too.* He wondered briefly why he was worried about something as little as that right now. Probably because he was trying to think of anything, but what was about to happen to him. He closed his eyes and braced himself as he heard the whip swish. Finally, the leather slithering ceased, then sang in the air. He bit his lip in order not to cry out as it cut into his flesh.

"You see that blood under you?" she asked.

Yeah right, like he could miss it since his face was right in it.

"Do you know who most of it belongs to?"

"Your boyfriend?" That comment earned him another lash of the whip. *Damn, she is one vicious bitch.*

"No, you smart mouthed fool. It belongs to your baby brother, Appolion." She laughed at the look in his eyes and knew she scored a point. "I honed my skills on him for hundreds of years. When he kept refusing to turn demon, his punishments were many. We used every technique we could think of, but he still refused to hurt any human. He's a stubborn, bleeding heart just like you. Appolion always got the same look in his eye you have right now. He's more like you than he will ever know."

"How could you? He was just a child!" he snarled. The whip came down again. This time, the pain was so bad he bit his lip and drew blood.

"I was right. You are just like your brother. He, too, refused to scream when he was being punished." Crack! "I tried and tried to break him, but he fought it." Crack! "We had to finally turn to more imaginative ways." Crack! "You would be surprised at how many demons are pedophiles."

That brought out a small cry of protest from him. While she couldn't break him with physical pain, she could with emotional pain. The mere thought of his brother being abused tore him apart, and she knew it. She was right. She was good at what she did.

"They love teenage angels. Lucky for them, we're not like humans. Those weak humans are only in their teens for seven years, whereas angels and demons are teens for many years. Until he finally grew to be a full grown male, your precious Appolion was very popular."

He fought against the restraints. "When I get my hands on you, Persephone, I'm going to tear you to pieces."

"You'll never have that chance. When we win this war, and we will win, I'll not only have you at my mercy, but I'll also have your bitch mate, Gabi."

"Don't talk about her. You aren't even fit to say her name." That threw her in a fury. She backhanded him before she started to use the whip on him again. Fueled by deep seated jealously she started calling him every name imaginable as she went into a frenzy. Finally, halfway through the beating, he lost control and let some cries of pain escape.

Exhausted and covered in his blood, she stopped. "I am going to give your precious princess to Beelzebub," she shrieked. "Do you know he has been taken with her since we all were in school? All those years you were mooning over me, while she pined for you, he drooled over her. It's like some bad love movie. He'd love a chance to finally screw her and he'll enjoy doing it in front of you."

"If he so much as touches her, I'll amputate his hands and feed them to him," Abdiel whispered, barely conscious.

She called in the guards. "Take him back to his cell and bring me the other one."

"No." He struggled to lift his head. "Leave him alone. He's already been hurt enough. I'll take his place."

Persephone's mouth opened in shock. "You're willing to take another session for him?"

"Yes," he gritted out between clenched teeth. "Just leave him alone."

She went over to the wall and pulled a set of pliers down. Walking toward him, she gave him a wicked smile. "You angels have always shocked me by how much you care for one another. It almost surpasses the affection you have for those lowly humans. I can't believe how you and the other angels let love and compassion rule what you do. That will be your eventual downfall."

"WHAT DO YOU MEAN there's nothing you can do?" Gabi shoved Michael in the chest before turning away from him in anger.

Michael raked his hands threw his hair as he paced around his living room. "Angels can't go into Hell. You know that just as well as I do. Just like we have protective fields around Heaven, the demons have put up their own barriers. If I took an army there and tried to infiltrate it, the shields would make them so sick they wouldn't even be able to move, let alone rescue anybody. I'm sorry, Gabi, but there's nothing we can do except hope the demons decide to release them on their own."

"Some consolation that is." Gabi wrapped her arms around herself. "The only time they ever release a captive is if they've already destroyed them. And the only reason they do it then is so they can terrorize us." Just the mere thought of finding Abdiel the same way they had found Haniel broke her heart. With an agonized moan, Gabi collapsed to the ground.

Rolling into a fetal position, she sobbed. They had Abdiel, and she could do nothing to get him back. The demons were hurting him and it was tearing her heart apart. She had never lost it like this before. She'd always been cool and in control of her emotions, a true ice princess. But that was before Abdiel melted the ice and found the way to her heart.

"If you won't go for him, I will," Rachael challenged their leader. "Unlike you, I'm no coward. I'll figure a way around these barriers."

Even in Heaven, her rage was evident. Lightning flashed through the sky, dangerously close to his house. She was teetering on the edge and the only one who could bring her back was in Hell.

"You step one toe into Hell and the demons will be on you so fast your little head will spin," Michael's voice held a warning. Every angel, including Abdiel, always backed up when they heard that tone.

Rachael however, took one step forward and glared at him. "How can you just sit by and do nothing? Don't you care anything about them?"

"Of course I do," he thundered. "Cam is my nephew, damn it."

Gabi rolled to her feet and stood there in stunned silence with Rachael. Gabi couldn't have been more shocked if Michael slapped her in the face. She'd never even suspected Michael and Cam were related. "Does Cam know you're his uncle?"

"No, none of them know, not even Ana."

She had the sudden urge to hit him again. "How could you keep something like this from them?"

"Lehor and I never had the best of relationships. When her children were born, we weren't even on speaking terms."

"How about after she was mentally destroyed? Why did you keep it a secret then?"

"I'm a leader. I can't afford to look like I'm playing favorites." Even as he defended himself, he couldn't look her in the eye.

"They needed you, Michael!" she yelled.

"They had their Aunt Amiteil to take care of them," he said lamely.

"Please, Lehor's sister is a cold bitch that never gave them a second thought. Ana and the boys were totally alone, and you know it. But then you should know all about Amiteil since she is obviously your sister, too. I should have known all along. You both share the same stone hearts."

"You're bordering on insubordination, Gabi." Michael's voice had taken on a cold edge. "You had better watch it."

"I'm going to tell them the truth," Rachael shot out heatedly. "As soon as I see Ana and the brothers, your precious little secret is going to be out."

"As Chief I forbid you both from saying a word." Michael pointed a finger at them.

Rachael gave him a scathing look. "You may be Gabi's Chief, but you're not mine. I never made any vows, remember?"

Michael stormed over to her and looked down into her eyes.

Even though he towered over her, Rachael stood her ground and didn't take a step backward.

"Whose side are you on, Rachael? Are you a demon or an angel?"

"I...I..." she stuttered. Suddenly, her anger dissolved and was replaced with grief. She looked so lost and small. "I just want my brother back. He's the only one that ever loved me and now I've lost him. I want Cam back, too. I'm so lost without both of them."

Then Michael did the most shocking thing of all, he took the small female in his arms and held her tenderly as she cried her heart out.

Gabi could only look on in stunned silence as he murmured soft words in her ear and stroked her hair while slowly rocking her.

He looked over her shoulder and met Gabi's gaze. "I always watched over them, even though I never let them know it. I know it was a piss poor substitution for what I really should have done, but I at least did that. I intend to start making up for it now, but I need you two to promise not to say anything to them until we get Cam and Abdiel back. Ana and the boys have enough on their plates right now without this being added to it."

Rachael pulled back so she could look at him and nodded. Michael used the pad of his thumb to wipe away a stray tear from her cheek.

Gabi was starting to feel a little awkward with the whole situation, almost like she was intruding on an intimate moment. Holy Moly, who was she kidding? She *was* intruding on an intimate moment and it involved Michael of all angels. If the situation wasn't so serious, she might have laughed.

"I know a way to get them back." He never took his gaze off of Rachael.

"How?" Rachael asked.

Gabi had the sudden urge to raise her hand and say, *Yoo hoo, grieving mate here.* Abdiel was in Hell and Michael was making nice with his sister. She was starting to get royally pissed off and she must have projected that fact because the two of them pulled away and shot her guilty glances.

"Pretty soon, the demons are going to know all about Rachael and her powers." Michael got back to business. "They will get that information from Cam and Abdiel."

"Abdiel would never break and talk under torture," Gabi protested proudly.

"There are plenty of telepaths in Hell able to rip that information out of their minds. The demons won't have to torture them to get it."

"He's right, Gabi. They'll find out about me, one way or another." Rachael wrapped her arms around herself.

"The way I see it," Michael added, "is when Lucifer's top general, Mammon, finds out Beelzebub actually gave away one of the Order, he is not going to be a happy camper. It won't matter to him that Beelzebub didn't realize you were a member. Beelzebub is going to be willing to do almost anything in order to save his own sorry hide. We will strike a deal with him. We bring Rachael and they bring Cam and Abdiel to the battlefield. Winner gets all of them."

"Are you crazy, Michael?" Gabi gasped. "You'll need an army to pull this off, and the council will never agree to this crazy plan."

"The council can go take a flying leap. Like I said before, I will right this wrong. Cam is my nephew and this is personal. As for the army, let me worry about getting it organized."

"I'll call to Beelzebub and tell him I want to meet him." Rachael went beside Gabi and took her hand. "Michael is right. They only have two of the angels. They'll want me, too. I will also let him know

Appolion and I can communicate telepathically. The demon will assume I can track him down that way."

"When is the last time you heard from Appolion?" Michael asked.

"A few hundred years," Rachael admitted. "Beelzebub doesn't know that though. I'll tell him I can find Appolion. The stupid demon won't be able to resist the chance to get all four of us."

Gabi jerked her head up. "No, you can't do this. It will destroy Abdiel if they get you, too."

Rachael pressed her forehead to Gabi's. "We just have to make sure we don't lose then. Abdiel is my brother and Cam is like a brother, too. I won't let them suffer in Hell. I know what it's like down there."

"Are you ready for this, Rachel?" Michael asked gravely. "Cam and Abdiel won't be in any condition to fight, and Appolion is still MIA. You're our biggest hope for success."

Gabi looked at her sister-in-law. She was so tiny and innocent looking. She held so much power in her small, delicate hands.

"Bring it on. Those demons aren't even going to know what hit them." Her blue eyes grew dark. "Nobody hurts my brothers and survives to tell about it."

WHEN PERSEPHONE FINALLY GOT bored with him, the demon guards had to carry him back to his cell. As soon as they entered it, the smell of vomit met them. Cam was curled up in the corner moaning softly. He'd gotten sick all over his clothes. One of the guards went up to him and hauled him to his feet. The young angel swayed on his feet as his head lolled back.

"You promised to leave him alone," Abdiel protested.

"Surprise," the guard sneered. "Demons lie. Who would have thought? We can't let you have all the fun, archangel. Persephone is going to enjoy messing up your friend's pretty face."

"The surprise is on you, asshole," Cam snarled as he jerked himself upright. "This empath's got a little bite in him." He smiled showing off a pair of fangs.

That didn't shock Abdiel as much as his eyes. They were still blue, but were a dark, deep blue and the blue filled up almost the entire area, leaving very little white, and were rimmed with black. The pupils looked just like the succubus', long and feline in appearance. His body structure had changed, too. His pants used to be several sizes too big and hung on his frame, now they actually fit. In the matter of hours, the angel had amassed several pounds of lean muscle mass. Gone was the scrawny kid, now replaced with a hardened warrior.

Cam bared his fangs and sank them deep into the demon's throat. Ripping out his jugular, he drank in its blood.

Abdiel was surprised when the blood didn't poison him. In fact, it seemed to give him even more energy.

Throwing away the monster's body, he turned to face the other guard. The remaining demon whimpered in fear. Cam smiled at him and wiped the blood off his chin. "Not as good as angel blood, but it will do for now."

"You're not supposed to be able to take in our blood," the guard protested. "It's poisonous to angels."

"Bad news for you. I was never good at following the rules." Cam licked his lips before he flashed his fangs again and bent his knees, preparing to launch himself at the remaining demon.

"Cam, stop," Abdiel yelled as panic welled inside him. "You don't know what drinking that crap will do to you."

"What will it do? Turn me into a monster? Oops, too late for that," Can retorted, however, he didn't bite the demon.

Abdiel was relieved to see he was still willing to listen to him.

They could hear other guards running toward the cell.

Cam grabbed the remaining demon by the head and twisted his neck in a way that would make Steven Segal proud. Six more demons rushed into the cell. Cam threw back his head and laughed, acting like he was actually looking forward to another fight.

Not that Abdiel really blamed him. After all they had been put through, it must feel good to give some back.

As the demons came into the cell, they stopped, horrified at the sight of their two fallen comrades. When they saw another demon with his throat ripped out, their jaws dropped in fear. They looked at Cam with a disbelieving stare. He used their hesitation to his advantage. Running at them, he tackled the closest one, bringing it to the ground. He straddled the demon and got in a few punches before the others dragged him off. He managed to pull away from their grip and stood with his fists up as the demons formed a circle around him. As they attacked him, the angel fought well, but he was hopelessly outnumbered and had no weapon besides his fists. They finally managed to take Cam down, but not before he took out four of them.

"You fuckers are so lucky I don't have my flame back," he told them as they pulled him out of the cell. "I would roast your asses, then make s'mores over your smoldering remains."

Abdiel cursed the demons that took Cam away. Then he cursed the demons lying injured in the cell. Finally, he cursed the demons coming in to drag their wounded away. None of it made him feel any better.

He then started to curse himself for failing Cam. As the archangel it was his duty to make sure all the angels under him were safe. Instead, he had royally screwed up, and now one of the few friends he had was morphing into some kind of monster. Remembering how innocent and kind Cam was the day he first came to their house, Abdiel had to blink back the tears. Even if he did manage to get them out of this mess, he would never be able to look Ana in the eye again. She had trusted him to protect her little brother, and he hadn't done a very good job.

Even if he could get free of the chains, he was useless now. Looking up at his mangled hands, he winced. Persephone had snapped every finger. That was after she had used the pliers to pull out every nail. Not to mention the fact his back was basically hamburger.

He let out a hysterical, half-mad laugh as he thought about what Michael would think if he saw him now. To think his Chief had actually thought he was to be some great leader who would help save the world. Some hero, he couldn't even save his best friend.

His only solace was that Gabi was safe. When he remembered her smell and the way her body felt around his, it helped to ease some of the pain. He knew he would never see her again. There was no way Satan would ever let him go. Not after he had dared defy his authority all those centuries ago. If anyone could hold a grudge, it was Lucifer.

He could only imagine how mad Gabi must be at him. He had gone off without letting her know what he was doing. She'd reminded him countless times how they were a team. That he was not alone in the world anymore. A small smile curved his lips. His little hellcat was probably spiting fire right now.

"WHEN WE GET ABDIEL back, I'm going to skin him alive," Gabi told her sister-in-law. She and Rachael were waiting in the same park where they had taken the males. Rachael had contacted Beelzebub telepathically and arranged a meeting. The demon had thought it would be fun to meet them at the scene of the crime. Tired of all the waiting, Gabi felt like screaming. It had been a whole two days since they had taken Abdiel and they were still no closer to getting him back than before.

Both females were armed to the hilt. Gabi had not only her crossbow, but several daggers and throwing stars tucked away. Rachael had a scabbard on her back with a sword. It had been Abdiel's when he was a young archangel in training. She also had two retractable blades attached to her wrists. Their biggest weapons were hidden in the trees around them. All seven of Cam's brothers kept a close watch on them. If the demons tried to pull a fast one, they'd be in for a nasty surprise.

Beelzebub flashed in front of them. With him were two of his generals. He didn't speak at first. He just looked at the two females with an evil smile on his face.

Gabi felt like she was being sized up in the slave market, but didn't betray that thought in her cold stare. He settled his gaze on Rachael.

His lip curled up in disgust. Rachael all but growled at him as she shot him a venomous glare. There was obviously no love lost between the two of them.

"Well, look who's a big girl now," he sneered at Rachael. "You called for me, so here I am. What in the hell do you want?"

"You know what I want," Rachel responded. "I want Cam and Abdiel released."

Bub laughed in her face. "Now why would I do that? What will you offer me in return?"

Rachael turned and directed her hands at one of the generals sending a ball of energy at him. The demon yelped in pain as it struck him in the chest and threw him backward. Bub looked scared for a moment before he turned to her and started to applaud mockingly. The general struggled to his feet and went to attack the females, but Bub held up his hand to stop him.

"I'm offering myself," she said coolly. "Not only will you have me, but I can track my twin brother. You know you'll never get Appolion without me. Without him, you will never have the completed Order of Four."

"Even if I were to trade them for you and you managed to get your twin that still wouldn't help me. We would need Abdiel and his little punk. We need all four of you, not just two." Bub held up four fingers in her face to prove his point.

She smacked them away. "We challenge you to a battle. Pick the place and bring as many demons as you want. Winner gets all four of us, loser leaves with their tail between their legs."

He looked at the two females uneasily. "Does Michael know you're proposing this deal?"

Gabi made a big deal of rolling her eyes. "Who do you think is amassing the army as we speak?"

Bub looked over at her with lust in his eyes. "I agree to your deal. However, I have one stipulation of my own. When you lose, I want Gabi, too. She will be mine to do with as I want."

"Fine," Gabi said without hesitation.

Bub reached over and stroked her cheek.

She shuddered, but held her revulsion in check.

"You don't know how long I have wanted you, princess," he whispered.

She gave him her most haughty, royal look. "The only one that calls me princess is Abdiel. He is the only male I will ever love. Whereas you are nothing but a slug."

Bub snarled in anger. "I could just take you now. You're just two females, and there are three of us."

Rachael pulled out her sword and pointed in at the two generals as Gabi grabbed a dagger from her waist and aimed it straight at Bub's black heart. The seven Lehor brothers came out of their hiding places with their weapons drawn.

Bub took one look at the situation and backed down. He let out an angry hiss at Rachael. "It must feel nice to have someone finally looking out for you, caring for you." He gave a snide smirk. "Do you want to know a secret, my little bitch? Appolion wasn't exiled. Your mother freed him. How does it feel to know she loved him enough to do that for him while she let you rot away in that bed? Do all these angels know what a whore you are? Do they know all the things Douma and Forcas did to you? The things they made you do to them? You're not the sweet, innocent thing they think you are."

"Shut your dirty, filthy mouth," Nathaniel yelled.

Bub ignored him, leaned forward and sniffed her. "I can smell you demon brothers' stench all over you even now. How can you possibly think Heaven could even want you when you're tainted?"

"She's been up to Heaven and Michael accepted her, you slimy bastard," Gabi spat. She felt a roar of anger ripping through her body. If they didn't need the demon for negotiations, she would have destroyed him herself. Rachael tried to keep on a brave face, but it was easy to see this devastated her spirit.

Bub continued his verbal torture. "When they realize Abdiel isn't coming back, do you really think they're going to let you stay around? They're going to send you packing so fast your head's going to spin. Then you'll be alone, just like before."

Derel pulled back the string of his longbow, an arrow pointed at Beelzebub's face. "Nobody talks to our new sister that way, you piece of demon trash. Just say the word, Rachael, and I'll shoot off his freaking face for you."

The demon backed down, realizing he had finally pushed the brothers to the end of their limit. "Fine." Beelzebub spat at her feet. "Go prepare your army. I'll send a messenger later to let you know the time and place."

"Agreed," Rachael said, never lowering her sword. "Just remember, if we don't see Cam and Abdiel, the deal is off."

"They had better be in one piece, too, or else," Gabi added.

"Or else what?" the demon asked.

Gabi gave Bub a look so cold and evil the demon shuddered. "Remember, I was the angel called on to destroy Sodom and Gomorrah." Her voice was pure venom. "If they're not brought to us whole, what I do to you will make it look like those two cities had it easy."

Bub looked downright afraid before he flashed himself and his two cronies out of the park.

Even though the demons were gone, Rachael remained rooted in her spot. She lowered her head in shame and refused to meet any of their eyes.

The youngest brother, Barakiel, came over and put his arms around her. "That demon doesn't know what he's talking about. We'll never leave you alone. You're one of us now. We love you, and that's not going to change even if we don't get Cam and Abdiel back."

Jophil and Cassiel came and stood on either side of her. They were the only set of twins in the Lehor family and had the honor of being born right smack in the middle of the age hierarchy. Although they were archangels like their older brothers, they weren't angel warriors. They were part of angel police force called the Enforcers. They were completely identical in looks right down to the long, blond bangs hung over blue eyes.

"Hey, don't pay any attention to anything that stupid demon said,"

Jophil soothed.

"Yeah, we'll always look out for you. Us twins have to stick together," Cassiel finished for him.

"What's Abdiel going to say when he finds out what Forcas and Douma did to me?" Rachael whispered.

Gabi's heart went out for her. She sounded so sad and ashamed. While Rachael tried hard to act as if nothing ever got to her, she obviously had more baggage than she ever let on. "Abdiel isn't going to blame you, and neither do we." Gabi gave her a fierce hug. "We love you, and that's never, ever going to change, no matter what."

All of a sudden, Barakiel yelled and crumpled to the ground. He started to let out sharp cries of pain as he rolled side to side. A fine sheen of sweat covered him and he grew deathly pale.

Rachael went to him and took him in her arms. She rubbed his back.

"It's Cam." Barakiel looked like he was about ready to get sick all over the place. "They're hurting him right now. Oh God, it's terrible. They're trying to destroy him. I can feel it."

"He's connected to Cam. He's feeling his brother's pain," Rachael explained to the others.

"Crap, what are they doing to him in Hell that's so bad it's affecting Bear this way?" Nathaniel asked, his face turning green.

"Come on." Gabi took charge. "We need to get him back to the house and into bed."

AS SOON AS THE demons started to drag Cam to the torture chamber, he got his fight back. Spinning around, he broke free from the two demons. He drove his fist in the face of one demon before he used a flying back kick to down the other. He knocked both the demons senseless in a matter of seconds. His freedom was short-lived as another group of demons ran and brought him to the ground.

Two of them pinned his arms behind his back while the rest took turns punching him. Closing his eyes and trying to concentrate through the pain, he sent out mental images to the demons. It worked. Some of the guards started to run around in circles, confused. He started to work mentally on the two that held his arms. He felt his powers returning to him, and he knew if he could get his hands free he might be able to throw fire.

Just when he thought he might have a chance, Douma and Forcas came storming up. Cam's head felt like it was going to explode when Douma brutally slammed a barrier in place. Forcas came up and pinched Cam's cheeks together forcing his mouth open.

When the demon saw his fangs, he hissed in surprise before he leaned closer to the angel in order to look at his eyes better. "Mammon, you better come and get a look at this," Forcas called, still pinching the angel's mouth open.

A tall, dark demon came forward. As soon as he got closer, the evil rolled off of him. It was ten times stronger than any other demon Cam had felt before. He was ashamed to feel himself tremble in fear.

Mammon looked straight into the angel's soul with his dead eyes.

Those black eyes pinned him in place and he couldn't look away because of the paralyzing terror. He felt the evil exude from the demon in waves. His body started absorbing the hate, anger and demon power. "No," Cam protested. "I won't let you make me one of you. You'll have to destroy me first."

"Fine." Mammon smiled coldly. "We'll do this the hard way."

A huge explosion of pain rebounded throughout the angel's skull. He felt every good memory, feelings of love and happiness, savagely ripped from his brain. Dimly aware of someone screaming in agony, he realized it was him, but couldn't help it. He never thought there could be pain this bad.

It felt like every cell in his body was exploding and dark pits of burning acid were left in their wake. He knew they were destroying the old him and replacing that Cam with a new one, an evil one. He tried to fight it, but felt his control and will drifting away into the darkness.

By the time Mammon released his mind, the only thing left was hate and anger. He wanted to destroy and kill, to feel the blood of his victims running down his throat, he wanted to bathe in it. He vaguely remembered he had a family, someone who loved him, but he found that did not matter to him anymore.

No, you are an angel warrior. You have taken sacred vows. You must fight this. You can fight this, he told himself. He focused hard on the little bit of love still left in him. He found that some of his control returned, and he even started to remember Ana and his brothers.

They threw Cam into a small cell, then slammed the door behind him. He got up from his hands and knees and looked around. He was surprised to find he hadn't been taken to a torture chamber. He was even more surprised to see there was a female angel sitting in the corner of the room.

He felt sick to his stomach as he realized what the demons had done. They'd thrown him in with a female thinking he would turn and attack her in his unpredictable state. The worst thing is he honestly didn't think he was above doing just that. In a panic, he turned to the door and pounded on it. "Let me out of here, you sick sons of bitches."

"They won't answer," the female said. "They never do."

Cam closed his eyes and laid his head against the door. He was shocked when the female came up and touched him on the shoulder. Her soft touch instantly made him full of lust. He found himself fighting the monster in him. *Get a grip, Cam. Don't give Mammon the satisfaction by letting yourself be turned into a demon.* "Get away from me," he gritted between clenched teeth. He didn't turn and look at her lest she see his fangs and be frightened.

"You're hurt," she gasped, caressing his wounds.

"Are you a healer?"

"No, I'm an archangel."

"Then my wounds are no concern of yours," he spoke harshly. She still was too close to him. He could smell her blood, hear it rushing through her veins. He started to breath hard as a red haze obscured his vision. His hold on his sanity slipped. If he could, he would have run from the room in order to put as much distance between him and the female.

All he needed was one taste. Just one little nip, then he would leave her alone. It's not like anyone would ever find out, and it wouldn't hurt her, much.

Losing control, he turned on her with a feral growl. Throwing her on the ground, he bared his fangs. She let out a terrified scream just as he sunk them deep into her neck. His last coherent thought was that the succubus had been right. Angel blood did taste so sweet.

Chapter Four

The monster that was once Cam was not gentle with the angel pinned under his body. She was strong, but he held her in a tight grip and drank her blood in long, deep drags. The piece of meat started to squirm even more. He grabbed her by the hip in order to hold her still. As soon as he touched that area, his head snapped up and his mind started to fire with memories. Memories that were not his own.

It was his brother Nathaniel and he was looking at this female with a small smile on his face and love in his eyes. Next, the female and Nathaniel were in a bed having sex and his brother was marking her. Finally, he saw Nathaniel alone, mourning the loss of his mate.

Cam rolled the female over and pulled down her leather pants just a couple of inches. When he saw what was on her flesh, he let out an anguished sob. It was the Lehor tiger. He had attacked Nathaniel's mate.

Shit, fuck, damn. Nathaniel's mate, this was your brother's female and you hurt her. You stupid piece of garbage. Shit, fuck, damn. Cam threw her away from him and ran to the opposite corner. He heard someone yelling in demon talk and was sickened to realize it was him. *Get a hold of yourself, do not let them win. You can fight this. You're an angel warrior.*

The problem was the demon in him wasn't going away. He could still hear himself spitting out words in the demon language and he wanted to get back at the female so badly he was clawing at the ground. He closed his eyes and prayed for relief.

"You're not alone. I'm with you, my son," a female's voice assured.

He opened his eyes and saw his mother standing there. She was surrounded by a soft golden light and wore a flowing, white dress. He scrubbed his face with his hands, not believing what he saw. *How can Mom be here? Last time I checked, she was still in Heaven catatonic.*

Yet, when she took him in her arms, she felt real. As soon as he was in her embrace, the demon thoughts went away. He closed his eyes and let her goodness wash over him, cleaning off all the evil thoughts Mammon had forced in him. "I wanna go home, Mama," he moaned, knowing he sounded like he was five again.

"I know, baby, and I wish I could take you there."

"They're going to destroy me, Mom."

"No, they cannot afford to let one of the Order perish. They'll try to turn you into one of them first. You must resist, my son. It won't be easy, but you must for all of our sakes."

"Why didn't you tell me what I really was?" Cam asked. "I might have been able to prepare myself better if I had known about my powers sooner."

She looked down sadly. "I was wrong about that. When you get home, you must go to your uncle. He will be able to help finish your training. Whatever you do, you must not trust your Aunt Amiteil. She is going to try to use you for her own political gain."

"I don't have an uncle," he protested. Maybe he really was imagining this whole thing.

"It's time for you to know the truth. Michael is you uncle. I'm his younger sister. We had a terrible fight before the day of my mating ceremony, and we never spoke as brother or sister again."

"Now I know this is one big hallucination," he muttered. "There is no way in hell I am related to the Chief."

"You're not hallucinating," the female angel said from across the room. She was holding a hand to her injured neck and looking at Lehor with awe. "I see her, too. It is the Lady of the empaths, my Nathaniel's mother."

Lehor turned and gave her a smile. "Do not give up hope, daughter. It will take years, but you will see Nathaniel again."

"Wait, wait, wait." Cam waved his hands in denial. "No offense, Ma, but the last time I saw you, you were staring off into space in the healing chambers. How is it you're here talking to me now?"

"My powers were once as great as yours. Michael is helping me channel them so I can come to you. I don't know how often I will be able to do this though. I can already feel my strength slipping away."

Cam started to say something back to her, but she vanished. He looked over at the female and saw her still holding her neck. He ducked his head and winced. He couldn't believe he had totally lost it and bit another angel. "I'm sorry," he said softly.

"I know," the female angel responded.

"Normally I don't go around attacking angels, honest. This demon just messed with my mind, and I wasn't myself."

"It was partly my fault. You did try to warn me to stay away. I recognized you as Nathaniel's brother and didn't listen."

"How come none of us ever knew about you? Nathaniel never told us he had a mate."

"My father had promised me to another male, but as soon as I met your brother, I had other plans. We didn't dare tell anyone we were in love."

"But you're marked. There's no way to hide that. Every male around you would have known."

Her smile was dreamy as she remembered. "It was the night I was captured. I had finally decided to defy my father, and I let Nathaniel claim me. We were going to tell his family the next day. Little did I know when I went out patrolling that night there was not going to be any tomorrows for us." She told him all about her. Her name was Belora and she was an archangel. She had been captured five years ago and had never found out what had become of her empath and healer.

"What do I look like?" he asked reaching up to touch one of his fangs.

"Your eyes look like a cat's." She narrowed her eyes as she sized him up. "Besides that and your fangs, you look like any other angel."

He twisted around to look behind him. "Oh crap, please tell me I don't have wings, too. I freaking hate heights."

She laughed lightly. "No wings. Don't worry you're completely wingless. You are safe in the knowledge you are still earthbound."

That gave him some measure of relief. "It must be lonely down here."

"That's the worst part of Hell," she confessed. "It's not the physical pain. It's being all alone."

Four guards entered the cell. Rather than wasting the energy it took to fight, he got up and walked over to them. They wrapped the Chains of Confinement around him. *Must have been that comment about roasting their asses.*

"Cam," Belora called.

He stopped and turned around.

"Tell Nathaniel I love him."

He nodded to her before they led him out. They took him to an empty cell. Inside were the guards he injured earlier. They were healed and looking for pay back. On impulse, he tried to blast them. As soon as he attempted to do so, the chains around him zapped him with enough force to send him sprawling backward. Even though the pain was agonizing, he scrambled to his feet. He didn't want to become their personal hackey sack. As long as he kept standing, they couldn't hurt him too bad.

That plan lasted for about two minutes. He managed to stay on his feet for the first half dozen blows. After that, they drove him to the ground. They viciously kicked him. One of them broke his nose, and he started to choke on his own blood. All of a sudden, someone hauled him up to his feet by the scruff of his shirt. Fuck, it was Mammon and he looked pissed.

"I just checked on the female I gave you, and I all I found was a little nip on her neck," he spat. "I am very disappointed with you. I guess you need another lesson."

Before Cam could fire off a smart comeback, Mammon slammed back into his mind. This time the pain was even worse than before. By the time Mammon was done with him, Cam was begging the demons to destroy him.

GABI SAT ON THEIR bed, holding Abdiel's pillow to her face, inhaling his scent. It had been weeks since the meeting with Beelzebub and they still hadn't heard anything. Slowly, bit-by-bit, her hope to get him back died away.

The Lehors had all moved into the house with her and kept a grim, silent vigil. Ana was pale and thin, a ghost of her former self. None of the brothers smiled anymore. Barakiel was the worst off. Somehow, he was receiving all of Cam's fear and it was affecting the empath so bad he could hardly get out of bed.

"Oh, God no, just leave him alone," Barakiel cried from the next room.

"I'm here, Bear," Rachael cooed. "It will be all right. I'll get Cam back for you."

Dear, sweet Rachael had comforted Barakiel these long weeks. Ana had been absorbing Cam's pain, as well, so she had been unable to aid her brother. Rachael had been taking care of him for her. In fact, Rachael took care of all of them. She was the one that brought meals to Gabi and Ana urged them to eat, the one who broke up the many fistfights the mentally unstable brothers were getting into, the one holding them together.

Rachael was not the silly, immature girl Gabi had first thought she was. Her new sister was a strong, capable female. She came at just the right time and was the only thing that gave Gabi the strength to go on.

Ana walked into her room and joined her on the bed. Her blonde hair was pulled back in a messy ponytail and she was wearing one of Cam's shirts. Dark circles rimmed her light blue eyes. "You want to know a secret, Gabi?" she finally asked, breaking the silence.

"What's that, Ana?"

"Cam was always my favorite. I know I wasn't supposed to have a favorite brother, but Cam and I were always the closest. We're more alike than anyone ever thought."

"I know, Ana. I've always known how much he means to you. Cam knows, too. He always talked about you and tried to do good by you."

"Something really bad has happened to him in Hell." Ana had big, fat tears rolling down her cheeks. "I can feel it. What are they doing to my baby?"

Gabi had no answer for her so she just held her in her arms and let her cry her heart out.

ABDIEL CLOSED HIS EYES and tried to think around the haze of pain. *How many days have we been locked up?* Since there was no daylight in Hell, he'd lost track long ago. Most of the time had been spent alone. After they had taken Cam away that first time, they never brought him back. Although he'd heard Cam scream plenty of times, it seemed to happen on a daily bases.

One of the more talkative demon guards had told him Mammon had made Cam his special project. Abdiel felt guilty for, while they'd almost seemed to forget about him, Cam was getting the worst of it.

Abdiel remembered the guard told him they hadn't been torturing him as much anymore because they wanted him healthy so he could fight in their little angel battles they had. He learned the demons liked to make captured archangels fight each other in a pit for entertainment.

"No, I'm not going back," Cam yelled from the hallway.

There was some scuffling sound and a big thud.

"He got away, get him," a demon called.

Abdiel heard footsteps, then the sound of a hand smacking against his door.

"Oh, look he wants his friend," one of the demons mocked.

"Cam, you fight those bastards," Abdiel yelled. "Don't you let them win. Remember who you are." He heard more scuffling, then the sound of them dragging him away.

"No, please," Cam nearly sobbed now. "Don't take me to him. I can't stand to be mind fucked again."

Abdiel waited in the ensuing silence, dreading what was coming next. Sure enough, about five minutes later, it came. Cam's screams of agony started to tear through Hell. Each one ripped through Abdiel's heart, slowly breaking his spirit. It went on and on, never seeming to end. He wondered how Cam was able to keep existing after so many punishments. The door to the cell opened and half a dozen demons walked in. One of them came and unchained him from the wall while the others roughly manhandled him to the ground.

Some of the dirt kicked up into his face and Abdiel choked on it, making his eyes water. "If you guys wanted a date, all you had to do was ask," he sputtered out between coughs.

"You were always a smartass," a gravelly voice declared from the doorway. "Some things never change."

Oh crap, that was another voice he would recognize anywhere. "Hey, Dad, didn't expect to meet you here. My birthday was a couple of months ago. Are you here to bring me a present? It better be good if it's this late."

One of the guards cuffed him hard in the head for his comment while another ground his knee deeper into the angel's back. Off in the distance, he could still hear Cam's screams and that added to his own terror. If his father was here, then whatever they had planned for him must not be good. Abdiel knew his father, Eurynome, hatred ran as deep as Lucifer's.

Eurynome stepped into view and Abdiel was hard pressed to hide his shock. The demon looked nothing like he had when he'd left Heaven. His skin was pitch black and oily in appearance. Razor sharp teeth were crammed so tightly in his mouth they stretched his jaw and distorted his face. The only thing that remained the same were his intense blue eyes, but they were now rimmed in gold. He was dressed in a tight fitting leather tunic with matching black pants.

"I know you have seen Appolion." The demon hunched down so he could look more directly into the archangel's face. "I will give you one chance to tell me where he is."

"I don't know where he is." He tried to draw in a breath, but only succeeded in sucking in more dirt. "Even if I did, I would never tell you."

The demon shook his head. "Abdiel, Abdiel, Abdiel. When are you going to learn you can't save the world? If you had looked out for yourself and not tried to play hero all your life, then you would have never ended up here. Now I have to punish you."

One of the demons ripped what remained of the back his shirt so his right shoulder was bared. That's when Abdiel noticed the black bag his father had in his clawed hand. The demon reached inside and pulled out a tattoo gun. The angel's heart thudded painfully in his chest. His own father was going to brand him. When a male angel marked his female, it was an act of love and a sign of dedication. This was different, it was meant to degrade and demean Abdiel. By putting his mark on Abdiel, Eurynome was marking him as his bitch.

"You do this, and I'll do everything in my power to destroy you," Abdiel vowed as he struggled wildly with the guards. It was a useless battle for they had a tight hold and weren't budging. Even if he hadn't been weakened from his captivity, he wouldn't have stood a chance.

"You won't live long enough to leave Hell, let alone destroy me," Eurynome chuckled. "You should be happy I'm giving you this mark. Now you'll match Appolion."

Abdiel roared in anger at the thought of his baby brother being abused. Grinding his teeth against the pain, he closed his eyes as the needle started to go in and out of his skin. The pain wasn't the worst part of it, the humiliation was. Putting the tattoo there was his father's way of saying, *I won. This male dared to challenge me and I beat him. Hell, I more than beat him, I broke him.* Halfway through Cam screams stopped echoing through the hallways so the only sounds were his harsh breathing and the laughter of the demon. When it finally stopped, he was covered in sweat and breathing rapidly.

Abdiel didn't even care when they dragged him over and chained him to the wall again. His shoulder throbbed in time with the beating of his heart. Closing his eyes, he refused to look at his father.

"Remember, son, I own you. You dared to defy me and I brought you to your knees for it." Eurynome's hot breath brushed the angel's cheek.

Abdiel tried to pull away, but was brought up short when his back slammed into the wall. There was the sound of retreating footsteps before the door slammed and he was alone with his humiliation. He didn't bother trying to crane his neck so he could see it, the last thing he wanted was to see what his mark of shame looked like. Even if he were by some chance able to ever get free, how would he be able to face Gabi again? The instant she saw him, the healer in her would know he had been tattooed. Worse yet, there was no way to ever get the mark off. The ink the demons used was resistant to any type of angel healing.

A bright flash of golden light bathed the cell and suddenly Lehor was in there with him Her appearance brought him abruptly out of his pity party.

She leaned forward until her light blue eyes stared directly into his.

He let out a disgusted breath. "Great, just what I need. Another freaky dream about Cam's mom."

She reached out and smacked him on the cheek.

"Ouch, that hurt," he said incredulously. "Knock it off, chick."

She smacked him again, this time a lot harder.

"You know, Cam never mentioned you had a violent streak."

"I'm sorry, but I needed to get your attention, archangel. My son is in trouble, and you are the only one who can help him."

Abdiel made a great show of looking up at his chained arms. "In case you haven't noticed, I'm in no position to help anybody."

"You must reach out with you mind and reach him that way."

"Cam can't communicate telepathically. They keep those chains on him all the time."

She let out a frustrated sigh. "You must use your powers then."

Abdiel gave her an aggravated look. "I don't have those powers. If I did, don't you think I would have used them by now?"

"You can visit him in your dreams. I will help show you the way." She gave him a beseeching look. "Please, Abdiel. He won't answer me anymore, and we are in danger of losing him. You are the only one that will be able to reach him now."

Abdiel had a ray of hope, the first one since they had been taken. "This is all real, isn't it? I'm not dreaming you."

"Well, it certainly took you a long time to catch on," she said tartly, displaying where Cam had inherited his smart mouth. "Now, are you going to help or not?"

"Of course I'm going to help. I'd do anything for Cam." This had to work. He knew it was Cam's only hope of survival.

She placed her hands on his temples. "Close your eyes and relax. Just think about Cam. Clear your mind and focus only on him."

He followed her instructions, shut his eyes and let his mind go. Slowly he felt himself leave his body and all the pain it contained. When he opened his eyes, he was in a dark room and no longer in chains.

He saw Cam huddled in the corner, his head tucked into his chest. The young archangel was nearly unrecognizable. Dressed only in his bloodied, ripped blue jeans, his bare chest was a mass of welts and cuts made from vicious beatings. He had his hands over his head and rocked back and forth, making soft mewling sounds. Suddenly, everything he had gone through seemed insignificant. It, in no way, compared to what Cam endured. "Cam, it's me, Abdiel. I'm here to talk to you for a while."

Cam whipped his head up.

What Abdiel saw in the young angel's eyes terrified him. They were completely void of expression. They were dead.

Cam curled up his lip and let out a demon snarl. "You're just another mind trick Mammon is playing with me." He snapped his fangs. "Go away and leave me alone."

"No, Cam, it's really me. I'm here in some dream state, but it is me."

He cocked his head to the side and studied Abdiel closely with his new cat eyes. His shoulders relaxed and he heaved a sigh of relief. He got up and hobbled closer. "Am I sleeping, too?"

"I think it's just me, otherwise you would still not have your injuries. I think I'm having an out of body experience."

"However you got here, I'm glad to see you." Cam couldn't stand any longer so he crumpled to the ground at Abdiel's feet. "It's too late for me though. I can't hold on any longer. The next time they get the chains off of me, I'm going to use my powers and destroy myself."

"Don't talk like that. Your family needs you. Ana couldn't go on without you."

"I can't fight it anymore, Abdiel," Cam sobbed. "I can take the whippings and the other physical torture. It's what Mammon is doing to me that's breaking me. He goes inside my mind and shreds it. My God, it hurts so bad."

"I want you to say the angel warrior vow every time he starts that crap. Use it to block out the evil. It will help you remember who you really are."

"I don't even remember it."

"Sure you do, kid. Say it with me."

They recited it together.

"I take the sacred vow of the angel warrior. With the shedding of my blood and thus the blood of my forefathers, I swear to give up all my privileges and freedoms in order to fulfill my duties. I promise never to waver in my devotion to my brethren and the human race. I shall always place their needs, desires and life before mine. I will always walk on the path of light, never venturing into the darkness and, if I do, I ask my fellow brethren to either bring me back or, if I refuse to return, destroy me."

"THIS IS FOOLISH AND you know it," Jehel said angrily.

"You've already told me that several times," Michael replied in clipped tones.

Gabi couldn't help but grin at the flippant way he was treating the council leader. They were in the main tent at the center of the command post set up in Siberia. As soon as Beelzebub had let them know where the battle was to take place and the day, Michael had started to gather angels and set up a battle plan. He'd been briefing Gabi and Rachael when Jehel had come storming in looking for a fight.

"The council has forbidden you to go ahead with this battle." Jehel was livid. He obviously wasn't used to having his authority questioned.

"The council can kiss my lily white backside," a voice spat out from behind them. Ana stood there flanked by her seven remaining brothers. She was dressed for battle in all white leather. She had two small swords that hung in hoops at her hips. The weapons were called sai and, much like tonfa, were used one in each hand. Standing there with fire shooting out of her eyes and her body tensed to attack, she looked like an Amazon warrior, all her fury directed at Jehel.

"May I remind you that you are a member of the council?" Jehel asked her coolly.

"No longer, I quit." She spat at his feet to prove her disgust. "If the council isn't willing to try and get its own angels back, then I want nothing more to do with them."

"You're just like your brothers," Jehel sneered.

"Thank you, that's the best compliment I ever got." Ana held her head up haughtily. "The only reason why we're in this mess is because my brother had to rescue *your* son. Cam traded himself for your little wimp and you thank him by leaving him to rot in Hell."

"Like losing your worthless brother is any big deal." Jehel treaded dangerous water. "We are all better off with both of them were they are."

The brothers went for their weapons. Gabi looked over at Michael and saw him simply cross his arms and lean back against the table, making no move to help Jehel. To the shock of everyone, it was Rachael who stopped the confrontation.

"He's not worth it," she said placing her body between them and Jehel. "We need to concentrate on getting our brothers back."

"I think it's time for you to go, Jehel." Michael smiled.

Jehel finally noticed the brothers. Gone was their usual carefree manner. It had been replaced with cold, hard rage. No one ever insulted one of their own. The five that were archangels lowered their weapons, but made no move to put them away. Derel was not as considerate. He kept his longbow armed and pointed at the elder angel.

"I'll make sure to inform the council of your wish to leave," Jehel said tightly before he turned to Michael. "This whole thing just reeks of nepotism. We all know that if it were not for the fact Cam is your nephew, this battle wouldn't be taking place."

When he heard the surprised gasps coming from the Lehor's, Jehel let out a satisfied grin. "So Uncle Mike never told you he's your mother's brother I gather." He stormed out of the tent.

"Michael, is he telling the truth?" Barakiel asked in a small voice.

"Yes." Michael finally dared to look at his niece and nephews.

"Are you that ashamed of us that you refused to claim us?" Ana snapped. "Or was it that you were so ashamed of our mother because of what happened to her?"

"Ana, that's not why," Michael placated. "I just can't afford to look like I'm favoring any of my warriors over the others. Honestly, I…"

Ana just held up a hand, dismissing him, her blue eyes on fire. She turned her back on him and walked out. The brothers followed. Michael closed his eyes in sad resignation.

Gabi almost felt bad for him. Almost. As soon as they left, she sank into a nearby chair. "Most angels think the same way Jehel does. Nobody is going to come and help us get them back. They have always acted like Abdiel was no better than his family. They're probably glad to get rid of him, too."

"Gabi, go look outside the tent," Michael ordered quietly.

She ignored him. "The only ones going to show up are Cam's empath friends, and all they'll do is barf all over the demons."

"Gabi!" Michael yelled in order to get her attention. Once he had it, he ordered again, "Go look outside the tent."

She obeyed him and went to the entrance. What she saw brought tears to her eyes. There were hundreds upon hundreds of angels getting ready for battle. More were flashing in every second. They went on for as far as the eye could see. Every type of angel was represented—archangels, healer, empaths, shifters, even some of the angel police force were present.

"Every single one volunteered. I did not have to recruit anyone," he told her. "Abdiel is one of the most respected and admired archangels."

Since she couldn't go out and thank each one of them individually, she ran and hugged Michael instead. "But everyone has always acted like they were afraid of him," she sobbed.

"That was before you tamed him and showed everybody he had a heart." Michael pulled her away so he could look her in the eye. "We will get him back for you, Gabi. I promise."

THE ANGELS WERE IN formation ready for the demons to arrive. Rachael and Gabi stood side by side at the front. The Lehor's stood right behind them, determined to protect them. The brothers were out for blood. The demons had taken one of their own and now there was going to be hell to pay. No pun intended. All seven of them were there, even Barakiel who had never been in battle before. There had been no argument when he insisted on coming. If you hurt one Lehor, well then, you had the entire clan to deal with.

Ana paced back and forth, spinning her sai so rapidly they were a blur. A flurry of emotions surged throughout her body, making it impossible to stand still. If she could only see Cam, she would feel better. No, she wanted more than that, she wanted him home, safe and in her arms. She needed to hear one of smartass remarks, to be able to yell at him for pulling some stupid stunt, to tease him about how scrawny he looked in his too-big jeans.

Her brothers started to bicker again, and she listened to them in an attempt to calm her mind. As stupid as it sounded, it was reassuring to hear their familiar banter.

"Why did they have to pick frigging Siberia?" asked Barakiel.

"Demons just love the cold. It gives them a break from Hell," Nathaniel shivered. He was sporting a nice shiner, courtesy of Ramiel. They'd gotten into it because Nathaniel had wanted to watch A&E while Ramiel wanted to watch Animal Planet.

"Are you sure about that?" Barakiel wrinkled his brow in confusion. "I thought it wasn't really hot in Hell."

"He's just pulling your chain, idiot," Derel drawled. He had refused to heal Nathaniel's black eye because he'd been pissed off at him at the time, too. He liked Animal Planet. "Don't be so gullible."

"I think they just love to see us freeze our balls off," Ramiel griped.

Ana shot him a dirty look. "Can we at least pretend we are a civilized family? There are other angels looking at us like we're freaks."

"Come on, Ana." Rachael turned to smile at her. "That's why I love you guys so much. I don't think I could take it if you guys were normal."

"Ah, guys." Nathaniel beamed at her although the smile never reached his eyes. "She likes us. She really, really likes us."

"Time to look lively boys and girls," Gabi called.

Demons had started to flash in. There were hundreds of them and they came in all shapes and sizes. There was even a pack of Hounds from Hell. They were the most vicious of demons. Fortunately, they had the only thing that could beat them, Hayyel and his pack of wolves.

Ana frantically scanned the opposite group, looking for Cam. Unable to spot him, she panicked. *What if they had already destroyed him?* She didn't think she could live with herself if they lost Cam. She should have told him sooner about his gifts, shouldn't have shielded him so much.

The two groups stood silent facing each other. The only sound was the wind blowing across the field. It whipped through Gabi's hair making stray strands blow into her face. She held hands with Rachael, the two of them looking every inch the powerful female warriors they were.

"You know the deal, Beelzebub," Gabi called loudly. "Show us Abdiel and Camael."

Ana was relieved when four demons dragged the two angels forward. They made a great show of forcing the two males to their knees. As soon as the demons released them, Cam fell forward on his face. Abdiel swayed, but managed to stay upright.

Ana's heart lurched when she saw Cam was not moving at all. She heard her brothers cursing loudly. Barakiel began to tremble. He grabbed his nanchukus so tightly his knuckles turned white.

"Ramiel, Nathaniel, you see those chains around Cam?" Rachael whispered. Both of them looked at their little brother with horror on their faces.

"Yeah, what about them?" Ramiel asked.

"They contain ancient dark, demon magic. They're using them to suppress his powers. The first thing you must do is get them off him."

She spoke with authority leaving no doubt in Ana's mind she was right.

"Consider it done," Ramiel replied.

"I hope you remember your end of the deal, Gabrielle," Beelzebub called back. "If we win, we get you and the female twin."

"Gabi, no don't do this," Abdiel cried in an anguished voice. "Please, I'm begging you."

"Persephone," Bub called behind him. "Show the angels what we do to those who do not keep their mouths shut."

Persephone walked up to Abdiel and uncoiled her whip. She brought it down on his back with a loud crack. The blow propelled him forward. With his hands bound behind his back, he was unable to catch himself. He landed on the ground next to Cam.

"You're going to pay for that one, witch," Gabi yelled. She brought up her crossbow and aimed it at Persephone. As soon as she shot it, the demoness dived to the side. The arrow narrowly missed her and hit a demon behind her.

Once she struck the first blow, both sides charged. The two armies ran toward each other with an ear-deafening roar. The demons and angels met with a surge of violence and mutual hatred.

Gabi, Rachael and the Lehor's fought side-by-side, trying to get to Abdiel and Cam. The two males were still on the ground and being trampled by the demons. Unfortunately, there were several demons between them and the two archangels.

ABDIEL WAS ABLE TO lift his head enough to see Gabi and Rachael fighting. He was proud to see that, even though Rachael was the smallest angel, she fought better than any other angel. She used one of his old swords and handled it as if it custom made for her.

Even though three demons surrounded her, Rachael showed no fear. One of the demons grabbed her from behind. She lifted her legs up and kicked the second demon in the chest hard enough to send it flying backward, then head-butted the first demon with the back of her head. The third demon tried to run, but she sent a lightning bolt and zapped him in the back. That dropped it like a ton of bricks.

Gabi was just as impressive. She had her crossbow slung on her back and was opting to use a short sword for hand-to-hand combat. A demon charged her. Releasing a blade in the tip of her boot, she kicked the fiend in the heart. The demon vanished as it retreated to Hell.

They were finally able to get to Cam and him. Abdiel could tell by the horror on their faces how bad he and Cam must look. He knew it was going to be ten times worse when they got a better look at Cam's altered appearance.

Gabi moved to untie his hands, but stopped and gave a cry of protest when she saw their mangled condition. She used her sword and gently sawed through the bindings.

He could feel her hot tears falling on them.

"What did they do to you?" she sobbed. As soon as he was free, she brought his hands to her lips.

"Forget about me." His voice was ragged with emotion. He thought he'd never feel her gentle touch ever again. "Whatever possessed you to make such a stupid bargain?"

"I promised never to leave you alone again." She brushed back his hair. "I will go with you anywhere, even Hell." She kissed him ever so softly.

Even though there was a battle of epic proportions going on around them, he felt like he had come home.

When she pulled back, there was a small smudge of his blood on her cheek. "Now I have a little score to settle with a certain female demon." She stood up, her expression lethal. "She dared to touch something that is mine."

There was nothing he could do but watch her fight. There was no way he could hold a sword, much less engage in a battle. But after seeing the way she handled herself, Abdiel knew he didn't have to worry about his wife. She was in Amazon Princess mode. Instead, he turned to see how Cam was doing.

GABI SCANNED THE CROWD looking for Persephone. All of a sudden, the demon came out of nowhere and backhanded her across the face. She barely dodged the blow from the whip that followed.

Gabi responded with a roundhouse kick that caught Persephone on the head. The demoness staggered back, dropping her whip. Gabi dove and grabbed it. Rolling to her feet, she turned to face her former rival. She lashed out and struck Persephone with her own weapon. "Doesn't feel too good, does it?"

Persephone's black eyes widened with fear when she saw what Gabi was capable of. "Have mercy on me, Gabi. Think of how long we've known one another."

"Have mercy on you?" Gabi asked incredulously as she lashed out with the whip again. "Like you had mercy on my mate?"

Persephone didn't answer. She simply rolled into a ball on the ground and tried to shield herself from any further attack.

Gabi struck her a few more times before she tossed the whip aside with disgust. Pulling out her short sword, she straddled the demoness. "If you so much as even think of Abdiel again, I will hunt you down and make you regret the day you were born," Gabi vowed. "My only regret is you're immortal, so this won't kill you." With those words, she buried her sword deep in the demon's black, shriveled heart.

Persephone let out of shriek of pain and was banished back to Hell.

Gabi felt her lips curve into a cruel smile of satisfaction.

ANA KEPT RUNNING HER hands over Cam, just to reassure herself he was really there. When he finally moaned in response, it was the best sound she ever heard in her immortal life. She watched Ramiel and Derel struggle to get the chains off Cam. Rachael came over and touched them. The locks clicked as they unlocked. Ramiel ripped them off and threw them aside.

As soon as Cam was free, he grabbed Derel. "You need to heal me now," he begged his brother.

Derel ran his hands over him. The healer let out an anguished sob. "I just can't heal you that quick, Cam. Your injuries are too severe. I've never seen anyone hurt this bad."

"In that case then, I'm sorry." Cam bent his head toward Derel's arm.

"Ouch, Cam, you just frigging bit me." Derel was indignant. "Ana, you want to lend a hand here? Cam is sucking on me like some kind of leech."

"What has gotten into you?" Ana asked him even as her heart started to pound hard with fear.

When Cam finally released Derel and looked at her, she gasped in horror. *Dear, sweet Lord, he has fangs. Sharp, hard, fully functioning fangs and he just used them to drink his own brother's blood.* Cam licked the remaining blood off his bottom lip and she actually began to shake.

She reached out to touch his teeth, to reassure what she saw was real, but he pulled back from her.

When Cam's wounds healed right before her eyes, she felt her knees go weak. This wasn't regular angel healing. This was something dark and evil. She looked into his eyes and what she saw there made her unleash a small cry of distress. They were filled with anger, hate and the need for vengeance.

She knew then her little Cammie was gone forever. She had gotten her brother back, but he was damaged, forever. Her skinny, dorky, little brother was now a mixture of archangel and demon.

"What happened to your scrawny butt?" Ramiel gaped. "Did they pump you full of angel steroids or something?"

"No, they did much worse," Derel answered. "They poisoned him with demon's blood and tried to turn him."

"That's not what caused all those injuries." Ramiel snapped. It was obvious he was just as upset as the rest of them. "You scanned him, Derel. Tell me what they did to our brother."

Derel only looked down at the bite mark on his wrist and refused to answer. His shoulders were shaking in silent sobs. Cam slowly got up to his feet. Ramiel grabbed him by the arm and gave him a questioning look.

"No, I'm not telling you," Cam said darkly. "Don't ever ask me again about what happened there."

Ana heard someone chanting, "Not my Cam. Not my Cam." She dimly realized it was her. "I should have protected you better," she rasped out. She wanted to cry so badly her throat ached from holding it back.

"I'm sorry, Ana Bana," Cam whispered. "We can talk more about this later. Right now, I have to fight. I need to make them pay for turning me into one of them."

Ana had worn his backpack into the battle. They always teased him about that ratty, old backpack. He carried it everywhere. They called it his Linus blanket. She took it off and handed him his tonfa.

He silently took them and ran toward the fight. He left the

backpack behind. A demon had little Barakiel pinned to the ground. Cam picked it up with one hand and yelled something in its face in the demon language right before he ripped its throat out. As soon as it vanished back to Hell, Cam helped Barakiel up to his feet before joining the battle.

"What did he just say to that demon?" Ramiel asked.

Ana knew because she had heard him say the words in English in her head. "He sent a warning, any demon that dares to harm one of us will be sent back to Hell in pieces." Unable to take anymore, Ana wrapped her arms around herself. Letting out a keening cry, she fell to her knees. Derel hugged her trying to give her some comfort. However, she was too far gone for that. She threw back her head and screamed in agony. The last little bit of innocence her family managed to hold on to, was gone forever. It died in Hell.

ABDIEL LOOKED OVER AND saw Cam and Rachael standing back to back. Cam was throwing off his flame destroying everything in sight. He was letting his anger rule him and it was spilling over to Rachael, making her powers erratic as well. If they kept going, the demons weren't going to be the only ones in trouble. With a curse, he ran toward them. "Cam it's over, we won," he shouted. It was true. The demons were flashing away left and right, retreating.

Rachael immediately obeyed and lowered her hand.

Cam kept firing.

Finally, Abdiel threw up a shield in order to stop him.

Cam slowly dropped his hand and closed his eyes with a sigh. "What's going to become of me?" he asked in a hoarse voice. "There is no place for me to go."

"You belong with us, Cam." Rachael threw her arms around him. "Gabi, Abdiel and I will always take care of you and love you."

Abdiel sighed with relief when Cam put his arms around Rachael and returned the hug. He could kiss his sister. She'd known exactly what the young angel needed to hear. He turned to where the Lehors were gathered. Their grief and worry was almost palatable.

Rachael tugged Cam by the arm and led him to Ana and his brothers.

Gabi walked up to him and placed a hand on his arm. "Let me heal you," she said softly.

He awkwardly pulled her to him and kissed her, trying to wash away all the bad feelings. They gained their freedom, but at a terrible price.

Chapter Five

Gabi sat on a chair between the cots that held Abdiel and Cam. She had already healed Abdiel, but Cam was a different story. What the demons had done to him could not be undone. He was forever going to be different. She put herself into a trance and scanned his body. Analyzing every molecule of his blood, she saw how it mutated. Although he was still an angel, he now stood with one foot in the demon world.

She still couldn't bring herself to give him the worst news of all. Unless he drank angel blood on a regular basis, he could succumb to the evil that was now a part of him. Their sweet, innocent Cam was gone.

There was one silver lining to the cloud. Cam's body now carried an antibody to the demon's blood. She was certain if she could isolate it, she could make an antidote to the poison. The demons would no longer have an advantage over them.

Michael came over and looked at Cam. The Chief's face was both sad and haunted at the same time.

Cam slept on, completely oblivious to his uncle's presence. Occasionally the young angel's brow would wrinkle as he was swept into another nightmare.

"Where is the rest of the gang?" Michael finally asked.

"Barakiel got his first battle injury and he wanted to show it off to the others before Derel healed it."

A ghost of a smile passed over his face. "They hate me, don't they?"

"Pretty much, yeah."

He ran his hand through his hair with a resigned sigh. "How bad was…I mean, what did the demons…crap."

Gabi arched her brow. "Are you trying to ask how injured Cam was?"

"Yes, I am."

"He was bad, Michael, real bad. It took both Derel and me to heal him. They did horrible things to him. What they did to his mind was even worse. Ana tried to scan him and he was so damaged in there it gave her a migraine. She's sleeping it off now."

Michael swallowed hard. "I really, really messed up."

"Yes, you really, really did."

He looked down at Cam again.

She could have sworn he teared up a bit. Having known him all her life, she never once saw him this emotional. Her anger melted away. "Look, Michael, you just need to give them time. I know Ana and the boys. While they may be mad at you now, they won't stay that way long. They don't have it in them."

"I guess that's more than I deserve right now." He ruffled her hair and left.

Gabi thought about the Lehor family and all they lost. She knew it was only going to get harder for them.

Raphael walked over to her. At the devastated look on her face, he opened his arms.

Without hesitation, she embraced her brother. A small part of her was shocked as she could count the times on one hand Raphael ever shown any affection.

"We are transferring all the injured back to the healing chambers," he told her when she finally pulled away.

"I thought the council didn't want anyone that was poisoned up in Heaven."

"I'm overruling them. With the high number of casualties, we need the extra magic the chamber provides."

"Listen, Raphael, about Cam—"

"Do you still trust him?"

"Of course I do."

"That's good enough for me." He gave her a kiss on the top of her head.

"I think I can make an antidote for the poison." She relayed what she found in Cam's blood.

When she was done, he nodded his head thoughtfully. "That just might work. It can't hurt to try. We need to work quickly, however. Several empaths were infected during the battle and they're in danger of losing their minds."

She flashed to the healing chamber and got rooms ready for the males. By the time she got back, Cam was awake and sitting. He wore sunglasses to shield his eyes from the other angels. He had his iPod cranked up as loud as it could go.

"How's Mr. Dark Angel doing?" He pulled out his ear buds.

"He's going to kick your ass if you keep calling me that," Abdiel grumbled.

"You're awake," she breathed as she leaned over to examine him.

Abdiel pulled her down with a growl.

Gabi giggled girlishly when he nuzzled the side of her neck. She loved it when he did that. Cupping the back of her head with his hand, he moved his lips to her mouth. When he nipped her bottom lip, she completely forgot they were not alone. She started to crawl onto the cot.

"Eww. Get a room," a disgusted voice said.

Gabi looked up with a gasp and saw the youngest Lehor brother shooting them a mischievous smile. He was completely dressed in Goth. His black pants had numerous zippers and loops and he wore a Good Charlotte tee shirt. The most shocking thing was his bright blue hair. "Hey, Barakiel." She sighed as she climbed off Abdiel.

Cam curled his lip at his brother. "What the hell have you done to your hair? You look like frigging Angel Smurf."

"Yeah, well with those sunglasses on you look like Billy Idol," Barakiel shot back.

"Come give me a hug, little brother." Cam opened up his arms. "I thought I would never see you again."

To Gabi's shock, the idiot fell for it. Barakiel went over to his brother ready to embrace him. As soon as he was close enough, Cam grabbed him and put him in a headlock. Barakiel struggled to get out of it until the cot flipped over and dumped them both to the ground. The two brothers continued to roughhouse.

"I swear if you bite me, I'll bite back," Barakiel gasped, his brother's knees on his chest, his breathing a struggle.

Cam cuffed him on the side of the head. "Please, with all the junk you eat you would probably taste like corn dogs and chips. Thanks, but no thanks."

Gabi started to laugh. She couldn't help it. Just seeing Cam act like his same old self made her feel so good. Pretty soon, Abdiel joined her. The two Lehor brothers looked over at them, no doubt wondering if they finally went looney. "I'm supposed to bring you both to the healing chambers," Gabi said, sobering.

"I'll pass, thank you." Cam's voice was full of panic. "I was thinking maybe I should just wait for you guys at the house."

"Ana figured that's what you would say. That's why she sent me to get you," his brother said with an evil smile. Barakiel flashed the two of them to Heaven before he had time to argue.

"Great," Gabi muttered when she saw Cam's sunglasses had fallen off during the wrestling. She snatched them up before she flashed herself and Abdiel to the healing Chambers.

Upon their arrival, she saw Cam rub his eyes and hiss with pain. The pure white light of Heaven was too much for him now. She quickly shoved on his sunglasses.

"What the hell, Gabi?" he snapped.

"I know this is all scary, Cam," she soothed. "But believe it or not, there is some good that can come from this."

"What could possibly be freaking good about this?"

"I think I can use you to make an antidote for this poison. You will be able to help countless empaths from being destroyed."

"No, thank you, I'm no lab rat," Cam growled.

"Just think about it, you could save you own kind."

"What, half-breed demon slash angels? I need to check around, but I'm pretty sure I'm the only one who fits that bill."

"I'm getting an assignment," Barakiel said quietly. "They need a new empath in Flint and I'm it. The last empath is in the insane ward with Mom and Dad because of this crap. Do you want that to happen to me?"

Cam gave him an aggravated look. "Don't—"

"All the empaths are in danger."

"—lay—"

"More and more of them are turning out of desperation."

"this guilt trip—"

"We all need your help, me included."

"—on me."

"Please Cam." Barakiel gave him the puppy dog eyes. "Do it for me."

"That's not fair and you know it," Cam sighed before he turned to Gabi. "What would I have to do?"

"I would just need to take some blood," she told him.

Cam blanched. "You mean you would have to stick me with a needle?"

She sighed. Angels were notoriously wimpy when it came to needles. They tended to become spoiled by the fact that healers could mend them simply by laying hands on them.

"I don't even want to hear it." Barakiel rolled his eyes. "We all got stuck this morning just so we could donate blood for your sorry hide."

Cam's brow wrinkled in confusion. "What are you talking about?"

"Gabi told us that you would need blood." Barakiel was talking to him like he was a child. "Since we didn't think it would be a good idea for you to go around vamping out on everybody, we donated ours."

"I must be losing it," Abdiel muttered in her ear. "All this is actually starting to sound normal to me."

"Can you still eat normal food?" Barakiel asked Cam.

"I dunno." Cam fiddled with his hair.

"I know where Ana has all the junk food hidden in her house. Let's go nosh." Barakiel grabbed Cam and started to drag him out of the room. "I'll bring him right back. I promise, Gabi."

As soon as they were alone, Abdiel turned around and captured her in his arms. "I thought they'd never leave," he murmured against her lips.

"I'm angry at you," she protested weakly. Her body was already arching in so she could touch every inch of him. The kiss he gave her was so soft and tender it made her want to weep.

He trailed his fingers down the side of her throat until he reached the front zipper of her jacket. She went to pull his shirt off, but he shook his head and took a jerky step back. Confused, she stepped toward him, only to have him pull back again. Then realization slowly dawned on her. When she had healed him, she found the tattoo that had been forced upon him. He had been in the healing sleep when she looked at it. It was his family mark, like the one he had placed on her, but his was surrounded by demon writing. When she had Michael translate it for her, a cold fury swept through her.

Property of Eurynome.

She could only imagine the shame he must have felt when his father did that to him. Abdiel was a proud male, even after all the centuries of being treated like a pariah, she had never once seen him hang his head in shame like he was doing now. She took his chin in her hand and tilted his head up so she could meet his gaze. The despair she saw there made her heart break.

"If I could heal it away, I would," she told him.

"I know," he replied in a broken whisper.

"You have nothing to be ashamed of. You made a tremendous sacrifice for one of your team members. Cam would have never survived captivity without you. He told me what you did for him."

"It wasn't enough. Look what happened to him. I'm his archangel, I should have protected him better. I failed him like I failed the twins and this was my father's way of reminding me of that."

"Cam's safe now and so is Rachael. Every demon you defeat from now on will prove your father wrong."

The look on his face said he was still unconvinced, but he didn't argue anymore. Gabi went to take off his shirt, and this time he let her. Her breath hitched when she saw he was still covered in blood and grim. "Wait right here," she whispered. She went into the adjoining bathroom and filled the large tub with of hot water. Stripped down, she stepped in. "Abdiel," she called seductively. "I'm waiting."

When he walked in and saw her waiting there his face darkened with desire.

She gave a sexy little giggle and watched him struggle to get the rest of his clothes off. When he was undressed, she crooked her finger at him. He reached out for her, but she shook her head and pushed his hands away. "You're still hurt," she whispered huskily in his ear. "Lucky for you. You have your own personal healer."

With gentle, loving hands, she carefully washed the blood from his back. Even though his wounds started to heal, there were still several red welts. She kissed each of them one by one, laving him gently with her tongue. Gabi smiled to herself at his moan, then moved around and straddled him so they were face to face. She grabbed his hands and slowly brought them to her lips, then took each of his fingers in her mouth and suckled them. "If you ever go off and leave me again, and I will destroy you."

He opened his mouth to answer, but hissed instead.

Her hand had trailed down and she was gently caressing his hard cock. When she looked at his face, she was amazed. His dark eyes were hooded with desire and his normally hardened warrior's face was soft and tender. The fact she had that power over him was heady.

She arched her back so her breasts were closer to his face and he took advantage. His tongue made several lazy paths over her nipple before he gave it a slight nip. Waves of pleasure mixed with pain shot through her body and she arched even more against him, urging him on. She continued to stroke his cock with one hand while her other gripped his shoulder for support. With a growl, he grabbed her rump to bring her closer and rubbed her core against his erection. He didn't enter her yet, instead he brushed against her clit. Now both her hands were on his shoulders and she couldn't help but undulate her hips against him so there was even more friction.

"You don't know how often I dreamed of this," he murmured against her flesh. "I would sit in that hot, putrid cell and remember how good your body felt against mine. How good you smelled. How sweet your flesh tasted." His hand dipped down so he could brush a finger against her opening. "I love it when you get wet for me and I don't mean from the bath water."

She would have blushed at his bluntness had he not been giving her such a longing look. "I missed you, too."

"Make love to me, Gabi."

She shifted her weight to take him. As his thickness filled her, she threw her head back with a sigh of happiness. Gabi found a slow, easy rhythm as she rode him, not wanting it to be over too soon. She wanted it to last forever because, now that she had him back, that was exactly what they had. Forever.

Much too soon she felt the pleasure building up in her, getting ready to crest. He must have sensed it too because he gripped her hips tight with his hands and took over control. With hard, quick thrusts, he brought her over in wave after wave of heaven. After a few more moments, he joined her.

"I thought I'd never feel like this again," he spoke against her throat right before he kissed it.

Already she was on fire for him again and, when she felt his erection against her leg, she knew that he was ready for another round, too. He tenderly dried her off, with a towel, his fingers lingering at all the right spots, then led her back into the bedroom.

She expected him to direct her to the bed, but instead he took her to wall and braced one hand on either side of her head, trapping her. The look in his eye was no longer tender, instead it was intense, almost animalistic. She knew that the first time in the tub had been for her. Now he was going to take her hard. He was going to regain his claim on her. Shivers danced over her body. It wasn't from fear, but excitement. Letting out a low growl, he leaned down and captured her lips with his.

HE KISSED HER, HIS body feeling like it was on fire. He wanted to touch every inch of her, to consume her. What had happened in Hell had torn him apart. Not only was he traumatized, but it had nearly destroyed him that Cam had been victimized, too. The terrible emptiness he felt could only be filled by her. By her love.

He picked her up and wrapped her legs around his waist. Pressing her back against the wall, he entered her in a hard stroke. He drove his cock in as deep as he could, wanting to claim every inch of her. She urged him on by digging her nails into his back. He pulled back and slammed into her again and again. As he took her, he buried his nose in the hollow of her throat, reveling in her sweet rose scent. He licked a bead of sweat off her neck, tasting the salty goodness as he caressed her satin skin.

He knew he wasn't being gentle with her, but she wasn't exactly being gentle with him either. She seemed to need this wild sex as much as he did. Her heels dug into the small of his back and he could feel her leg muscles staining to pull him in even deeper. When he looked at her face, he saw her cheeks were flushed with desire and her green eyes were seductive, beckoning for more. She made soft mewling sounds that coordinated perfectly with his thrusts.

When she came, she threw back her head and cried out. He covered her mouth with a kiss so that her sounds were muffled. As soon as her body started to tighten and spasm around him, he joined her. Semen shot from him as she tightened around him, milking his cock dry. He still held her in his arms when they were finished while they both caught their breath.

"I need to get going," she sighed regretfully. "They should have the lab set up by now, and I have work to do."

He nodded and let her slide down his body to the ground. Giving her a quick peck on the tip of her nose, he turned to get dressed. She had been thoughtful enough to have a change of fresh clothes waiting for him. It felt good to get rid of his old clothes because they reeked of Hell.

They made their way to the laboratory situated in the center of all the healing chambers. Gabi pushed open the glass doors and they entered a cold and clinical room.

Watching the numerous angels bustling around the room in white lab coats, his jaw went slack with shock. It seemed so human, not at all like the mystical healing techniques he was used to seeing. Hell, there were even microscopes and test tubes lining the walls.

Gabi smiled. "This isn't the first time demons introduced poison into the war. In fact, almost every human disease has been invented by demons. We built this facility several hundred years ago in order to keep up."

"I'm sorry. I thought humans were the only ones that practiced this type of healing," he admitted.

"Please." She gave a small chuckle. "We were the ones who taught the humans their modern medicine. They just don't know it."

Barakiel came through the lab doors. Cam followed, dragging his feet.

Even though his sunglasses covered his eyes, Abdiel knew his gaze was sweeping the lab, looking to see if anyone was gawking. However, everyone seemed oblivious to their presence.

A male angel rushed over to Gabi's side. Small in stature, his head, topped with a mass of tangled brown hair, barely reached her shoulder. His lab coat was wrinkled as were the rest of his clothes. Appearances aside, he carried an aura of authority around him. He was clearly the one that ran the entire lab.

"If Camael is ready, we have everything set up and ready to go," he said. "If everything goes as expected, we could have the antidote ready in as little as an hour."

"That quick?" Abdiel asked.

"Yes," Gabi nodded. "We are considerably more advanced than

humans. Something that could take them months to accomplish, we can do in hours."

A tall, brunette female walked over and handed Cam a travel coffee mug. "Come with me and we'll get your blood."

"What's this?" Cam eyed the mug, suspicious.

"I'm sorry, sir," the female's voice was no-nonsense. "We will have to take a considerable amount of blood, and your body is going to need to replace its fluids."

"I can't drink this, Gabi," Cam argued. "Not in front of all these angels."

"Why not?" Barakiel growled. "You vamped out on Derel right in the middle of a battlefield of hundreds of angels. Why let a few lab dorks freak you out?"

"Thank you for the compliment." The female shot Barakiel a filthy look. "We'll go to the table over in the corner so nobody will see you. Besides, for all they know, all that's in that cup is Starbucks." When Cam still looked doubtful, she added, "I'll give you juice and a cookie after."

Barakiel grabbed Cam by the elbow and led him over to the examination table.

Abdiel watched amazed at how the youngest bother handled Cam. With a few well-placed jokes, he made it seem like there was nothing abnormal going on. It was obvious that the youngest Lehor was the peacemaker of the family. He suspected that's why Ana sent Barakiel in the first place. Cam finally drifted off to sleep, his body exhausted after all the abuse it had suffered. Barakiel gripped his hand and finally let his true emotions show.

Abdiel went over and pulled up a chair next to him.

"He's never going to be the same again, is he?" Barakiel ducked his head trying to hide his tears from the archangel.

"No." Abdiel felt a lump well up in his throat. "I'm sorry, but Gabi said the change is permanent. I should have tried to stop the succubus from making him drink the blood, but he was starting to become comatose. I didn't know what else to do."

Barakiel's eyes snapped up and bore into his. "Don't have any regrets. You brought our brother back to us, and he's not like Mom and Dad. That's what's important. All this other crap, we can deal with. We're family, and we stick together through good and bad times."

The female lab tech came over and gave Barakiel a cookie. Patting him on the head, she walked away.

"I'm not a child." Barakiel called after her. He bit into the cookie.

"Cam's very lucky to have you guys as family," Abdiel said softly. "You should all hate me now. It was my brothers that did this to him."

"Dang it, archangel." Barakiel shot him an exasperated look. "Those things that did this to Cam and you, aren't your brothers, we are. You and Rachael may not share the same blood as us, but we couldn't love you anymore than we do. Any one of us would gladly sacrifice ourselves for you two."

Abdiel was shocked at Barakiel's speech. The mature words were in complete contrast to his dark Gothic look. This little empath who had just completed his training was able to put both him and Cam at ease. They both fell into a comfortable silence as they watched Cam sleep and waited to see if his misfortune could be the miracle all angels had prayed for.

Chapter Six

CAM HUNCHED OVER THE TOILET AS THE LAST OF THE DRY HEAVES painfully wrenched their way through his body. Dumbass that he was, he'd taken a gander at himself in the mirror and, what he found staring back at him, sent him diving for the can just in time to lose his lunch.

He was one of them, a demon. By all rights the council should send him right back to Hell where he belonged. The only reason why they probably hadn't already done so was because he was part of their precious Order of Four. Or maybe his dear old uncle had intervened on his behalf.

One thing he learned from his time in Hell was if you kept your trap shut and pretend to be invisible, you learn all kinds of neat things. Another thing he learned was not to sleep too deeply. Too many nasty surprises could be sprung on you if you were caught with your guard down. As soon as Michael started talking with Gabi back on Earth while they stood over his cot, he woke up and heard every single word they said.

It was true, Michael was his uncle and never claimed them as his. Cam could care less about himself, but the fact the Chief rejected his brothers and Ana, pissed him off. They never did anything wrong. In fact, every single one of them devoted their lives to the *good fight*. Now his family was falling apart and it was all his fault. When little Bear started to cry in the lab, he wanted to pull his brother in his arms and comfort him, but he didn't know what to say.

Don't cry for me, Bear. Don't you see? The real Cam is dead. They destroyed and buried him in Hell. All that stands before you now is a worthless piece of shit. That's what I am, too, a worthless piece of shit that does not deserve any of their compassion or love. They didn't know how close he had come to turning. He had been about ready to lick Mammon's boots and give in, just to stop the torture.

Only Abdiel knew that. Abdiel had grabbed him and pulled him back from the brink. The one who reminded him what he was and the sacred vows he had taken to protect. He also knew that Abdiel would never tell anyone about what really went on down there. Even though he didn't deserve it, Abdiel respected and loved him too much to do that.

As soon as the antidote had worked, everyone was jumping up and down for joy. Yippy skippy! Now the demons couldn't poison angels anymore. Oh yeah, it came a little too late for his sorry ass. While everyone else was able to skip around free and untouched, he was seriously fucked up both physically and mentally.

Although all the change hadn't been bad. He was wearing Nathaniel's leather pants and one of his long sleeved black shirts. Normally the clothes would have hung on him. He'd bulked up and filled the clothes out. He wasn't scrawny anymore. Maybe it was time to ditch the jeans and tee shirts and dress like all the other archangels.

He didn't feel like a real archangel though, regardless of what Michael thought. Sure, he could fight as well as anyone, but he was still a freak. He felt like he was a confused mixture of angel parts, a tad of empath, mixed with a sprinkle of telepath, with a dash of archangel. Oh, and don't forget the heaping spoonful of demon, too. Now he knew what a platypus felt like. Obviously, Michael must agree with him somewhat because he never held the formal naming ceremony for him that all archangels had.

He felt Ana's presence the minute she entered his room and his gut tightened with guilt. It was her blood he drank earlier. He knew it the second he sipped it from that cold, clinical mug. All of her emotions, feelings and memories slammed into him like a sledgehammer and he learned something never suspected before.

Their Ana was lonely. She devoted her entire life to raising them and, now that Barakiel was leaving, she felt she had no more purpose. Ana wanted nothing more than to find a male and settle down to start her own family, but no male ever gave her a second glance. If her cold demeanor didn't run off suitors, her eight brothers did.

"Hi, Ana." He walked out of the bathroom.

She turned and gave him a fake, sickly smile. "How are you feeling?"

Let's see, he thought. *I have a pounding headache and a queasy stomach that I suspect is from being in Heaven. All I can think about is getting into a good fight and getting laid, not necessarily in that order. What does that make you think of your little brother, sis?* However all he grunted was, "Fine."

"Cam—"

"Look, Ana, I said I was fine, and I meant it. Your little Cammie is doing just peachy. Let it go already."

"Don't lie to me." Ana narrowed her eyes. "I can feel all the anger and confusion rolling off you."

"Yeah, well I've had a bad hair day." He sat on the edge of the bed and started to pull on his black combat boots.

"Are you planning on going somewhere?"

"No, it's just always good to be prepared. There are enemies everywhere."

"But we're in Heaven. You're perfectly safe here."

"I'm sure that's what Abdiel thought the day his brothers and Lucifer almost destroyed him."

"That was different. Surely you don't think anybody up here would want to harm you."

"That's bullshit and you know it!" He ground his teeth together and got control of himself. "Douma and Forcas knew I was going to be alone and away from the house that day. How did they know that? Someone with insider information had to tell them. Who was it, Ana?"

She looked down at the ground before softly answering him. "We think it was Anfial. Ramiel said that she took off the day after you were captured and neither he nor Daniel have heard from her since, no one has."

Cam closed his eyes as he took in this latest piece of news. Another empath had turned. Even though he was now supposedly an archangel, he would always be first and foremost an empath, and it hurt him his own kind was suffering. He realized now that the Empath Guild hadn't been blowing hot air all along. Ever since his mother had been incapacitated, there had been no one to lead the empaths, to provide them with structure, to stand up for their rights.

He had paid the ultimate price for that, too, and it had all been thanks to another empath. If he ever got a hold of Anfial, he'd wrap his hands around her throat and squeeze her until that annoying voice was shut up forever. Just thinking about her pissed him off so bad the mirror in the bathroom shattered as his powers surged.

He heard Ana gasp and, when he caught the look on her face, he turned away in shame. She had the look of fear on her and it wasn't fear for him, it was fear of him. He cursed under his breath and breathed several times until he got control of himself. "Sorry," he finally said.

"You have to learn how to control the rage," her voice was laced with worry.

"Tell me, Ana." He stood and walked over to face her. "What did you find when you scanned me? Don't try to tell me you didn't do it either. I know you too well to believe that for one minute."

"I don't want to discuss this right now." She refused to look him in the eye.

"You detected evil in me?" he demanded. When she refused to answer, he gave her a slight shake of the shoulders. "Damn it, Ana, I deserve to know the truth."

"You already know the answer," Ana said dully. "We can stand here and act stupid all we want, but we both know you're part demon now. Cam, you're something our world has never seen before. An angel that was able to fight conversion to full demon. You may have some evil in you, but your heart is still angel. Don't ever forget that."

"I just want things to go back to the way they were before," Cam cried in a ragged voice. "I don't want to be special. I don't want to be part of the Order. I don't want to be part demon. I just want to go back to being my old, dorky self."

"I know you do, sweetie." She pulled him into a hug.

He closed his eyes and allowed himself to feel the familiar comfort her arms offered. "They are all idiots," he whispered against her hair.

"Who?" she asked as he pulled away from her.

"You are the most beautiful and smartest female I know." He cupped her chin and made her look at him. "Any male in his right mind would gladly fight through the eight of us for you."

"Have you been reading my mind?" She shot him an irritated look.

"No, I have not been reading your thoughts." Technically, that was the truth. "You're very good at shielding your mind. Hayyel taught you well."

"You better be telling me the truth. Come on, we have to go. Michael is passing out commendations for the battle and he specifically asked that you be present."

"Fine, but only to show how grateful I am to the warriors that fought to free us, not because Michael asked me to. Right now, I wouldn't spit on our dear uncle if he were on fire. But we sit in the back where no one can see us. Step outside for a second and let me finish getting ready."

As soon as he ushered her out, he locked the door using his mind. Pulling the piece of paper out of his pocket, he thoughtfully fingered the numbers on it. He knew he shouldn't even be considering calling her, but he also knew he needed to find some way to release all the emotions boiling up in him. He dialed the number before he lost the courage. As soon as he heard her voice, his body tightened in response.

"It's me." He cringed when he realized he was licking his lips in anticipation.

"What does my little puppy need?" She had laughter in her voice.

"You know what I need." He gripped the phone tight, hating

himself for admitting such. They arranged to meet later that night at a neutral bar.

Neutral bars were usually dingy hole in the wall places. Frequented by rogue angels and demons, there was a no fighting rule in place that was more fragile than any Middle East peace treaty. Although no alcohol was served there, it was a hot bed for illegal activity. No self-respecting, law-abiding angel would ever set foot in one, but Cam did not particularly care about that right now.

He left his room and followed Ana to the ceremony hall. When they reached the huge double doors, he could hear they had already started. *Great, nothing like walking in late to call attention to one's self.* He was going to crack the door just enough to slide in when Ana pushed both doors wide open. Every angel in the hall looked at them, including Michael who stood at the front. He turned to shoot a dirty look at Ana only to discover she snuck away to sit with Derel.

"Camael, we have been waiting for you," Michael called.

It started slowly sinking in for him. Every archangel was present and standing at attention at the front of the hall. They had their swords drawn and pointed down. Michael held a sword flat balanced between both hands. On either side of him were Gabi and Abdiel, both smiling. It was an archangel naming ceremony. It was *his* archangel naming ceremony.

He slowly walked forward, his boots making the only sound in the hushed hall. Having attended all five of his archangel brother's ceremonies he knew exactly what to do. Once he reached Michael, he went down on one knee and bowed his head.

"Wait!" a voice called out in the back.

Cam whipped around toward the source and saw his Aunt Amiteil rushing forward. *Now what?* He somehow did not think she was coming up to give him a welcome home kiss.

Once she reached them, she bowed slightly to Michael. The Chief was giving her a look of warning, but she ignored it. "Before you continue, Michael, the empaths have one request to make," she spoke loudly so all of her words carried through the hall.

"Amiteil, don't do it." Michael growled so low only the three of them could hear.

"We would like Camael to be our leader."

Cam clamped his jaw together so it didn't drop open with shock. What the hell was his aunt thinking? He was the last one that should be a leader. He was so screwed up right now he couldn't even manage his own life, let alone every empath's. He stood up and faced his aunt. "What is this, some sick joke?" he asked softly, before he opened his mouth to show her his fangs. "Look at me. I'm some monster, not the next leader of the empaths."

"No, you are our savior," she replied, loudly. "You are the only one strong enough to lead us through these hard times. Our kind are in disarray. We need someone to stand up for us, to protect us when no one else will."

He knew she was painting him into a corner. When she put it that way, there was no way he could refuse her. That bitch was smarter than he gave her credit for.

Think carefully before you accept. She thinks you are too young and will turn to her for council. She intends to control you and use you as her own personal puppet, Michael's voice warned in his head.

Is that why you are finally having my naming ceremony? So I will be one of your archangels and under your control? Cam snapped back.

No, I do it to honor you. Not only have you sacrificed a lot, but you have proven yourself worthy.

I'm freaking touched. So you will claim me as one of your archangels, but you are too ashamed to claim me as your nephew. He slammed off contact before Michael could respond. His mind raced. *Maybe some good could come out of this. The empaths did need someone to stand up for them and to lead them. With Ana's help, I might be able to do it.* "I accept with great honor," he shocked everybody by saying in a loud, clear voice.

"Of course, I will council you until you are fully ready to lead."

Amiteil bowed.

"No, I take full leadership now. Today." He took one look at his aunt's shocked face and bit back a smile. *Check fucking mate, bitch.* She had no choice but to nod to him before she went into a full bow at his feet.

Every empath in the room followed suit and bowed to him, even Barakiel. Cam swallowed a mouthful of bile as the repercussions of what he just did hit him like a sledgehammer. Holy crap, he wasn't ready for this. He looked at Ana, and she must have read the panic in his face.

It will be fine. I will help you. You won't face this alone.

Her soft, gentle voice soothed him and gave him courage. He waved his hand over the group of kneeling empaths. "Rise now, my fellow empaths, and know you are now facing a new time. Gone are the days where we go unprepared into battle." Holy crap, were these words of wisdom actually coming from his trap? All that time alone in Hell with nothing to occupy him but his thoughts must have done some good. "Keep your heads and hopes high. I vow to you all that I will do everything in my power to make sure all empaths have a brighter future."

This brought a roar of cheers from all the empaths. He knew then he did the right thing. Even if the mere thought of leading them did scare the piss out of him. He turned and saw that Gabi and Abdiel were both so shocked at his speech their jaws dropped. He just gave them a little, sheepish shrug.

"Now that we have cleared up that matter, shall we continue with your naming ceremony?" Michael said once the cheering had stopped.

Cam could have sworn the Chief actually looked impressed with him. Cam nodded and once again, knelt at Michael's feet.

"Do you accept this sword?" Michael raised the blade.

"Yes, with great honor."

All the archangels banged their swords on the marble floor. The sound echoed through the hall.

Michael lowered the sword and Cam kissed the blade, symbolizing the weapon was now his most treasured possession.

"Do you accept the title archangel?" Michael continued.

"Yes, with great honor."

Again, the archangels hit the ground with their swords.

Michael lowered the sword.

This time Cam wrapped his hand around the blade. He squeezed it tightly until blood trickled down and dripped onto the gold floor. "I swear a blood oath to always protect the human race and my fellow angel brethren from Lucifer and his followers." Cam recited the archangel oath that was as old as time. Different from the angel warrior oath Abdiel and he had recited in Hell, this vow was taken only by new archangels. Even though he was never taught the words, they poured from his lips easily because they were ingrained into his heart, his soul. "I will always put their needs before my own and willingly sacrifice myself if necessary. I vow to never use my powers for evil and always remember the ones who have fallen before me."

"Rise archangel, Camael, and be accepted by you brothers," Michael instructed.

Cam rose and took the sword from Michael. As soon as he turned around, all the archangels saluted him by raising their swords into the air. Cam followed suit raising his up, too. The entire hall erupted into a loud cheer. To Cam's shock, the cheering continued for several minutes. Never in history had there ever been such a response to a new archangel.

As soon as the naming ceremony was over, Cam rushed outside. When he found who he was looking for, he let out a whistle. Barakiel stopped and shot him a guilty look. *Sorry, I got to go do something,* the coward mouthed to him. Cam shook his head and pushed his way through the crowd until he got to him. He grabbed Bear by the front of his shirt and eyeballed him. "Why didn't you tell me what the empaths had planned?" Cam asked in a deceptively calm voice.

"They told me at the last minute. I didn't have time to find you."

"You could have told me this way." Cam thumped his finger on Bear's head to show what he meant.

"You know I can't initiate a link, Cam. Only a telepath can do that."

"Remember when we were little and we used to talk to each other in that language nobody else could understand?" Cam waited for Bear to nod before he continued, "Our lips were not moving. We were talking in our minds, little brother."

Bear grew pale and shook his head in denial.

"You must have forgotten about that. Just like you forgot that half the time when I got into trouble for moving stuff with my mind, it wasn't me, it was you."

"Why are you making this stuff up?" Bear smacked his brother's hand away. "Do you get your jollies out of freaking me out?"

"No, Bear, it's all true."

"Screw you. I don't have to listen to this crap." He shrugged out of Cam's grip and stormed away, shooting a heated look over his shoulder.

Cam left the area before he had to deal with anymore of his brothers and made his way to the infirmary. Ever since the visions in Hell, he had a burning desire to visit Lehor. Not that he really believed for one cotton-picking moment it really was his mother who calmed him in Hell. He just needed to see her for himself, to really put this issue to rest.

He opened the door to her room and found her sitting in the same chair she was always in. He walked over and switched on the television set, not that she would watch it, but it made him feel better to have her staring at that rather than the plain white wall.

He went down on his knees and looked her straight in the eyes. Well, as much as he could through his dark glasses. He itched to take them off so he could see her even better, but remembered how much the Heavenly glow hurt and left them on.

He searched for any signs of life, but saw the same thing he always saw since she had been destroyed, nothing. "Mom, it's me, Cam," he whispered. Her dull blue eyes didn't even give the smallest flicker of recognition. He reached out and tried to touch her mind with telepathy. All he got was a strange jumble of words. *Box, dog, teacup, boys...* He pulled out, unable to bear hearing her insanity.

Her hair was still beautiful, so long it formed a puddle of gold in her lap. He laid his head in it, nuzzling the softness like he was a five-year-old baby again. "I'm scared, Mom," he confessed. "I think I'm turning into a full demon. It will kill Ana if I do. Everybody is expecting all these great things from me, and I honestly don't think I can be what they want me to be. If they all only knew what was going on inside of my head, they would all despise me. I have such evil, vile thoughts. It's almost like there is a monster inside of me, eating me up from the inside out."

She continued to look out vacantly.

Not that he had expected her to answer. "I sometimes think that you and Dad were the lucky ones." He made the vile admission with his eyes down. "If I had become catatonic like your two, at least then I wouldn't have to live with the guilt. I should have been stronger. I should have been able to fight the demon blood. Instead, I let it take over me. I was weak."

He realized his mother's lap was wet because he'd cried all over her. Dear God, he was weak, one second in the presence of his mommy and he was blubbering like a baby. He brought her cold, lifeless hand to his lips and kissed it. "I've got to go now, Mom. I'll come back soon."

He got up and walked out of the room, wiping his eyes on the way out. He closed the door and turned around to find Nathaniel standing there. Crap, he had been trying to put off telling his brother what he found in Hell, but it looked like now was as good as time as any. Bear already hated him. Might as well shoot for a deuce.

"Hey, Cam." Nathaniel smiled. "Visiting Mom?"

"Yeah, figured since I was in Heaven, I might as well stop by." Cam grabbed his brother by the arm "Look, there's something I gotta tell you. I saw Belora when I was in Hell. I talked with her."

Nathaniel turned pale. "You saw Belora? She's alive?" When Cam only nodded his head, Nathaniel grabbed him by the shirt and pushed him against the wall. "Tell me everything, Cam, now."

"She's in a cell chained up. She's been there ever since they captured her."

"Have they hurt her?"

"I bit her." Cam closed his eyes against the sudden hatred he saw on his brother's face.

Nathaniel started to punch him.

Cam made no move to defend himself. He let his brother give him the punishment he deserved. It didn't stop until Nathaniel finally got control of himself and threw him away with an agonized cry.

"How could you, Cam?" he yelled out. "Why Belora? I love her."

"I know you do." Cam wiped away the blood from his bottom lip. "As soon as I knew she was yours, I stopped. I'm sorry, Nathaniel. It was right after they turned me, and I didn't know what I was doing."

Nathaniel reached down and hauled him back up to his feet.

Cam winced, totally expecting another beating. However, Nathaniel pulled him into a tight embrace. When Cam realized he wanted the hatred over the compassion, his stomach dropped. "I'm sorry, I'm sorry, I'm sorry," he babbled repeatedly as his big brother sobbed in his arms.

"I don't know you anymore." Nathaniel pushed Cam away and left.

Cam walked off in the opposite direction. He just needed to get the hell out of there before he ran into someone else. He made it as far as the lobby before he literally, ran into someone else. He instinctively wrapped his arms around that someone to prevent them from falling and was shocked to feel the soft curves of a female.

"Oh, I am so sorry," she exclaimed as her deep green eyes widened in embarrassment. "I am such a klutz."

"That's all right," he replied as he drank in every inch of her with his gaze, from her deep red hair right down to the dainty ankles peeking out from under her white dress. "You're Haniel's sister, aren't you?"

"Yes, my name is Amadeaha, remember? We met at your house, although I must say you have changed a little bit."

"What can I say? I've been eating my spinach." She let out a small laugh that seemed to dance over his skin like raindrops. He even found himself smiling back at her despite his crappy mood.

"You can let me go now. I don't think we have to worry about me falling anymore," she informed with a mischievous twinkle in her eyes.

"Yeah, right. Sorry about that." Once he released her, he expected her to run away, however she continued to stand there and smile. He noticed that Jehel was off to the side, with another male, both of them giving him an angry glare.

"I'm afraid my father and Uncle Jehel don't approve of me talking to you," she confessed.

"They probably know I'm a bad influence."

"Lucky for both of us, I don't give a rip what they think."

That last comment made him laugh for the first time since capture. She stood on tiptoe and gave him a soft kiss on his cheek. She smelled like lilacs. He'd forgotten how much he loved that smell. He had a tree that grew outside his window back on Earth. Every spring he would leave his window open just so he could smell it. "You're really going to tick them off by doing that." He tried not to notice how strained his voice sounded.

"They are just going to have to get over it. I wanted to thank you for finishing my brother's mission for him. All he had left is his honor."

She then walked away, leaving him feeling an odd emptiness. He resisted the urge to go after her. She was a female, sure, but she was an angel and he was not worthy of her anymore.

He knew now that was why he had lashed out a Bear earlier. His brother was everything he used to be, a small, geeky kid without any real responsibility. He would give anything to have the old him back. Most angels would give their hind teeth to have the power he now held, and he just wanted to turn his back on it all, but his damn honor wouldn't let him.

Like Haniel, his honor was all he had left.

EVEN THOUGH HE KNEW he shouldn't be doing it, Cam went to the neutral bar that night for his date with the succubus. He couldn't help himself, even though he was supposed to be the leader of the empaths and an archangel, the demon part of him still screamed for some release. And right now, the demon part was stronger than the angel part.

As soon as Cam entered the bar, he scanned it for danger. There were several demons seated at tables, but they didn't pay him any attention. He returned the favor by walking by them without a second glance. Several rogue angels were scattered about the place. They eyed him nervously, but after taking one look at his huge, opposing frame clad in all black and the sword strapped to his back, they all hastily turned and looked down.

"We don't want any trouble here, archangel," a demon from behind the bar called.

Cam turned to him and hissed, baring his fangs.

Startled, the bartender jumped back. The bottles behind him rattled.

"I promise to be a good, little boy," Cam growled in a deep voice.

The bartender filled a glass and pushed it toward him. "Here, it's on the house."

He eyed the drink suspiciously. "What is it?"

"Pure angel blood, female, too." The demon's hands shook.

Cam smiled to himself, pleased he was able to get that kind of reaction from others. He took off his sunglasses for the first time that day. As soon as the bartender saw his eyes, he trembled even more.

He drank the blood and was instantly lost in its sweetness. Since he was not related to the blood, it carried no thoughts or memories. Instead, it gave him an instant high as the power and lust rushed to his head. The injuries Nathaniel gave him earlier healed. The demon behind the bar looked at him with pure terror. Cam let the empath part of him soak up that emotion. For the first time in his immortal life, he found himself liking the taste of fear. He pulled out a fifty and slammed it on the bar. "Give me another."

Slender hands wrapped themselves around his chest. "I'm here for you, puppy," she purred in his ear.

He pulled her into his lap and pinned her to the bar before roughly kissing her. He felt her tongue slide into his mouth and slowly explore his fangs, perhaps reveling in what she helped create. Shielding her from view with his body, he slipped his hand under her short skirt and discovered that all that separated her from him was a tiny pair of panties. When he nudged them to the side to stroke her wet folds, she moaned loudly in his ear. Slipping one digit inside her, he brushed his thumb against her clit. With a sigh of pleasure, she started moved her hips in a slow sensual pattern. Their kissing grew more frantic as she rode his hand, her juices coating his fingers. He knew he really shouldn't be finger fucking her in the middle of a crowded bar, but it was a turn on having others watch him get her off.

"Come for me now," he commanded into her ear. She obeyed him, throwing her head back and unleashing a cry that carried across the room.

He eyed a nearby tabletop and was half tempted to throw her on top of it and have his way with her right there. He knew that she would not protest. Hell, she probably would enjoy the audience more than he would. However, he wasn't about to give more of a show to the whole bar.

He jerked her to her feet and led her to the bathroom. It was dark, dingy and filthy like the rest of the bar, but he didn't care. He had barely closed and locked the door before she was on him. She started to tear at his clothes, but he stopped her hands. "Don't rip my shirt again."

She then literally climbed up him to get to his neck.

How frigging hot was that? Wrapping her legs tightly around his waist for leverage, she sank her fangs into his neck. Hissing with pleasure, he slammed her back against the wall and ripped her underwear off. Freeing himself from his pants, he thrust into her. She never let go of his neck, feeding on him as he pounded into her furiously. If he closed his eyes tight enough, he could imagine it wasn't her he was with. Instead, he was with a female angel, one with deep red hair and flashing green eyes.

After a few moments, Lilith rolled her head back with a moan. "I have never tasted better," she panted. Her bright eyes glowed eerily. "Your blood makes me feel so alive. It's so strong and yet so sweet. Do you know what they are calling you? The Empath King. I'm fucking one of the most powerful angels in Heaven."

He didn't answer her because he was a little too occupied with her body. Looking down at the column of her white throat, he licked his lips. The urge to bite her was so strong his fangs ached. He remembered Abdiel warning him not to drink demon blood and tried to fight his thirst. But as he climaxed, he lost control. With an animalistic roar, he pierced her throat with his teeth and started to drink deeply.

It wasn't until much later that he left the bathroom. Lilith was still in there humming softly to herself and covered with even more bite marks than he was. Slipping on his sunglasses, he marched down the center of the bar like he owned it. He mentally sent out a challenge and three demons fell for the bait. As he got to the door, he felt them follow. He smiled to himself as he walked outside.

He almost stopped dead in his tracks when someone nudged his mind. Whipping around, he halfway expected to see Douma or Forcas there. They weren't. Deciding he must be losing his mind, he went outside and waited for the three demons. He was happy to hear them coming out. He so needed a good fight.

CAM WALKED QUIETLY THROUGH the house trying not to wake anyone up. He didn't feel like explaining where he was all night. He winced from his many bruises because he had taken a beating. He'd still won the fight and pummeled the crap out of those three demons. Still, his eye was swollen shut and, since he couldn't very well ask Gabi to heal it and the thought of drinking his own family's blood repulsed him, a good old fashioned ice bag was going to have to do the trick.

Just as he was closing the freezer door, the kitchen light turned on.

Busted! He turned around and saw Abdiel leaning against the counter. Deciding to play it casual, Cam slipped on his sunglasses and smiled. "Hi, Abdiel," he said brightly. "You're up kind of late."

Abdiel wasn't fooled for one moment. He walked over and pulled off Cam's sunglasses. Turning the younger angel's face side to side, he examined the bruises and scrapes. When he saw all the bite marks, he cursed in displeasure. "Where did you go?" Abdiel snapped.

"Some neutral bar." Cam yelped in pain when a concerned finger probed his injured eye. "I wasn't the only archangel there, you know."

"That still doesn't make it all right." Abdiel pushed the ice pack to the other angel's face. "Those places are dicey at best."

"I dunno, it kind of reminded me of the tavern Luke found Han Solo in."

"How did you get all the bite marks?" he shot back sarcastically.

"Rough sex," he winced as the words slipped out.

"Damn it, Cam. What are you thinking? Did she give you the shiner, too?"

"No, I picked a fight with a few demons after I was done with her. Look, why are you riding me so hard about this? If one of my brothers showed up like this, you wouldn't say one damn thing."

"Your brothers don't have a huge bounty on their head," Abdiel said between clenched teeth. "What if Douma and Forcas had been there? We can't afford to lose you."

"Yeah, wouldn't want to lose a member of the freaking Order. That would just be tragic."

"This has nothing to do with the Order. We can't afford to lose you because we all care for you too much. I know what they did to you down there. I could hear it. It would destroy me if I knew that you were going through that again."

"I can take care of myself, Abdiel. You just have to trust me on that one." Cam started to go up the stairs, but hesitated, tapping his hand on the banister. "Abdiel, don't think I've forgotten what you did for me in Hell. If you hadn't come to me, I would have been lost. I also wanted to thank you for not telling anyone about how close I came to turning."

"I just figured that was between you and me and could stay that way. No one would understand everything that went on there."

"Why are you up so late? Is it because you have nightmares, too?" He knew the other angel didn't respond because they both already knew the answer. There were no pleasant dreams in their future. That possibility was smashed the minute they had entered Hell.

Cam went into his room and stopped dead in his tracks. On the bed were several shopping bags full of clothes. Opening the card that sat on top, he smiled. *I knew you were wanting some new duds so I took the liberty of picking these out. Love ya, Rachael.* He moved the bags over enough to lie down.

He tried to sleep, but every time he drifted off, a memory of his torture came rushing back leaving him drenched in sweat and out of breath. Cam stared off into the darkness, cursing himself for being weak. He was supposed to be a strong, macho archangel and here he was wishing that Ana would come and comfort him like she used to when he was a small child.

Just slow down your breathing and try to focus. It will help the panic pass, a male voice directed in his head.

Cam sat up, shocked. The voice almost sounded like Abdiel's yet it was slightly different. It couldn't be the archangel though. He was the only one that could initiate a telepathic link besides Rachael. *Crap, Douma and Forcas must be messing with my mind.*

No, I am not Douma or Forcas. The voice was angry now. *I'm insulted that you would think that. My demon brothers are complete assholes.*

Cam laughed aloud. *They're not on my MySpace Friend's list either. So who in the hell are you?*

I'm not in Hell anymore, thank you very much, and I'm Appolion.

No frigging way. Cam's mouth dropped open in shock. *No offense, but why are you contacting me and not Rachael?*

My family is so dysfunctional that we should be on the Springer Show, Appolion replied dryly. *I saw you earlier tonight at the bar and immediately sensed you were a telepath. I know you live with Rachael and Abdiel. I was hoping you could answer some questions for me.*

So that had been the mental push he felt earlier. Cam settled back on the bed and told him everything. He explained the Order, told him about his and Rachael's powers and how Abdiel fit in. He even divulged what happened to him in Hell. Appolion listened thoughtfully and even interjected some humorous observations of his own. Cam slowly began to like and trust him and soon was telling him about his transformation. Since Appolion was trapped between both worlds, too, he completely understood.

We have been talking for hours and you have not tried to talk me into coming back. Appolion seemed surprised.

Hell. Cam sent back, *if it weren't for the vows I took as an archangel, I would be tempted to join you in exile. I feel like a freak most of the time, even around my sister and brothers. They would probably be relieved if I left.*

I need to hit the sack. Appolion yawned in his head. *I have to work tomorrow. I'm going to leave the link up though so you can talk to me anytime you want. Just you though, tell Rachael not to even try reaching me. Even though you claim she and Abdiel are cool, I am just not ready to deal with any of my family yet.*

After what you shared with me about your parents and brothers, I don't blame you. Cam smiled when he imagined how pissed Rachael was going to be. *Thank you for letting me vent. If you ever need me for anything, let me know.*

Chapter Seven

GABI WOKE UP AND INSTANTLY REACHED OVER TO ABDIEL'S SIDE OF THE bed only to find it cold and empty. She sat up and saw him standing in front of their bedroom window, a dagger in his hand. The soft, early morning light cast harsh shadows across his face as he scanned the street in front of their house. "Did you sleep at all last night?"

"Sure, I just woke up not too long ago." He never looked away from the window.

"You're lying to me. You've not even taken your boots off, let alone come to bed."

"Yeah, well, sleep is overrated anyhow," he snapped, still refusing to turn around.

Gabi juggled her options in her head. She did not know the best way to approach him. She was afraid that if she pushed him too hard, that he would just shut her out. However, she was also afraid that if she didn't help him face his fears that they would take over both of their lives. She finally decided on the latter option. It was time for her mate to talk about what happened. "What was Hell like?" She pretended not to notice his annoyed expression.

"It was Hell. What do you think it was like?"

"Were you and Cam kept together? Did you, at least, have each other?"

"No, they separated us almost from the first day. I could hear him while they were torturing him though."

She felt a small sense of victory when he came and sat on the bed with her.

"It was horrible, hearing him suffering and not being able to go help him."

"Did they keep you chained up the entire time?" When he only nodded, she continued. "They didn't feed you guys at all, did they? I saw the way Cam attacked his food when the healers first brought it to him."

"No, I only got a couple of meals some female demon left for me. You want to hear something real pathetic? At the time, I actually thought it might have been my mother."

"You may be right." She reached over and stroked his hair. "Did you know Appolion wasn't exiled? Your mother just told him that. She really set him free."

"Where did you hear that?"

"Beelzebub rubbed it into Rachael to hurt her feelings. Unfortunately, it worked."

A brief flash of anger went through his dark eyes. "I wish he'd stayed long enough during the battle so I could have paid him back for that one. I noticed both he and my brothers hightailed it out of there as soon as things got hairy."

"Do you know why they decided to fixate so much on Cam? Was it Douma and Forcas that messed with his mind?"

"No, it was Mammon who mind raped Cam. He decided to make him his *special project*."

As soon as she heard Mammon's name, her stomach flipped over in fear. Every angel knew about the most powerful and ruthless demon in Hell. No wonder Cam had been so damaged when they got him back. "How did he find out Michael was his uncle? Did Mammon tell him?"

"Cam won't admit it, but his mother came to him and comforted him while he was down there. She told him. Mammon just had fun rubbing in the fact that Michael never wanted to claim him."

"How horrible." She remembered how the other Lehor's reacted to the news. "How could no one have known they were related?"

"You forget how disorganized things were in the angel world back then. We were the first class of students to be formally educated in the school, remember? It wasn't until after the fall of Lucifer that the council was even formed. Most angel families didn't really even know each other. They all lived their own separate lives. The few angels that did know the truth about Michael probably knew they better keep their mouths shut."

"Until Jehel opened his big trap," Gabi spat venomously. "The little maggot loved the reaction he got from Ana and the boys."

"That's okay. He got his. Did you see his face when the emapths made Cam their leader? He looked about ready to explode. This means Cam will be sitting on the council now."

"Cam's got a whole lot of responsibility all of a sudden. I hope he can handle that coupled with everything else that has happened to him."

"Ana will help him with the leadership stuff. She's good at that sort of thing."

She noticed the dark circles under his eyes. She doubted if he had slept more than a couple hours since his return home. The few times he let his guard down enough to sleep, nightmares woke him. "Are your dreams about what they did to Cam?" she asked gently.

"Sometimes," he admitted. "Other times I dream about what might happen in the future if we don't stop it."

"Stop what?"

"That super demon Rachael told us about. She was right. It's real and it's going to come for us all."

"You need to sleep, Abdiel. You look terrible."

"I don't know if I can anymore. I worry that if I fall asleep I'm going to wake up back in Hell."

"Here, lay down with me," she urged. "I'll stay awake and watch over you. I'll make sure you don't go anywhere."

"I'm fine, honestly," he protested, even as he let her pull him down.

Gabi put his head in her lap and brushed her fingers through his hair. He fell asleep within a couple of minutes and she kept her promise to him. She sat there and watched over him.

THEY'D BEEN SITTING AT the kitchen table eating lunch when Cam finally rolled out of bed and joined them. As soon as Gabi saw him, she knew he'd been up to no good. He had a nice black eye he made no attempt to hide in addition to a split lip. Several scratches ran down the side of his face before they disappeared into his black turtleneck shirt. He was pale and his hands shook as reached for the plate of sandwiches.

"I talked to Appolion last night," Cam said casually.

Rachael and Abdiel's heads snapped up like someone slapped them.

Cam seemed unaffected by their reaction. He just sat there and ate, acting like everything was normal.

"What do you mean you talked with Appolion last night?" Abdiel finally asked.

"He called me on the physic friend's network line."

Rachael jumped up and slugged his arm. "Why didn't you come and get me?"

He winced. "I got a little sidetracked." Cam had the good graces to look guilty. "You know how I can get a little chatty sometimes."

"Just how long did you talk with him?" Gabi asked, more than a little annoyed.

"I dunno." He shrugged his shoulders. "Couple hours."

That was the final straw. She was going to strangle him. First, he'd taken off last night without telling them where he was going. Then, he stayed out all night raising hell and now this. Not to mention he was trying to hide numerous bite marks. As soon as he walked into the kitchen with his black eye, she scanned him for more injuries. She was no idiot either. She knew how he had gotten chewed on, that little perv. Now he was sitting there admitting he had spent hours talking to someone that claimed to be Appolion without any real proof the voice was telling the truth.

"You just can't talk to anyone that pops into your head." Abdiel looked ticked as well. "You can't be sure it was Appolion. It could have been anyone."

"It was your brother," Cam said firmly. "He sounds almost like you, Abdiel."

"Why would he contact you?" Gabi shook her head in confusion. "More importantly, why now, after all this time?"

"He saw me last night and figured out who I was." Cam said evasively. "I think he's reaching out now because the demons have been trying to capture him lately. I guess up until then, they pretty much ignored him since he left."

"What exactly did you tell him?" Abdiel he leaned back and crossed his arms.

"Everything," Cam admitted, refusing to look at Abdiel.

Gabi groaned. She was really getting sick of Cam's impulsive behavior.

"Did he tell you where he's been all this time?" Rachel frowned. It was obvious she was more than a little hurt that her twin had not contacted her.

Cam shook his head. "He refused. He's afraid I would tell you guys."

"Would you?" A month ago, Gabi would not have asked that question, but she didn't know what Cam was capable of now.

Her doubt seemed to hurt him. "Of course I would Gabi. I told you he contacted me, didn't I? Just because I've done a few stupid things doesn't mean I'd deliberately hurt Rachael and Abdiel."

Gabi instantly felt guilty. Even though he was going through tough times, Cam was still Cam. He still had his sweet, tender heart. He just hid it beneath layers of shame, guilt and hate now.

"Did he tell you why he won't connect with me?" Rachael looked completely crestfallen.

"He says he doesn't want anything to do with his family. After what his brothers and parents did to you guys, he's a little bitter." Cam gave Rachael a little smile and reached out to squeeze her hand. "Personally, I think he was trying to protect you. He went through a lot of crap, and he was trying to shield you from it."

Gabi got up and hugged Rachel, her heart breaking along with the female. If what Cam said was true, then part of her understood why Appolion would cut off contact with his twin. Their link had been so strong Rachael would have suffered alongside him during his abuse much like Barakiel had with Cam. Another part of her wanted to slug him for hurting her so much. Until they had brought her home, Rachael had been alone in the world.

"Do you think you could talk him into coming home?" Abdiel asked.

"Right now, no. Douma and Forcas have him scared of Michael and you. They told him you guys are hunting him down."

Gabi was so sick of hearing those two demon names. Come on, they really needed to get a hobby and not one that involved breeding a super demon.

"What has he been doing all this time?" Rachael obviously was trying to be strong and hold her tears back. "How has he been surviving?"

"He's very good at shielding his presence from both demons and angels."

When Cam mentioned that, Gabi remembered that's what he had done for them on the first day of the riot.

"He's been living like a human for centuries. He even works human jobs. He's been a doctor, policeman, firefighter and a paramedic just to name a few."

"That would explain the paramedic uniform he was wearing," Gabi mused.

"For someone that claims to not to be an angel, he sure seems to be very protective of humans," Abdiel said hopefully. "Every job he's ever had has been geared toward protecting or healing."

"I agree." Cam nodded. "He has a lot of guilt and feels like he needs to do penance. No demon would feel that way."

Gabi reached over and tilted Cam's face toward her. He scowled, but made no move to stop her. She touched his black eye before she pulled down the collar of his shirt to look at the bite marks. She cursed softly under her breath when she saw how vicious they were. She had seen succubus bites before, but never this many. "Is this what I think it is, Cam?" She looked up and met his gaze. "A penance?"

"I don't know, maybe," Cam admitted with a small shrug.

"What for? You did nothing wrong."

He shifted his gaze away from hers. "We all have sins to pay for. I'm no different."

"What could you have possibly done to deserve this?" her voice cracked. "This succubus was downright brutal with you."

"You would be surprised at what I'm capable of."

"Was it the same succubus that came to you in Hell, Lilith?"

"It's not like I keep a little black book filled with demon names."

Abdiel ran his hand through his dark hair as he heaved a deep sigh. "You need to be careful. I don't trust that female demon at all. You should have heard the way she went on in Hell. She's got a weird fixation with you."

"So what if she does?" Cam responded quietly as he looked down at the table. "It's not like any female angels are going to be lining up to be with me. What female would want to be my mate now?"

"I had plenty of them asking me about you after your naming ceremony," Gabi argued. It was true, too. She had to leave the hallway just to get away from them.

"They're only interested in me because I was just named leader of the empaths. They don't even care about me because I'm, well...me. You understand what I'm trying to say?"

Gabi did. She couldn't count the times males had approached her in the past just because of her position within Heaven. It had hurt every time to know that they wanted her power, not her. "If you want me to heal you, just let me know." She instinctively knew he would refuse any help from her.

"I'll be fine." He downed the rest of his sandwich in one hungry gulp and got up. "I'm going to the gym."

"I'm coming, too." Rachael popped up and ran to join him.

"No zapping each other," Abdiel yelled. "Weapons and fists only."

They both groaned in protest, bringing a smile to Abdiel's lips. It soon faded as he stared down at the ground deep in thought.

Gabi knew he was replaying the conversation in his head. She also knew he was upset to hear Appolion was afraid of him. She climbed onto his lap and put her head on his chest, trying to give him some comfort. "It sounds like your baby brother is as stubborn as you are," she teased.

"I'm not stubborn," he protested.

She laughed right in his face. "You are the most stubborn male I have ever met." She softened the comment by kissing his neck.

"I don't think we're ever going to get him back," he sighed.

"Don't give up on him yet." She reached up and brushed the lock of hair off his forehead. "He did contact Cam after all, and he did it because he knew he lived with you. That's a big step forward."

"Great, just what we need," he drawled. "Two males with a serious guilt complex lamenting together. They'll probably form a rock band and sing sappy ballads."

"You got to wonder why Appolion decided to come to Detroit. Personally, I think you and Rachael are drawing him here. He may be scared of you, but he still wants to be close."

"He's out there all alone, Gabi." Abdiel played with her fingers. "He's just as hunted as we are, and he has no one to protect him. At least we have each other."

"As long as you and Cam don't go running off and play hero on your own again."

"I promise no more stupid stunts." He kissed the corner of her mouth before holding her so tight it almost hurt. "I can't stand to go through being apart from you again."

She wiggled her hips in his lap, smiling when she felt him respond. He slipped his hand under her shirt and nudged her black, lacy bra up so he could cup her breast. When he softly feathered her nipple with his thumb, she arched her back and let out a soft whimper. He kissed her long, slender neck just the way she liked. Grabbing, his dark hair tight in her hands, she tried to pull him closer, even as she did that wiggle thing again against his cock. He unzipped her pants and his hand softly caressed her already wet flesh.

"I need you now," she declared. Every since he came home, they hadn't been able to get enough of each other. It was as if they were making up for lost time.

Getting up, they stumbled their way to the closest room, never breaking off their kiss. It was the office. A large oak desk occupied the center of the room. It was huge, more than large enough to accommodate both of them. He shut the door behind them and locked it. "Strip," he commanded. His lips curled up into a rakish smile.

With a small giggle, she obeyed him, shedding her clothes in record speed. He did the same thing, baring his muscular body for her appraisal. She was pleased to notice he no longer tried to hide his tattoo from her.

Grabbing her by the shoulders, he spun her around and gently bent her over the edge of the desk. "Hold on and close your eyes," he ordered as he ran a finger down her spine, making her shiver. "If you disobey me, I'll stop."

Whimpering with desire, she did as he asked, closing her eyes and gripping the edge of the desk so tightly, the wood bit into her fingers. The surface felt cool against her bare flesh and teased her nipples. Her breath came out in pants as she waited and waited for him to do something. He kept her in suspense and that only increased her desire as she imagined the ways he planned on pleasuring her.

Just when she thought she couldn't wait any longer, his tongue caressed her inner thigh before traveling up further. A shriek of pleasure burst from her lips as his velvet touch caressed her clit in slow sensual paths. Shocked, she let go of the desk and opened her eyes. He instantly stopped.

"You're not obeying me, Princess." He blew on her swollen flesh, the cold air teasing her even more.

"Sorry, I'll obey," she whimpered. "Don't stop." Closing her eyes, she held the desk again. As soon as she did, he resumed his sweet torture. His tongue speared inside her before slurping up her fluid. He devoured her like she was his last meal. Teasing all parts of her flesh with his lips, tongue and teeth, leaving her sweaty and weak with desire. Her hips gyrated against his face and, even though she was embarrassed by her wanton behavior, she couldn't stop herself.

When she came, it was so intense she couldn't hold back her screams of pleasure. He continued to love her with his mouth until she came twice more. She bit her lip to hold back the loudest of them, not wanting the others to know what they were up to, but it was hard. He pulled away and she waited with baited breath to see what he planned next. Gabi jumped when the tip of his erection pushed against her entrance. She waited for him to plunge into her, but it didn't. Instead, he teased her by barely brushing against her. She thrust her hips back, but he pulled back, not taking the bait.

"Abdiel. Please."

"Please, what?"

She let out a growl of frustration and thrust her hips back again. "I need you."

"You need what?" His cock entered her, but just barely before he pulled it out again.

"I need you inside me. Now stop teasing me," she snarled.

"You're cute when you get angry." Gripping her hip for leverage, he finally thrust all the way into her.

She let out a gasp as he filled her. Gabi started to open her eyes, but remembered his warning and squeezed them tightly. The last thing she wanted now was for him to stop.

"I love you so much, Princess." He started to make love to her at a fast urgent pace.

Gabi urged him on by tilting her backside up so she could take him in even deeper. His balls slapped against her clit, causing ripples of pleasure to dance down her body. His grip on her tightened as he got closer to the edge. She started to thrust back, meeting his halfway. With a loud groan he came, his hot seed spurting inside of her. After a few more strokes, she joined him. She screamed so loud there was no way Cam and Rachael didn't hear her, but she didn't give a damn anymore. She was so overcome with desire that all her inhibitions were gone.

Afterward, they both stayed in place as they caught their breath. He was still inside her and she could feel him getting hard again. She smiled, eager for their next round. Something in the other room hit the wall so hard the entire house shook, followed by a thud that sounded suspiciously like a body hitting the floor.

"Ouch! Damn it, Rachael, Abdiel said no zapping," Cam yelled from the gym.

Gabi laughed as they pulled apart, the mood totally spoiled. "When this is all over, we need to get away for a few days."

MUCH TO RACHAEL'S DELIGHT, she got to go patrolling with them that night. Much to her dismay, big brother Abdiel took one look at her racy outfit and made her change. It was dark before they started slowly walking the streets, with Cam in the lead scanning for demons. They all had their weapons out and ready. Rachael still had Abdiel's old sword. He offered to have a new one made for her, but she refused. Gabi could tell it touched him that she wanted to use something that had been his.

"Hey, Cam," Rachael called out after several minutes. "It's my turn to scan for demons."

Cam gave her a conflicted look and Gabi could almost hear the hamster wheel in his head spinning as he mulled it over. He'd always been the one to search for the demons. Gabi knew he felt it his responsibility to lead the way into battle.

"But I'm the empath," he finally said in a lame voice that was very close to sounding like the old Cam.

Rachael made a big show of rolling her eyes. "I'm very good at tracking demons. I've had a lot of experience in that area, in case you forgot."

"You heard the lady," Abdiel called, a small smile playing on his full lips. "Switch places."

Cam sighed before shrugging his shoulders. He came and stood by Gabi.

She reached up and took off his sunglasses, ignoring the irritated look he gave at her actions. "Quit hiding your eyes from us," she ordered as she slipped the glasses in her jacket. "Personally, I happen to think your eyes are beautiful."

"I agree," Rachael responded never taking her gaze off the street ahead of her. "Do you know they sell contacts on the internet that make humans eyes look like that?"

"Great." Cam smiled, showing he really wasn't offended. "It's good to know the internet likes me. It's such a reliable source after all."

"You should try signing up for a dating service on it," Abdiel added. "Maybe that would get you to leave that succubus alone."

"Yeah, I could just see the profile now." Cam held his hand up and cocked his head to the side, like he could almost see the ad. "Single male angel with psychotic disposition seeks like-minded female."

"Don't forget to add she needs to bring a fire extinguisher on the first date." Abdiel clapped Cam on the back as they laughed.

Rachael stopped walking and started jumping up and down in excitement, her blue eyes practically glowing. "Oh goodie, there are demons nearby."

Gabi couldn't help but smile at her sister-in-law's enthusiasm. "Come on, boys," she said. "Let's go find those demons so Rachel can zap 'em."

APPOLION WAS WALKING THROUGH the city patrolling, which was totally stupid because he'd never gone out and actively hunted demons before. He'd always kept his head down and only fought when absolutely necessary. Yet here he was, acting like he was some lame archangel protecting the world from evil.

He had been perfectly fine until Abdiel came to Earth. Appolion had known the instant his big brother left Heaven and he'd been drawn to Detroit like some pathetic loser. He cursed the small part of him that wanted to run to his brother, hoping for love and acceptance. The last time he had tried that with a family member, he ended up bitch slapped, laughed at and spit on.

He really meant to leave Detroit once Abdiel had seen him, then Rachael showed up. He missed his twin so much it hurt. Every time he felt her call him, it had been torture not to respond to her, but he didn't want her to know what happened to him or what he'd been forced to do. He was too ashamed to show her that side. He would still give anything just to be with her for five minutes. When he had cut off any contact with Rachael, it was like he lost a piece of himself.

When Abdiel asked him to come home with him and his female, Appolion almost agreed. He was so sick of living all alone with only the occasional human for a friend he was willing to face Michael. But he'd been too scared to leave the life he lived all these centuries. What would Abdiel think of him if he knew about all the things the demons had done to him? What if he couldn't enter Heaven after being tainted by Hell? What if he really was a demon even though he fought turning?

He knew he shouldn't have contacted Cam. It was just when he saw him at the bar and remembered the angel lived with his siblings, Appolion seized on the opportunity. He still could not believe they actually thought he was part of their stupid super hero team. He may be a telepath, but he didn't have any powers like Rachael or Cam. *Nada, zip, nothing, what you see is what you get.*

Appolion stopped dead in his tracks when he felt something breathing on the back of his neck. He whipped his guns out of his waistband as he spun around. He let out a foul curse as five Hounds from Hell greeted him with snarls. The demon dogs fanned out, surrounding him. "Just flash out of here, you idiot," he muttered under his breath. He knew he couldn't do that though. If he didn't send these demons back to Hell, they would find some innocent humans to prey on.

He started to hum, then stopped and rolled his eyes when he realized it was *Who Let the Dogs Out?* He sighed. *Okay, it's official folks, I'm losing it.* The Hounds continued to slowly circle him, but they made no move to attack. He kept his guns aimed and cocked even as he grew more apprehensive from their behavior.

Several throwing stars flew out from the night and buried themselves into his body. Instantly, Appolion's entire body felt like it was burning from the inside out. He furiously dug at the stars trying to rip them out. Several different voices started to scream and cry in his head. Clamping his hands over his ears, he tried to shut them up, but it was useless. The tormented wailing continued. Remembering what Cam told him, Appolion realized he had just been poisoned with demon blood.

He fell onto the street, lying on his back, as he writhed around in agony. Someone walked up and placed their foot on his chest, pinning him to the ground. He barely noticed them until they stomped on one of the stars and ground it deeper into his body. When he saw who it was, Appolion stifled the whimper to avoid showing his fear.

It was Forcas and Douma was right behind him. They both smirked.

Rachael, help me. He knew he had no right to call out to her, but he could not go back to Hell.

Appolion, is that really you? she responded.

The soothing concern in her voice gave him some comfort, despite the fact those damn voices were still shrieking in his head. *Please, Rachael, don't let them take me back there.* He knew he was being pathetic by begging his sister to come save him, but he was too desperate to care.

Don't worry, we're coming.

Her reassuring words helped calm him down some. "Get your fucking foot off me, you son of a bitch!" Appolion yelled to Forcas. His brother ground the weapon even deeper into his chest causing Appolion to groan in pain.

"Look what the dogs dragged in, Douma," the demon said. "Here we were, looking for Abdiel and his crew and we get a little bonus. You always were good at hiding your stench, Appolion."

"You know you're both still dickheads. Some things never change."

Forcas kicked him in the side of the head. "You're still the same cocky, little shit, too. You'll soon change your tune when you find yourself in your old cell in Hell."

"Please, Forcas, don't take me back to Hell." Appolion cringed at the pathetic groveling tone his voice had taken. "If you have any compassion in your heart, you'll do me a favor and destroy me instead."

Even as he asked the question, he knew it was hopeless. His brothers would never give up a chance to watch him suffer. They were going to take him back to Hell. His life was once again going to be filled with torture and abject loneliness. The poison pulsated through his body. He arched his back as another wave of pain hit him. Foam seeped from his mouth. His vision clouded as the screaming voices threatened to split his skull.

A flurry of arrows rained down, hitting the Hounds. The demon dogs howled in pain as his brothers started to curse. Appolion lifted his head and was shocked by what he saw. Four tall warriors walked toward them. There were two males and two females, and they were all dressed in black leather. As they marched side by side down the center of the street, they made formable sight.

Appolion smiled when he recognized Rachael, Cam, Abdiel and Gabi. His sister had not let him down, and judging by the expression on the other angels' faces, his demon brothers were in big trouble. He suddenly felt like a little kid being saved from the neighborhood bullies. "My big brother is here and he is so going to beat you up."

Of course, Douma and Forcas didn't get the joke. Forcas just gave him another swift kick before they turned and got ready for battle.

Chapter Eight

*C*RAP, CRAP, CRAP, DOUBLE CRAP. ABDIEL GROWLED IN ANGER. Rachael had been right, Appolion was in a world of trouble and, as usual The Brothers Grimm were behind it. He was lying on the street yelling in pain as Forcas stood over him stomping him in the chest. Abdiel heard Rachael curse foully behind him. While part of him was appalled his sweet, little sister knew such language, another part of him totally agreed with her. That was their Appolion that was being treated like he was nothing more than a cockroach being stepped on.

Gabi fired her crossbow at Forcas causing the demon to jump away from Appolion in order to avoid being hit. At the same time, Cam threw several small throwing daggers at Douma. The demon brothers ran in the same direction as the Hounds. Retreating, for now.

As soon as the demon was no longer pinning him down, Appolion rolled to his knees and put his head between his hands. He made no move to stand up. Instead, he rocked back and forth and moaned.

Damn it, the bastards poisoned him. "Gabi, do you have the antidote with you?" Abdiel asked.

Gabi nodded, her bright green eyes flashing with anger when she saw all the throwing stars sticking out of Appolion. Blood was slowly oozing into his dark blue tee shirt that had the name of a human firefighting company stamped on the front.

Appolion obviously hadn't lost his sense of humor, however. He raked them over with his gaze before throwing out snidely, "In all that frigging leather you look like rejects from the Hell's Angels biker gang."

Cam snickered as they ran to help his smart mouthed ass.

Rachael started to remove all the stars, letting out small cry of distress with each one she yanked free. When she saw the wounds left behind, she touched each area lovingly.

Appolion flinched at her touch, but let her continue. They all heard the snarls indicating the Hounds were coming back.

"You guys help Appolion," Cam said. "Rachael and I will be doggy bait."

"Douma and Forcas are still close," Appolion gasped between clenched teeth.

"That's the story of our life, big boy," Cam said drolly. "Don't worry. Rachael and I can handle ourselves."

Appolion managed a ghost of a smile before another wave of pain hit him. He barked, "Take my guns with you. They're over there on the ground."

Cam walked over and picked them up. He handed one to Rachael before giving a dubious look. "What good are these going to do? Human weapons never work against demons."

"The bullets are infused with holy water. It's one of the few things that can take down a Hound from Hell." Appolion wiped away the blood that dripped from his nose.

"I think you've been watching too many late night horror movies, little bro," Abdiel said doubtfully. "That stuff doesn't work against demons. It's just a myth."

"Have you ever tried it before?" Appolion shuddered when Gabi wiped his face. "Trust me, they work. I buy them from the black market."

Cam shrugged before he started running toward where the Hound's howls were coming from.

Rachael shot a worried look at her twin before she followed. After a few steps, she stopped and turned around. She ran back to Appolion and threw her arms around him.

He grunted in pain when she slammed into him, but he still hugged her back.

She pulled away and left to help Cam.

Abdiel saw her wipe away a tear with her finger. "Come on, Appolion. We need to get you out of the street before Forcas and Douma come back." He went to help his brother up.

Appolion avoided his hands and struggled to his feet by himself. He managed to stumble a couple of steps before he crumpled to the ground.

Abdiel let out an aggravated sigh at his brother's stubbornness.

Gabi shot him an I-told-you-so look.

"Fuck, this hurts," Appolion snarled. He looked over at Gabi and cringed. "Sorry about that, Abdiel. I'll try to watch my language around your female."

"I'LL MAKE SURE TO cover my ears next time," Gabi said sarcastically. She grabbed him by the back of the collar and dragged him behind the shelter of a dumpster.

"I forget how strong female angels are," Appolion gasped. "I've been living around humans too long."

Gabi saw him foam at the mouth again and realized he was getting worse. She pulled the antidote out of her pocket and tapped the side of the syringe. When she rolled up Appolion's shirt, he pulled his arm back, his eyes wide with fear.

"What the hell is that?" His voice was horse with panic.

Abdiel knelt down so he could look his brother in the eye. "It's just the antidote. I know it's hard, but you just have to trust us. We would never hurt you. If you can't believe in me, then believe in Rachael. If I so much as harmed a hair on your head, she would zap me into the next century."

They locked gazes for several tense moments before Appolion reluctantly nodded his head. "Aren't you going to wipe the injection site with alcohol?" he asked incredulously.

Gabi rolled her eyes. "You're immortal, remember? I could lick the needle and nothing would happen to you." She injected him before he could change his mind.

He laid back and seemed to relax a bit as the antidote started to work its way through his system.

Abdiel went to the front of the dumpster to watch out for Douma and Forcas. Off in the distance, a gunshot resounded.

"Whoo hoo!" Cam's voice echoed through the streets. "Take that you demented, twisted Lassie wannabe."

"I guess holy water does work after all." Gabi stared laughing.

Appolion joined her. "I should go see if they need help." He started to get up.

Gabi stopped him. "No, you're still wounded. You need to be healed and this time I'm not letting you get away until I've helped you," she said firmly.

"I've had worse, honestly."

"I know you have." She gave him a tender smile. "You still carry some of those injuries. Let me take those away for you."

"I'm not worth the hassle." Appolion looked down.

Even in the dark, she could still see his face redden with shame. "Of course you are." Gabi rubbed his arm. When he did not pull away, she took that as a good sign. "You're Abdiel's brother, that's enough for me."

"So are Forcas and Douma," there was a small hitch in his voice.

"You and Rachael are nothing like Douma and Forcas."

That seemed to convince Appolion enough to allow her to lower him onto his back again. "It's all a waste of your time," he still argued. "If you're doing this because you think I'm part of that Order thing, you may as well save it. I don't have any mad skills like Rachael or Cam. All I have is telepathy and telekinesis and even those powers aren't as strong as theirs."

"What about that thing you did to the demon that made it choke?"

"Oh you mean the Darth Vader thing?" He shook his head ruefully. "That was just a jazzed up form of telepathy. I just made the demon think it couldn't breathe."

"You forget you can also shield your presence from others."

"That was just a survival mechanism." He sighed when she gave him a doubtful look. "I figured out how to do that little trick when I was real young. It's better if you go unnoticed in Hell."

She smiled sadly at him before she put her hand over his eyes and put him in a relaxed state. It would have been better to put him completely asleep, but she only had a thin thread of trust from him to begin with. Somehow, she knew if she knocked him unconscious and dragged him back to the house, it wouldn't be the start of a good friendship. The demons would be coming back soon, so she had to work quickly and get as much done in the little time she had.

Gabi closed her eyes and slipped into a trance. Her heart lurched when she realized just how damaged he was. Numerous wounds were scattered throughout his body, both internal and external. Some were so vicious and old she didn't know how the poor angel survived so long. The pain must have been horrific.

She paused when she felt the energy force that was held down by his battered body. It was stronger than the ones she felt in Rachael and Cam, much stronger. Appolion was as powerful as his twin had predicted. He just didn't know it yet. She hesitated only a moment before she healed the area around his energy field, releasing his powers. He was in for one hell of a shock. He may not want to be a hero, but he was.

Gabi worked fast knowing that time was running out. She was a great healer. Unfortunately, Appolion was one of the worst cases she had ever seen. She still tried to be as meticulous as possible. Working from the inside out, she fused together flesh and bone trying to make him whole again. A fleeting part of her wondered when he had ever been whole. With an aggravated growl, she pulled out as she sensed Douma and Forcas coming down the street. There was so much more that still needed to be done.

Appolion gingerly sat up.

As he flexed his shoulders, she could see his shocked expression. It was probably the first time he was able to do that without pain. Hot tears spilled unchecked down her face.

He saw them and his jaw dropped. "Nobody but Rachael has ever cried for me," he said in awe. "I'm not worth it."

"Quit saying that," she told him. "You're a wonderful angel with a pure heart, and don't even think of arguing with me about that. I was inside you, Appolion. I saw what they've done to you, and yet you never gave in and turned."

He reached out and placed his palm over her stomach. "You shouldn't be out here fighting. You're pregnant."

"No, I'm not," she argued as her breath left her. "I would know it."

"Sorry, Charlie." He grinned, showing off an adorable set of dimples. "But in case you forgot, I was born healer, too. You're definitely preggers."

"Well when you put it in such medical terms, how can I argue?" she shot back tartly. Her hand still went protectively over her stomach. With a quick search, there was no doubt in her mind, he was right. She was having Abdiel's baby

"I better go help Abdiel," he said gruffly, standing up. "Douma and Forcas are getting closer."

"Appolion," Gabi called.

He looked at her.

"Rachael wasn't the only one that wept over you. Abdiel did, I saw how he was right after your father took you to Hell. It devastated him. Then I held him in my arms while he cried over losing you again just recently. He never got over not being able to save you and Rachael." She saw a mixture of emotions pass over his face—pain, confusion and finally, hope.

He gave her a little smile, then went to help Abdiel.

ABDIEL HAD JUST UNSHEATHED his sword when Appolion came up and stood by his side. "You doing okay?" he asked his younger brother.

"Never better. Your female is a great healer." Appolion pulled out his own weapon.

Abdiel scowled when he saw its wavy blade. It was a kris and a demon one at that. "Where did you get that?" He pointed to the offending weapon.

"I lifted it off a demon I dusted." Appolion shrugged. "It's not like I can go and order a custom built weapon like you can. I have to make do with what I can get. Demons don't carry around fancy swords like you archangels."

"Oh great, I don't even want to know what other demon weapons you have tucked away, do I?"

Appolion gave him a wicked grin before he pulled out various weapons from every pocket of his blue cargo pants. There were several different types of daggers, throwing stars and a set of brass knuckles. Every single one of them was fashioned by demons.

"I've seen you fight, little brother. You're far too good of a warrior to be using weapons like that. Demons have never done quality work."

"I'm not a warrior," Appolion scowled slightly. "I'd just as soon hop into my little rabbit hole and wait for all the fireworks to be over."

"I can tell," Abdiel said sarcastically. "Everybody walks around with an arsenal that would make Steven Segal proud."

"Funny," Appolion mused. "I was trying to impress The Rock." He tilted his head up and sniffed loudly. "Do you smell singed dog hair? I think Rachael zapped herself a demon."

"She's going to be impossible to live with now," Abdiel groaned.

"Don't worry," a voice said from the darkness. Forcas came into the view, Douma at his side. "You three won't be seeing that much of each other in Hell and that's where you're going back to. I think we'll take the Empath King, too. Mammon misses him so much."

Appolion gripped his kris so tight his knuckles turned white. "Hey, Forcas. Hey, Douma," he spat their names like foul curse words. "Why don't you go take a flying fuck. Tell Mammon to take one while you're at it."

"Such language, Appolion. You're going to shock your new angel friends with a mouth like that." Douma tsked. "Of course, you've got to wonder what they would say if they knew what you did to that female angel back in Hell. You remember, I'm sure. It was right before you left us. Now what was that angel whore's name?"

"Ambriel. Her name was Ambriel," Appolion's voice shook. "You know damn well what her name was and she wasn't a whore."

"Enough of this talky talky crap," Abdiel interrupted, more to put an end to the mental torture inflicted on Appolion than anything else. "Are we going to fight or what?"

"Isn't this just epic?" Forcas laughed, showing off his jagged teeth. "Brother against brother. Human filmmakers would just love it."

Appolion started calling them every foul name in the book. When he used up all the human ones, he switched to an ancient demon language and used those, too.

Once he was finally quiet, Abdiel gave him an amused look. "Done?"

Appolion nodded.

Forcas let out a primal roar before he ran to attack Appolion. The angel met the demon halfway. Their swords met with an ear-shattering clang. Soon the two exchanged blows and parries at a rate so fast it was almost impossible to follow. Abdiel took this all in from the corner of his eye. He kept his main focus on Douma. His demon brother stretched out his arm and crooked his fingers forward, beckoning Abdiel.

The archangel shot the demon a look of disgust. "I can't believe that you just did the *come hither* thing with your hand," Abdiel said incredulously. "How lame can you be?"

Douma tried to shoot off a ball of energy, but Abdiel easily deflected it. When the demon saw his dark magic wasn't going to work, he resorted to hand-to-hand combat. That was a big mistake, fist and blades were what Abdiel was best at.

When Douma raised his sword in order to strike, Abdiel easily dodged to the side while bringing his blade across, cutting the demon's belly. Spinning around, the archangel stuck the demon's arm next with his sword.

Douma shrieked as he pulled back the stump. The demon's curved blade was on the ground, the steel glinting in the moonlight. A disembodied, bloody claw still clenched the hilt.

The demon tried to flash away, but Abdiel held up a hand and put up a shield.

Trapped, Douma yelled in terror.

Abdiel turned to help Appolion, but soon realized the angel didn't need it. Forcas was a mass of cuts and gashes. The demon tried feebly to fight back, but Appolion was too quick. Although the angel's skills were rough and undisciplined, they were a force to be reckoned with. It was easy to see how his young brother had survived all these years on his own.

When Forcas tried to retreat back to Hell, Abdiel stopped him, too.

Appolion looked up at the archangel in awe. "I didn't know you could do that." He smiled at the sight of his two demon brothers quivering in fear as they lay there helpless, side-by-side on the ground.

"Neither did I." Abdiel turned around at the sound of running footsteps.

Cam and Rachael stood there panting as they surveyed the scene. Cam gave the carnage an appraising look. Rachael's narrowed eyes remained focused on the demons as she whispered something low under her breath in demon speak with an angry hiss, her bottom lip trembling slightly.

"Hey, Cam," Appolion called out with a wicked grin, the smile never reaching his eyes. "Douma needs a hand. Ya wanna give it to him?"

Cam gasped in laughter. "He always wanted to be Satan's left hand man."

"You guys are killing me with these corny B-movie lines." Rachael tightened her grip on her sword and stepped closer to her older brother.

To Abdiel, it was clear she was terrified of her demon brothers. It was also clear she tried her best to hide it.

"What are you going to do with them, Abdiel?" Gabi asked quietly.

"I'm going to end this right here right now," Abdiel gritted between clenched teeth. "I'm sick of us always having to live in fear and always having to look over our shoulders. These two have done enough damage. Cam, Rachael, I want you guys to destroy them."

"Are you sure?" Gabi put her hand on his shoulder. "We could call in Michael. He would do it for you."

"We're your brothers," Douma yelled, his demon eyes wide with fear. "You may talk a big game, but we all know in the end your soft heart won't be able to destroy your own family."

"After what you did to Cam and Appolion, you are no longer my family," Abdiel snarled. He looked at Appolion for his consent.

The angel nodded his head before he whispered, "Please, do it. I'm begging you."

"How about you, Rachael?" Abdiel murmured. "I'll understand if you can't."

Rachael was already raising her hand. "For Cam and Appolion, I can do anything. After all the pain these two maggots have caused, it would be my honor to rid the world of their existence."

He turned to ask Cam if he could do it, but saw the question wasn't necessary. Cam's eyes were glazed over in fury and hate. He obviously hadn't forgotten it was Douma and Forcas that turned him into what he was. The only reason he probably hadn't already released his flame was out of respect for him. Abdiel looked over at Gabi.

She nodded before she said, "I love you."

"Do it," Abdiel ordered Cam and Rachael.

The two of them turned their upturned hands toward the demons. Rachael took Douma while Cam took Forcas. It was no surprise to see the cold, deadly gaze on Cam's face. However, the fact Rachael wore the same expression showed how deep she hid whatever abuse she suffered, too. Gone was the usual caring and compassionate female, now replaced by a warrior seeking vengeance.

When the energy hit the demons, it slammed them into the wall of a building. The monsters withered and screamed in agony as the energy started to rip them apart from the inside out. The two demon bodies pulsated and shifted into gruesome shapes as their cries became more pitiful. Finally, just as it seemed it would never end, Douma and Forcas blew up.

Abdiel pulled Gabi to his chest and shielded her as body parts, blood and gore rained down on all of them. When he looked up at where his two brothers had once been, there was nothing left but blackened, smoldering ashes. He sighed in relief as he realized they were finally free from Douma and Forcas and their evil.

Chapter Nine

GONE THEY WERE, GONE FOR GOOD. *NOT SENT BACK TO HELL ONLY to return again another day, but destroyed forever.* His brothers would never be able to hurt him or anyone he loved ever again. So why didn't he feel relieved? He should be happy, and instead he felt cold and dead inside.

"It's all right. It's all over," Gabi cooed in his ear. As always, she knew exactly what he was thinking and how he was feeling.

Abdiel held her tight and looked over to Rachael and Appolion. The twins were holding onto each other for dear life while she sobbed. Appolion stroked Rachael's hair and murmured to her, trying to calm her down. Meanwhile, Cam stared at the piles of ash with a sardonic smile on his face. Abdiel could see him running his tongue over one of his fangs.

"You made me into a monster and it came back to bite you in the ass," Cam whispered at the smoldering remains. He didn't seem to realize he ranted in a low voice. "You should have just left us alone, but no, you had to come and try to take me back to him. I'm never going back there, never. Mammon is never going to mind fuck me again. I won't let him."

Abdiel closed his eyes as the guilt sank in. If anyone was the monster, it was him. He destroyed his own brothers tonight. They may have been demons, but they were still family, and he ruthlessly cut them down. Worse, he used his own baby sister to do it.

"You are not a monster." Rachael picked up his thoughts and pulled away from Appolion in order to look at her older brother. "I wanted to destroy them even more than you. I've never told you what they did to me, Abdiel. I was too much of a coward."

"Ray," Appolion gave a slight shake as his face softened with concern. "You don't have to do this."

"Yes, I do." She wrapped both of her arms around herself and briefly averted her eyes before she brought them back up to capture Abdiel's gaze. "It's time he knew. When we first got to Hell, the first thing they did was separate Appolion and me. They didn't put us in cells. They put us in our own bedrooms. But with the locks on the door, the effect was the same."

"They didn't want Ray and I to have even each other," Appolion added, his voice sounded so sad and hollow like he still felt the sting of the separation. "They knew if they kept us from each other, we'd be weaker, and they were right. But they didn't know we could talk to each other telepathically. For a while, we were able to do at least that."

"Douma and Forcas would come into my room," Rachael spoke so softly it was hard to hear her. "They said it was stupid of them to go looking for a willing female when they already had one waiting for them."

"Oh dear, God, please no," Cam whispered as the impact of her words were enough to finally pull him out of his trance. "What did those two bastards do to you?"

"They would take turns with me," Rachael continued. "I tried not to cry, but it hurt so bad. After they were done, I felt so dirty. I just didn't want to even exist anymore. They came and did that to me every day for a whole year. When I tried to tell Mother, she didn't believe me. When I told Dad, he just laughed in my face and told me that if I knew what was good for me, I would keep my mouth shut. So you see, Abdiel, I had more reason than you to want them destroyed."

"Is that why you put yourself in that frozen state?" Gabi asked. "So you could get away from them?"

"I honestly don't know how I did that." Rachael shrugged.

"I did it," Appolion stated. "The entire time they were violating you, I knew it. Like I told Gabi earlier, I was born a healer so I just urged you to go to sleep. I thought if you were out of it, they would leave you alone. Unfortunately, I was only ten at the time and didn't know what I was doing so I made the urge too strong. I didn't mean to make it permanent."

"Okay, I'm just going to state the obvious here," Cam said, shaking his head. "You were only ten, dude. No freaking healer I've ever known could do anything close to that until after they reached adulthood."

"That just goes to show you how pathetic I am." Appolion snorted. "I started out with some pretty nice gifts, but they've gotten weaker as I've gotten older. I guess it sucks to be me."

"You're wrong, Appolion," Rachael argued. "I saw it in a dream and you know my dreams are never wrong. You are the Destroyer."

"Please, give me a break," Appolion gave the entire group a disgusted glare. "The only thing I can destroy is a large pepperoni pizza. How many times do I have to tell you angels? I'm not part of your little club and I'm no hero. I don't have special powers, see?" He held up his hand and pointed it off to the side to prove nothing would come out of it. A huge ball of energy shot from his hand and blew up the garbage dumpster. Appolion was so shocked, he fell flat on his butt, his mouth open, his eyes wide.

Despite the grim situation, Abdiel almost laughed at his brother's dumbfounded expression.

"What the hell?" He looked down at his hand like it truly offended him.

"I tried to tell you," Gabi said meekly. "Remember the first day when we met and I told you an injured angel could not heal other angels? Well, I guess the same thing goes for all your gifts. When I healed you, all of your powers came pouring out."

"Well just put them back in," Appolion growled.

Gabi gave him an aggravated look. "I can't do that. As a healer you should already know that."

"I said I was born a healer. I never said anything about being a healer." Appolion got up and started to pace. "Sorry, I know you're supposed to be some great and mighty healer, but I've never had a lick of formal training in the art of healing angels. Over the centuries, I've been to four different medical schools for humans, but I don't know bupkis on angel anatomy."

"You're just mad because you've just realized everything I've been telling you is the truth." Rachael pointed an accusing finger. "For the first time in your immortal life, you may have to put somebody else's needs before yours, and you can't stand that. Do you know how much you hurt me when you cut all contact with me?"

"That's not fair, Ray." Appolion stopped pacing and gave her a hurt look. "I was trying to protect you."

"Oh save it, Appolion." She gave him the hand. "You can say that you were trying to protect me all you want, but we both know that's bull. How about after you left Hell? You weren't being abused then, but you still kept me out of your mind. Why?"

"Do we really need to go through all this now?" he snapped.

"I was all alone down there!" She ran up and slugged him hard in the chest. "How could you do that to me?"

"Because I couldn't trust you wouldn't lead the demons to me!" Now he was just as angry as her, and his blazing blue eyes bore into hers. "Face it kiddo, we come from some seriously messed up DNA. Mom turned, Dad turned, Forcas turned, Douma turned, and it's just a matter of time before we do, too."

"Do you really think that?" Abdiel interjected. "You honestly think that just because of our family history the three of us are damned?"

"We are beyond damned, big brother," Appolion redirected his glare. "We are thoroughly fucked, and the worst thing is now that Rachael and I are full strength, we're going to be difficult to defeat."

Abdiel wanted to shake some sense into his brother, but stopped himself when he remembered that not too long ago he felt the same way. Before he met Gabi, he shut himself away from the world, just like Appolion. He now realized he had been a first class idiot. His family wasn't the ones who had beaten and deserted him. His family was standing in front of him now.

He looked over at his beautiful mate who would always stand by him no matter what. He then turned to his baby sister. Even though she'd suffered just as bad as any of them, she refused to let the past rule how she lived in the present. Shifting his gaze to Cam, who he loved like a brother even though the kid had been to Hell and back, literally, Abdiel knew he would always have his back. Finally, he focused on Appolion. Poor, scared, moronic, Appolion. If his little brother had stopped worrying about turning long enough to really think everything through, he'd realize he was wrong. Demons don't go to medical school and devote their lives to helping humans, but he knew the younger angel wasn't ready to hear that, yet.

"I'm not going back with you," Appolion told him, his jaw set in defiance.

"Nobody asked you to," Abdiel said with a casual shrug of his shoulders.

Appolion acted shocked his older brother agreed. It seemed to take some of the wind out of his sails. He recovered and shrugged his shoulders. "Your high and mighty council would put me in chains the second I even tried to enter Heaven."

Abdiel had to concede to himself that his brother was most likely right. There's no way the council would look the other way with Appolion like they did with Rachael. Appolion had been free from Hell for years and never attempted any contact before now. They would view him as a suspect spy or worse, a rogue. Abdiel knew that, even though it was going to tear his and Rachael's hearts apart, they were going to have to let their brother go. "If you ever want to come home, I'll always be here for you."

Appolion gave him a dismissive wave of his hand and turned around to leave. After a few steps, the angel stopped, turned and looked at them. "I really did miss you guys," he admitted in a strained voice.

Rachael threw herself into his arms and the two hugged for several minutes. When they finally pulled away, she fixed him with a stern look. "Promise you won't cut our telepathic connection again. I need to be able to talk with you so I know you're all right."

"I promise to talk with you whenever you want to." He smiled sadly down at her.

Cam walked up and offered the guns.

Appolion refused to take them. "Keep them. I have plenty more. Ask that bartender you met the other night where to get replacement bullets. Mangus knows all the connections to the local black market. Just make sure your council doesn't find out you have them."

"Why would the council give a rip about that?"

He raised a dark brow, his grin snide. "The council thinks using holy water is too human from what I hear. Angels can be so hypocritical."

Abdiel took his long sword and handed it to the younger angel.

Appolion took it with a confused look. "What's this for?"

"I want you to have this. You need a proper weapon if you're going to be out here alone."

"I can't take this. I know how you archangels treasure your swords. You guys treat them like they're your—" He stopped and flashed a guilty grin in the female's direction. "You treat them like they're your right hand."

"You're more important to me than any weapon. I just hope someday you realize that."

Appolion took the sword and looked down at the gleaming blade. He opened and closed his mouth a couple of times.

As usual, Gabi, the diplomat, found a way to ease the awkwardness. "Why don't you tell Abdiel the good news, Appolion?"

"You sure?"

She nodded.

He announced, "You and your mate are having a baby, Abdiel."

"Really, is he right?" Abdiel grabbed Gabi and made her look at him. When she smiled in response, he pulled her into a tight embrace.

"It's going to be a boy," Appolion added. "He's going to have Rachael's blue eyes."

"You mean your blue eyes, too." Abdiel smiled when his brother gave him a dismissive wave. "Maybe he'll sing his own soundtrack, too, just like his Uncle Appolion."

Cam snickered. "The last thing we need is another angel karaoke machine."

"Please," Appolion rolled his eyes. "Don't let him hang around with his Uncle Cam too much or else the kid will be hooked on hockey and female demons. Keep the kid around Rachael. She'll make sure he's halfway decent." With those parting words, he flashed out, leaving them standing there alone.

THE FIRST THING GABI wanted to do once she got home was take a nice, long shower and wash all the demon gore out of her hair. As soon as she flashed herself into the kitchen, she heard the TV blaring. She turned and frowned at the others. "Did one of you guys forget to turn the set off?"

"It's Ana." Cam sighed.

Now why the hell was she here at this time? They all went to the living room. The usually graceful and regal angel was sitting with her head hanging off the end of the couch and her feet propped up against the back. Her hair was loose for once, and Gabi couldn't help but admire how beautiful it looked when it was free. The honey-blonde locks were soft, curly and streaked with both highlights and lowlights. Gabi wondered why Ana chose to always pull it up in a tight bun when most females would give their hind teeth for hair like that.

Instead of her usual formal white, she wore a pair of blue jean shorts and a Red Wings shirt. She had fuzzy, pink bunny slippers on her feet. All around her were wrappers from various candy bars and empty chip bags. She pumped candy into her mouth. Gabi and the other three angels just stared in shock.

"You guys stink." Ana never took her gaze off the TV.

"We've been kind of busy tonight," Cam said warily. Obviously, her uncharacteristic behavior was throwing him for a loop.

"I know. You guys destroyed some demons." She made a sarcastic yippie motion with her finger. "Quick someone call CNN. It's not going to do any good you know. There will be more stepping up to take their place. Demons reproduce faster than bunnies."

"Well aren't you in a foul, rank mood," Cam snapped. "Besides it wasn't just any demons, it was Douma and Forcas."

"Oh." Her blue eyes grew wide. "I just picked up that you destroyed some demons. I didn't know it was The Brothers Grimm."

"What do you mean *picked up* Ana?" Cam narrowed his eyes. "Only a telepath could do that."

She took off one of her bunny slippers and threw it at him. "Because you're big spinster of a sister is good for something besides wiping snotty noses and getting you guys out of trouble. Did it ever occur to you that you might not be the only telepath in the family?"

"Since when have you been a frigging telepath?" Cam asked.

"I've had *some* ability, but it's always been very weak." She shot him an accusing glare. "But now thanks to you my mind has more traffic in it than Woodward Avenue."

"What did I do?" Cam threw his hands up.

Rachael gave a knowing chuckle. "When you kept going into her mind, you inadvertently taught her how to create and maintain a psychic connection. Way to go, Einstein."

"But I didn't do it on purpose." Cam pointed the pink bunny at Ana. "She never told me she was psychic."

"That's because I didn't even know myself, not really." Ana rifled through the empty wrappers before finally finding a full one. She ripped it open with her even, white teeth. "I always assumed it was wistful thinking on my part. Remember, Mom was such a powerful telepath and I've always wanted so bad to be just like her. Like I told you before, the power was very weak. I kept telling myself I was imaging things."

"Is that why you're on my couch pigging out?" Gabi smiled at the sight of the prim and proper angel putting an entire peanut butter cup in her mouth at once.

"No, it's not the reason why," Ana said in a garbled voice. "But you guys really need to take a shower before we talk anymore. You smell like burned garbage and it's making me lose my appetite."

"I can tell," Abdiel drawled.

Ana raised one long, elegant middle finger up at him.

Cam hooted in laughter before tossing the bunny slipper back at her head.

IT WAS SEVERAL MINUTES before they had all cleaned up and met in the living room again. Rachael had gotten a whole gallon of ice cream out of the freezer and her and Ana were eating it straight from the carton. Cam sat on the other side of the room with a travel coffee mug in his hands Rachael had forced him to take. With each sip, his color improved and the shakes started to leave. Abdiel sat down on the couch and Gabi settled into his lap.

"Cam," Rachael said slowly. "Every time we're home, you get all cranky and pasty looking. Is the house making you sick?"

"You're a telepath so you should already know the answer to that question," Cam's tone was as sour as the look on his face.

"It's the protective spells isn't it?" Gabi suspected as much for a while, but hadn't brought it up until now.

"Yeah," he admitted. "The little monster in me doesn't like the shielding chants. It's no big deal though I'm adjusting."

"We could weaken them," Abdiel offered. "It might help some."

Cam shook his head. "You've got to protect Gabi and Rachael, not to mention the future Baby Dark Angel. Don't worry about me. I'll deal with it just fine."

Abdiel put his hand protectively on Gabi's stomach. Even though it was still flat and there was no indication a baby was in there, he didn't doubt Appolion's words for a second. *Wow, I'm going to be a father.*

"I'm all out of food," Ana complained.

"I'll go get you my stash from my room," Cam offered.

"That was your stash." She held her stomach. "I think I'm going to be sick."

"Serves you right, you little hog," Cam shot back with an amused glint in his eyes. "Are you going to tell us why you've gone on this bender or not?"

"I got sacked," Ana wailed.

Rachael threw her arms around the crying female and tried to comfort her.

"I thought you quit the council. How can they fire you?" Cam was clearly angry anybody would upset his sister.

"Not from the council," she sobbed. "They told me my services as a justice angel are no longer needed."

"It's because of me isn't it?" Cam closed his eyes and sighed in disgust.

"Actually you're name didn't even come up in the conversation. They refused to tell me why. I just got my walking papers."

"Come on, Ana, cheer up," Gabi urged. "Don't let those jerks get you down."

"It's not just that, Gabi," Ana said with a delicate sniff. "Today I dropped Bear off at his new home in Flint. It wasn't until I met his big, bad archangel and his Britney Spears lookalike healer that it finally settled in. All my brothers are gone."

"His healer looks like Britney Spears?" Rachael asked.

"Yes, the early skinny one not the later post-Kevin one."

"Okay, back on topic guys." Cam rubbed his forehead. "Why would the fact that we are all gone bum you out? I would think you would be glad to get rid of us."

Ana took a shaky breath. "I sat there in that cold, empty house and realized that after all these years, I have nothing. My whole life has always been you boys, the council and being a justice angel and now, all that's gone. I'm nothing but an old spinster. I may as well go out and buy twenty cats and get it over with."

"You know what you need?" Rachael announced. "A girl's day out. Tomorrow, you and I are going to get all gussied up and hit the mall.

Nothing like shopping yourself silly and having male humans ogling you to make you feel better."

"Please, Rachael," Ana said dryly. "No male has ever ogled me, demon, angel or human."

"That's because you've always kept you best assets hidden," Rachael argued. "You need to let that gorgeous hair of yours down more. Not to mention you've got a killer set of gams. You borrow one of my skirts and we'll see how much attention you get."

"No way, Ana," Cam ordered. "You're not stepping foot outside of the house in one of *her* outfits. I forbid it."

"You forbid it?" Ana arched a brow. "You forget that I was the one who changed your diapers, little male."

"Abdiel," he groaned. "Ya wanna help me here?"

"Sorry, bud." Abdiel thoroughly enjoyed the archangel's discomfort. "You're on your own."

"Rachael, stay away from my sister. You're a bad influence."

Rachael wrinkled up her little, button nose and stuck her tongue out at the young archangel.

Cam stuck his tongue out back at her.

Abdiel let out a loud bark of laughter. Cam was easily six-foot four and every inch hard muscle. His black tee shirt and leather pants added to his badass look and that was even before you tossed in the fangs and borderline psychotic attitude. The sight of him sticking his tongue out like a kindergartner was hilarious. Soon the entire room cracked up, Cam included.

"I wouldn't nag too much if I were you anyways, Cam," Ana said. "Not with the way you've been carrying around with that female demon."

Cam's jaw dropped open before he recovered and snapped it shut. "You know about that, huh?" He looked down at the ground.

She released an aggravated breath. "I knew the very first time when we came to pick you up from that warehouse."

"Why didn't you say anything?" Cam startled to shuffle his feet.

"What was I supposed to say?" Ana shot him an incredulous look.

"Hi, Cam, nice to see that you finally got laid. That would have been just a little awkward."

Gabi ducked her head into Abdiel's shoulder so Cam wouldn't see her laughing at his completely dumbfounded look. Abdiel wasn't as considerate. He smirked right in the young archangel's face.

Cam shook his head before he leaned forward and put a bullet on the coffee table. He sat back and shot a questioning look at his older sister. "Do you know what this is?"

"Duh, it's a bullet." She shrugged her shoulders as she looked at him like he'd lost all of his marbles.

"It's just not any bullet, Ana." Cam fixed her with a stern look. "It's a bullet that's been infused with holy water."

"Where in the hell did you get that?" She picked up the bullet and looked closer at it. "Did you go to some freaky vampire fan convention or something?"

"We got them from Appolion tonight." As he talked, Cam watched her face closely, looking to see what her reaction would be. "Guess what? They work. What I want to know is did you know anything about this? Appolion said the council knew all about holy water working."

Ana gave him a hurt look. "Do you really think I would keep something like this from you boys? My God, Cam, every day I worry something is going to happen to you or one of your brothers. I would never hide a potential weapon from you guys. I love you too much."

"What about angel's blood?" Cam took her hand in his and gave it a slight squeeze. "Do you know anything about that being sold on the black market?"

"Why would that be sold on the black market?" Ana's face grew pale. "Aren't you the only one who needs it?"

"No Ana, it seems rogues and some demons use it in order to delay the change."

Gabi cast a worried look at Ana before she added. "Is it possible some members of the council kept this from coming out? Would there be anything for them to gain from keeping us in the dark?"

"Yes, I can see certain members using this information to manipulate others."

"How would that help them?" Rachael asked.

"For starters, they now know a major weakness of a member of the Order." Ana went over to Cam and gently stroked his face. "They know Cam needs angel's blood to survive. They could possibly hope to manipulate the market and control Cam by cutting off his supply. We didn't tell anyone we were donating our blood to him, so they may think the black market is the only way he can get it."

"What do they have against the Order?" Gabi wondered.

"I have some ideas," Ana snapped. "Give me a few days to prove them though. They've gone and pissed me off which is a big mistake."

"Would you mind watching over Double and Trouble here for a few days, Ana?" Abdiel pointed at Rachael and Cam. "I'm taking my mate on a honeymoon. Now that my brothers are dust, we might actually get some time off."

"Go have fun, you kids deserve it," Ana replied with a wicked smile.

Cam and Rachael started to argue they didn't need a babysitter, but it was a waste of their breath. Abdiel already flashed himself and Gabi out of there.

Chapter Ten

"SUCK ME, EMPATH KING."

Cam was back at the neutral bar again, and this time, he was with three succubi. He had slipped Mangus a wad of cash in order to use the demon's back office, and it was a damn good thing he did. It would have been a might bit crowded in the bathroom. Cam still didn't know how he ended up with the trio. It had originally only been him and Lilith going at it, but after a few rounds, the blonde demon had left. The others had slowly come in, one by one, and Cam wasn't about ready to turn down a free meal.

Right now, he was only using one of the females, a real flexible redhead. He had her pinned down to the ground in the missionary position. *An oldie, but a goodie.* The other two were sitting close by, naked, watching.

One of the voyeurs, a tall brunette, must have gotten sick of waiting her turn because she came up to Cam and stretched out over his back. Cam moaned, aroused further by the sensation of her soft body and breasts pressed against his back while yet another warm body writhed as underneath him. Cam reached his hand back and stroked her finely shaped rump, lest she think he didn't appreciate her efforts, all the while still screwing the first demon. He could feel the redhead tighten around him as she started to come.

"Suck me," she commanded again.

So Cam bit her in the neck. He meant only to take a little bit. He already drank so much demon blood tonight that everything was starting to get hazy, but she grabbed him by the back of the head and jerked his fangs deeper. Cam both tasted and felt her come then, and it was enough for him to join her. The brunette reached down and gently squeezed his balls, giving him the orgasm of his life. He felt her fangs sinking into his back as she drank from him even as he was feeding off the redhead.

No sooner had he finished than the brunette grabbed him by the shoulder and threw him on his back. Before one could say, *what da fuck?* she'd already straddled him and was riding him. The fact he was already hard and ready to go again didn't surprise him. Ever since his transformation, he couldn't get enough sex. In fact, he craved it almost as much as blood. But he was tired, damn tired. He'd let the demons take too much of his blood. Derel had warned him about this when he saw Cam coming home almost every night with bite marks. He'd said if he let them feed too much from him or if he took in too much demon blood, it could throw his whole body out of whack. Dumbass that he was, Cam had gone and done both tonight.

As soon as the brunette finished using his body, he scrambled to his feet and pulled his clothes on. The room spun in slow, lazy circles and his head felt fuzzy. He'd never been drunk before, but he was pretty damn sure this is what it felt like. He steadied himself by putting a hand on the wall and tried to act casual. "I'll be right back," he told his demon posse. He would just go out, drink some angel blood, then be back in shape. He wasn't about to call it a night yet.

The one female demon he hadn't taken yet came up and pressed her naked body against him. "You can't leave." She pouted and ran her hands over the bulge in his pants. "I haven't had my turn."

Cam chucked her softly on the cheek. "I'll be gone for only five minutes. Just make sure that you're ready for me when I come back."

"What are we supposed to do while we're waiting for you?" The brunette frowned.

"Keep yourselves occupied." Cam smiled as a wicked thought came to his addled mind. "Better yet, keep each other occupied." He left the room and made his way down the hallway, stumbling several times because some asshole had made the floor wobbly. He started to make his way to the bar and stopped dead when he saw his brother Mael was sitting on one of the stools, nursing a very macho soda. Cam groaned. He'd forgotten Mael had insisted on coming with him tonight.

Mael was the third oldest Lehor brother, but he was by far the biggest and meanest looking. Not that either of the attributes helped him a lick tonight. He pulled the short stick and was put on Cam duty. Cam didn't feel one bit sorry for him. He wouldn't be here at if it weren't for all the brothers meddling. They had decided Cam would be taking a babysitter with him whenever he went to the bars at night.

So for the last week, Cam had to put up with one of them tailing him wherever he went. The last thing he needed was for his archangel brother to see him in this condition. He leaned against the wall, trying hard to ignore the fact there was some sticky substance on it, and weighed his options. He could go up to the bar and get the blood he desperately needed, but then Mael would know for sure he was blood drunk. The last thing he needed was to give his brothers more ammunition against him. So he decided to go with plan B, hide in the shadows and hope Mael got sick of waiting and left.

Since he had nothing better to do with his time, Cam slowly took in the bar. *What a freaking dive.* The tables all had rough wooden tops that looked like they'd never seen a wet cloth while the filthy floors were covered in dirt, grim and God knows what else. The entire joint reeked of demon and garbage.

Several demons were sitting around the bar talking in their freaky demon talk. About a dozen rogue angels were there as well, each of them casting nervous glances in Mael's direction. There were a handful of archangels as well. They were the lowest of the low among their ranks. Most other archangels would never trust them enough to turn their backs on any one of them. They were treacherous leeches, every single one of them, and his brothers knew he was mingling with them on a daily basis. *No wonder they are looking at me like I'm some loser. I've hit rock bottom, hard and fast.*

Mael jumped and almost grabbed his sword when a small succubus came up from behind and playfully tugged at his long ponytail.

Cam recognized Lilith's sister.

She gave Mael a wide smile, showing off her fangs. "Mind if I take a seat?" She nodded to the stool next to him.

Mael gave an indifferent hug. "Just promise you won't bite."

Her laughter was soft and light. "I'll be a good, little demoness. I just figured since we're both waiting for our siblings to finish fucking like bunnies we might as well keep each other company."

"Please, don't hold back, tell me what you really think," he said sarcastically.

"If you want pretty foo-foo, then you'll have to find one of your female angels."

The bartender set a glass of angel's blood in front of her.

Cam felt a little guilty about eavesdropping on his brother's conversation, but not enough to show himself. He noticed Mael gave the succubus a disgusted glare as she gulped down the angel's blood.

"Don't look at me like that," the dark haired female said. "I didn't ask for this any more than your brother did. I was only twelve when my parents took me to Hell."

"I'm sorry." Mael shifted uncomfortably in his seat, an uneasy look on his face. "How much longer do you think they'll be?"

"Who knows?" The female rolled her eyes. "The last time I checked, he was with not only my sister, but two other females.

Cam wasn't about to give himself away by correcting her. He'd been with three females, but Lillith hadn't been one of them. In fact, he hadn't seen her since she left the back room earlier. *Now where had that little demon taken off to?*

Mael choked on his cola. "You guys take turns with him?"

Cam smirked. *See I'm not you're dorky baby brother anymore.*

"Your brother, Cam, is *very* popular Not only does he do amazing things with his hands, but his blood is unlike any other."

"What do you mean?" Mael asked sharply. "Not the hands thing, that was T.M.I., but what's so different about his blood?"

"It is so full of life and energy it makes you high." She sighed wistfully. "It's like the Red Bull of angel blood."

"Sorry, sweetheart," he said blandly. "But Cammie's going home as soon as he comes out."

"Well, seeing how your brother is already taken, I guess I'll have to settle for you." She stood and tugged on his hand.

Yes, go with the nice little succubus, Cam thought privately. *That way I can get my damn blood and get back to my fun orgy.* When his brother shook his head, refusing, he almost growled in frustration.

"Thanks, but no thanks." Mael jerked his hand away.

Her eyes flashed with anger. "Well aren't you so high and mighty. We'll see how arrogant you are when your brother is back where he belongs." She spun around to walk away.

Mael reached out, snagged one of her wings and dragged her back to him. He twisted the wing in his hand, trying to make her more cooperative with pain. That plan backfired when she gave him a seductive smile.

"Oh, pain. Pain is good, archangel. It turns me on. Just ask your little brother."

He pulled out a dagger and spun it in his hand before he slammed it through her wing and pinned it into the wood table.

She unleashed a demonic cry. Several patrons looked their way before turning away. It was best to mind one's own business at neutral bars.

He grabbed her wrist and twisted her body awkwardly until she faced him. "What are you talking about when you say Cam will be back where he belongs?"

"Lilith wants to take him back to Hell with her." She panted from the pain. "The other day while Cam was screwing her, he made the mistake of calling her the wrong name.

"Who's Lilith?"

"That's my sister's name." She bared her fangs at him in anger. "Us filthy whores do have names you know."

"So, is she jealous over another succubus? Did he make a mistake and forget what demon slut he was with?"

"No, worse, he called her by an angel name. Does the name Amadeaha mean anything to you?"

Cam cringed. He hoped Lilith hadn't heard him when he made that little slip. It seemed she had caught it and it pissed her off.

"What does your sister have planned?" Mael continued to grill the demoness. When she hesitated in answering, he twisted the dagger in her wing.

"She's set up a trap for him and she's going to take him home with her tonight." She yelped. "She's going to drain his blood so he'll be too weak to fight back."

"She's going to be able to drink that much of his blood?"

"No, she has the other succubi back there right now to help her. She knows your brother has no qualms about taking more than one of us at a time." She gave him a malicious smile. "You see, your brother is no better than us. He's a whore just like me. That's why he has a pair of fangs and eyes like a succubus. He's one of us and that just kills you, doesn't it, archangel?"

Cam recognized the dangerous glint in his brother's eyes. The demon saw it, too, but too late.

Mael took the dagger out of Lilith's sister's wing and buried it deep in her chest. She screamed right before she flashed back to Hell.

Cam smiled at his brother's actions. Mael really was one badass.

The bartender, Mangus, walked up to Mael. "I heard what she said," the demon rumbled. "I've already had one of my staff go lock the back door so they can't sneak him out that way."

"Thank you. You know for a demon, you're not half bad."

"Yeah, well for archangels you and your brother are not half bad. Just don't let anyone know I'm a big softie."

Cam curled his lip. He didn't need their help. He could handle anything those damn demons threw his way. He'd show them that, too. Pushing himself from the dirty wall, he sent out a mental, *Fuck you*, to a group of demons sitting at a nearby table. Then he headed for the door. Walking became even more difficult for him and the room spun even more.

Cam hid his condition well. He marched down the center of the bar with his long, black leather trench coat flaring behind him, acting as if he could rip apart anything that came in his way. The entire time he was saying the same chant that all drunks say in their heads when they're trying to hide their condition, *Maintain, maintain, maintain.*

He stopped once he was outside and waited for the demons to join him. They did not disappoint. Soon they came spilling out of the bar and formed a tight circle around him. Cam was only slightly annoyed to see Mael was following them. Maybe once his brother saw he could fight on his own, he would leave him alone. Cam curled his lip at them. "Good work, boys. I didn't think you'd have the guts to fight me."

Moving so fast nobody could see him, Cam flipped over the closest demon until he was behind it. The demon tried to scamper away, its glowing red eyes wide with fear, but the archangel kept it firmly in his grasp. Cam ripped into the demon's throat and drank deeply from the fiend before he finally let it slide to the ground. As soon as the monster hit the street, it vanished back to Hell.

The other four demons started to shake with fear. But they weren't ready to retreat yet. One pulled out a gun and shot the archangel square in the chest.

The angel staggered back a few steps before he straightened up and gave the shooter a disgusted look. "You just shot me," Cam stated the obvious. "With a bullet dipped in demon's blood. Hey, guess what, dumbass? It's not going to work. I've drank about ten gallons of the stuff already tonight."

Cam tried hard to ignore the fact his words were coming out slurred now. He knew the gunshot did some damage because the warm blood from the wound soaked into his shirt. He swayed on his feet before shaking his head slightly to clear away the fog. Mael shot him a worried look so Cam shot him the bird in retaliation and giggled. *Since when do*

I freaking giggle?

Mael swung his long sword sideways at the shooter. The demon's head came cleanly off its body and rolled on the ground.

Cam glanced down and smiled at it before he looked up in alarm. "Quick, Dael, muck down." He raised his hand.

Mael quickly translated his brother's muddled language and hit the dirt.

Cam released a ball of fire, hitting the demon about ready to strike Mael with its sword. The demon was blasted across the street before it slammed into a building. The remaining two demons finally had the good sense to flash themselves out of there. Cam looked over at the bar just in time to see Lilith walk back inside, her eyes flashing with anger. Her little plan hadn't gone so well after all. *So the bitch was trying to set me up. How rude.*

As soon as they were alone, Cam sank to his knees, laughing hysterically. He couldn't help it, the dumfounded look on his brother's face was suddenly the funniest thing he ever saw. *You're not maintaining very well.* Mael went over and grabbed him by the collar hauling him to his feet. Cam tried to stand up, but found his legs weren't working very well anymore.

"Are you drunk?" Mael asked disgusted.

"Blood drunk," Cam slurred. "No alkie haulie for angels. Lucky for me, demon's blood is better than whiskey if I get enough of it."

"Idiot," Mael muttered, his mind racing so fast he was sending out thoughts to Cam without meaning to. *Great, now I'm stuck figuring out what to do with my injured, idiot, drunk brother. I can't very well take him back into the bar. While most of the demons tend to leave him alone out of fear, with him being injured, it would be a whole different ballgame. Even with Douma and Forcas destroyed, there is still a huge bounty on Cam's head. Taking him back to the house is out of the question, too. Ana's there and, if there is one thing I fear, it isn't evil demons, it's the wrath of Ana. I can't even try to sneak Cam back into the house now that Ana's a physic.*

Finally, Mael spotted an empty car. He dragged Cam over, touched the lock and opened it up. With the door ajar, he threw Cam in none too gently.

Cam thunked his head on the way in and there was no mistaking the satisfied grin on his brother's face when he mumbled, "Ouch."

Mael got into the passenger side. "You've really got to stop pulling this stuff. It's time to end this pity party."

"Sorry, I just lost control tonight." Cam curled up into a ball and pretended to sleep.

Mael jerked him up roughly. "That's bull and we both know it. While you were occupied with the enemy, I had a little talk with the bartender. He told me you're in there almost every night and the routine is always the same."

"Fine, so what? It's the only way I can sleep at night. Every time I close my freaking eyes everything comes back in a flash." Cam started to do that babbling thing drunks do. "I see the ones that we left behind in Hell. I should have figured out a way to get them out. Crap, Nathaniel's mate is down there, and I bit her. I took my own brother's female, threw her down on the ground and fed off of her. What kind of monster does that make me? I barely stopped myself before I really hurt her."

"You were able to control yourself in the end," Mael reminded.

"Sure, now I just buy blood every night that probably came from either her or some other poor angel in chains," Cam slurred his words even worse. "I'm no idiot. They have to get that blood from someplace. I can try to fool myself all I want, but there are no willing donors giving out blood anymore than there are cows giving up burger patties."

"Speaking of blood, you need some, Cam. Not only do we have to dilute all the demon's blood you sucked down, but we have to replace all the fluids you gave to those demon whores." He pulled up the sleeve on his shirt and put his wrist by Cam's mouth.

He weakly pushed it away. "No thanks," he could only talk in a whisper because he was getting so weak. "It skeeves me out when I have to drink from family."

Mael pulled out one of his daggers and made a deep slash into his own wrist.

Cam still tried to fight him at first, but the smell of the blood was too enticing. He grabbed his arm and, as he started to drink, things went black for a moment.

When Cam came too, his mind less muddled, he noticed Mael's injured arm clutched to his chest. Too much damn blood came from it. "Let me see your arm."

Mael shook his head. "It's okay."

"Let me see it, now."

He relented.

Cam cursed. There were several deep bite marks surrounding the original cut. He hated himself at that moment for attacking his own brother.

Mael gave a half smile. "It's no big deal."

Cam grabbed a scarf from the backseat and wrapped it around his brother's injury. "It is a big deal. I almost gnawed your arm off."

"Please, even with fangs, your puny butt couldn't take me on."

"You want to know a secret?" he asked, his voice clearing up. "Even though we destroyed Douma and Forcas, their super demon is still coming for us."

"Why would you say that?

"It's been calling to me." Cam shuddered. "Not just at night either. It comes during the day, too. It wants me to completely turn and join up with it. It says if I don't, it will not only destroy me, but you guys, too."

"Are you sure it's for real?"

"Oh yeah." He nodded. "I can feel the evil from it. It's unlike anything I've ever felt, and I met some real gems when I was in Hell. Don't worry though. I told It to piss off. I'm not going to turn. Not only do I have you guys to think about, but I took vows and I'll never break them."

"I know that, little brother. We all do." Mael put his hand on his brother's shoulder.

"What the hell?" Cam looked over at the bar.

Mael followed his gaze. "Is that Michael?"

"It sure is." He slipped off his sunglasses so he could see better. He discovered his new demon eyes gave him great night vision. "What the hell is the Chief doing with an illegal arms dealer? A demon one at that?"

"Oops. Oh, crap. Duck, Abdiel!"

Abdiel brought his head down just in time for the football to sail overhead and into Nathaniel's hands.

"Sorry." His smile begged to differ. "I didn't expect you guys to poof in right in the middle of us."

"Why are you all crashing here? Don't you have homes of your own?' Abdiel asked with an aggravated tone he really didn't feel. During the week he and Gabi were gone, he actually started to miss everybody.

"Surprise," Rachael yelled from the kitchen. "Ana's called a family meeting. Consider it your welcome home party."

Abdiel laughed. Even though she was right and it was just family, the entire house was full to capacity. A few months ago, he had been alone in the world and now he had more brothers and sisters than he knew what to do with. Not that he was complaining.

"Hey, Barakiel," Gabi called. "You changed your hair back."

The young angel looked up and smiled. "Yeah, my new archangel Uriel likes it better this way."

Gabi went and sat across from him at the table. "I've known Uriel for years. Is he being good to you? Because if he's not, I'll have a talk with him."

"No, he's really cool. In fact, he didn't even order me to change my hair. He just asked nicely. It's my healer that's driving me batty."

Cam gave a snide chuckle. Bear rolled his eyes.

Now that the youngest Lehor was blond again, Abdiel was taken aback by how much he looked like Cam. *Well, Cam, before he got a new pair of choppers and about fifty pounds of lean muscle mass.*

"I know every healer," Gabi said. "Which one are you stuck with?"

"Tiffany."

Now it was Gabi's turn to laugh. She quickly recovered and patted Bear's head. "I am so, so, so sorry."

"Tiffany isn't even an angel's name," Bear groused. "She refuses to tell us her real one. She's the biggest airhead. Her only concerns are shopping and what color to paint her nails. I feel like I've moved in with Paris Hilton."

"You've got to tell them what you did to her cat." Cam slapped him on the back.

"She brought this pure white, longhaired Persian cat with her. The other night she made me mad, so I shaved it bald."

"That's cold, man," Abdiel could barely get the words out he was laughing so hard.

"The bad thing is for some reason it made that stupid cat like me even more." Bear shook his head, clearly dumbfounded. "Hairball won't leave me alone."

"Where's Ana?' Gabi asked as soon as they all stopped laughing.

"She's at her new job," Cam replied. "She said she would be here as soon as she could."

"Ana got a new job?" Abdiel asked with a raised brow.

"Yup, she's a cop now." Cam jumped when Ana flashed in.

"The proper term is enforcer, fang-head," she snapped, her hand on her hip. She wore an enforcer's uniform, black leather pants and a short, cropped black leather jacket with blue trim.

On her hips, she had something on that Abdiel had never seen any enforcer wear before— guns.

When she saw his expression, she patted them. "Mael picked them up for me the other night. Don't worry. We got some for you guys, too.

It wouldn't be fair not to share."

"Since when do you use black market weapons?" Abdiel asked, more than a little shocked. Ana was the last angel he would have ever suspected of illegal activity.

"I'm not about ready to let those demons get a hold of one of us again. If that means we use weapons the council doesn't approve of, so be it."

"But you're walking around with them in the open," Gabi pointed out. "You're kind of rubbing it in everybody's face."

"What are they going to do, fire me? Besides my new boss, Jacob, has ordered a whole bunch himself. When he found out there was something we could use against demons and the council had been hiding it all this time, he was pissed."

"What else did you find out, old wise one?" Abdiel crossed his arms.

Ana opened her mouth, then closed it. She seemed to be trying to find the right words. "I found out a lot and most of it is not good. Nobody knows about my telepathy, so I was able to get inside them and find out things."

"That's just rude, Ana," Cam teased as he wagged a finger at her. "It's not nice to snoop in other's minds. It's just a gross abuse of your powers."

"Give it a rest." She batted his finger away. "Desperate times call for desperate measures. I've found out some pretty scary stuff. The council, in particular Jehel, wants to break up the Order. He knows if you guys are as powerful as predicated, you will have more control in Heaven than he does."

"Is he really that power hungry?" Gabi asked.

"He deliberately set Dina up to be captured in order to get Cam. Is that hungry enough for you?"

"You mean to tell me he risked his own son in order to get me?" Cam had a disgusted look on his face.

"Yes, and that is not even the worse part of it. He was working directly with Forcas and Douma in order to put you guys out of commission. They struck a deal the demons get you guys and Jehel doesn't have to worry about the Order unseating him."

Rachael came into the kitchen along with the rest of the males and they all stood around. "How low is Jehel willing to go?"

"Oh believe me, he has gone much lower before." Ana breathed heavy. "You four are not the original Order. There were four other angels before you. The first two were your parent's, Abdiel and Rachael. In fact, your dad was the original Destroyer."

"Appolion is just going to love hearing that one," Rachael muttered.

"Who was the third one?" Cam asked as he stared to pull at his hair.

"It was Mom." Ana reached out and pulled his hand down. "But as soon as I mentioned the original Order, you knew that. We've always known Mom was a strong telepath. That's why you and I have developed such strong skills. In time, I think Bear will gain them, too."

"Oh hell no." Bear gave a vigorous shake of his head. "I'm just a simple empath."

"That's what I said at first, too," Cam said grimly. He looked at Ana. "Jehel set up Mom and Dad, too, didn't he? He wanted Mom destroyed so she wouldn't be a threat to him anymore."

When Ana nodded her head, all eight brothers started to curse. "That doesn't make sense," Mael snarled. "Mom was destroyed after Abdiel's parents defected to Hell. The Order had already been broken up."

"He still felt Mom was a threat. He didn't want to risk losing any of his precious power," Ana said bitterly. "The worst part is I can't even prove any of this. All I have is wild accusations that no one is going to believe." She turned to look at Abdiel. "I've got even worse news I'm afraid. They have declared Appolion a rogue and have put out a search on him. The archangels that are working for the justice angels have already come here to Earth to start hunting."

"Good luck," Rachael scoffed. "My brother is very good at shielding himself. They'll never find him."

"Yes they will, Rachael," Ana said firmly. "The justice angels have the best trackers in Heaven looking for him. They will find him, and they have orders to bring him in, willing or not. There is some good news, however."

"My brother is being hunted down like a dog. How could anything be good about that?" Abdiel growled.

"Well as you all already know, Jacob is the Chief of the enforcers. He's suspected that Jehel has been dirty for years, but he could never prove it. When I came to him with our problem, he was more than happy to help. Appolion is now wanted by the enforcers, too."

"How is that supposed to help?" Rachael wailed.

"Because now I can go hunt for him." Ana couldn't have shocked her brothers more than if she had run down the streets of Heaven buck-naked. "I'll go and convince him to come in peacefully."

All at once, the kitchen was in an uproar. Abdiel, Rachael and every single brother were arguing they should be the ones to go fetch Appolion. Everyone agreed it was much too dangerous for Ana to go out there alone.

"Enough," Ana finally yelled. "I'm going and that's final. Abdiel, if you or Rachael go, Appolion will view it as a betrayal and he will never trust you again."

Abdiel hated to admit she was right. If Appolion thought his own family deceived him again, he might do something stupid.

Ana turned and looked at Cam. "I need you to stay in contact with Appolion. You and Rachael are the only connection we have to him now. If he cuts you off because he senses you're after him, we lose one of the best advantages we have against the justice angels." Ana pinned each of her brothers with a steely look. "As for you lunk-heads, back off! This is my assignment, not yours."

"Look, Ana, it's going to be dangerous out there," Ramiel started. He was the oldest brother and, because of that, obviously decided to be their spokesman. "Not only do you have demons coming after this guy, but now some overzealous angels, too."

"I know you boys want to protect me," Ana said softly, "but this is something I have to do. For years, I sat on that council and tried to live up to its expectations. Now, after all this time, I find out that it's all been a lie. That they were the ones that made Mom and Dad the way they are today. Don't you see I have to do something so some good comes of all this? Abdiel brought Cam home to us. The least I can do is bring Appolion back to him."

"You don't owe me anything, Ana." Abdiel didn't want to see her hurt either.

"I know I don't. If you want to know the truth, I'm looking forward to getting out there and mixing it up a bit."

"Little Miss Uptight Ana, getting down and dirty with some demons?" Bear smiled, breaking the tension in the room. "I'd pay money to see that."

Ana ignored her youngest brother and turned to address Cam. "I need you to contact Appolion right now and let him know about the justice angels. We can't afford for them to get to him first."

Cam nodded before he closed his eyes. After a minute, he winced. "Damn, he's pissed. He's yelling all kinds of nice things in my head."

"Tell him not to worry, I'm coming for him."

"Consider it relayed." Cam opened his eyes wide, his message simultaneously aloud and telepathic. "Dude, if I tell her that she'll kick my ass."

Ana narrowed her eyes. "What did he say?"

Cam took a deep, steadying breath. "He said, *yippi, diddly, diddly, doo! Some female empath is coming to save me. Now I have nothing to worry about.*"

Her mouth opened and closed several times, her light blue eyes wide with disbelief. "That arrogant jerk," she finally managed to strangle out. "Tell him to come into my mind and say that to my face."

Cam smirked. "He said, *no way, Jose.*" It was obvious he enjoyed relaying these messages a little too much.

"Well isn't that real mature."

Abdiel ducked his head trying to choke back his laughter. The coughs that surrounded him told him the brothers were doing the same thing. It was kind of funny seeing someone stand up to Ana for once.

"Great," Cam groaned. "Now he's singing in my head and its Blondie's *One Way or Another.*"

"Oh," Rachael gasped. "I like that song."

"No, dude," Cam argued with the unseen Appolion. "I won't tell you what she's wearing. That's my sister."

Ana went over to Cam and stalked him, completely forgetting he was just the messenger. "You tell that no good, pig of a male that I *am* coming for him." Her brother got up and quickly backpedaled until she him pinned against the counter.

"He wants to know if you're going to able to drop the bon-bons long enough to do that." Cam put his arms up in anticipation.

"Stupid jerk." Ana hit her brother several times in the chest and stomach.

"Ouch, Ana, stop. He's gone."

Ana gave him one last slug for good measure before she walked over and pulled some files out of her bag. "Fine, let him be arrogant, it'll be easier that way. Appolion just thinks he's smarter than me. But little does he know, I've figured out his little secret."

Abdiel was actually starting to feel a little sorry for his brother. He'd never seen Ana this riled up, not even the time when Barakiel sneaked and got his nose pierced. Her cheeks were flushed and her pink lips were pressed tight together with anger. A thick lock of her blonde hair had escaped the usual immaculate bun and was swinging in front of her eyes.

Ana didn't even bother to brush it out of her way. She finally gathered up several newspapers and slammed them down on the table. Some of them were so old they were cracked and yellowed.

"What's your big plan, Ana?" Cam asked, still rubbing the spot in his chest where she hit him. "Are you going to keep signing him up for newspaper and magazine subscriptions until he finally turns himself in?"

"Don't worry," Abdiel drawled. "She'll still remember to renew

Cosmo for you."

"Mr. Dark Angel made a funny." Bear smiled.

Abdiel went up to him and ruffled his hair.

"This is how I'm going to get Macho Pants," Ana declared proudly.

Gabi and Abdiel started sorting through the newspapers. He could see they were old articles on several different serial killers. Was Ana trying to say that his brother was a murderer? He instantly dismissed the thought. If she really thought Appolion had done these killings, she'd have just let the justice angels have him.

"I'm sorry, Ana." Gabi had a small frown on her lips. "I just don't get it."

"Maybe this will help." Ana pulled out a paper from one of the files. "I compiled a list of places Appolion has lived in the past using both the information he gave Cam and reports of unauthorized angel activity. When I compared the dates and locations, I found a pattern. I think he's been hunting down serial killers."

"Are you sure?" Rachael looked through the paperwork.

"It would make sense. We all know most serial killings are either the work of demons or humans are under strong demon persuasion."

"That little booger." Gabi turned to smile at Abdiel. "What was all that talk he was shooting off about keeping his head down and hiding in his rabbit hole?"

"Don't forget, he claimed he was no hero, too." Abdiel knew that he had a stupid grin on his face, but he couldn't help it. He was proud of his baby brother. Appolion was out there helping his mortal brothers even though he had to do it all alone.

"How's all this going to help you find my brother?" Rachael wrinkled her nose in confusion.

"I just need to figure out where there is a killer active and wait for him to show up."

"Ana." Abdiel rubbed his head. "Do you have any idea how many serial killers there are active at any given time?"

She held her head up. "I didn't say it would be easy, but it's all I got. It just may take a little time."

"Thank you for going to save my little brother."

Ana ducked her head, embarrassed by the gratitude.

"I just have one last question," Rachael said. "Who was the Control over the original Order?"

"I was," a voice answered from the kitchen doorway. Michael stood there tossing a baseball from hand to hand.

Bear gave a small yelp, shocked by the Chief's sudden appearance.

Abdiel saw Mael and Cam exchange a look before Cam fixed the Chief with a hard stare.

"You were the Control?" Gabi asked her lips forming an O. "Why didn't you tell us about the other Order?"

"There's a lot they're not telling us, isn't there Michael," Cam snapped. "But then that's nothing new is it?"

Abdiel knew finding out Michael had been his uncle after all these years was a big blow to Cam, but he still was shocked at his behavior. The young archangel would hardly even look at the Chief before, and now he was snarling at him. In fact, it looked like Cam was thoroughly pissed at Michael and was two steps from attacking him.

"Back down, boy," Michael's voice was low, but full of menace. There was a reason why he was the biggest, baddest archangel. "If you have a question, why don't you just ask it?"

"Fine," Cam snapped. "Did you know about the holy water or the angel's blood?"

"I thought the holy water was just a myth. As for the angel's blood, yes I did know about that."

"So you knew all along and never said anything?"

The younger angel's teeth ground together, but Abdiel was proud he maintained his cool.

Cam glowered, "How could you keep something like that from us?"

"It was a matter of security. If a bad angel were to use it to hide their going rogue, they would be able to spy on us, or worse. Do you honestly think that I like the idea of those demons draining captured angels dry? Those are my warriors they are doing that to."

"What were you doing at the neutral bar the other night?"

"I was doing a couple of things." Michael walked over and stood toe-to-toe with Cam. "One was having to scare a certain succubus away from one of my nephews."

"Look, Michael—"

"No, you listen, that female demon has an obsession with you."

"That's ridiculous. She does not."

Michael grabbed Cam's cell phone out of his pocket and started to scroll through the history. "Yeah right, that's why she called you fifteen times today and it's not even evening. Lilith sucked you dry of blood the other night, knowing full well you were going to pick a fight with those demons. She wants you to be captured again."

"Now you're beginning to sound like Mael. She wouldn't do that. She's a succubus. I'm just another lay to her. She just understands me better than anyone else right now."

"Surprise, she's a demon." Michael smacked Cam on the forehead as if he were trying to beat some sense into him. "She would love nothing more than to have you become her own personal pet in Hell and believe me, it wouldn't be as fun as it sounds. Stay away from her. Lilith's one dangerous chick."

"Since when do you give a flip about what happens to any of us, *Uncle Mike*?" Cam asked with heavy sarcasm. "I think I liked it better when you ignored us."

"If Mael hadn't been there last night, you would have been in big trouble. You're losing control and you're going to drag your entire family down with you. I'm not asking you to stay away from that female demon, I'm *ordering* you to do so. You're still an archangel and I'm still your leader, no matter how you feel about me otherwise."

"Fine, I'll stay away from that particular succubus," Cam conceded angrily. "But you have to tell me one thing first. What the hell were you doing talking to an illegal arms dealer?"

"Let's just say I'm no longer following the council's dictates. Everything Ana just told you is true. Jehel and several others have betrayed us all." Michael ran his hands through his mane of dark blond hair and started to pace. "The powers of Heaven are now divided."

"Are we going to have a war?" Abdiel remembered the last civil war that took place in Hell when Lucifer revolted.

"Nobody's formally declared it, but we're coming close. The council wants to either have total control of the Order or disband it. As leader of the angel warriors, I cannot allow that. The Order is supposed to help balance the power while protecting mankind. The council members want to use it to promote their own agendas."

"So what are you going to do now, Michael?" Cam was still shooting him dark looks.

"The better question would be what are *we* going to do?"

He gave him suspicious glare. "What are you talking about?"

"You, Raphael and I need to visit all the angel warriors' homes and see where their loyalties lie."

"You're crazy if you think I'm going anywhere with you."

"I think it would be good for you to get away from everybody and get your head together. This mission will do that."

"So you get me back from Hell and all of a sudden you want to be my protective uncle now?" Cam shook his head in disgust. "Are you going to insist we spend quality time together now? We could go to the ballpark, maybe go bowling together or better yet, I could sit on your lap while you teach me how to drive a car."

Rachael let out a loud peal of laughter. When everyone in the room turned to look at her, she quickly recovered and coughed into her hand. "Sorry about that." She blushed. "I just got a visual of that last one in my head."

Michael and Cam continued to give her identical looks of annoyance.

Now that Abdiel knew they were related, it was easy to see how much a lot of their expressions and movements were the same. In fact, Cam looked a lot like Michael, especially now that he'd gone through the change.

Michael turned back to Cam. "The way I see it is until you get a grip on yourself, your dear Uncle Mike is going to be on you like white on rice, kiddo. I'm not about ready to stand by and watch my nephew slowly destroy himself. You need to remember you're the leader of the empaths now. You have responsibilities and other angels looking up to you."

"I've been trying, Michael. I've been going to all those stupid council meetings, haven't I?"

"Yeah, and you've been making a great impression, too." Now it was Michael's turn to lay on the sarcasm. "Especially when you make that game show wrong answer buzzer sound whenever Jehel talks. Now get ready to leave because Raphael is waiting for us."

"All right, I'll go." Cam snapped his teeth together. "But just for the record, this totally sucks."

"Noted." Michael gave him a brief smile before he turned to the others. "I need to know where all of you stand. Are with me or the council?"

"You know I will always stand by you, Michael," Abdiel said formally. He bowed down to the Chief, showing his allegiance.

The brothers followed suit, all swearing their loyalty and sword arm to Michael.

Cam came up last, he bowed the lowest. "Please forgive me for doubting you, Michael," he said without lifting his head. "I swear to follow wherever you lead me."

Barakiel was still sitting at the table. He looked over at Rachael and mouthed, *so much drama*, then rolled his eyes.

She clapped her hand over her mouth to hide the smile.

Bear stopped grinning when he realized Michael looked at him. "Sorry?"

Michael rubbed his head like it ached. "You need to formally declare your side too, Barakiel."

"Oh, yeah right." He hopped down and bowed at Cam's feet and became as serious as a heart attack. "I vow to always stay by your side, my Lordship."

"Bear get up, you don't have to bow to me," Cam sputtered.

"Yes, he does," Ana said, then bowed to him. Since she was no longer a justice angel, she was now considered an empath, too.

Cam had no choice but to awkwardly acknowledge their pledges of loyalty. It was clear he had a lot to learn about leading and it seemed like Michael had decided to be the one to teach him.

"Who else do you think will be on our side?" Abdiel asked.

"The entire force of the enforcers, all the angel warriors, half the angels in Heaven and half the shifters." Michael tossed the baseball over to Ana who looked surprised, but easily caught it. "The big problem is I suspect that Jehel has some rogues and demons on his side."

"So do we." Cam flashed his fangs.

"Were you really the original Control?" Gabi asked as Abdiel came and wrapped his arms around her.

"Yes, I was." He looked at the Lehors. "I have never forgiven myself for losing your mother. When they destroyed her and your father, I decided the next Control would be better prepared. That's why I worked so hard to make sure Abdiel was ready."

"You knew all along that I was going to be the Control? What else do you know?"

"I know lots of things. Like Cam shouldn't offer his help so much because someone is going to take him up on his offer when he least expects it. I also know Ana needs to pack an extra pair of pants with her before she leaves. Heck, I even know that Rachael should always make sure she's alone in the room before she dances to her iPod. The one thing I don't know is whether we're going to be able to beat the council. We need to prepare for hard times. I cannot guarantee all of us will survive."

Rachael put her hands on her hips and cocked her head to the side. "You're one confusing angel, Michael."

"He's right about one thing." Abdiel hugged Gabi tighter. "Even though we destroyed Douma and Forcas, that was just the tip of the iceberg and now we don't just have demons to worry about. We're going to have to fight our own kind."

LATER THAT NIGHT, ABDIEL lay in bed on his side with Gabi pressed to his chest. They had just finished making love and they were both naked. His hand was slowly caressing her softly rounded hip. Up and down, up and down, his fingers gently teased.

"Are you worried?" she whispered into the darkness. Her voice was warm, like honey.

He leaned down so he could drink in her scent. *Roses.* It mingled with the smell of their lovemaking. "I'd be a liar if I didn't say I worried about you and the baby, but I have no regrets."

"None?"

"My God, female, don't you realize I would walk through the fires of hell to be with you?"

"Yes I do." She rolled over. Her long, slender fingers danced across his chest. "I just like to hear you say it."

He responded by tickling her. She wiggled underneath him while she let out peals of laughter. When he finished, she lay under him panting for air. He let out a hiss as her movements aroused him. When she realized this, her beautiful green eyes became dark with desire. He used his lips and teeth to tease the side of her neck, right where he knew she loved it.

"It scares me to think of how close I came to never having you," he admitted. "If Michael hadn't sent me to be your archangel, I never would have realized how much I love you. I'd still be sad and miserable if it weren't for you."

She cupped his face in her hands and drew him in for a deep, sensual kiss. "But he did send you to me, Abdiel. Neither one of us will ever be alone again."

About the Author

Stephani Hecht is a happily married mother of two. You can usually find her snuggled up to her laptop, creating her next book.

eXtasybooks.com